Francisca and the Boys

By

Alfred Arroyo

Strategic Book Publishing and Rights Co.

Copyright © 2013 Alfred Arroyo. All rights reserved.

No part of this book may be reproduced or transmitted in any form or by any means, graphic, electronic, or mechanical, including photocopying, recording, taping, or by any information storage retrieval system, without the permission, in writing, of the publisher.

Copyright 2006-2011
Alfred Arroyo
Library of Congress Catalog
Card # 99-93740

Strategic Book Publishing and Rights Co.
12620 FM 1960, Suite A4-507
Houston TX 77065
www.sbpra.com

ISBN: 978-1-62212-325-4

Francisca and the Boys

Dedicated to
Alejandra Francisca

AUTHOR'S NOTE

The Great Depression of the late 1920's and early 1930's caused suffering to families in every station of life, but more so to the immigrant who had no particular knowledge of the way of life in the United States. Immigrant families of the various nationalities that entered the United States for the first time suffered equally, for poverty did not pick it's victim according to national origin. Each family head approached the problem in his or her own particular method.

Readers should be aware that this novel was not written to give acceptance or support to a way of life that is presented here, but that in reality this WAS the way of life for some families of that era. There is no message or protest intended here other than there were and are inconsistencies in life facing us all.

This novel depicts the lives of the Delmonte family headed by Chamaco Delmonte who, in his own way, managed to keep the family above the poverty levels of the time. Circumstances eventually cause the family reins to be handed to his wife Francisca, giving her the task of bringing up their two sons, David and Nicolas, by herself.

The Delmonte family happens to be of Mexican descent, as is this author, who therefore has used his own life experiences to set this story in place.

Part one of this book is a revision of the first *Francisca and the Boys,* included here as the first twelve chapters of the entire volume. Corrections have been made and twelve more chapters have been added to the original twelve.

Alfred Arroyo

Objectionable language will be found in much of the dialogue in the following pages, but without it most of the realism in the story would be lost.

Finally, to those readers who might be offended for any reason in the content of this novel, I sincerely apologize.

Alfred Arroyo

INTRODUCTION

The words across the upper portion of the double plate glass windows were painted in white script lettering on a dark blue background that read "Nick's Club Delmonte". Beer signs adorned the corners of the windows in blue and white. A large electric sign hung outside above the entrance with a huge blue ribbon imprinted on to a white plastic background announcing this bar's most prestigious product, Pabst Blue Ribbon Beer On Tap.

   The larger windows were to the left as you entered, and to the right was a single window advertising the same product with only the name "Nick's" painted across the top. The serving bar occupied the west wall to the left when entering the establishment. This bar was a semicircle of mahogany colored wood with a wide rounded arm rest attached from end to end. A dozen or so stainless steel bar stools with black plastic leather cushions surrounded the bar. About half of those cushions were either ripped or cut and begged replacement.

   Three sections of mirror combined into one rested on the back bar against the wall. An old metal cash register took up the center, with whiskey bottles lined on each side in double rows and labeled with their appropriate brands. Glasses were neatly stacked according to their capacity on the top surface, all this seeming a double quantity due to the reflections in the mirror.

   There was a telephone booth squeezed in between the bar and the front windows, a public phone accessible to all patrons.

   A brown, fading cloth hung low in curved and waves across the full length and breadth of the ceiling, secured by thin hanging wire to the original metal section above. The cloth was sprayed in part with white luminous paint and sprinkled with particles of confetti-like material, evidently to give the illusion of a clear night sky.

Nick invariably looked for this illusion while in a typical state of inebriation, but as much as he tried he could never find it. He seriously thought of tearing down the cloth ceiling more than once but would ultimately relent. *After all,* he thought, *it gives the place a little character.* The upper ceiling was in terrible shape anyway, so perhaps it would be best to leave things as they were.

The place was clearly a remnant of the prohibition era, the days of gangsters and "moonshine". There was an unbelievable amount of equipment in the basement that had at one time been used for the making of moonshine. There were copper vats and coils undisturbed for years. Dust and cobwebs clung to these artifacts so neatly stacked in a far corner of the room.

The basement was dank and dimly lit by a single light bulb. Looking from the steps down as you left the upper floor, the far wall was very dark and hardly visible. The light from the small bulb fell short of the wall by five or six feet, giving the wall an eerie and ominous appearance as it loomed into view.

On this far wall, a boarded and nailed door was in surprisingly good condition. Next to it, about a foot to the left, a window was firmly entrenched within a frame of wood on bricks. The cracked glass on the window was black from accumulated dirt but seemed to be holding up well. An iron frame with vertical bars was bolted and cemented into the brick surrounding the window's rotting wooden frame.

By close observation one could see through the dirt covered glass and make out the supports of a stairway leading up to the side walk, where the old entrance was covered by iron grating. Here was absolute evidence to a once existing, and very busy entrance to this thriving speakeasy of the past. Even the peephole at eye level on the door was still in place.

Francisca and the Boys

A small walk-in cooler underneath the stairs housed and cooled the barrels of beer with attached hoses and coils for service to the bar above.

Canal Street, running north and south, and 18th Street, running east and west came together not more than a block from the Chicago River about three miles from downtown Chicago. Nick's, located on the northwest corner of the intersection, was situated directly cross-corner from the Hendrickson Bottling Company, a distributor of soft drinks and supplier to a great number of businesses throughout the Chicago area. The Company had been a good source of revenue to this particular bar in the past, and Nick looked forward to a continuing relationship.

The bar would not open for business until the finishing touches on the interior of the place were complete. Although Nick had permission from the local Police District to open his doors, he remained closed until the liquor license would arrive through the mails, thus to avoid any legal misunderstandings.

The floors and walls were cleaned and painted. The bar was sanded down and varnished and the torn seats on the stools were replaced with new plastic leather covers. A half dozen tables, with four chairs for each, were brought in. New liquor, beer, and soda stock was ordered to supplement what had been left by the previous owners. A regulation pool table was installed toward the rear and center of the floor, complete with accessories, all to the convenience of potential clientele. Payment to play the game of choice would not be necessary. Nick's reward would show up in the cash register from liquor sales, while the customers remained busy and interested.

In the meantime Nick placed a large, hand painted sign on the window that read, WILL OPEN SOON UNDER NEW MANAGEMENT.

Nick felt pleased with himself for having acquired the business for a mere three thousand dollars. It included all equipment and existing stock plus three remaining years on the lease with option to renew. He was sure the sellers were also pleased at making such a deal because, by the looks of the place, business was not exactly booming. Nick was confident he could draw and cultivate new clientele once the establishment was completely organized and opened for business.

In a couple of months, on August 6, 1955 Nick would turn thirty two years of age. He thought it was time to go into business for himself, thus not having to work for others ever again.

After his discharge from the Navy, Nick had done a stint at driving a taxicab for a few years. Eventually he became disheartened at the politics involved in the operation of a cab business. Cab driving, in fact, was a dangerous vocation due to the many holdups and beatings that a number of drivers had sustained in the past. Nick himself had been in such a situation not too long ago but managed to escape unscathed and with a lot more respect and fear of the job thereafter. Nick sold the cab and began looking for a type of business that he could enjoy and bring in revenue as well. He thought he might have found it in the tavern business.

In the interim, Nick had held various jobs as a driver of one type or other. Bus driver and motorman on streetcars for the city, truck driver, beer and soda delivery, laundry pick up and delivery. Finally Nick took a job as a bartender, a job that he embraced wholeheartedly.

A fellow by the name of Richard J. Daley was running for Mayor of the City of Chicago on the Democratic ticket this year. It was the only ticket that meant anything in Chicago since Nick could remember, going back to the days of Mayor Edward J. Kelly, a powerful political boss of his day, nonetheless a good Mayor during his administration around the late thirties and early forties.

Nick was not too enthusiastic when it came to politics, but he knew it was somewhat of a necessary evil, for politics and business were closely related in this great City of Chicago.

Francisca and the Boys

Everything was in order now and the doors to the bar could be opened at anytime during the first week of May. Nick leaned back on his perch behind the bar and surveyed the establishment from stem to stern. He was pleased with himself and felt anxiety as the opening day drew near.

Nick's thoughts reverted to another time.

ONE

Between 21st and 22nd Streets on a lot parallel to Arapaho Street stood a huge oak tree rising at an angle to perhaps twenty feet before abruptly curving upward and branching out in all directions. The white of the inner wood shown brightly, evidence that the outer and upper side of its trunk had been extensively trampled. The bark had been torn away by footwear belonging to the neighborhood children. In contrast, the underside of the enormous trunk still had strong rough bark, intact and undisturbed. Large roots spread out from the trunk over a large area of ground surface, digging in at various locations, while gripping the ground with a might patterned by this towering perennial plant.

This was "The Tree". The tree known to every kid within a radius that had no boundaries. The tree was the meeting place, the gathering place. The place where you could find your friend, your partner, your chum or buddy, after school or any hot afternoon during summer vacation.

The school yard on 24th Street contained all the necessities for a playground. There were swings and slides, merry-go-round, teeter-totter, and chinning bar. One drawback though, the ground was covered with cinders. This made playing dangerous in a sense that the slightest fall was conducive to the appearance of unwanted cuts and abrasions.

So, the playground of choice would be the lot where the tree stood, leaning to one side in its curious position. In the immediate area surrounding the tree the ground was so soft and loose from trampling that there was absolutely no danger of injuries.

You could climb the tree with very little effort, or with good balance you could walk it upright if you were not afraid to try. This tree represented freedom to every kid that came in contact with it, whether they knew it or not.

Thick ropes hung from the branches of the tree. One rope dangled from a thick branch to nearly touch the ground. On this rope you could pull yourself up as far as you dared, then release the grip enough to enable you to slide down to the ground, if you cared to risk the burning of your palms. Another rope was tied to the same branch separated by a few feet from the other and knotted at intervals to accommodate the grip of any would-be "Tarzan of the Apes", ready to swing through the air and feel the freedom of being airborne if only for a few seconds. Of course there was the high-flying seat swing that allowed you to touch the dangling leaves and branches while swinging high, nearly to the level of the branch to which the swing itself was tied.

This was "The Tree", in all its grandeur and glory, waiting to be stepped on and used by any kid that felt the urge to fly.

On this particular warm June afternoon of 1934, and the beginning of summer vacation, a group of neighborhood children played on and around the tree. Davy Delmonte was stretched on the branch where the knotted rope was tied. He was swinging the rope to his younger brother Nick. While standing on the upper curve of the tree, Nick grabbed the rope and pulled several times to make adjustments prior to swinging to the ground. As he pushed himself away from the tree he commenced yodeling his imitation of the mournful cry of "Tarzan of the Apes". After a few times of swinging back and forth in the air, Nick let go of the rope landing safely a few feet from the tree.

Emilio Chacon clambered up the tree followed closely by the brothers Ricky and Freddy Carrizales, first cousins to the Delmonte brothers. Each boy waited his turn, and after each turn the boys would return to repeat the established routine. Except for profuse perspiration on their faces, the boys remained indefatigable.

Davy, becoming weary of tossing the rope to the would-be Tarzans, let everyone know that he was about to abandon his perch.

"I'm coming down, you guys," Davy announced, "somebody come up and take my place!"

None of the others made a voluntary move to relieve Davy of his station. As luck would have it, at this very moment Mary Moya appeared from beyond the fence that separated the lot from the adjoining property. As she walked toward the tree Mary waved and shouted, "Nicky, I was by your house, I was looking for you!"

Nick, sitting in the landing area after his jump, called back, "I'm over here, Mary!" Signaling with a wave of his arm he shouted, "Come 'ere!"

Mary half walked and half ran to where Nick was sitting.

Mary would turn thirteen by the time school would start in September. She would be attending Cole Junior High School now that she had completed her sixth year of grammar school.

Nick was promoted to sixth grade after passing with average grades. He would be twelve years old the following year.

Mary's full name was Maria Elena Moya, but all Spanish names were summarily changed to their English translations by the teachers at the school. Before long the children would prefer them over their Spanish sounding names. Thus the names of these children of Spanish and Mexican heritage would soon become Mary in place of Maria, Nicolas would remain the same in pronunciation but the spelling would change to Nicholas, Federico would become Frederick etc.

As a rule, Mary wore trousers while at play, but on this particular day she was wearing a print cotton dress with flared skirt held tightly at the waist by a sewn-in elastic band. Her bosom filled the upper half of her dress quite extensively, for by age twelve she was already comfortably endowed.

As Mary walked toward the tree, play came to a complete stop. All heads turned in her direction, all eyes glued on every single motion of her gait. Suddenly Mary stopped and raised both hands to her mouth as she let out a somewhat restrained scream.

There was a heavy thud followed by a loud groan from beyond the tree trunk. Davy, while turning to look at Mary, had become careless and loosened his grip on the branch supporting his outstretched body. He fell heavily among the roots protruding from the ground at the base of the tree. He lay spread-eagled, face down, legs opened wide. Davy moaned and groaned loudly as tears flooded his cheeks.

The children stopped their play instantly and moved toward Davy as one. A circle was quickly formed around him as he squirmed while laying on his side. With both hands between his legs he held tightly to his testicles, opening and closing his bent knees repeatedly. Davy now became hysterical and was screaming at the top of his lungs.

"Ouch, it hurts, it hurts," Davy yelled, "my balls, my balls!" He rolled over a few times as if the motion might ease the pain, but the pain did not subside and he continued to scream.

Ray Lucero arrived, strolling in from the alley side of the lot and promptly gave his full attention to his fallen pal. Taking Davy by the arm Ray tried raising him gently, but Davy refused to budge.

"Hey, Russian," Ray called to Emilio, "give me a hand!"

Emilio at eleven years of age had large hands and broad shoulders and was only an inch or so shorter than Ray's nearly six feet of height.

Ray's Spanish background was evident in his green eyes, fair skin, and reddish brown hair. He would be fifteen on his next birthday, making him the oldest of this band of youngsters. He was gentle and quiet and well respected by most of the group. Ray was one of the "big guys".

Emilio, better known as the Russian by the kids in the neighborhood, had flaming red hair, blue eyes, and large freckles covering his entire face and ears and extending back to his neck and shoulders on white, almost transparent skin.

His true biological ancestry was in fact Russian, but he had been adopted and raised since infancy by Spanish speaking parents and brought up in the culture that was so apparent in all of these children, that of an Hispanic background.

The rest of the group consisted of a majority having a mixture of Spanish and Indian blood or "Mestizos", the distinction given to the vast majority of people living throughout the Latin American countries in this hemisphere.

With one arm each around Davy's waistline and the other under his legs, Ray and Emilio carried him toward Arapaho Street with home as the ultimate destination.

As Davy was carried past Mary, she innocently inquired, "Does it hurt a lot, Davy?"

Mary was genuinely concerned but was rather naive with her question. She reached over to touch Davy, but he snapped his head to one side avoiding her glance and her touch.

Without replying, Davy managed to repress an urge to swear and instead hung his head and groaned a little louder.

All this time Emilio was wearing a huge smile, finding the entire situation extremely amusing.

Ray and Emilio the Russian, holding tightly to their damaged friend, walked toward Davy's house. As they walked, Emilio turned to Davy and asked, "Did you hurt your pee-pee?" Then releasing an enormous guffaw he moved his head up and down for emphasis.

"Shut up, you fuckin' asshole!" Davy yelled at the Russian, "and stop shaking me, you're hurtin' my balls!"

Again, Emilio taunted Davy. "How's your 'huevos'?" he asked using the Spanish word for eggs, and another guffaw.

Of course, Emilio Chacon meant no harm, for he was one of the gentlest of souls with a happy-go-lucky attitude as portrayed by his enchanting and humorous personality. He was younger than Davy who was nearly thirteen, but as large as he was in stature, he tended to hang out with the smaller guys, like Nick and Freddy who were closer to his own age.

Davy was carried away and the trio could no longer be seen. As if by magic, and in one motion, the kids returned to their play.

Mary climbed the tree trunk followed closely by Nick. She wore no socks and as she clambered up the tree the heels of her feet would pop out of her unlaced tennis shoes. Her skirt slipped up to her waistline when she bent her knees for the climb revealing her upper legs. Her thick smooth thighs complimented her muscular calves as she climbed inadvertently exposing her fluffy white bloomers.

Shoulder length coal black hair dangled precariously over Mary's thin sallow face as she continued up the tree. She bent forward reaching down with her finger tips to steady herself making sure that her knees did not touch the surface.

Nick, following directly behind Mary, stretched out his arms and gripped her by the hips while shouting with glee, "Wait for me, Mary!"

Mary reached the upper curve of the tree trunk and turned enough to pull Nick up by the suspender of his overalls. Laughing loudly she called, "Come on, Nicky!" At the top curve of the tree they stood close together.

As Nick stood at the top he felt the tip of his penis touch his pants at the crotch. He looked down to see the bulge between his legs and tried pushing it down with his hand only to have it grow larger. He stuck his right hand into his pocket and pushed down on his penis as he slowly bent his knees going into a squatting position. He tried frantically to hide the erection that had so suddenly appeared. Mary bent down toward Nick and asked him, "What's the matter Nicky, are you tired?"

"Yeah," Nick lied, "you go ahead, Mary, I'll be right behind you!"

The dampness of her hair touching his face as she leaned toward him, and the fresh smell of soap emanating from her body made the sensations he was feeling more acute. Nick had touched her stomach and her hips while on the way up and now had an overwhelming urge to embrace her. However, because of his total embarrassment he reluctantly refrained from doing so.

What Nick was experiencing at this moment was totally innocent and without malicious intent, in spite of the braggadocio that he and his buddies usually displayed when discussing the opposite sex.

The sensations that he was feeling would not go away. He contemplated and searched for his next move in the recesses of his mind. He found nothing.

Mary, in compliance to Nick's request, stood up and took hold of the knotted rope. After making the customary adjustments with her hands, she pushed away from the tree, bending her knees as she went swinging through the air.

Nick took a quick glance at Mary, but instantly turned away to avoid eye contact. At that moment he was desperately trying to rid himself of this erection that he had experienced so suddenly. Managing to finally control his unexpected stimulation, Nick stood up to take his turn on the knotted rope.

Freddy Carrizales was now on the upper branch swinging the rope to those below. He was perspiring profusely due to his turns at the knotted rope, he welcomed the break. With one hand under his cheek and the other free to manipulate the knotted rope, Freddy made himself comfortable.

In the meantime Mary had dropped to the ground. As she did so, she fell in a sitting position with her legs thrown upward revealing her underwear with slight tear in the center of her bloomers.

On seeing this, Freddy immediately sat up, straddled the branch and shouted, "Hey, Mary, I see your twat!" Then in repeatedly sing-song he continued, "I saw your twaat, I saw your twaat!"

Mary in consternation shouted back, "Shut up you goddam pig, you didn't see shit!" She stood up and pulled down her skirt. She felt no particular embarrassment, only anger at the audacity of Freddy's remarks.

Meanwhile, Nick attempted to hide the embarrassment he was feeling, for himself as well as for Mary, by trying not to notice what had transpired between his two friends.

Finally, Nick swung away from the tree and landed in the same general area where Mary now stood. He wiped his brow and grinned, a rather forced grin at that, since his feelings at this point were a mixed bag to say the least.

It was late afternoon now, and the sun seemed willing to touch down somewhere behind the buildings of downtown Denver. The tree no longer cast a shadow, and the leaves had stopped reflecting sunlight. The buildings' silhouettes appeared in the distance and soon darkness would be replacing daylight, the daylight that these children cherished for so many hours throughout the day.

After taking a couple of swings on the knotted rope Freddy's older brother, Ricky, opted to relax by sitting on the seat swing the rest of the afternoon.

Emilio returned from his mission of mercy and took a few turns on the knotted rope.

Nick and Mary walked to the alley and turned east to 22nd Street in the direction of Mary's home. Their conversation was highly animated.

TWO

At about six the next morning Nick was awakened by the noise reverberating from the city water truck spraying the curb on Arapaho Street just below the living room windows. A swath of sunlight penetrated the glass on the window, resting directly on Nick's face. He felt the heat as the brightness of the sun went through his eyelids.

Nick had been relegated to the couch since Davy's return from the hospital. Their once shared bedroom was now solely occupied by Davy, who at this very moment was stirring and about to wake up from a miserable night.

Nick sat up rubbing his eyes as he tossed his legs over the side in preparation for his morning routine. As usual, he put his shoes on first, then slipped into his overalls tying the suspenders around his waist and letting the front bib fall over the knot. Next, he put on his worn and frayed denim shirt. Untying the knot in front, he then carelessly tucked in the shirt and finally hooked the buttons on the bib to the brass loops on the suspenders.

Rare was the kid in the neighborhood who wore underwear, and Nick was no exception. No socks were worn either. Tennis shoes were the order of the day. Torn shoes were usually held together with adhesive tape until, with any luck at all, a new or better pair came along. During the hot summer months bare feet were not uncommon.

Hearing a slight groan and a grunt, Nick walked into the bedroom to check on Davy.

Davy was on his back with his head resting on two pillows, with knees up and legs opened wide. Turning his head Davy looked at Nick as he came through the doorway.

"I think they cut off my dick," Davy began to explain, "I can't feel nothin'!"

Nick's eyes widened and his mouth dropped open as he whispered, "Wow, let me see!"

Davy pulled back the sheet exposing the area of the wound. Nick could see a trace of blood coming through the bandage at the spot where presumably the tip of his penis should be. Nick's eyes grew wider as he stared down between Davy's legs. Now Davy groaned a little louder.

"Davy, wait, don't wake anybody up 'till I get out uh' here!" Nick told him, "I'm going to the market with the guys!" With that he turned and quietly sneaked out the back door.

The family rented the five room second floor flat with access to the roof via the rear porch. Often the brothers would go up to the roof to throw stones onto the shed roof across the back yard or to just generally horse around. At times they would peek into the next door neighbor's window one floor below just to see what was going on in the bedroom.

This morning Nick climbed the wooden ladder and pushed open the trap door at the top. He intended to walk on the roof toward the front of the house and look over the edge for Emilio and Freddy who were to pick him up. Sticking his head through the trap door Nick caught the aroma of fresh green weeds. Unmistakably the odor of freshly cut marijuana plants. He peeked over the flat roof as the rest of his body came through the trap door.

Three quarters of the roof's surface was covered with carefully laid out buds and leaves attached to short stems and resting on large sheets of canvas. Now Nick understood what the commotion of the night before had been. He had seen someone carrying something on their shoulders up to the roof. Through the open kitchen door he watched momentarily but thought nothing of it at the time.

On the roof, Nick took a few deep breaths to take in the aroma that he liked so much. It was a strong, fresh odor and much better than when it was being smoked by his father and his father's friends. Nick was accustomed to the smell of marijuana, for it had been somewhat of a family staple as far back as he could remember.

Stepping around the hemp, Nick walked to the front of the building to see if the guys were coming. Sure enough, Emilio and Freddy were less than a block away. Freddy was pulling a four wheeled wooden wagon as they walked west from 22nd Street.

Nick took his right forefinger and thumb to his lips and blew a short shrill whistle. The guys looked up and waved as Nick turned and ran to the escape hatch.

The boys met directly across the street near the tree. They turned in the direction of the city's business district, heading for the Produce Market Exchange situated just outside the main drag at 16th and Market Streets. They continued west on Arapaho then turned north on 18th Street. They crossed Lawrence and Larimer then turned west on Market Street. There they could see the trucks and horse wagons backed into the docks that serviced the single story wood frame buildings

The area was bustling.

Nick, Freddy and Emilio already had their routine mapped out, for they had done this many times in the past. They approached the docks and pushed their empty wagon underneath a dock platform near a horse wagon.

Now Freddy would approach the horse with a tidbit, calming him down by feeding and petting him. The other two would now begin their surreptitious activity.

Nick took his position under the horse wagon as Emilio wandered about in the general area as if looking for damaged goods on the ground. Walking back to the wagon with a couple of cucumbers in his hands, Emilio was ready to board the horse wagon to relieve it of some of its contents. Freddy continued to feed and pet the horse to keep it calm. He seemed to be having some success.

Nick waited patiently under the wagon for the produce to begin dropping. Emilio, waiting for a signal from Freddy, swiftly surveyed the entire area in the vicinity of the docks then placed one foot on the wheel hub of the wagon. They looked at each other and simultaneously whispered, "Now!"

Within seconds Emilio was in the wagon to begin dropping produce of every type over the side. Nick raked it into the gunnysack down below. In two to three minutes Nick had made enough trips with the sack to fill the wooden wagon. The boys quickly departed from the parked horse wagon without incident and richer by a few pounds of produce.

On this particular day the boys had managed to accumulate a variety of fruits and vegetables. There were apples, oranges, grapefruit, tomatoes, lettuce, cucumbers, and onions. Included were two good sized cantaloupes and a fairly large watermelon that topped off the take.

The watermelon was broken across the middle when Nick caught it with the aid of his knee as it fell from above. By breaking the fall, he avoided a completely smashing disaster.

The small wagon was fully loaded and covered with an empty gunnysack. Pieces of broken wooden crates were placed over the entire load. The wire wheels of the little wagon were wobbly and unsteady under the heavy load, but with Nick at the helm, and his companions pushing from behind, everything was going well.

As the boys began their journey home, Emilio remarked, "I need a smoke, let's look for butts!"

The trio, retracing their steps, pulled the heavily loaded wagon along the curb. By the time they reached the end of the block, Emilio had already found several cigarette butts. He stopped momentarily to tear off the ends where others had placed their lips., being conscious of the fact that germs could be transferred by way of the cigarette butt from someone else's mouth.

Francisca and the Boys

"You guys got matches?" Emilio asked.

"Yeah, I got some," replied Freddy, pulling half a dozen stick matches from his pocket.

"Wait 'til we get in the alley, you guys," Nick intervened, "and we can sit down for a while."

The boys crossed Larimer Street and turned in at the first alley. They walked to the middle of the block and picked a spot next to a high wood fence. Sitting on the alley cement the boys leaned back against the fence and made themselves comfortable. Legs propped up and arms resting on their knees the boys lit up.

Nick took a look at his trimmed cigarette and found the brand name on the paper. "Hey, I got a Lucky," he said. "What did you get?" Then he took a long drag and inhaled deeply.

"Mine don't got nuthin'," Freddy answered.

"This one's a Twenty Grand, man," offered Emilio.

After a few minutes of silence and a few puffs on their butts, Emilio was the first to speak.

"Nicky," he said "have you smoked any *grifa* yet?"

"Nah," replied Nick, "I'm scared to try it, I think it puts you to sleep, have you?"

"Nah, not yet," Emilio answered, leaving open the possibilities for future experimentation.

Freddy entered the conversation, "It does put you to sleep, because when Alvino smokes it, after a while his eyes get real small. I think he sleeps with his eyes open." Alvino being his step father, his mother's common law husband.

The conversation continued and the subjects varied. Now it would turn to Mary Moya.

Emilio was the first to bring up her name.

"Man," he said, "Mary sure looked nice yesterday by the tree, first time I seen her wearing a dress."

"Yeah," cut in Nick, "she smelled good too, I was real close to her and I started to get a hard-on."

Emilio guffawed in his usual manner and slapped his knees as he did so. Freddy also laughed loudly, then giggled as he put his hands to his mouth.

Nick smiled and continued talking, "Yuh know, when I was walking with her through the alley yesterday?" Nick paused for effect. He continued, "Well, she was telling me that somebody in her house had done dirty things to her."

Emilio and Freddy stopped giggling and both looked at Nick in anticipation of what would be coming next.

Nick continued, "I think she got screwed or raped, or something like that."

Nick refrained from using the stronger word, "fucked" because of his respect for Mary and in his mind he could not associate Mary with anything dirty.

The other two boys now stared at Nick, waiting for the rest of the story.

"She couldn't tell me everything 'cause she began to cry," Nick said, "I didn't know what to say, I just left her on 22nd and I went home."

There was a long period of silence as the boys smoked their butts and just looked downward, each with his own thoughts on this thing that had happened to their friend. In spite of the fooling around that the group engaged in, they were all concerned about one another.

Freddy broke the silence by asking, "How's Davy, anyway, is he home?"

Before Nick could answer he was interrupted by Emilio, "Yeah, how's his peter?" And he laughed as he slapped his knees one more time.

"He thinks they cut off his dick," replied Nick, "I don't know, but he sure had a lot of bandages wrapped all around his prick, and his balls, and all over, we won't know until the bandages come off!"

Emilio became unusually serious for a few minutes and remained quiet. Suddenly he broke out into his usual type of humor by shouting, "Now he's gonna be a girl!" followed by his knee slapping routine.

"Come on, you guys, let's get goin'," Nick finally said

Nick stood up and went to the wagon and dumped the wooden pieces to one side and pulled the gunny sack back. He then broke off a piece of watermelon and took a bite of the juicy red interior. The others followed suit.

The consummate buddies began their trek back to the neighborhood. Leaving a trail of watermelon rinds, the boys continued down the alley looking for junk and empty bottles.

Bottles were a good source of income, wine bottles in particular since there were more of these to be found. They quart size paid two cents apiece while the pints paid only half a cent, therefore you had to look twice as hard to make a penny.

Whiskey bottles were good but they were beginning to show up with stamped printing on one side which read, "No deposit no return". Half gallon beer bottles were good for a nickel but the no deposit printing was beginning to show up on them also.

Milk bottles were another good source, but you had to steal them from porches very early in the morning before the milkman arrived. Sometimes if the milkman arrived first, then you would naturally enjoy the fresh milk he left, then take the empty bottle.

Metals were another good source of income. Aluminum was acceptable but hard to find, iron sold but was too heavy to carry, so the boys concentrated on finding copper which was easier to find and brought in the most money.

Emilio volunteered to push the wagon while Nick pulled and guided. Freddy got stuck with the gunny sack over his shoulder with a few bottles in it. The boys trudged along talking and laughing and generally horsing around. They approached the electric transformer station that occupied the whole corner at 21st and Lawrence and covering about a quarter of the block. They found numerous pieces of copper cable and some strands of insulated wire which would certainly help to supplement their income.

Repairs had been recently been made at the station and pieces of copper wire had been left in the alley just outside the station fence.

The boys filled the gunny sack with all types of copper pieces and wire strands. The heavy pieces of cable would earn them enough to pay their way in to the Zaza theater to see Buster Crabbe in the next chapter of "Flash Gordon".

Emilio stopped for a moment and pulled a cigarette butt out of his shirt pocket and lit up. "You guys wanna smoke?" he asked.

Nick replied, "Nah, not me."

"I'll take a couple o' drags from yours," Freddy told him, Emilio was agreeable.

A little ways down the alley the boys stopped at the rear entrance of the candy factory. By now the aroma was sweet and strong and it tingled their olfactory senses, making their taste buds swim in saliva.

The boys pulled in their wagon and parked it just inside the rear driveway and walked toward the opened rear door. They could see clear through to the front of the building to the street where the front door was also open.

Inside there were wooden racks about ten feet high holding metal trays that were lined with small candies recently covered with melted chocolate. The racks stood against the walls on both sides of the room and a long conveyer belt turned in the center carrying candy to be processed further toward the rear.

There were empty candy boxes piled next to the loading platform ready for trash pick up, and candies of many types strewn in and around the trash can.

Freddy climbed the loading platform, walked to the opened door to look around and take in some of the delicious aroma, and perhaps to steal some candy if no one was looking. The large woman working on one side of the belt looked up from her job momentarily and smiled at Freddy. She quickly turned her eyes back to her task of pouring melted chocolate over the white candies on the trays being carried along on the belt. The woman wore thick cloth gloves and poured the hot chocolate from a long heavy ladle.

There were three other women along the length of the conveyer belt, each performing a required duty in the manufacture of the product.

A man worked at the end of the conveyer belt taking candy filled trays and placing them on the racks. Every now and then he would stop the belt by pushing a button so as not to become overwhelmed then restart it after catching up.

As the conveyer belt was stopped for a moment, the man took three cooled chocolates in one hand and quickly handed them to Freddy.

"Here," the man said, "you better get out of here before the boss shows up."

Precisely at that very moment the owner of the factory was walking toward the rear of the building.

Freddy jumped from the platform calling excitedly, "Jiggers you guys, here comes the guy, let's blow!"

Shoving one of the candies into his mouth Freddy handed one each to the others and ran to the wagon. Picking up the handle, he strained to get it to roll just as Emilio stepped in behind and pushed. Nick stepped in next to Emilio to help, while throwing a full box of candy on to the wagon.

Just as the boys were pulling out of the factory yard, the owner, a short, heavy set man with blond hair parted at the center and flopping around his ears, stepped out to the rear platform shouting, "Get out o' here, you goddam Spicks!"

The trio turned east into the alley as the man continued his verbal assault with arms flailing, "Go back to where you belong ya dirty Spicks!" he screamed at the top of his lungs.

On hearing the last remark Emilio stopped abruptly and went back a few steps to confront the man, all-be-it from a safe distance. Taking his right hand clenched into a fist, Emilio gestured by pumping it several times in front of his crotch with legs in an open stance and shouting back, "Here, you fuckin' fat ass!" then turning quickly and running to catch up with his buddies, knowing full well that the man would not follow. Even if he followed, his weight would allow him only a minimal distance of pursuit.

After running a short distance the boys stopped at the end of the alley and turned right on 22nd Street looking back to see if they were being followed. There was no one in sight They felt safe enough to slow down the pace. The boys stopped at the first gangway they encountered on 22nd Street. They parked their wagon and walked into the space between two buildings. Nick proceeded to open the box of candy he had been carrying from the candy factory. He examined its contents to see if it might be edible.

"Look, you guys," Nick said, presenting the exposed candy to his partners, "how do they look?"

The candies were whole and with a slight tinge of dryness of the outer skin.

"They look OK to me!" Freddy spoke up.

Nick took one of the candies and broke it in half with his fingers. He examined the center closely, smelled it and took a small bite.

"It tastes ok, but I don't know," he said more to himself, a doubtful look crossing his face, "there might be worms in there but I don't see nuthin'."

Emilio reached into the box and took a candy in each hand. He raised his right hand with a candy between his thumb and forefinger and held it up to the light as if to look through it. Rolling it several times in his fingers he said, "Well, guys, worms or no worms!" and summarily tossed it into his mouth and began to chew.

The others followed his lead without further doubt as to the edibility of the candy. The boys stood around until most of the candy had been devoured. Suddenly they were all feeling full after piling the candy on top of the watermelon they had eaten earlier.

Without further word the trio moved out of the gangway to complete their journey home.

As they began their walk toward home, Emilio took one more piece of candy and shoved it into his mouth. He chewed on it for a little while then stuck his fingers in his mouth and pulled out an elongated piece of caramel. He held it up and dangled it to make it appear as if it was a living worm.

"Look guys," Emilio exclaimed, "it's alive!"

Freddy immediately crossed his eyes and grabbed his stomach, making a face as if to vomit.

Emilio put the caramel back in his mouth and broke out to his usual guffaw while slapping Freddy on the shoulders.

"You fuckin' idiot," Freddy shouted, "you're nuts!"

The journey came to an end in Nick's back yard where the boys proceeded to divide their load of produce.

The bottles and copper wire would be stored in the woodshed and would remain there until there was enough junk to sell at the junkyard on Friday afternoon.

Since the election of Franklin D. Roosevelt in the early 1930's, the era of the so called Great Depression, the jobless soon began to find work due to programs instituted by the new President. However, in Francisca's world, everything remained the same.

Francisca was never reluctant to accepting food items brought home by her sons. She never questioned them as to the origin of their contributions because she fully understood that these things were absolute necessities. A contribution to the household in any form was welcomed and perhaps encouraged by silence and passivity and prayer.

When speaking of poverty, Francisca Delmonte was a history of poverty within herself. She had known poverty as a toddler in Mexico and as a growing child in El Paso, Texas. What she and her family were experiencing now could not be compared to the poverty and misery of past years. Now she was thankful for what she had, even if it was just for the moment.

Francisca was brought to the United States at a very tender age by her mother Silvina. The revolution in Mexico had forced Silvina to seek ways of survival after her husband had been conscripted into military service for one side or the other, which side Silvina was never really sure.

Francisca was brought up in the poorest section of El Paso being oblivious to what constituted poverty. She learned English in elementary school but only managed to reach and finish the fourth grade. After an altercation in which Francisca winged a heavy stone to the head of one of the teachers, she was dutifully expelled and never to see the inside of a school again.

So in comparison, yes, these were fairly good times.

There were not many rules that Nick and Davy had to adhere to, but the ones that were in place had to be followed to the letter or the consequences would have to be met.

Swearing and smoking were not allowed much less the drinking of alcohol. Coming home after nine o'clock curfew was punishable by a whipping with a razor strop or a belt or whatever happened to be handy at the time. If the offense was grave or it involved outsiders, like the police, then the punishment was a little more stern. Then the punishment would include kneeling on the floor, in a corner of the room with arms crossed and held away from the body, back straight without movement of any kind, not even whimpering or coughing. Sometimes a cold bath in the tin tub was thrown in for good measure if the punishment was warranted by the offense.

Francisca, as a child, had been whipped with a cat-o-nine-tails by her step father, and it was difficult for her to break away from what was considered normal during her own childhood, not completely understanding that it had been physical abuse. She still carried the scars on her back and buttocks due to the whippings. As far as she was concerned, her sons had it pretty easy. She now had modified the punishment to avoid injury to her boys.

Francisca and the Boys

Nick placed his share of the produce on a small table near the kitchen sink. Nothing would be touched until it was thoroughly washed.

There was a large stack of flour tortillas on the kitchen table and the aroma of melted cheese in fried beans in the air. The pan of rice was on the stove, covered with a plate and steaming hot. Nick attempted to remove the plate from the pan to catch a whiff. He abandoned the idea after burning his fingers.

The *molcajete* was on the table full of ground green peppers, with tomato and garlic mixed and ground into a delicious *salsa*. These were food staples that never varied and they sustained the family quite well.

"Wash your hands and sit down!" Francisca told Nick with authority.

Nick knew better than to ever question Francisca's authority, he complied.

At times Francisca would swear at the boys when she was irritated, but always in Spanish because she thought English swear words sounded vulgar.

Nick went to the stove with a dishcloth in his hand to use as a pot holder. He picked up the hot water pot and poured water into the wash pan in the sink. He refilled the pot and placed it back on the stove to remain in perpetuity. He washed his hands like he was told.

Nick sat down to a plate filled to the edges with beans and rice and with as much *chile* that he cared to add to his food. Nick would never let a meal go by under any circumstances. So in spite of the watermelon and the candy, he proceeded to indulge.

A groan was heard coming from Davy's bedroom, then his voice, "Ma, oh ma!"

Francisca walked into the bedroom with Nick close on her heels.

"What is it," Francisca asked Davy, "and stop saying ma, ma, you sound like a goat!"

Francisca felt terrible that this accident had happened to her son David, but she was not about to let him know her true feelings. She was very strong in that respect and she continued to maintain the facade so as not to pamper Davy too much during his illness.

"I have to pee, ma, how am I gonna do it?" Davy told Francisca.

His mother was very close to laughing but she managed to maintain her composure, "Just wait a minute and I'll get you a *basinilla,*" She went to the porch and brought back a porcelain urinal with a curved loop handle.

Davy protested, "But ma, how am I gonna pee?" He was still under the illusion that his penis was missing.

Francisca pulled back the cover and helped Davy sit up in bed. She placed the urinal between his legs. "Look," she explained, "see that little hole in the bandage, just pull back the bandage a little bit and aim for the pot!"

Davy did what he was told and breathed a sigh of relief when he saw the flow of urine come through the hole in the bandage. He urinated slowly for the swelling was still apparent, and managed to evacuate his bladder with his mother's encouragement. When Davy was finished, Francisca took the urinal and handed it to Nick and said, "Here, go empty it in the toilet."

Francisca turned to Davy and said, "Let me tell you what the doctors told me about your *huevos.*"

Davy responded with, "Maaa!"

"Shut up and listen!" admonished Francisca.

Nick stood there, still holding the urinal and he would not leave until he heard about his brother's injury.

Francisca continued, "When you fell you hit the bone that is up here," she pointed to herself in more or less the corresponding area to Davy's injury. She continued, "The bone did not break but you hit it hard enough to make your pee-pee swell up."

Davy was feeling embarrassed at this point so he looked downward and scratched his head.

"So," continued Francisca, "your thing swelled up so much that they had to cut off the skin hanging from your pee-pee."

On hearing this, Davy began to sob and the tears rolled down his cheeks.

"Wait, let me finish," she told Davy turning him gently by the shoulder, "it's called a circumcision, and when it's through healing you will be as good as new!"

Davy was not thoroughly convinced about the being "as good as new" stuff, but he accepted his mother's explanation. At least he still had something to hold on to, he thought, not completely understanding the irony in his thinking. Davy managed to laugh to himself.

There had been no swelling to the testicles and no fractures found in the pelvic area, no open wounds around the pubis, contusion to the base of the penis with extreme swelling due to trauma, removal of redundant prepuce recommended to relieve pressure. All this according to the doctors at Denver General Hospital.

Nick walked away and completed his assigned chore with a great load lifted from his shoulders. His big brother would be alright, but the best part of it all was that all his parts were still in place.

THREE

The stitches had been removed from around the corona of Davy's penis, and like his mother had predicted, he was as good as new. So much so that the brothers were now up to their old selves again wrestling and roughhousing in their bedroom.

Grabbing and gripping each other the boys rolled around on their bed. Now and then they would fall off stopping long enough to return to the soft mattress and resume their antics. Trading and switching body holds, the boys finally ended up in a position where each had a scissor hold around the head of the other. Ankles were tightly held together in a crossed position with the opponent's head between the knees. While Davy was the bigger and stronger of the two, Nick managed to hold his own while they were locked together.

"Ya give, Nicky?" Davy asked in a breathless second.

"Naw," replied Nick, barely able to get the word out.

"OK then, you asked for it," Davy shot back. Davy then released a flatulent gas that he had been holding in reserve, loudly into Nick's face as he burst into a frenzy of laughter. Nick found the strength to pull his head out of the scissor grip screaming, "Davy, you fat pig!" and jumping off the bed he continued, "I'm gonna tell Ma, you stupid ass!"

The boys continued to laugh loudly lying on their backs and trying to catch their breath.

"Let's go see if any uh the guys are outside," Davy suggested.

"OK, let's go," responded Nick.

Nick and Davy had been across the street around the tree several times in the last few days but for some unknown reason it was no longer as much fun as the first week of summer vacation.

For one, Mary had not been around since Nick escorted her home in tears. Notwithstanding the fact that Mary was of the opposite sex, the boys considered her to be one of the guys. She was missed by them all, but by Nick in particular to whom she confided so much, and vice versa.

There were a few things that had to be attended to before leaving the house so the boys began their preparation. Nick pulled out his cigar box full of marbles from under the bed and began the selection of those marbles that he intended to lose and those he intended to play only in case of emergency. He picked the scratched and chipped marbles and placed them in a Bull Durham bag along with his "glassies." which were to be used first. The newer ones were placed in a separate bag along with his "boulder" which was used for "breaking," and his "shooters."

The shooters were two agates, one the size of an ordinary marble used for shooting in a large ring, and the boulder, used for power when breaking. Davy went through a similar routine but he dumped all of his marbles into a leather pouch closing it with its leather thong at the opening. Each boy stuck a sheepskin knuckle pad in his pocket.

After dressing and washing up, the boys went into the kitchen to see what they could find to eat before embarking on their adventures of the day. Their mother was in her bedroom presumably resting comfortably, so the boys quietly tiptoed around the kitchen making as little noise as possible.

Davy removed the pot of beans from the icebox while Nick brought out the tortillas. They each made themselves a taco of cold beans on tortilla covered with plenty of hot sauce. They poured the remaining milk from the quart bottle making sure they each had an equal amount then put the empty bottle in the sink. As they chewed on their tacos, the boys heard a slight stirring in their mother's bedroom. Knowing that Francisca was about to awaken they hurriedly downed their milk and quietly walked out the rear door while still holding firmly to their tacos to finish on the way to their next stop. Through the back yard to the alley and around to the corner to Arapaho and 21st Street, giving themselves enough time to finish eating their tacos before meeting up with any of the guys.

Mr. Ransom was unlocking the door to his drugstore on the corner of 21st and Arapaho. He greeted the boys with a cheerful, "Hi kids!"

The boys responded, "Hello Mr. Ransom."

Mr. Ransom was a very tall black man with very short grey hair and a cheerful, yet serious disposition. He also happened to be the uncle to Earl, one of the boys' closest friends who at this particular time was visiting relatives out of town.

On one occasion within the last few months, when a few of the boys were playing "kick the can" in the street in front of the store, someone got the idea of pounding on the large front windows then running to hide before the owner came out. On about the third or fourth pounding Mr. Ransom was ready and waiting. Nick happened to be one of the culprits during this particular episode and he got caught.

As Nick ran through the alley with Mr. Ransom on his heels, he scaled a wooden fence. Sliding over the fence on his stomach he caught a long sliver of wood that became imbedded in his chest between the muscle and the skin.

Mr. Ransom had caught up with Nick and brought him back to the store to turn him over to his parents. Under the circumstances, the druggist decided to take him into the store to attend to his injury.

Nick had stood in the store with tears in his eyes while sobbing uncontrollably, more from fear and shame than any pain Eventually Mr. Ransom had removed the sliver from Nick's chest while receiving a solemn promise from his young captive never to repeat the window pounding again. To this day Nick had kept his promise and now gave Mr. Ransom the respect that he deserved.

Francisca and the Boys

The boys crossed the street toward the lot now, each carrying a full stomach. Ray Lucero was there straddling his bike. He owned the only bike in the immediate surroundings with balloon tires and bright chrome fenders. It was a Schwin.

Rick and Freddy and Emilio were there shooting marbles "just for fun". The serious or "for keeps" games were usually held between Twenty Third and Twenty Fourth Streets a half block from the school. Other players, from the east and the north sides of town would eventually show up to join in the games.

Ray turned his bike around and told the others, "See you guys by the school." He rode off as the rest of the guys began their two block walk.

At Twenty Third and Arapaho there was a fairly large area in front of a fenced-in lot where the ground was hard and smooth, having been pounded down by the players to insure that the marbles rolled smoothly whenever a game took place. There were already a few boys shooting marbles in two large circles that had been scratched on the ground surface for that purpose.

Ray had already drawn a circle of his own by the time the others arrived, and had been practice shooting for a while. He was the best player of the group, but on a good day, almost anyone could be a winner. The rest of the boys arrived and immediately began shooting for practice without the benefit of a circle.

Four boys on the other circles were finishing up their game with some arguing amongst themselves.

There were three Irish kids from Five Points, an area about eight to ten blocks from Twenty Fourth Street School and out of the district. A well known tough guy and trouble maker by the name of Joe Spino was also there He came from the North Side, from beyond the railroad tracks on the other side of the viaduct. Joe Spino was called "Little Joe" because of his short stature and muscular build. But in spite of his size, Little Joe was mean and aggressive, therefore he was considered to be one of the "tough guys." He was of Italian descent and at about age twelve, he was also pugnacious to no end.

The first game had ended and now all the boys were standing around to see who would be "in" when the next game would begin. Little Joe and two East Side boys would play from their group. Ray, Davy, and Nick entered from the local group.

Each boy would ante up five marbles to be placed in the center of the six foot ring, but first they all must "lag" or shoot to a straight line scratched in the ground about ten feet away to see who would come the closest and be the first to "break"

Nick shot with his small agate and stopped at about three inches from the line. One by one each boy shot to the line. Nick was closest so he would start the game by shooting first into the circle and breaking the marbles that were bunched together in the center. He placed his knuckle pad at the outer edge of the circle and prepared to shoot with his large marble, the "boulder".

Suddenly Little Joe stepped up and stood inside the circle directly in front of Nick blocking his shooting path.

"No boulders!" exclaimed Little Joe.

Nick stood up from his crouched position and asked, "Why not, we didn't make no rules?"

Little Joe reiterated with authority, "I said no boulders!" He placed his hands on his hips and put his face directly in front of Nick's looking him straight in the eye.

Nick was on the verge of responding when Ray stepped between the two, convincing Nick to use a smaller shooter to save the peace. Nick reluctantly agreed but only because his friend Ray had asked him to, not because he was afraid of Little Joe.

Nick made the break with his medium sized agate, spreading marbles in every direction and hitting three marbles out of the ring. His shooter rolled out of the ring thus eliminating a second chance shot until his next turn.

Little Joe shot next and managed to hit two marbles out of the ring, his shooter rolling out of the circle in the process.

Davy shot next for a couple of good ones, as did the two kids from the east side of town. Now it was Ray's turn to shoot.

Francisca and the Boys

Ray cleared a spot on the outer edge of the ring with sweeping motions of the palm of his right hand. He then placed four fingers of his left hand just outside the circle, balancing his body with one knee on the ground, his fingertips touching the ground with left wrist higher up.

Ray took his first shot at a small bunch of marbles not yet dispersed. His shooter scattered the marbles as it hit the center of the bunch. Several marbles rolled out of the circle from the force of the shot, his shooter sticking on the spot. He then methodically continued hitting most of the marbles out of the ring one by one. He purposely left four marbles in the ring letting his shooter roll out, thus "scratching" on purpose so that his buddy Nick would have something to shoot at.

Nick cleared the ring of the last four marbles and picked up his shooter along with his winnings. He was ready for the next game.

At the instant that Nick stood up with all his marbles Little Joe walked up to Nick and pushed him hard to the ground shouting, "You fudged you fuckin' Spick!

Nick jumped up ready to fight but before anything happened, Davy was on Little Joe aiming a roundhouse right that landed squarely on Little Joe's forehead. Little Joe staggered backward and stopped for about a second or two to regain his composure. He attacked Davy like a bull seeing red.

As Little Joe went on the offensive he lunged head first at Davy who was waiting for him. Davy stuck out his left hand jamming his fist square on the nose of Little Joe. Then Davy swung another right hand that landed on Little Joe's left ear. Little Joe went down As he fell he went forward, head down, directly into the wooden fence separating the lot from the sidewalk. Little Joe stood up crying and swearing.

"I'll getcha, ya fuckin' Spick," Little Joe shouted at Davy, "ya got all dees guys here right now, but I'll getcha!"

"Get outta here before I really kick your ass, you fuckin' Wop," Davy answered as he made a threatening motion toward

Little Joe. Little Joe turned the corner and ran north on 24th Street.

"Hey, I could have taken him," Nick said, "I ain't afraid of him!"

"Yeah, yeah," Davy razzed Nick, "we know you could."

The guys smirked and laughed giving Nick the benefit of the doubt.

Nick felt pretty good that his big brother had stuck up for him but he didn't care too much for the ethnic slurs that the combatants had tossed at one another. Oh, he used them himself whenever the occasion called for it, but an uneasy feeling persisted when he did, for he knew exactly how it felt, for he had been called a Spick and a dirty Mexican more than once in his young life.

All the guys went back to playing marbles with the exception of Ray. The kids from the east side refused to play against him because he was just too good. Ray dropped out of the games without complaining stood around to watch.

The games ended with satisfied winners and non-complaining losers. It was closing in on noon time, a good time to head for home and make preparations for swimming at the bathhouse. Ray left on his bike. The Irish kids walked east toward Five-Points, and the rest walked two blocks west to the tree.

At the tree the boys stood around and talked for a while, they soon separated, each going his own way.

Davy and Nick walked across the street to their house. Nick turned and shouted to Freddy and Emilio, "See ya at the bathhouse, guys!"

"OK," they shouted back in unison.

Francisca was sweeping the living room floor when the boys walked in the front door.

"Look what time it is," she said, "go in there and make your bed and wash the dishes and throw the garbage out." She kept sweeping as she spoke without looking up.

There were no rugs on the living room floor and only a few furniture items. A long davenport couch rested against the wall just below the living room windows. To one side stood two straight backed wooden chairs with black leather upholstered seats and a narrow table holding an alarm clock stood between the chairs. Against the opposite wall across the room stood a black Singer Sewing Machine with a sturdy wood stool in front of it. Family pictures hung on the walls along with a mirror large enough to reflect the upper half of one's body.

Finally, a large wooden trunk, reinforced by inch-wide metal strips all the way around, occupied a space near the dining room entrance. The half round cover of this trunk was closed, a strong looking padlock hung at the center.

Neither of the brothers cared for dishwashing, so there would have to be some dialogue as to who would do what in the execution of their chores.

"Let's lag for it," suggested Nick.

"OK," Davy responded, "let's go outside."

They each took a marble of equal size and stepped out the back door to the yard.

Davy took a piece of tree branch and scratched a line on the ground and asked, "You wanna shoot or throw?"

Nick, knowing full well that he could not out-shoot Davy, answered, "Let's throw." In the end, Davy won the throw anyway so they walked back into the house, instinctively knowing what each was to do.

The boys would save the garbage can for last since it took two to carry it by the handles.

Nick wore a disgusted look throughout his ordeal as a dishwasher but managed to complete his self-imposed sentence at the kitchen sink. After washing the dishes and pans Nick dried everything with a drying cloth and placed it in its proper place and finished by sweeping the kitchen floor for good measure.

Davy also completed his share of the deal by making the bed and picking up and arranging all the loose clothing into two wooden boxes on the floor that were there for that purpose.

Francisca came into the kitchen and told the boys, "I'm going to make some *quesadillas,* and after you eat I want you to take a bath."

As if purposely synchronized, the boys spoke as one, "But Maaa!"

"You gotta take a bath," she insisted.

"Ma," Davy said, "we're going to the bathhouse today and they got showers!"

"Yeah!" echoed Nick.

"Alright," Francisca told the boys, "but you have to wash your feet, look how dirty and stinky they are!"

The boys had no choice but to comply or risk the chance of not going swimming at all.

The boys ate their *quesadillas* with cold water to wash them down. They took out the garbage can and dumped its contents into the building's designated ash-pit. On returning they immediately commenced the process of feet washing in the galvanized tub that was also used for bathing and the washing of clothes.

Davy and Nick retired to their bedroom to wait until 3:15pm before leaving for the bathhouse. To kill the monotony they shot marbles on the bed, shooting the marbles into the pillows then stopping to count them over and over. It was nearing time to leave.

The doors of the bathhouse would open at 4:00 o'clock sharp and it was just 3:30 when Nick and Davy arrived. The line from the entrance near the corner was already as far as the alley.

Kids from eight to fifteen were allowed to enter but the eight year olds must be accompanied by someone to take responsibility for their behavior. Many older "brothers" and "cousins" were put into service by youngsters arriving without proper chaperones.

As the doors swung open, the wild bunch of kids shoved and pushed their way in, screaming and hollering in anticipation. As each boy passed the counter he was given a mini bar of soap and directed to the locker and shower rooms. No towels were issued, so if you wanted to dry off after swimming, you would have to bring your own towel or share someone else's. The only option left would then be to dress while dripping wet, which many of the boys did.

Soon the shower room was fogged with steam as everyone was soaping, scrubbing, rinsing and preparing for examination by the lifeguard before entering the pool. No wash cloths were allowed so scrubbing was done by hand.

The madness continued as the boys compared their penises for size, or how much fuzz or hair this one or that one had around the pubic area. Leaving the showers for the pool was indicative that you were ready for the first cold plunge, but not before the lifeguard checked out your body for any dirt or sores that might contaminate the water.

Most of the bigger kids would take their first dive from the corner of the pool on entering the pool area. The smaller ones would walk to the shallow side and slip into the cold water very slowly.

All the guys from the neighborhood were at the bathhouse with the exception of Ray, for he felt that he had outgrown the bathhouse and felt uncomfortable swimming in the nude with all the little kids present.

For the last few weeks Ray had opted to forego the bathhouse. He was now channeling his energies in other directions. His sexual urges were beginning to take effect therefore his interests had now turned to girls.

Freddy, Ricky, Emilio, Nick and Davy were all cavorting at the deep end of the pool, diving under and splashing each other. There were kids of all sizes enjoying the moment for what it was worth.

Nick took a dive and swam a ways underwater coming up at about mid pool. To his surprise he was suddenly face to face with no other than Little Joe Spino.

"Hey, Spick, my little brother's over here," Little Joe told Nick, "he's gonna kick your ass!"

"Fuck you, you fuckin' asshole," Nick replied, "I ain't scared of him or you either!"

At that very moment Davy's head popped out from underneath the surface of the water and he went straight toward Little Joe. Nick stopped Davy's advance with a hand motion and said, "Let' 'im alone, he just said his little brother was gonna kick my ass."

"You wanna fight 'im, Nicky?" Davy asked.

"Fuckin' ay!" replied Nick emphatically.

Arrangements were made for the four of them to meet in the alley across the street. Davy passed the word along to the guys that there would be a fight after swimming.

On hearing the news, Emilio rubbed his hands together with glee and remarked, "Oh boy!"

Nick was nervous not knowing what to expect since this was the first time he ever heard that Little Joe had a little brother. Looking around the pool Nick tried finding Little Joe's brother among the bobbing heads but had no luck since Nick had yet to meet him. In any event he was not about to back out from the coming encounter with his would-be adversary. He continued to swim and to enjoy himself while hiding his anxiety successfully.

Suddenly the lifeguard's whistle blew signaling the end of the hour and time for everyone to leave. If you were not out of the pool within a specified time after the whistle, you would be sprayed with a hard stream from the cold water hose.

The guys met in the locker room where everyone dried off and dressed. All were anxious to see a fight and to see how Nick would handle himself. Everyone gave Nick words of encouragement as they dressed. They were all prepared to fight in case of any interference during Nick's coming encounter.

The guys walked across the street together and into the alley. The "other side" was already there consisting of four or five boys plus the participant in the coming main event.

A circle was formed by the spectators as Nick and his opponent entered the arena. Joe Spino's little brother was a replica of his big brother, just a slight smaller.

As Nick mentally prepared himself for combat there was a sudden burst of action from across the circle. The little brother was rushing toward Nick with flailing fists, landing several blows all around Nick's head and face. Nick felt the sting of the boy's fists and for a moment his vision became a blanket of colors. He broke away from the onslaught, stepping back to recuperate. His vision cleared just as his adversary was coming in for the second attack.

Nick could hear the noise around him but only now and then could he discern a voice that he could recognize. At that particular moment everything was just a din. Nick saw his opposition ready to attack once more. The boy lunged one more time.

Nick suddenly remembered a trick he had learned from Davy. As the other boy rushed at him, Nick fell to the ground and sticking one leg out he forced his own body to one side. The kid tripped over Nick's leg and fell face first to the ground. Quickly, Nick jumped up from his stretched position and straddled the boy on the ground, flailing both fists over the boys head and neck.

The boy was now with his face and stomach on the ground with Nick aboard him like a rider on horseback.

"Let me up and fight fair!" the boy screamed as he attempted to hide his face in the ground.

Nick now took the boy's left arm and twisted it behind the back, pinning it in a hold. He grabbed the boy's right arm tucking it between the boy's body and his own right knee. Now Nick began punching with his free right hand over the kid's head and neck. Nick had no clear shots to his face.

Nick shifted by loosening the boy's left arm and tucking it inside the knee as on the other side. Now he took the boy's hair with his left hand, turning his face to inflict punishment. He pummeled the boy on the right side of his face repeatedly, so much so that his right hand became numb and was beginning to swell. The boy's face was now a swollen pulp with blood covering him from forehead to chin. The boy could no longer scream, all he could do was whimper.

Nick felt someone pulling him off the boy's back and holding his arm so that he could no longer swing. He stood up and stepped away for an instant, then he swung his right foot into the fallen boy's stomach area with great force. Nick looked around in search of Little Joe in the crowd. He spotted him and went after him with fire in his eyes.

"Call me a spick again, you rotten motherfucker!" Nick shouted.

The guys all stepped in and held Nick back.

Little Joe dragged his brother to one side and helped him stand. Little Joe had tears in his eyes.

The crowd dispersed drifting in different directions. The guys walked toward the neighborhood praising Nick as they walked along.

Nick felt his left eye swelling and turning to his cousin Freddy he asked, "Do I have a black eye?"

"Na," replied Freddy, "but it's real red." It was evident that his eye would be black and blue by morning.

Suddenly from out of the blue there was a shout, "Viva Nicky boy!" It was Emilio the Russian, whooping it up in celebration of Nick's victory.

FOUR

The guys gathered at the tree to decide what they should do for the rest of the evening, they had until nine o'clock curfew. It was six thirty, not much time before dark. Fireworks could be heard coming from around the corner on 22nd. The decision was made to meet on the corner after reporting home from swimming. They dispersed.

As the brothers crossed the street they noticed a parked automobile in front of the house. It was a 1929 Ford with big round headlights and a wheel attached to the rear. It had four doors and wide running boards on the sides. The boys stepped on the running board to look inside and saw that the interior was of all black leather. They oohed and aahed before jumping off unaware that the car belonged to their father. They climbed the porch stairs and ran up to their second floor flat to check in with their mother, Francisca.

There was a strong aroma of burning weeds in the hallway, unmistakably the smell of burning marijuana. Immediately the boys knew that their father was home. As the boys rushed into the living room, their father stood up from his chair to greet them. It seemed like a very long time since the boys had seen him, but in reality it was only one week.

Nick and Davy ran in screaming, "Chamaco!" They had never learned to call him father or dad since he was hardly ever at home. The boys picked up on the name Chamaco from others, and it stuck.

Chamaco grabbed each boy around the waist as they jumped up on him in their excitement at seeing him again. They kissed his stubbly cheeks and messed up his hair, laughing with him as he set them back on the floor.

"*Ya cabrones*, go see what your mother has for you inside," he told them. Then they ran to their bedroom where Francisca was separating new pants and shirts according to each boy's size. Her personal bonanza was already put away in her closet, but she was wearing a dissatisfied look on her face. The boys sensed that not everything was going well but they didn't dwell on it for they had learned from past experience not to ask questions. Everything was on their bed including new tennis shoes and a pair of patent leather shoes for each and at least a dozen pairs of knee length socks, something that the boys did not like to wear.

"We're going out for a while, ma," Davy told his mother, "we'll be home on time."

"Alright, but be careful with those firecrackers," she replied.

The boys kissed their mother and ran back to the living room to see their father one more time before leaving.

"We're going out to play, Chamaco," Nick told his father.

"Don't call me Chamaco, *cabron,* call me papa," his father said in mock seriousness. Nick looked at his father on the way out and smiled. The boys walked out heading for the corner at 22nd and Arapaho to meet the guys.

Chamaco, whose given name was Estanislao Delmonte, had been called "El Chamaco" since his younger days of gambling and carousing in El Paso, Texas and across the border in Juarez. He was seventeen when he left his home in Monterrey, Nuevo Leon, Mexico to find a way of life in the American border towns where the American dollar circulated quite freely. He was dubbed "El Chamaco," meaning "The Kid", because of his age and always youthful appearance. The name stuck to this day at age thirty four.

Chamaco sat in the living room accompanied by some of his friends and cohorts. There were his two brothers-in-law, Jesse and Albert, who traveled with Chamaco wherever and whenever he had "business" to attend to. Jesse was thirty six years old and was Chamaco's closest confidant, and Albert was in his middle twenties and usually served as chauffeur when on their so-called "campaigns." He also happened to be an excellent mechanic.

Jimmy "El Mocho" was there, alternately smoking his *frajo* of marijuana and drinking whiskey from a tin cup with his left hand. Jimmy had only one arm and one leg each on the opposite side of his body. His left leg was cut off just above the knee and he walked with the aid of a homemade wooden leg, fashioned so as to rest his leg stump on a surface to fit, while a continuing piece of the wooden leg went upward to be used as a handle. His right arm had been severed at the shoulder.

Jimmy had been "hooking" trains as a youth when he fell under the wheels causing the loss of those extremities. He was over six feet in height, balding and extremely heavy. He was fair skinned with Mongolian type features and, according to him, he was a true "Chicano." Jimmy had no family of his own so he attached himself to Chamaco and his crowd, becoming a trusted friend.

Jimmy was also the distributor of the *grifa* that was sold in cigarette form after final processing of the marijuana.

There were others who followed Chamaco, who had become their established leader, but there were no others here today.

After drinking and smoking and conversing for a couple of hours, the gathering broke up.

Chamaco and Francisca finally found themselves alone. They looked at each other with that longing that both suffered so much when they were apart. Without speaking they embraced and kissed, holding each other for what seemed an eternity. They slowly made their way to the bedroom and made love.

Francisca was two years younger than Chamaco. At thirty two she was still beautiful and voluptuous, having lost nothing of her beauty after the birth of her children.

Chamaco was an inveterate womanizer and could not resist the tendency as much as he tried.

Francisca knew this and tolerated his activities. He was now the same man that he was when they first met fifteen years earlier when she was just seventeen. Their love was solid, but at times the relationship was embattled and frustrating.

As they lay in bed Chamaco said, "Pancha," using a synonym for her true name, and his favorite, "I'm going to Chon's for a little while, do you mind?" Chon's was the local bar two blocks away on Larimer Street.

"Yes I mind, you just got home and you want to leave already? I'm going with you," she told him.

Chamaco slipped his right arm under and around her neck, pulled her toward him and kissed her on the cheek.

"You know what they say about women that hang around places like that, Pancha, and besides, I won't be long. I'm just going to make a few connections and I'll be right back."

"I don't care what they say about women who hang out there, anyway, it's always the men who say it, no?" She continued, "Besides, I might as well be your whore, all you do is bring me things and give me money, then you use me and leave."

"*Vete, vete pues*, I can't stop you from going," Francisca told him.

Chamaco got out of bed wearing only his BVD's and went to the kitchen to prepare his bath in the galvanized tub. The flat was not equipped with a bath tub, or even electricity. Kerosene lamps were strategically placed throughout the house and they were lit as they were needed when darkness fell. The water closet consisted of merely the commode with a high water tank and its pull chain.

Francisca came to the kitchen to help Chamaco fix his bath. By taking two kitchen chairs and placing them in front of the tub, she fashioned a curtain by tossing a sheet over the backs of the chairs. "What are you covering me up for, you already know what I look like naked," Chamaco told his wife.

"Yes, but the kids don't, they might walk in at any time," she said, "do you want them to see your skinny ass?" Chamaco laughed loudly and Francisca smiled.

Both were in a good mood and were somewhat happy to be back to a semi-normal relationship. Francisca still had doubts about the connections Chamaco claimed he was going to make. What kind of connections, she wondered. She had a pretty good idea what those connections might be and they certainly were not business. She formed a plan in her mind as she moved around the kitchen.

Chamaco was in the tin tub with his knees high over the edge, soaping, and rinsing with fresh water tossed over him by Francisca.

"*Vieja,*" Chamaco said to Francisca, "we will be going to the farm to work in the beet fields in a few days, and I'm taking you and the kids. When we get back we will move into a better flat with electricity and a bath tub."

"I don't want to live in a flat, I want a whole house where I can live and move around as I please, without nosey neighbors watching everything I do," replied Francisca. She was referring to the neighbors living on the first floor whom she never saw except when they were peeking out the windows.

"You will have it and more, my love," Chamaco told her, and meaning every word.

Since their marriage more than ten years earlier, Francisca was never wanting for any of the real necessities of life. There was always a decent place to live, with food on the table provided by Chamaco. At times there were lulls when her husband would disappear for days or weeks, and on occasion for a month or more, but there was always that revival of love and life itself whenever he returned. He would never count the money that he gave her and it was never in numerical order when he did. He would hand her rolls of bills that could hardly be held with two hands, always keeping enough to continue his activities outside the home.

Francisca's wooden chest held the secret to her husband's successes in the many ventures that he was engaged, illegal as they might be. The chest contained a future for herself and her two sons should anything happen to her beloved husband.

Chamaco was dressed in a dark suit with white shirt and black tie and ready to leave the house. He took enough money to enter the games at Chon's place and have some drinks while he was there.

"Why do you have to dress like a lawyer to go to a dump like Chon's?" Francisca asked mockingly. "To make some impressions," he replied, "you have to make these *sayos* believe that you have a lot of money to lose."

Francisca understood that from past experience, but she was fishing for any weakness in the sound of his voice or the expression on his face. She didn't see or hear anything that she could pinpoint, but she knew very well that it was there, somewhere. Chamaco kissed her several times on the eyes and cheeks and finally on the mouth, then walked out the door.

* * *

The building on the corner at 22nd and Arapaho was three floors high and it divided into two sections of front and rear. The side entrance led into a hallway separating the sections which contained a flat on each floor. The front entrance accommodated the front of the building while the rear flats each contained its individual rear porch.

All the flats were occupied by medium to large families, and the side entrance and middle hallway were always the center of much activity. Today was no different. It was buzzing, with laughter and screaming from children and adults as well. As the guys arrived to join the festivities, firecrackers of every size and shape were being tossed into the street by the children as well as the adults. The noise was deafening and the confusion was unnerving but the joy that was apparent was gratifying.

There were chairs on the sidewalk occupied by older adults enjoying the celebration. Some kids sat on the iron railing alongside the building while others just ran back and forth covering their ears as they ran.

Francisca and the Boys

Mary Moya was there, leaning against the railing and laughing as usual, for in spite of her enormous problem she maintained the facade of a normal and happy girl.

Mary was an only child with plenty of time on her hands, always dreaming and scheming of ways to escape the misery that fate had dropped into the repertoire of her young life. Her father had left home when she was just a toddler, and her mother, who was not much older than herself, was content to live on, changing boyfriends whenever it suited her.

A police squad car pulled up near the corner and two uniformed policemen stepped out and walked toward the crowd at the side entrance. Three or four of the guys ran down the alley fearing that the police were there because of the continuing raucous.

A policeman asked no one in particular, "Is there a Jonathan Moreno anywhere around her?"

The unwritten law of "no information to police" was quietly adhered to as everyone remained silent.

"I know him," Mary spoke up, "third floor rear, he's up there right now."

"Thank you honey," said one of the cops as he drew his pistol from its holster and went upstairs by the side entrance. The other officer went to the alley and entered the back yard, swiftly running up the back stairs with his pistol in his hand.

Suddenly Mary felt a certain glee and joy within herself. She was getting even with the son-of-bitch that had raped her. Nick, who had been standing next to her all this time immediately understood what she had done. Nick glanced at Mary looking for her eyes, Mary looked straight into his eyes and gave him the slightest of nods. Now Nick understood completely, and smiled while looking away.

"Let's go by the tree," she told Nick

As they walked Nick asked, "Is he the....."

Mary didn't let Nick finish, "Yea, the dirty bastard, I hope they hang his fuckin' ass!"

Mary didn't usually swear much unless provoked or if she had a sound reason for it. In this case she was so happy, that as the saying goes, she was "fit to be tied."

Mary continued talking as they walked, "You know, I told my mother what happened and she didn't believe me. She stood there just looking at me and calling me a liar. I cried so much, I didn't want any of the guys to see me after. My eyes swelled up so much...." Her voice trailed off.

Nick kept very quiet. He felt sorry for her and he was again feeling those strong urges that he had felt when they had been climbing the tree together. Mary was wearing the same dress she had worn the last time he had seen her.

Nick walked up to the tree ready to climb when he suddenly stepped back. Wiping his hands on his pants he exclaimed, "Ah, shit, look what they done to the tree!"

Grease of some sort had been smeared on the tree trunk all the way up to the curve. Who did it or why was a mystery, but the deed was done and now they would have no tree for the rest of the summer.

Nick and Mary walked through the lot to the alley and turned toward the noise coming from Mary's building.

"Let's stay here for a while until we're sure the cops are gone," Mary told Nick. They stopped behind the abandoned house next to the lot and went into the woodshed.

All the guys had been here at one time or another, usually when it rained or if they wanted to rest without having to go home.

Mary sat on the cardboard pieces that were on the ground, propping up her legs, causing her skirt to fall back. Nick remained standing and soon had his right hand in his pocket one more time.

Mary noticed what was happening and knew that Nick now had an erection. She told Nick, "Come over here." He sat next to her as she took his hand and shoved it down to her breasts and told him, "Rub them a little bit."

Francisca and the Boys

Nick began to pant and waited for Mary to continue telling him what to do next. He was having his first sexual experience and was waiting for Mary to lead. She reached over with her left hand and unbuttoned his fly. Nick was frantic and seemingly wild as she reached in and took hold of his penis. He was uncontrollable now.

Mary stood up and told Nick, "Come on Nicky, hurry up and take off your pants!" In the meantime she removed her bloomers and stood up against the wall with her legs opened.

Nick took off his pants and stood close to Mary, who pulled him closer to her, and resumed to guide his penis into her vagina. Nick penetrated and felt the warmest and most wonderful thing he had ever felt in his life.

"Pump Nicky, pump in and out," Mary kept saying. But Nick's inexperience showed when after two or three pumps, he slipped out and ejaculated all over Mary's legs. He held her very tight for a few moments then relaxed and looked away. He had no words of explanation for what had just happened. It was his first time.

Mary was a little disappointed because she did not complete an orgasm, but at least she taught Nick something that he would remember for a long, long time. They dressed and buckled up and continued their stroll toward the crowd in silence.

The guys were already back from their run through the alley. "What happened, Nicky?" Emilio asked, "Did somebody go to jail?"

"I don't know," answered Nick, "I wasn't here."

The word got around soon enough that John Moreno had been picked up and arrested for breaking into a store on Larimer Street. His partner had been caught and had given the police his name as the accomplice.

Nick and Davy left the area while the fireworks were still going strong, and it was nearing nine o'clock, their inevitable curfew. The crowd was beginning to thin out as the youngsters left for home. The older boys stuck around to continue in the festivities.

The brothers walked in the house with time to spare. Their mother had some cooked sweet rice in milk ready for the boys so they wouldn't go to bed on an empty stomach. They had the rice pudding with toast saturated with butter off the hot stove plate. After eating, the boys retired to their bedroom and went to bed, not to sleep, but to play around and just talk.

The boys finally slept and the clock on the small table showed a few minutes before midnight.

Francisca would now prepare to pay a visit to Chon's on Larimer Street.

Francisca walked the two blocks slowly to Larimer Street carrying a black leather bag under her left arm. Arriving at Chon's, she went to the door and was recognized instantly by the bartender as Chamaco's wife. The bartender invited her in, but she refused to enter and asked only if he would call her husband to the door. The bartender walked to the rear and returned shortly to tell Francisca that her husband had left earlier. She thanked him and went around the corner. She stepped into a darkened doorway next door to Chon's and waited.

After some time, Francisca heard talking and laughing down the street. A couple was walking toward her, evidently on their way to the bar. The woman was walking on the inside from the street and on the outside was none other than Chamaco himself, just as she expected.

The woman was a well known prostitute and the current waitress at Chon's establishment. As the couple approached the doorway where Francisca stood, she stepped out, holding a square object wrapped in cloth in her right hand. She swung her right hand still holding the object and planted it squarely on the woman's forehead. The woman went down hard and with such force that on landing on the sidewalk the back of her head hit and bounced, adding to the punishment that had already been inflicted. Francisca then stooped over her victim and hit her twice more, once on each side of the head. As she raised the makeshift weapon one more time, she was about to administer the 'coup de grace' when Chamaco stepped in and pulled her away from the fallen woman.

"Pancha." he was screaming, "stop, you'll kill her!"

"That's what I want to do, leave me alone," Francisca replied.

"No Pancha," Chamaco pleaded, "you can go to prison, please go home."

"I don't care," Francisca was livid.

"What will I do without you?" he asked.

"You should have thought of that before you started fucking around with this whore bitch."

"How about our kids, your sons!" Chamaco told her, almost in tears now.

Francisca stopped struggling abruptly and stared at Chamaco with steely eyes. Without another word she turned away and headed for home.

Chamaco went to the door of the tavern and called the bartender out for a minute. He explained the situation to him without lying as to who was involved.

"The woman needs help right away," he nervously told the bartender.

"OK, Chamaco," the man told him, "take it easy, you go home and I'll take care of it."

Chamaco reached into his pocket and handed the bartender a handful of bills, and gave him a tight hug around the shoulders and said, "*gracias compadre*," thanking him for his help.

Chamaco walked away going in the opposite direction from where the woman lay unconscious.

Chamaco walked the full block and turned the corner going south on 22nd. He could see and hear the commotion occurring on the next block where there were still a few of the neighbors tossing firecrackers into the street. Chamaco arrived at the building on 22nd and greeted the people who were still in a festive mood as he walked by. Some recognized him and greeted him, others didn't, particularly the young. He turned the corner toward his house and at about this time he heard the faint wail of sirens in the street. He gave a sigh of relief at the much welcomed sound and prayed as he crossed the street for home.

Francisca had arrived in less than five minutes after the incident. She walked in the door and went straight for the kitchen cabinet where Chamaco stored his whiskey. She pulled out a bottle of gin and poured herself a tin cupful, dropping into a chair at the kitchen table. She took a large swallow of the gin forcing it down. She held her breath while it went down and felt a terrible burning sensation. Every area from her mouth to her throat through her esophagus down to her stomach was on fire. She took another drink that went down a little smoother. She then pulled the wrapped house brick from the black bag and placed it on the table. The cloth around the brick contained blood and strands of hair, she proceeded to unwrap the brick, then took it out to the yard and dropped it on the pile where she had picked it up early that evening.

Francisca came back indoors and stopped at the table to finish the rest of the gin in her cup, which she did in one large gulp. Now she was beginning to feel dizzy. She took the bloody rag and soaked it in kerosene then stuffed it into her kitchen stove and set it on fire. After carefully storing the kerosene can, she threw a lighted match into the stove and immediately a long flame shot up consuming the rag. She replaced the cover on the stove and dropped back onto the chair to contemplate what she had done.

Francisca poured another cupful of gin. Her brain was now doing somersaults and her vision was becoming impaired. She tried standing, but couldn't. Francisca was not a drinking woman so she didn't realize how little alcohol it took to make one drunk. The room began to reel as she placed her head to rest on her arm at the table. She had easily consumed about ten ounces of gin, and without the benefit of a chaser. Tears streaming down her cheeks, Francisca passed out into the outer limits of never-never land.

As Chamaco crossed the street to the house, he made the sign of the cross, praying that the waitress from Chon's establishment would not die. He walked into the house and in the dim light of the kerosene lamp he could see Francisca at the kitchen table, one hand on a tin cup and the other under her head as a pillow. Chamaco was extremely distraught, nervous, and dripping in perspiration. He ran to Francisca's side fearing that she might have done something drastic. He soon found that she was just drunk to the gills.

Chamaco picked his wife up bodily and carried her to the bedroom, placed her on the bed and proceeded to undress her. He laid her back on the pillows and brought in a pan of cold water and washcloth and began to put cold packs on her forehead. He smoothed back her hair and kissed her, and while sitting on the bed next to her, he began to weep. He slumped over while still dressed and fell asleep with his feet still on the floor.

Nick and Davy were up early the next morning. They each took a turn to use the water closet.

The kerosene lamp on the kitchen table was still lit but flickering like it was ready to go out. It must have been on all night, the boys guessed. They sensed something was very wrong but were not quite sure what it was. Hearing a moan coming from Francisca's bedroom, the boys looked at each other, wondering what was going on.

Chamaco exited the bedroom still wearing his pants and shirt all mussed and wrinkled. Half his shirt tails were hanging over his pants, the other half was still tucked inside the belt and he was in his stocking feet. He had kicked off his shoes during the night while half asleep, but that was the extent of his preparation for bed the night before.

The boys stood at their bedroom door with mouths ajar still trying to figure out what was happening. They had never seen their father out of bed ahead of Francisca.

Chamaco went to the toilet and retrieved the bed pan and took it to the couple's bedroom. In just a short time later the boys could hear Francisca heaving and vomiting with tremendous difficulty.

Chamaco called the boys into the bedroom and told them, "Take some money and go to the store for milk and corn flakes, your mother's not getting up for a while."

Francisca was leaning over one side of the bed with her head hanging low while moaning and groaning, much like Davy when he was recovering from his penile injury. She made an attempt to look up at the boys but quickly turned back to the pan and heaved again. Her stomach was empty now, so the only thing left were the symptoms and the agony.

Davy took a dollar bill from the bedside table that was strewn with bills of every denomination up to fifty. The boys dressed and left for the grocery store.

Chamaco went to the kitchen and brewed up a concoction of hot tea with half an ounce of gin, a few squirts of lemon juice and the slightest touch of sugar. He brought it in to his wife and coaxed her to drink it along with two aspirins.

Francisca was at first reluctant to drink, but after the first taste she proceeded to drink it slowly, for it had a very pleasant taste.

Francisca asked, "What was in that, it was good?"

"The hair from the tail of the dog that bit you," replied Chamaco.

FIVE

The entire family remained indoors the day of Francisca's hangover. Chamaco catered to his wife's every whim this day, without complaining but with a rather subdued attitude. He felt his guilt so much deeper than Francisca, knowing full well that it was due to his own actions that the episode of the night before had been triggered.

Nick and Davy were notified that they would be moving to a town called Eaton to stay for the rest of the summer. Eaton was located fifty to sixty miles north of Denver and was near the farm where Chamaco had signed on his crew to work the fields in preparation for the harvest

The boys didn't like the idea of leaving their friends nor having to settle in a place that was unknown to them. However, this would not be the first time the boys would be moving to a new location, for now it had become commonplace to move from place to place, it having been done repeatedly during their young lives.

The boys could remember, and often talked about, how as toddlers they had been placed in the care of the nuns at the Sisters of The Sacred Heart School. There they had lost, almost completely, the Spanish-speaking background which they had identified with since birth. After leaving the school, the boys began somewhat of a re-transformation in regaining the understanding of the Spanish spoken to them by their parents. Soon Davy spoke Spanish with a mixture of English in order to communicate with his mother and father. Nick stuck to English even when spoken to in Spanish. A practice that he continued into adulthood.

The boys were allowed to go out later that evening. It was Saturday, and the fourth of July just a couple of days away. There would be plenty of fireworks this particular evening

Chamaco chose to remain at home to continue caring for his wife who certainly was in need of it.

Francisca was sitting up in bed now and was recovering fairly well from the affects of the night before. She got out of bed and stood on her feet for a few seconds, she felt a slight dizziness and sat back down. She composed herself and was ready to try again as she stood up one more time. Succeeding in her first attempt to go to the water closet, she decided to stay out of bed.

Soon the couple was sitting at the kitchen table conversing in low tones, trying to rectify to one another the part that each played in the actions of the night before. They came to a peaceful conclusion without argument and decided to put everything behind them, and as always, when situations like these occurred, there would be reconciliation.

There was a knock at the front door, Chamaco and Francisca looked at each other. Francisca's heart sank as Chamaco got up to answer the door. Was it the police? She was beside herself with very taut nerves. Suddenly a slight trembling seemed to have activated within her entire body.

There was a clear view to the living room door from where Francisca was sitting. She stared with apprehension attempting to distinguish the figure at the door. She heard her husband say, *"Pasale,"* as the huge hulk of Jimmy "El Mocho" appeared coming through the front door.

Francisca breathed a huge sigh of relief and felt as though a whole new dawning had appeared in her immediate future. She was ecstatic, yet attempting to control a mixture of emotions. She remained seated waiting for a sign from Chamaco. There was none for the moment.

Did Jimmy have some news?

Did he even know what happened?

Francisca and the Boys

Francisca thought of every possible situation that could develop after her night of horror. She finally stood up and began to brew a pot of coffee for Chamaco and his guest. In reality, she was building an excuse to go in and listen to the conversation. Jimmy walked out the door before the coffee was done. Francisca felt relieved, for now she could talk to Chamaco alone. She poured coffee for Chamaco and one for herself. He walked back to join her in the kitchen.

Chamaco sat at the kitchen table and tasted his coffee. No cream no sugar, as he liked it.

Francisca poured her own coffee with cream and sugar and stirred while waiting for Chamaco to speak.

"She's alive." Chamaco told his wife.

At those words Francisca fell back into her chair spilling some of her coffee. She dropped her chin to her chest and sobbed softly.

Chamaco continued to speak, "Her eyes swelled up and she can't open them but she will be alright. She told the police she don't know who hit her."

Francisca whispered softly, *"Gracias a Dios."* thanking God over her sobs.

Chamaco moved his chair closer to hers and put his arm around Francisca's shoulders. "Try to get some rest," he told her.

Francisca said nothing wiping her eyes with opened hands. She took a sip of coffee then left the table. She went to her altar and knelt to pray.

Chamaco and Francisca were devout Catholics within self imposed perimeters. He would make donations whenever it was affordable by entering a church and dropping a donation into the poor box, kneeling in a pew for a short prayer and leave. He didn't care to listen to the preaching of any priest or to spend to much time on his knees.

Francisca would attend mass on occasion but she avoided getting involved in church activities simply because her time belonged to her family. Her worshiping was done in private at her ever-present home altar with its religious pictures and statues illuminated by a perpetual vigil light.

Belonging to a particular congregation required the type of devotion that neither he nor she could offer in good conscience.

Prayer was not always the ideal solution to problems that at times seemed to accumulate in great numbers, Chamaco thought. A living had to be made, and with a wife and two growing boys to support, his efforts were focused on the reality of the present. But then again, there were problems with no evident solutions where even the profound atheist would turn to prayer.

Francisca now found herself in such a predicament. As much as she wanted to destroy the life of the woman whom she attacked, she was looking for redemption through prayer, hoping that the woman's life would be spared. She would go to church and burn a votive light asking for the recovery of the woman who's name she did not even know. Today she would learn about the woman's condition and in the meantime she would light another candle on her personal altar, there in the corner of her bedroom.

Francisca's remorse and anxiety clearly showed on her face, yet she had concluded that it was an uncontrollable temper that caused her to plan and deliver the attack in question. In her mind, jealousy was never a consideration. Was she being a hypocrite? After all, the woman was just another prostitute. But she was also a human being etc. etc. Francisca's mind was now in total and complete turmoil. In her glossary of emotions she found inconsistencies and contradictions, but she was not about to go into deciphering the complexities of life. She would continue to pray.

Nick and Davy were home well before their curfew laughing and playing as usual.

Chamaco would now gather the family around the kitchen table. He had something to say.

Francisca returned shortly from her prayer vigil. She scrambled four eggs in a frying pan and refried a small amount

Francisca and the Boys

of beans, heated a half dozen tortillas and sat the boys down to eat. She divided the food evenly into two plates and served each boy individually to avoid argument. The boys sat on opposite sides of the table with an empty chair next to each of them.

Francisca poured herself another cup of coffee and sat next to Nick. Chamaco soon returned holding a medium sized brown paper bag then placing it on the table. He refilled his coffee cup and sat down next to Davy. No one seemed curious about the paper bag so no questions were raised.

"Now," Chamaco said looking at each of the boys, "we will be moving to Eaton to live for a while until *la limpia* and *el desahijue* of *el betabel* is finished and we might stay for *el tapeo*. It's the same farm we worked for two years ago. If we stay for the topping of the beets, you kids will have to go to school in Eaton or Ault at least for a few weeks." Chamaco continued, "We have to start by next week so we will leave here Tuesday morning, the fourth."

Chamaco knew that the Fourth of July was a favorite holiday of the boys because of the noise and the fireworks, but there were many reasons to expedite the moving. He felt he and Francisca were not completely in the clear yet and wanted to leave Denver as soon as possible.

The boys looked at each other and both made a disagreeable face at the same time.

Davy protested, "But that's the fourth of July!"

His protest was ignored.

Chamaco told the boys, "when you're through eating just put your dishes in the sink and go to bed."

Nick complained saying, "Chamaco, I'll have a nightmare if I go to sleep full."

"You can stay up for a while, but in your room," Chamaco said pointing to their bedroom door.

Chamaco then turned to Francisca and said, "Do you think your sister Lucy will take this flat if we give it to her? It's much better than the one they live in now, that place is really a dump if you ask me," he continued, "you can give her the beds and the stove and all the rest of the stuff that you don't need."

"Then what am I going to do without the beds and the stove and I need everything," she said in a serious tone, but she was fishing for information from Chamaco.

"Pancha," he said, "we can't carry all this stuff in the car anyway. So at least Lucy can benefit a little, she could use all of this. There's already a stove and a heater at the house in Eaton and we can take care of the rest as soon as we settle down. We'll take one mattress with blankets and your trunk. We can throw it on the roof of the car tied down with rope."

Francisca received the answers she was looking for and half smiled. After clearing the table, the boys disappeared into their bedroom.

Francisca wiped the table with a damp cloth, put the cloth back in the sink and returned to finish her coffee.

Chamaco took a sip of his coffee then reached over, taking the brown paper bag and dumping the contents on the table as Francisca looked on in amazement. There were bills of denominations from one to twenty strewn the full length of the table.

During the times that Chamaco was gone from home and prior to the incident on Larimer Street, he had made stops in places like Brighten, Fort Lupton, Greeley, and Fort Collins and as far as Cheyenne, Wyoming, finding the enclaves of the local gamblers in each town or city.

Somehow a gambler new a gambler when he saw one, usually sensing the vibrations by the mode of dress or speech, recognizing certain expressions in body language and showing a respect ordinarily not found in the average man. Chamaco was well received where ever he went because of his congeniality and his willingness to play the game.

Sitting at the poker table or shooting at the dice table for six, eight or ten hours was no great feat. Walking away a winner was the hardest part of the game. Chamaco was an average

Francisca and the Boys

poker player and played on shear luck and would usually walk out 'even' or as a winner. Now when it came to dice, he was considered to be one of the luckiest players for he rarely lost. But craps was his game and only because he had it perfected.

There were ways to win at dice that required some psychology and some slight of hand, and Chamaco had perfected both ingredients.

At first he would gain the confidence of everyone involved. Then by carrying enough money for the purpose, he would have a short losing streak. Soon he would make a comeback and begin to play for bigger stakes. The interest in the other players would gain momentum and then he would begin his slight of hand. He would shoot the dice and switch to a loaded one with the same hand motion when it became necessary. He always made it a point to switch when the stakes were high. At times he would switch both dice and shoot the winning points in one toss and quickly gather the dice to avoid detection. At times a suspicious player would ask to see the dice, and the dice he would receive were perfectly legal. Chamaco's slight of hand was so perfect that in the years he had played the game, he had never made a mistake.

Chamaco and Francisca began to count the money on the table, making stacks of ones, twos, fives, tens, and twenties. Total count amounted to two thousand three hundred and forty eight dollars.

Francisca had never seen that much money at one time in her entire life. Even the modest savings of a few hundred dollars that she had put away over the last two years did not compare. That stash lay at the bottom of the wooden chest to be used only in extreme emergencies.

After the stock market crash of 1929, and the losses and closings suffered by banks all over the country, the Delmontes felt some vindication in not having used banks at all, ever. Whatever was available to the luckier ones would usually go into safety boxes or under mattresses at home.

Francisca and Chamaco sat at the table making plans for the move to Eaton. Chamaco had become nervous and slightly irritable while sitting, and his anxiety was beginning to show.

"Pancha," he said rather sheepishly, "I would like to take one more *tiro* at the crowd at Chon's."

"Chamaco?" she looked at him with a questioning stare.

"Vieja," he continued, "please listen to what I have to say before you fly off the handle."

At that very moment Francisca lost all hope of keeping Chamaco at home he continued to talk, "It's Saturday night and the place will be full of people with money. My friend 'The Greek' from Broadway will be there with a couple of *sallos* and there will be others from out of town."

As Francisca was about to protest, Chamaco held up his hand and said, "All I need is a hundred dollars, you can put the rest away."

Francisca stared at him without blinking an eye. She knew she had lost this argument but she was not about to give in that easily.

"Aren't you satisfied with the money you brought home?" she asked.

Chamaco was seeing an opportunity to add to his winnings before leaving Denver. His inner greed had taken hold and he was prepared to feed and thrive on that greed for better or for worse.

"Francisca," Chamaco now addressed her by her true name and ignoring her question he said, "I give you my word I will not stray." He crossed his heart with his right hand touching his fingers to his lips then raising it high to show the piety of his intentions. "I will not go without your permission," he concluded.

The love Francisca had for this man could hardly be contained as she stood up and walked to where he sat. Her eyes were moist but she managed to hold back imminent tears.

"Go," she told him as she leaned over and kissed him tenderly on the cheek, "may God watch over you."

Francisca and the Boys

Chamaco stood up and kissed her on the eyes and nose and finally on the lips before leaving the house.

Chamaco walked out the door at approximately 11:00 PM. He was coughing loudly and releasing large amounts of sputum as he walked toward Chon's.

Francisca immediately blew out the kerosene lamp on the kitchen table and checked in on the boys as she passed their bedroom. She walked straight to her altar and lit another votive light and she knelt to pray.

The votive lights on the altar illuminated the bedroom enough for Francisca to see and move around comfortably. She depended a great deal on these candles, to light the way for Chamaco as well, and to bring him home safely.

Francisca went to bed with a feeling of anxiety and apprehension. She was not comfortable with her husband's apparent uneasiness before leaving the house. Other than the occurrences and developments of the last two days, there seemed to be something else on Chamaco's mind, but as hard as she tried, Francisca could not detect what it might be. She lay in bed thinking of the money that was now at the bottom of the wooden chest understanding full well that there was a certain amount of danger in the methods Chamaco used in acquiring this money.

Chamaco and Francisca were both poor and uneducated when first they met many years ago. She had now conformed to the "feast and famine" style of living, and at this particular time it seemed to be turning for the better.

Working for others was not a consideration for Chamaco, for to him every employer and every person in authority in any part of the world was still a *cabron*. Whatever methods he used to accomplish some level of financial success, he was not reluctant to trying for after the crash of 1929 people were either starving or turning to crime for survival. Chamaco was not about to let his family suffer. But even the great depression in the United States could not compare with the poverty and the misery existing in Mexico, where people were dying of starvation and politicians were maneuvering for position to better rape the country of its resources. These politicians and military leaders of his home country headed Chamaco's list of *cabrones.*

Thus the emigration of thousands upon thousands of Mexicans, looking for means of survival, descended en masse upon the agricultural fields of the farmlands in the United States.

Chamaco attached himself to the methods of the average agricultural worker by working in the fields with the rest while applying his expertise to other avenues of escape. Considering the pittance for pay that was given to these workers for such hard and strenuous work, to Chamaco this type of work was for slaves. Chamaco decided to use the farm labor as a cover for his illegal activities. He became an organizer of sorts by forming his own group of workers and acquiring season contracts with farms in need of help. He traveled throughout the western and mid western states that were in the harvest of such things as potatoes, tomatoes, corn or sugar beets. He always made sure that the contracts were fulfilled and never complained about the pay, thus building trust with the farmers and avoiding any suspicion that might be directed his way.

Chamaco soon became well known and respected throughout the field working communities by both the farmer and the worker.

Besides marijuana sales and gambling there was also a specialized system of shoplifting that Chamaco and his cohorts were engaged in. It could only be applied during cold weather when overcoats or topcoats were necessary to keep warm. The targets were usually large department stores in the cities, and small clothing stores in the smaller towns. For the most part, attendants in the smaller towns where one person, more than not, would be alone in the store.

The routine used in committing the act of thievery necessitated the cooperation of at least three individuals with one of them being a woman. While a man and the woman negotiated with the clerk or shop keeper for, say, shoes or a dress, the third party would roam the racks of men's suits looking for and picking something suitable to lift.

The best time would be when the woman would sit down to try on several pairs of shoes. Before deciding on one particular pair, she would sit at the fitting chair and while placing her foot on the stool she would nonchalantly raise her skirt high enough for the salesman to become interested. Before long there would be two men's suits neatly tucked away inside the third party's buttoned overcoat while the unsuspecting salesman was still busy fitting shoes and getting an eyeful.

Chamaco and his brother-in-law Jesse along with Jesse's wife Nena were the three that usually worked the routine and had perfected it over the years. Francisca had been a member of the trio in years past, but her children were growing up and they needed attention. Most of her time was now spent in her home where, you might say, she was semi-retired.

Everything would be repeated from town to town and perhaps in more than one store until the back seat of the automobile was filled with clothing of all types and sizes.

The stolen articles would be taken back to the farm where they were separated and stored until Sunday when all workers were at rest. On this day, trips would be made from farm to farm where everything was sold at half the price showing on the price tag..

Thus, the supplemental income was "earned" keeping Chamaco and his family at a decent level of society and having no qualms about what he did and never being self-conscious about his way of life. He did what he did because that was what he knew and what he practiced, that was his vocation.

Among his friends and others who knew him, Chamaco was well liked and respected. Then there were the authorities who also knew about Chamaco, some who also liked and respected him, but were always on the lookout for the opportunity to arrest him.

Francisca was up and around when she heard the front door open. It was about eight thirty in the morning. Chamaco walked in and headed for the bedroom. He emptied his pockets on the bedside table placing two large rolls of bills carelessly on the top. As usual, the bills were put together at random and not arranged in any particular monetary order. His shirt was soaked in perspiration and he looked very weak and pale. Beads of sweat rolled down his face and neck as he removed his clothing down to his shorts. He dropped on the bed on his back, arms outstretched and legs open, completely exhausted.

Instinctively Francisca knew that Chamaco was ill and needed attention. He began to cough as Francisca came in with the bed pan placing it on the bed where Chamaco could reach it. He coughed violently for a few seconds then expectorated a great deal of mucus from his lungs and throat. He spat into the bed pan then fell back on the pillow closing his eyes and breathing deeply. Francisca forced Chamaco to take a spoonful of cough syrup then began to wipe him off with dry towels. Now she began to apply cold compresses to his face and neck, over his shoulders and across his chest, alternately soaking and wringing the wash cloth and one of the large towels.

"Gracias vieja," he said when he felt the cool cloth on his skin, "it feels good."

Francisca felt Chamaco's forehead with the back of her hand. "You don't have a fever, that's a good sign," she told him.

"Take that money and put it away," Chamaco told Francisca, "there's about four hundred dollars there."

Francisca stuffed the money into an empty pillow case and shoved it under the bed. She would take care of that later, but for now, she must attend to her husband's needs.

"I should go bring Doctor Alanis so he can look at you," Francisca told him.

"No, Pancha," he said, "he's not in his office today, it's Sunday, and anyway, I'll be alright, all I need is some rest."

The coughing stopped and Chamaco went into a deep sleep.

Francisca pulled the pillow case from under the bed and emptied the contents onto the kitchen table and began to separate

Francisca and the Boys

and count. Her count reached a total of six hundred eighty dollars as she then took the money, placed it in a glass jar and stored it on the top shelf of the kitchen cabinet. So much for Chamaco's estimate of four hundred dollars.

Nick walked out of the bedroom rubbing his eyes, "I'm hungry, ma!"

"OK," she said, "wash up and I'll make you a breakfast 'Americana'.

Davy heard what she had said as he walked out of the bedroom and immediately exclaimed,

"Oh boy, hot cakes!" And he was right.

As the boys washed and prepared for breakfast Francisca mixed the batter for hot cakes using the necessary ingredients from her ready mix bowl on the shelf. She also prepared her own syrup by melting *pilonsillo* and mixing it with *canela* tea. Butter was not necessary since neither boy cared for it anyway.

Davy had a stack of four hot cakes with syrup while Nick had a stack of three and one egg, also with syrup poured over everything, including the egg.

After breakfast Francisca directed the boys to bathe and dress in their new clothes and warned them not to leave the house before noon. The theaters on Curtis Street would not open until around one. The boys complained about having to dress up, but to no avail. She gave each boy a dollar, to their great surprise, and simultaneously each exclaimed, "Wow!"

There were two movie houses next door to each other on Larimer and 17th. One was called the Jazz and the other the Zaza. These theaters had been recently converted from vaudeville to moving pictures and they were now including talkies. The Zaza still maintained a little of the vaudeville flare by holding amateur night once a week along with the regular feature, a cartoon, and movie tone news.

A feature stretched into chapters would be shown on Sundays, one chapter per week. Saturdays brought cowboys such as William S. Hart, a silent movie hero, or the latest talking picture stars such as Tom Mix, Buck Jones, or Ken Maynard, to name a few.

Not too long ago Nick and Davy were broke and the only way to gain entrance to the movies was to volunteer for amateur night. They were introduced on stage and began to sing a duet of "Springtime in The Rockies." At about half way through the song the boys forgot the words and stopped suddenly, looking at each other for help. The master of ceremonies stepped in and saved the day by announcing, "Let's give the boys a big hand folks." Each was given a bar of candy and directed to find a seat in the auditorium.

The boys had a decision to make, for now they had money to attend the Orpheum to see King Kong, or go to the Zaza and not miss the next chapter of Flash Gordon with Buster Crabbe. They opted for the Zaza.

At the Zaza there would be chapters plus one silent short, probably Charlie Chaplin, a cartoon of Micky Mouse, and the Movie Tone News, which always showed first.

Noon rolled around and the boys went out to meet the guys by the tree. Freddy and Emilio were there, and Ricky was walking down the street toward them.

Emilio had only four cents. He asked, "Anybody got a penny?" Nick gave him a dime in exchange for the pennies and said, "Keep the rest for candy." Nick was in a generous mood and as long as he could afford it, he felt good that he could help his buddy make up the difference of one penny to pay the entry fee at the Zaza. The Jazz and Zaza were five cents and the Orpheum and the Denver and the rest of the big movie houses were all fifteen cents. None of the guys were much interested in first run movies anyway, as long as there were chapters and cowboys, they were all satisfied.

The guys killed time until the Movie Tone News was almost over so they could come in close to the start of the cartoon, which always came on next. They arrived at the theater and each paid his way in. There was very loud talking and now and

Francisca and the Boys

then a scream from the younger kids. The auditorium was dark and it took a while for the guys to accustom their eyes to the darkness. Soon they could see a little, enough to make out the figures inside and to find seats. All seats toward the front were occupied so the guys found a completely empty row toward the center near the rear. They made themselves comfortable and began ripping the candy bar rappers open ready to settle down.

Nick looked around from his angle to see who was there and hoping he might get a glimpse of Mary Moya. He thought he had seen her as he walked in but he wasn't sure. Then he spotted her sitting closer to the wall across the aisle. There was a man sitting next to her and she was busy talking to him, so Nick couldn't make a connecting glance. Nick decided to just wait a while then he would try to catch her eye.

About halfway through the movie Mary got up from her seat and walked toward the rear. She spotted the guys as she went by and stopped for a second to let them know she was going to the ladies room and she would be right back.

Nick's secret about his sexual encounter with Mary was still that, a secret. No one knew unless she had mentioned it to someone but, in Nick's mind, that was very doubtful. Mary soon returned and sat one row behind the guys. Nick thought of their time together in the wood shed. Soon he was sexually aroused again but all eyes were on the screen so no one noticed his condition. He pushed his penis down between his legs and crossed them tightly. He glanced at Mary several times more, and the more he looked at her, the more aroused he became. Nick began to move his upper body slowly back and forth causing his penis to slide down and up between his legs. He was panting, but ever so quietly that no one noticed.

Nick caught the slightest odor of Mary's soap penetrating the warm air in the theater and he squeezed his penis so tight as to cause him to ejaculate. Just as Nick glanced at Mary one more time, she looked at him and smiled. Nick smiled back and he sank back into his seat after that wonderful ordeal he had just experienced.

The movie was soon over and the lights in the auditorium were turned on. Everyone was laughing and shouting and getting ready to leave. The younger kids were already running up the aisle and out the door.

Mary stood up and reached over touching Nick on the shoulder as she told him, "I'll wait for you outside, Nicky." Nick turned and nodded in affirmation.

Nick left his seat, a little bit sticky but no worse for wear. No one had noticed anything and there was nothing visible on his clothing. There was a slightly wet spot on his right inner pants leg, but no one knew it was there. All the guys got up and started inching their way toward the exit.

Mary Moya was patiently waiting for the rest of the guys in front of the theater.

Mary talked to all the guys, giving each a little conversation but she drifted toward Nick as Nick drifted toward her. The entire group started walking back to the neighborhood slowly, with Mary and Nick together a few steps behind.

"How come you're all dressed up in all new stuff?" Mary asked Nick.

"My father brought it when he came home and my ma made us put them on," Nick replied as he pulled on the front of his shirt.

"You look nice," she said.

"Ma gave us some money, too," Nick told her, "she gave us a dollar each, me 'n Davy." Nick pulled the change from his pocket and showed it to Mary.

"I've got some money too," Mary said to Nick as she showed him a five dollar bill.

"Wow, where'd ya get that?" he asked.

"Nicky," she said, "I'll tell you if you promise not to tell. You can't tell nobody, Nicky." now saying it with a more serious tone in her voice.

"I won't," he said, "I didn't tell nobody about what we did in the clubhouse, did you?"

"Of course not," Mary replied rather sternly

"OK," he said, "go ahead.

"Well, I was sitting next to this guy in the show and he started touching me. First my knee and I didn't say nothin'. Then he went up higher with his hand and I pushed it away. Then he pulled out the five and showed it to me and said, 'I'll give it to you if you play with it', then he pulled his prick out of his pants. I told him to give me the five first and he did."

"Then what?" Nick asked her in bewilderment.

"Well, I jacked him off!" she replied as a matter of fact.

Nick became even more bewildered as he looked down shaking his head from side to side.

"Come on," she told Nick, slightly tugging at his arm, "let's catch up with the guys, and don't say nothin'."

It was mid-afternoon when the group dispersed after lingering a few minutes at the tree. No plans were made to meet later. Nick and Davy crossed the street for home.

Francisca was busy packing clothes and other essentials. Except for a few dishes and cooking utensils most of the kitchen ware would be left behind.

There was beans and rice on the stove and a stack of, still warm, tortillas on the table wrapped in a large dishcloth. There was also a special treat for the boys in a covered frying pan plus the inevitable hot sauce in the *molcajete.*

His curiosity getting the best of him, Davy lifted the cover on the frying pan to find two extra large, toast brown pork chops.

"Wow, look at this, Nicky!" he exclaimed.

Nick walked over to look and as his eyes widened he shouted, "Oh boy, let's eat!"

The boys sat and gorged themselves to their utter satisfaction, washing everything down with ice-cold lemonade, which was another unexpected treat.

The boys checked the time and found that they still had three hours before curfew. It was only six o'clock with still plenty of time to have some fun. They left the house and crossed the street to the tree where they separated. Davy went east to Broadway in the direction of Ricky's house and Nick crossed the lot passed the tree to Mary's house through the alley.

As Nick passed the wood shed behind the abandoned building, he noticed a bicycle wheel showing through the cracks in the fence. He stopped and peered through the gate to make sure. It was unmistakably Ray Lucero's bike with its chrome fenders and balloon tires. He opened the gate very quietly and stepped through. Peeking through the small window on the shed wall, Nick could see two figures laying on the cardboard floor squirming and grunting.

Ray was on top of Mary with his pants down to his ankles while Mary had her legs wrapped around his buttocks while completely naked from the waist down. Her breasts were out of her shirt and Ray's lips were fondling and sucking on her nipples.

Nick immediately became aroused and deep down he wanted a share of Mary, but somehow, he thought, it wasn't the right thing to do. He took another look through the window and saw Ray now very stiff and still, while kissing her and embracing her very tightly.

Nick became so aroused that he finally unbuttoned his fly and let his penis pop out and he proceeded to masturbate.

He soon walked through and out the gate without being noticed and headed through the alley to his cousin Freddy's house on 23rd Street.

SIX

After a full day and a full night of bed rest, Chamaco was feeling much better. The cough had subsided and the sweating had completely disappeared. A sponge bath by Francisca the night before and some home made soup garnished with the hottest sauce imaginable had rejuvenated Chamaco enough to allow him to leave the bed. He ventured into the kitchen in a rather weakened condition but no worse for wear.

"I feel good now, all I needed was some rest," Chamaco told Francisca over coffee.

"I don't care," she said, "Doctor Alanis opens at ten and we're going to see him today."

She was emphatic, and insistent to a point that Chamaco could not very well argue.

The boys were awakened and given breakfast.

"After you eat," Francisca instructed the boys, "I want you to ask Mr. Ransom for empty boxes so we can finish packing. Your father and I will be back in about an hour. Don't go anywhere, you stay right here." She pointed down to the floor for emphasis.

"OK ma, yea ma," the boys nodded in unison.

Chamaco dressed in preparation for his visit to Doctor Alanis' office. The doctor's second floor office was located just a few doors from Chon's bar on Larimer Street. Larimer was lined with small businesses of many types for it was the business district of this racially diverse neighborhood. It was a two block walk to Larimer if you were to walk straight down 21st Street. Francisca chose to go to 22nd instead and walk the extra block thus circumventing the location of her ill fated encounter of a few nights ago.

Dr. Alanis, a South American type, spoke English with a heavy Spanish accent identical to that of Chamaco's. Francisca spoke English without an accent other than slang and colloquialisms that had been entrenched in her vocabulary since childhood. In reality, she spoke better English than her husband or the doctor. They chose Spanish as their language of communication.

After the usual pleasantries Dr. Alanis asked, "which one of you is the sick one?"

Chamaco was about to explain his problem to the doctor, but he only had a chance to open his mouth slightly and blink his eyes before Francisca went into her spiel.

"Doctor, Chamaco is very sick and he acts like it's nothing," Francisca said, "he's had a bad cough for more than a week and he's spitting a lot of stuff from his lungs. He was sweating for two days and he was having bad dreams."

"But he didn't have a fever," she added as an afterthought.

"You should have taken up medicine, Mrs. Delmonte," Dr. Alanis said to Francisca jokingly but with respect.

He touched Chamaco on the elbow and said, "Come in here and take off your shirt," as he led him into the examining room.

Francisca sat on a chair in a small waiting area while the doctor examined Chamaco. She could see through the open door that Dr. Alanis had a stethoscope in his ears and was running the other end up and down Chamaco's back and chest. He sat down at his desk and pulled out a prescription pad and began to write.

Chamaco came out now fully dressed and sat down next to his wife.

"Chamaco," the doctor began, "I'm prescribing a sedative that you must take before you go to bed. It will help relax your body so that you can sleep comfortably without tossing around at night. It is most important that you get a great deal of rest and that you follow directions according to the label on your medication bottle." He looked over to Francisca so that she would take note of what he was saying and then he turned back to

Chamaco saying, "Your lungs are extremely congested and you are in danger of contracting pneumonia or even consumption if you don't take it easy. I know what your life-style is like, and I recommend that you try cutting your activities to a minimum. Also, the smear of your sputum will be sent out for laboratory analysis and it should be back within a week. We must make sure that tuberculosis has not set in."

Neither Chamaco nor Francisca mentioned the fact that they would not be in town the following week, but Chamaco had the foresight to take the doctor's business card so that he could make contact by telephone at a later date.

"Thank you very much doctor," Chamaco said, "how much will that be?"

"Five dollars," replied the doctor.

Francisca opened her black leather snap purse rummaging through bills and pulling out a five dollar bill. She handed the five to Chamaco who in turn gave it to Dr. Alanis, both men smiling at the humorous position they all found themselves in.

"One more thing," the doctor admonished, "you must cut down on alcohol intake. Alcohol will not help the situation in any way." Then he smiled a broad smile as they shook hands and said their goodbyes.

This doctor had been their family physician since the boys were toddlers and they had become very close friends over the years. The couple's faith and respect in him was unconditional and uncompromising.

Stepping out of the doctor's doorway, Chamaco took Francisca's arm as if to walk toward 21st Street, but she pulled her arm away saying, "No, I'm not going that way, you go ahead if you want to, not me."

"Pancha," Chamaco told her, "you have to go by there sometime, come on." He tried to persuade her, but to no avail.

"The blood is barely dry and you want me to go there already?" she asked. "No senor, not today and maybe never." She was adamant.

The fact of the matter was that no one had bothered to clean up the blood that was dry but very visible on the sidewalk where the encounter took place.

Inevitably, Francisca won out and the couple returned home by their previous route. On their arrival home they found Francisca's sister Lucy and her entire family already there to help in the packing and to see what she was about to inherit after the move. The boys had managed to acquire a half dozen cardboard boxes of different sizes from Mr. Ransom. The packing soon began in earnest. Once the packing was finished, there wasn't much left to do except wait until morning to load up the car.

Lucy agreed to take the flat with the furnishings that Francisca was leaving behind. Francisca decided to leave the chest behind also, but with the understanding that Lucy was to hold it and take good care of it until she returned.

"Lucy, I'm leaving my *castana* with you until after the beets," Francisca told her, "just make sure you take good care of it for me. I'm leaving the padlock on it, so just put it in a corner where nobody will fool with it. There's nothing of value in it, all it contains is the stuff mama gave me just before she died and some personal pictures and things."

"Don't worry, I'll take good care of it. Anybody that touches it will have to answer to me," Lucy said, "and by the way, I appreciate very much that you gave me all this stuff."

"You don't know how much it hurts me to leave everything, but at least you and your family can benefit from it. All I can say is that Chamaco better make good on his promises, or else!"

Francisca concluded with a weak laugh.

Francisca decided to leave the hope chest behind because it would be too cumbersome to carry, even on the roof of the car. She remembered seeing people traveling to California with their cars and trucks loaded down with their belongings a few years back. She was embarrassed to give the impression that her family was totally poor, as did the "Okies" of their particular era. Even so, there would still have to be some things, such as the mattress and blankets, tied to the car somewhere on the outside.

Davy came to his mother and asked, "Ma, can we go out after everything's packed, this is our last day."

"Yes," replied his mother, "but I want you to go to the hardware and get me a roll of string."

Francisca gave Davy a quarter for the twine and urged him to hurry back. "Don't let them cheat you," she told Davy as he ran out the door, "you should get some change back."

Davy returned with a ball of twine, and he did get back some change that he turned over to his mother.

Promptly Nick and Davy, along with Ricky and Freddy, were out the door on their way to meet the rest of the guys.

Chamaco helped around a little bit, but there wasn't that much more to do, so he went out to see Albert to make sure he would be there early the next morning, for Albert would be doing most of the driving between Denver and Eaton. Albert lived in a two room apartment with his girlfriend "Goldie" Romero on Curtis near 26th Street. Goldie had bright natural blond hair with blue eyes and small freckles around her nose. She bragged about being a full blooded "Chicana" and made sure that everybody knew it. More than once she had been accused of being a *bolilla* and she resented it. She was known as a "hustler" and did not like being called a whore or a prostitute. She knew what she was and was not ashamed of it. She also contributed to the welfare of Albert who in turn had no complaints whatsoever. Chamaco knocked and Goldie answered the door wearing only her slip. He couldn't help staring at her breasts, since she was not wearing a bra, and the shape of her nipples protruded through the silk material. She was five foot two with an exceptional figure and a face that could be called beautiful.

"Hello Goldie," Chamaco greeted her, *"como estas?"*

"Muy bien," she answered, *"pase,* please come in." Albert walked up behind Goldie to greet Chamaco..

"We want to leave early in the morning," Chamaco told Albert,

"I came to make sure that you don't forget. If you want to stay by the house tonight you can, or better still, drop me off at home and you can bring the car back with you, then pick us up early tomorrow."

"OK," Albert said, "just let me put on a shirt."

Chamaco was Albert's idol and trusted him implicitly, as Chamaco trusted Albert. Even with that trust in mind, Chamaco couldn't help picturing Goldie next to him in bed. He quickly eliminated the thought from his mind, for he didn't want to give away his thoughts by the look in his eyes.

Albert drove Chamaco home and returned to the apartment.

Chamaco decided he needed extra rest, so he would stay home, go to bed early, and start out early the next morning.

* * *

All the guys were on 22nd Street in front of the big building. Emilio was hitting fly balls to the guys out in the street. After three clean catches the batter had to give up the bat to the next guy in line. The game went on for an hour or so, soon the guys were beginning to become overheated and were all in need of a rest.

Ray Lucero was hitting the fly balls when he hit a foul ball that sailed and landed on the roof of a three story building across the street. Everyone was relieved, for now they had an excuse to quit playing.

There were means of access to the roof across the street but nobody was in a mood to volunteer. Among the younger kids was a boy whom everyone knew as "Peedy", and was about eight or nine years of age. He ran across the street and climbed a drain pipe to the second floor fire escape. No one stopped him because he had done this same thing several times before and none of the guys seemed concerned. He walked up the fire escape to the third floor and finished the climb to the roof by way of the same drain pipe that extended to the rain gutters on the edge. Peedy finished the climb and found the ball. He reached back and tossed it into the street below.

All the guys raised their hands and thanked Peedy for his trouble. Peedy walked around on the roof for a little while then decided it was time to come down. He got on his knees with his back to the alley so that he could straddle the drain pipe and slide down to the fire escape. As he pushed with his right foot to test the gutter, it gave way, and suddenly Peedy was falling to the pavement below. As he fell, Peedy reached for the electric wires running along the back of the building down the alley. There were sparks, and Peedy's body shook as he hung on to the wires, then he fell to the alley pavement.

The guys all rushed to where Peedy now lay. Nick was first to get there and as he touched Peedy, he could feel a slight tingling going through his own body.

"Peedy, Peedy," cried Nick. There was no answer.

Peedy lay with his arms and legs twisted grotesquely as a result of the fall, and there was a pool of blood forming under his head.

Soon the sirens could be heard. Fire trucks arrived at the scene and Peedy was given immediate attention. An ambulance arrived and two men dressed in white jumped out, pulling a stretcher from the rear of the ambulance.

Peedy was administered oxygen by way of tank and mask, but there was no life in the small, frail body. His hands were charred and curled from the electrical shock he had absorbed. Peedy was dead.

Peedy's body was placed on the stretcher and covered completely with a white blanket. The stretcher was placed aboard the ambulance and driven away.

All the guys were in shock, some to a point of turning pale white. Some were in tears. Nick was crying uncontrollably. Ray Lucero put his arm around Nick's shoulders trying to help him ease the pain. The guys stood around dumbfounded.

A police car arrived and soon Peedy's mother was being taken to the hospital where Peedy would be. She was screaming in terror, "Peedy, my baby, my baby!" The police car disappeared.

It was getting close to the middle of the afternoon and Nick and Davy had plenty of time to spare as far as curfew was concerned. Davy, Ricky, and Ray went east through the alley toward the school ground, and for once, Nick noticed, Ray did not have his ever present Schwin with him. He was actually walking with the rest of the guys. They stopped to look at the spot where Peedy had fallen, looking up at the electrical wiring going lengthwise along the alley. Two of the wires were bare where Peedy had tried to hold on at the time of his fall. There was a large pool of blood, very fresh on the alley pavement. The guys stepped around it and continued their walk to the school ground.

Everybody else had dispersed and gone their separate ways. Nick turned toward home and decided to walk through the alley in the opposite direction. As he was about to enter the alley, Mary Moya appeared from nowhere. Nick had stopped crying but there were still a couple of sobs that he had to eliminate in order to become himself again. He wiped his eyes and tried to smile at Mary.

"Nicky," Mary told him, "what are ya gonna do, are you going home?"

"Yea, we're leaving tomorrow and I have to help pack," he said. In effect, he just wanted to go home long enough to stop the sobs that he still had difficulty controlling..

"Can you sneak out after while?" she asked.

"Yea," he responded. Nick looked at her curiously and immediately became sexually aroused.

"Meet me by the wood shed in about an hour.

"OK," said Nick, and they separated.

SEVEN

Albert and Goldie arrived at Francisca's house early the next morning.

Francisca had hot fresh coffee ready made for those who might want some. Cups, spoons and milk and sugar were on the table with fresh bakery rolls. She made oatmeal for the boys and advised them to eat for there would be no more food until their arrival in Eaton. Davy drank straight milk, because "it looks like spit," he would say of his refusal to eat oatmeal.

Goldie walked in and poured herself a cup of coffee. She added milk and sugar and reached for a roll over Nick's shoulder, rubbing her breasts against his back as she did so. Nick turned his head at about the same time and was confronted by a crevice between two large flesh bubbles. He took a deep whiff of the perfume she was wearing and his immediate instinct was to stick his nose between her tits. He didn't, but Goldie sensing that Nick was enjoying her closeness, planted a kiss on his forehead, leaving a set of red lip prints in the center

"Ah, come on Goldie," protested Nick.

"Shut up or I'll kiss you on the lips," she kidded as she walked away.

Goldie was wearing a thin silk blouse that was transparent enough to show her tight fitting brazier with her breasts breaking out at the edges. Nick and Davy laughed out loud as Nick grabbed his crotch and whispered to Davy, "I got a hard-on."

"I'd like to fuck her," Davy said in a whisper. They laughed again. With this arousal Nick thought of his final sexual encounter yesterday afternoon with Mary Moya in the wood shed behind the abandoned building.

Nick and Davy usually shared their secrets, but this one he wanted to keep to himself, for two reasons. One, it was a very personal experience that he wanted for himself only. Two, he had made a solemn promise to Mary not to reveal any of this to anyone. Today he was extra careful not to give away his thoughts to his brother Davy.

Nick's mind wandered. He had come home and washed his face with cold water and had forced his sobbing to stop. He was anxious to go back and meet Mary for he already knew what she had in mind.

When Nick arrived at the woodshed, Mary was waiting for him. This time she had brought a large bath towel and spread it on the cardboard floor. When Nick walked in he found her completely undressed, stark naked. He couldn't believe the beautiful sight before his eyes.

Nick had been aroused before walking into the shed. He removed his pants without being told. Mary laid on her back on the towel and motioned for Nick to come to her.

"Nicky, get on your knees then lay on top of me between my legs, go slow."

Nick did as he was told. Mary took his penis in her hand and found her vagina for him. He penetrated and found himself in a world of warmth one more time. He was completely and absolutely enthralled.

Mary wrapped her legs around his buttocks and told him, "Pump in and out, slow."

As Nick pumped, Mary held him close to her, tightly with her legs to avoid him from popping out as before. He ejaculated twice and each time he waited for a new erection. On the third time, Mary went wild. She pumped upward fast and furious while holding tightly to Nick with her legs. She finally completed an orgasm as did Nick.

In the last few seconds Mary had taken Nick by the hair and kissed him hard on the lips, pushing her tongue into his mouth as far as it would go. This was another new experience for Nick. It was over. Nick was no longer afraid or ashamed.

Unknown to him at the time, this sexual encounter with Mary had served a therapeutic purpose to his well being after the devastating accident to Peedy earlier that day.

Nick's thoughts were interrupted by his mother's voice, "Let's start loading."

Davy stood up immediately and went to help, Nick stepped into the water closet locking himself in. He masturbated, then walked out relieved and ready to go to work.

The mattresses out of each bedroom were rolled and tied and placed crosswise on the roof of the car and tied underneath on the inside. A suitcase was pushed onto the right fender and tied to the headlight. Full boxes were forced into the rear passenger section, to the floor as tight as they could fit. A shoe box wrapped several times around with twine was placed on the floor between two of the larger cardboard boxes, then covered with a pillow case filled with underclothes.

Francisca told the boys to take special care of that box. Under no circumstances was it to be moved by anyone but herself when the time came. The box held all the money that she had been entrusted with, over time, by her husband. The house was now a hive of activity and conversation and planning.

Besides the entire Delmonte family and Francisca's brother Albert with Goldie, others had arrived. There was Francisca's younger sister Lucy, with her spouse Alvino, her older brother Jesse and his spouse, Nena. Jimmy was there. Of Lucy's four children, only Freddy was able to get up early enough to come and see his cousin and buddy Nick, leave for new territorial grounds.

The small coffee table that once held the alarm clock was pressed into service but instead of coffee it held a bottle of gin and a bottle of whiskey, surrounded by glasses and cups of different shapes and sizes. The house was a cloud of smoke from front to rear and the strong odor of marijuana was everywhere.

The weeding of sugar beets would have to be started by the beginning of the coming week. Everyone had to be on the farm and ready for work by Monday morning. Alvino had a car, so he would take a second group to Eaton. They would sort it out later, but everyone would make sure that they would get there one way or another.

Chamaco finally stood up and declared, "We must get on our way, *vamonos!*"

Everyone stood and shook hands and embraced, saying their goodbyes.

Chamaco shook hands with Goldie, taking a quick glance at her cleavage. The glance went unnoticed, but Francisca was there with her ever present watchful eye.

Goldie, wearing a skirt split on both sides, with high heels and no stockings, had sat most of the morning on the davenport, crossing and re-crossing her legs. Eyes would glance ever so slight in her direction by the men to catch a glimpse now and then, including Davy and Nick.

There was a rule of thumb that Goldie followed quite strictly. That was, never involve a family member as a customer in her business. She reserved most of her energy for the *sallos* or "marks", for there was a lot more to prostitution than just sex. There was the enticing and the deceiving that was so necessary in the extracting of money over and above the price of the sex act itself. Sometimes it required that she use supplementary means, such as the use of alcohol or drugs in order to complete a job. She would also use the threat of blackmail if it happened to become necessary.

Francisca trusted Goldie so much that she always treated her as a daughter and always called her *hija*, the Spanish word for daughter. Over the years Francisca managed to acquire a certain fondness for wayward women and would help any that needed it. She was always ready to offer lodging or money, or advice if nothing else, to any young woman in need.

Goldie herself would not give any attention to the men in close proximity to Francisca's family. She respected her a great deal, not to mention that Francisca's reputation was well known in regards to Chamaco's infidelity.

Nick and Davy climbed aboard and sat in the rear seat with their legs resting on the boxes underneath. It was not exactly comfortable, but to the boys it was going to be just another day of fun. Albert kissed Goldie goodbye and climbed behind the wheel, Francisca sat in the middle in front, and Chamaco, the last to board, took the front seat at the end.

Albert threw a small bundle of his own clothes into the rear at the boys, playfully hitting Nick on the head with the soft bundle. He stuck a small wrapping of tools under his own feet and was ready to go. He used the spark and choke levers to start the car, then put it into gear and slowly pulled away. In just a few minutes the 1929 Model A Ford was through Denver heading north on the highway toward Fort Lupton, Greeley and places north.

One stop was made for water, gas and oil check, and within a space of two and one half hours they were pulling into East Eaton, as it was known by the locals west of the tracks. To the Chicano population it was known as "Ragtown."

The small dilapidated town was situated east of the railroad tracks from Eaton proper, and, as most of its residents felt, it was called East Eaton just to give it a semblance of recognition.

The main street of the town, located a few yards from the tracks, ran about an average city block from one highway exit to the other. On the south end of the main street stood a large grain storage bin just outside of, what you might call, the "main drag." The rest of the street contained the local bar, better known as "La Cantina", on one side, and a grocery store across the street on the south corner. A few frame houses lined each side of the street

At the north end the street an embankment curved up which ran for a block or so overlooking a stock yard and corral of days gone by. The bull pen was still in place and the kids of the town used it for play during the day.

It was rumored that there had been a hanging in the bull pen area, so the local kids would stay away after dark.

There was a Catholic church on the northwest corner where a priest would celebrate mass once a month, if the locals could get him to show. Usually the word would get around about a week ahead of time that the Father would be coming.

The cattle car track ran along the bottom of the embankment and circled around to the unloading platform that still existed next to the corral. It was a town of the old west for sure.

There was an alley behind the main street with nailed wooden crosses planted into the ground representing the locations where the body of each victim had been found after a stabbing or a shooting. At the alley entrance there was a windowless wooden structure that was used as a church by the local group known as "The Hallelujahs". Services were conducted on Saturday nights and the singing could be heard throughout the town.

There was scattered housing on the outer edges of the large stock yard of yesteryear. The yard now contained a softball field with backstop and a few wooden benches simulating a grandstand.

Softball games were held here on weekends when they were scheduled with surrounding towns or the High School from across the tracks.

La Garra translated to "Ragtown" by the residents of East Eaton.

Chamaco rented the largest house on the highest elevation of the embankment. It had a yard and a driveway.

Albert pulled the car into the driveway and stopped just short of the outhouse standing a few feet away at the end.

Beyond the yard was a field covered with small stacks of hay that would soon be gathered and stacked into one large pile closer to the farmhouse about a half mile away.

Francisca and the Boys

The boys jumped out of the car as soon as it came to a halt and ran to the outhouse to urinate. Davy got their first, but as he opened the door, he slammed it shut again because of the stench.

"It stinks like shit Nicky, you can't breath in there," Davy said.

They both stepped behind the outhouse to leak in the adjoining field.

"Come on kids, let's get this stuff inside," Chamaco called.

The boys obeyed as they ran back to the car and began to help unload.

Nick looked for the shoe box but it wasn't where it had been placed. He ran inside to tell Francisca, but she already had it under one arm. Nick felt relieved.

Francisca walked in the rear door of her new home, however temporary. The kitchen was small but usable There was a window on each side of the room, one to the left at about the center of the wall and one on the right near the corner next to the adjoining wall. In the far left hand corner, a large heavy looking coal burning stove with six covers rested about a foot from the wall. It had a fire compartment on the left, facing it, with a clean-out door just underneath the grating. The oven door was a few inches to the right. The cast iron covers were slightly rusted from lack of use, but Francisca saw great possibilities in the huge stove. The stove pipes went up and through the low slanted roof.

There was no kitchen table nor chairs, but a tall narrow table was situated next to the kitchen entrance which looked like it might have been used to hold pans with water for dishwashing. There was no indoor plumbing, but the hand water pump could be seen just a few steps from the doorway in the back yard.

Three fairly wide shelves were built into the wall studs, one on each side of the kitchen, and the third next to the living room entrance opposite the stove.

The living room was very large with similar shelves attached at strategic places around the room. In the very center of the room stood an enormous pot-bellied stove used for heating the house.

On the front wall was the front entrance, and to the left, a double window, with a single window to the right allowing for plenty of light and, at the moment, much heat.

There were no inner walls anywhere in the house, thus no insulation or covering of any type. Francisca pulled old cardboard and crumbled newspapers from in between the wall studs that had been used in an attempt to insulate the walls.

Francisca shook her head from side to side.

"What do you think, Pancha?" Chamaco asked her.

"Two things," she answered, "first, I will not spend any time in this house when cold weather comes around. Second, we need something to sit on."

Chamaco smiled.

There was a long wood stool outside the kitchen door in the yard. Chamaco dusted it off and dragged it into the kitchen. He pulled the tall narrow table closer to the stove.

"We can use this for now until we get a table and chairs," he told his wife. "We're going out to buy some groceries. Albert is going with me, we'll be right back," Chamaco announced.

"OK, but hurry," she answered, "the kids are getting hungry, and bring a broom."

Chamaco and Albert drove away.

Francisca ordered the boys to place all the boxes in one corner of the living room. The bedrolls were dropped on the floor next to the bedroom entrance. Everything was now in the house and all that remained was to sort it out.

"Go out and see if you can find some wood for the stove," Francisca told the boys, "if you don't find any you're going to starve," she kidded.

The boys ran out the front door and down the embankment whooping it up. It was after the noon hour and the sun was shining brighter and hotter, or so it seemed.

Francisca unpacked two kerosene lamps that had been carefully wrapped in rags and old newspapers. She wiped off slight leakage of kerosene from the outside of the lamps and wiped the inside and outside of the glass chimneys. She placed one on a shelf in the kitchen and the other in the living room. She found the box containing the kitchen paraphernalia and proceeded to pull out utensils.

The most important thing was the board and rolling pin that were used in the making of tortillas. A pan for cooking beans and a frying pan. A larger pan for mixing the doe and a few plates and cups. Everything was transferred to the table in the kitchen.

After several trips the boys had a decent pile of wood in the back yard. Most of it was old boards but with a few dried out tree branches.

Francisca took several rags and wiped off the surfaces she could reach in the kitchen. Then she paid special attention to the stove, wiping it clean from top to bottom several times with damp cloths. She moved the grate handle several times to release old ashes and unburned lumps in the fire compartment. She opened the clean-out door to check for residue, there was none. She was now ready to cook.

Chamaco and Albert drove across the tracks and parked in front of the Eaton general store. A sign on the glass door read, CLOSED FOR THE 4th.

After all the planning, Chamaco had failed to take into consideration the fact that it was a national holiday. There would be no sense in driving to another town for evidently it would have been the same result. For a moment Chamaco contemplated reading and learning some American History. Perhaps someday, he thought.

They drove back across the tracks and parked in front of La Cantina. Stepping in the door they were greeted by a tall red faced, grey haired gentleman.

"Buenas tardes muchachos," the man greeted them in Spanish.

Chamaco and Albert nodded, returning the greeting, *"Buenas tardes."* They each ordered a beer and sat down at the bar.

Noting that they were strangers, the bartender asked, "Are you here to work?"

"Yes," Chamaco replied, "but I think we picked the wrong day for moving, everything is closed around here."

"What do you need?" asked the man.

"We need to buy some groceries," replied Chamaco.

"If you go to the corner," he pointed south, "across the street, you'll find some things. I don't know all she's got but she has a few things. Just go around the corner to the side door and knock. Dona Amalia is always there. She'll open for you."

The man's Spanish was exceptional, with a trace of the sing-song accent that was so common in the Spanish-Americans of the western states. He spoke in English to Albert with a western style twang, yet with a trace of a Spanish accent.

"Where are you from?" he asked Albert.

"We came in from Denver," Albert replied. Albert's English was without a trace of an accent, having been brought to Denver from El Paso at a very tender age. He spoke more English than Spanish since he had been brought up in the State of Colorado, attending public schools in various sections of the state. His education had been limited to the sixth grade but it was enough for him to be able to establish a dialogue in either language.

"Well, you know, this is a Chicano town and you're always welcome here. The *gringos* from across the tracks don't like us, but we survive," the bartender said as a matter of fact.

"Thanks, thanks a lot," Albert told him as he arose to leave.

Chamaco also got up from the bar stool and thanked the man, *"Muchas gracias amigo!"*

Chamaco and Albert walked out the door. They walked across the street and headed for the grocery store on the corner. They knocked on the side door. A very short and very heavy woman appeared. She seemed to be in her middle fifties. She waddled when she walked due to the concentration of weight in here thighs and legs. She wore a dress with long sleeves and down to her ankles, and a white apron covered the entire front of

Francisca and the Boys

her body. The flesh from her feet and ankles slightly overflowed the edges of her house slippers. She walked with great difficulty.

Chamaco explained his situation to the woman, and could she help. Yes she could, "Please come in," she said.

Chamaco went down his mental list asking for items as they appeared behind his eyes. She had pinto beans, eggs, potatoes, flour, lard, baking powder, and salt. She had no coffee or milk so he took six bottles of soda-pop. They would stop at La Cantina for a few bottles of beer. Chamaco added a couple of boxes of cookies and asked for candy bars. She had none, but plenty of penny candy. He declined the candy.

Chamaco asked if she had any hot green peppers. She opened a bin below the counter and took a look, she was out.

"But I have *chile seco*," the woman told Chamaco.

"Good," he said, "give me a little bag full."

She scooped up the dry red Japanese peppers and put a scoopful into a brown paper bag.

Chamaco looked around for fresh tomatoes and didn't see any, but he spotted canned tomato on the shelf and asked for two cans. It took the woman a little time to add up the list.

"That will be, let's see, three dollars and fifty cents," she said.

"Where do you buy your coal and wood?" Chamaco asked Dona Amalia.

"A man comes around selling it from his truck," she replied, adding, "but not today, it's the fourth of July and everybody is in Greeley or Lupton for the fireworks. But I have two bushels of coal, I can sell you one for twenty five cents if you want it."

"Oh yes, *gracias*," Chamaco told her, "you are very kind,"

"Here," she said, "It's here on the floor by the stove, I can't lift it."

Albert walked around the counter and brought out the bushel.

Chamaco gave Dona Amalia a five dollar bill and said, "Keep the change, we appreciate your help very much, we can't thank you enough."

Dona Amalia protested mildly but accepted the extra money graciously.

The car was loaded with groceries and as they drove off Albert mentioned to Chamaco, "These people are very nice,"

Chamaco replied, "yes, and that's why they are so poor."

It took Francisca about an hour to have cooked food on the table. There would be no beans because they would take too long to cook. They settled for scrambled eggs with bacon bits, fried potatoes, hot sauce and hot tortillas that Francisca whipped up in a very short time.

The table was high for tortilla rolling, but Francisca stood on a small footstool that was found in the back yard by the boys. The stove covers were clean and perfect for cooking the tortillas. The heat from the stove was unbearable, but that was the nature of things when working in the kitchen. Francisca did not complain.

EIGHT

Francisca and her family were finally settled in Eaton, but not to her complete satisfaction. She acquired beds for herself and for the boys along with tables, drawers and cooking utensils.

She laid linoleum floor coverings in every room and hung curtains on every window, transforming the house from a dusty shack to a comfortable and livable home.

The boys' bed was set up in one corner of the living room, which would also serve as a couch during the day if necessary. Her own bed was tucked away behind the wall, in the bedroom, as far from the bedroom entrance as possible since it had no door. She hung a long heavy drape at the entrance for the sake of privacy.

Francisca's major problem now was the lack of bathing facilities, which she was accustomed to not having anyway, and having to pump her water by hand. With that she could live, but her biggest complaint was the outhouse, which she abhorred. It smelled so bad that she would have to hold her breath almost the entire time she occupied it. Even after scrubbing the wooden seats and dumping fifty pounds of lime into the pit, the stench persisted.

For evacuating purposes Francisca would force herself to use the outhouse, but if it was just a matter of urinating, she preferred to go in the ditch separating the back fence from the hayfield beyond, taking a cue from her sons.

Francisca's mind was already made up, she would be back in Denver by the last week in August. School would reopen in September and she was going to make sure that the boys would be educated in one place, and for all practical purposes, that place was Denver.

Nick and Davy had a complete playground and front yard stretching from the embankment clear across to the ball field backstop. They had already investigated the corral and the bullpen, which were very handy for exerting energy and having fun. Now it was time to look the rest of the town over.

The boys walked through the alley behind the houses on the main street, stopping at each wooden cross that was either nailed to a fence or driven into the ground. They stared in wonderment. How did this person die? Who killed him? Taking for granted that it had been a man. They continued down the alley with a slight shiver in each of their spines. The boys walked around the corner at the town grocery store and headed back up the main street of Ragtown.

La Cantina had its doors wide open but no customers could be seen. It was too early in the day, but there would be some action later this evening. It was Friday and the beginning of the weekend.

The boys passed a small group of children playing in the front yards of the homes across the street from La Cantina. Two girls of about their own age were sitting on the doorstep of one of the houses. The boys half waved and said hello as the girls immediately stood and walked toward them. In less than a blink of an eye the four were in deep conversation, asking for information and giving information in return.

The girls, Sally and Rosy, belonged to the Martinez family and had lived in Eaton all of their lives. Sally was fourteen and Rosy was twelve, and they attended the grammar school across the tracks.

After a few minutes of conversation, the boys decided to be on their way. They were aware that their mother would be missing them very soon.

"We gotta go," Davy said without explanation.

"OK," Sally said with a smile, "why don't you come back when it gets dark. By that time there'll be a lot of people around here. The tavern will be full and you can see everything from here. We can watch 'em dance, and you can hear the music clear across the street."

"We'll try," Davy told her, "bye."

Nick was staring at Sally all the time that she was talking. Her long jet black hair parted at the center and went down the sides of her face, touching the outer corners of her eyes and hanging past her shoulders to her waist. Her face was thin, with wide mouth and thin lips, a slender nose and large brown eyes. Her skin was extremely bronzed due to the effects of the sun. Her true skin color was a light sallow showing around the edges of her eyes.

Nick compared the sisters in his mind. Rosy's facial features were almost identical to those of her sister, except that they appeared a bit thinner. Her hair was also waist length, but it was held by a bobby pin above each ear as it ran back behind her shoulders. It was light brown at the roots and gradually changed to a lighter, almost blond shade at the ends. Rosy was very skinny, without a trace of a bosom. Her eyes were green and moved from side to side very fast, almost constantly. She didn't talk much.

The boys started to walk home and the girls joined them as far as the corner near the Catholic church. They stopped for a moment and Nick said, pointing, "That's where we live, where the car is sticking out."

"Oh yea," Sally told them, "that house has been empty for a long time, come back later if you can make it, bye."

Nick and Davy responded at the same time, "Bye."

The boys climbed the embankment to the small road leading to their house. The car sticking out of the driveway was unfamiliar, but as they approached the house they soon found that the car belonged to Alvino, Ricky's and Freddy's stepfather.

The house was full of people again, just like in Denver. The crew that was to start work on Monday had arrived while the boys were out evaluating their new location. Francisca and their aunt Nena were busy cooking for everyone before the gang must leave to settle down in the bunkhouse on the farm.

Arrangements had been made for Jesse and Nena to stay in the two room house at the farm, which in reality was not much more than a shack with kitchen facilities consisting of a short four plated iron stove and a small table. The crew would bed down in the bunkhouse just a few feet behind the first building. It had a two tier wooden bunk built against the wall on each side of the room.

At Francisca's, all of the men were standing or squatting in the small back yard smoking marijuana while pouring and drinking beer out of half gallon bottles. There was a bottle of gin for those who cared to mix their drinking. Smoke permeated the area but floated away steadily in the summer air, and the smell was strong.

Francisca and Nena served a huge meal to the satisfaction of everyone concerned. After the meal the men prepared to leave for the bunkhouse. They boarded Alvino's car and drove away to the Anderson farm.

Nena remained behind to help Francisca with the dishes after which Francisca would accompany her to the farm and help her get settled. It was now getting toward late afternoon and Chamaco took the opportunity to walk down to La Cantina to have a beer and talk to Juan Montoya, the owner of the bar.

Since their arrival and during the week Chamaca had made friends with many of the local people and was now known fairly well. He greeted and was greeted in return by the red faced bartender he had met on the first day here.

"Is Juan anywhere around?" Chamaco asked the bartender.

"No, he isn't here, he won't come in 'til later tonight," the bartender told him.

"Well, maybe you can help me," Chamaco said, "I need one more man for the field contract that I have with a farm in Ault, do you know anybody that wants to work. It would be for the rest of the summer."

Francisca and the Boys

The bartender said, "Yes, I know somebody that needs work, but he's still a very young man, would that make any difference."

"No, not if he's big enough, and what do you mean by 'very young'?" asked Chamaco.

"Well, you can see for yourself, let me get him for you." he answered. The bartender walked to the door and spoke to one of the children playing outside. The child ran across the street and soon a tall gangling young man appeared at the door.

"Manuelito, do you want to work beets for the rest of the summer?" asked the bartender.

"Yea," replied the young man.

Then the bartender said, "This is Manuel Martinez, I don't know your name."

"Oh *perdon* that I failed to introduce myself," Chamaco apologized, "everyone calls me Chamaco." They shook hands all around.

"How old are you?" Chamaco asked Manuel.

"I'm seventeen, I'll be eighteen in a couple of months," replied Manuel.

"OK, we start Monday morning, can you be at my house by five o'clock? I live in that house above the cattle track," Chamaco offered.

"Yea, I'll be there Monday in the morning. I know the house, I saw when you were moving in," Manuel said.

It was settled, and Chamaco had his sixth man, counting himself.

"Thank you," Manuel said to Chamaco. Then he turned to the bartender and said, *"Gracias Don Jesus"*

Chamaco returned home to prepare for the short trip to the farm. The boys asked to stay behind because they wanted to join the Martinez girls. They were curious to see and hear the activity that would be going on in the tavern.

"Alright, you can sit outside with the girls but don't go anywhere near that tavern," Francisca warned the boys, "and as soon as you see the lights from the car, make sure you get home right away."

"Yea ma, we will," Davy said.

"We will ma," Nick repeated reassuringly.

Chamaco and Francisca drove off taking their aunt Nena to her new temporary home.

Nick and Davy waited until dusk before taking their walk to the main street. They wanted to see and hear the action that Sally and Rosy had promised.

The boys lit the kerosene lamp and placed it in the center of the kitchen table and lowered the wick slightly as per instructions from their mother. It was a warm night so neither boy bothered to put on a shirt. The bib overalls fit nice and loose to allow air circulation around the back and sides. Taking a short cut, the boys ran down the embankment, jumping the old track below in two strides, then headed toward the main street. Turning the corner at the church they spotted the girls sitting on the door step. They waved and the girls stood up to greet them.

The lights from the tavern flooded the street through the open door. It was only a little after seven and the juke box was already blasting western music at a high pitch. There were only two customers at the bar, but it was still early. By dark, automobiles and trucks were pulling up in front of the tavern. Soon the bar was full of men from the surrounding area along with three scantily clad young women. There was dancing, drinking and arguing that would continue into the night.

Car lights appeared at the end of the street and did not make the turn toward the bar. The car continued up the small road above the embankment.

Nick said, "There they are Davy, we better go."

"Yea, my mother and father are back, we'll see you tomorrow," Davy told the girls.

At that precise moment a car pulled up in front of the girls' house and a tall young heavy set man of about twenty five or so stepped out.

Francisca and the Boys

"That's my brother Sam," Sally said to the boys.

Sam worked road construction for the state and was just arriving home from work.

"Hi girls," Sam said. Then he asked playfully, "Who are these guys?"

"This is Davy and Nicky," Sally said, "they just moved in up the hill."

"Oh, you're Chamaco's boys, huh," Sam said.

"Yea," Davy nodded.

Sam had already been acquainted with Chamaco through the local politician, Enrique Archuleta, better known to the residents of East Eaton as Henry. As in all small towns it did not take very long for the population of Ragtown to know that there were newcomers in town, secrets were hard to keep.

A voice from inside the house said, "I'll see you guys Monday morning, I'm gonna be working for your dad."

There was a surprised look on both the boys' faces as they turned to where the voice was coming from.

"That's my brother Manuel," Sally said, giggling. Soon everyone was introduced and the boys were on their way home.

Francisca made hot chocolate and toasted tortillas on the hot plates of the stove, a snack before bedtime.

"Go to bed now, you have to get up early in the morning," Francisca told the boys.

"But ma, tomorrow's Saturday, why do we have to get up early?" protested Davy.

"Never mind, just go to bed," Francisca was firm.

"Aw, heck," Nick exclaimed.

"Watch your mouth, Nicolas," she pronounced his name hard and deliberate.

By seven thirty the next morning the Ford was pulling out of Eaton headed north on the main highway. The boys were in their Sunday best including long pants with a belt to hold them up, patent leather shoes and knee length socks. They were uncomfortable but excited about taking a trip.

Francisca wore a sleeveless black silk dress with flared skirt to just below the knee. She had on silk hose held up by garters, and black high heeled pumps. She carried a large scarf to use as protection over her shoulders to ward off the morning chill.

Chamaco had on grey pants with white shirt and black tie and wore brown pointed oxfords. He draped his, likewise grey suit coat over the backrest of the front seat.

Francisca had "withdrawn" fifty dollars in small bills from her shoe box before securing it safely under a loose floor board under her bed. The house was secured with padlocks on front and back doors. No one was told about the coming trip so both, Chamaco and Francisca, felt good about the security of the house.

It was still morning when the Delmonte family arrived in Cheyenne, Wyoming. They stopped for breakfast at a restaurant on the outskirts of town.

"Oh boy," exclaimed Davy, "I want hot cakes."

"Me too," echoed Nick.

"Alright, but sit down and be quiet," Francisca warned them.

All had breakfast and now prepared to continue the journey. Chamaco paid the bill and left a generous tip of twenty five cents.

Again they headed north.

About a mile from the Wheatland, Wyoming city limits, the car turned east on a side road. Nick and Davy were beginning to recognize the territory.

"Hey, look, I remember that place," Davy said pointing at a farmhouse off the road.

"Yea, me too," Nick chimed in.

Soon the names of towns and locations began to stir memories in the boys. Places like Torrington, Wyoming and Scotts Bluff, Nebraska, and the Indian reservation they visited years ago.

They particularly remembered the rumors of the time that the Indian tribes took their dogs and tore them apart for food while still alive. In reality, the true rumor, which was still only a rumor, was that starvation was so prevalent during the depression that the tribes were forced to kill and cook their domestic animals for

Francisca and the Boys

food to avoid starvation. That might have been a more plausible explanation if, in fact, there was any truth to the rumors at all.

Nick and Davy kept up their conversation.

"Scotts Bluff is where grandma died in 1929," Davy mentioned.

"Yea," Nick said as he pictured his grandmother Silvina laid out in her coffin in the living room. He remembered being picked up by someone and held over the body to kiss his grandmother. He shivered and whimpered at the cold touch of his lips on her cheek, but he did not cry.

The car slowed and pulled into a short driveway leading to a modest looking white house. It was the main house of the Estrada farm. Chamaco stepped out of the car and walked to the front door. Juan Estrada was waiting at the door to greet him.

"Hello Chamaco," Estrada said, "*como estas?*."

"*Bien gracias*," answered Chamaco as the two shook hands.

"Call your wife in," Estrada told him and turned in, saying "Estela, Pancha is here."

Chamaco and Francisca disappeared into the house. Nick and Davy disembarked and began to run around the building and through the yard. Behind and to one side of the house was perhaps a full acre of marijuana plants, growing unimpeded to a possible height of six feet or more. The buds bloomed thick and dark green, almost purple in color, on several stems of each plant. The boys walked through a labyrinth of plants, enjoying the flapping of the leaves and the strong evergreen smell.

The Delmontes and the Estradas conversed for more than an hour and had refreshments.

"Ask the boys if they want some lemonade," Estela told Francisca.

Francisca opened the front door and called to the boys, "You want some lemonade, kids?"

"Yea," was the simultaneous retort.

The boys ran in but slowed down when their father cautioned them to be polite. They swallowed their drinks without removing the glasses from their lips then turned and walked slowly toward the door and suddenly burst out screaming and yelling.

Their business finished, Chamaco and Francisca came out, after their goodbyes to the host couple, and boarded the car for the trip home.

In this farming area the boys had first learned to use the weeding hoe and the beet thinning hoe. The weeding hoe had a long handle and it was fairly easy to cut away weeds when cleaning around the sugar beet plant because it could be done standing and walking. But the thinning hoe was short and it must be used in a stooping or kneeling position in order to cut away excessive plants, so that one plant alone remained at perhaps eight to ten inch intervals. Later the single plant would produce one large, single sugar beet that would later be processed further and finally into sugar.

The boys remembered the back pains after each row of beets was completed. Now they were preparing for another crack at it on Monday morning.

Manuel arrived at the back door at 4:45 Monday morning, making sure he would not be late.

Nick and Davy were up and ready to go. Although they were not obliged to, it was their choice to be in the fields instead of at home They enjoyed the adventure and also appreciated whatever earnings their father would decide to allot them. The boys had spent much time in a field of one kind or another in the past and had learned the intricacies of the cultivating of each product simply by participating.

By 5:30 a.m. the Ford was pulling into the front yard of the small house on the Anderson farm. The weeding hoes were placed against the bunkhouse wall so that every worker could pick one to his liking. The weeding was begun in earnest on the twenty acre sugar beet field stretching out behind the buildings in rows of one quarter mile or more in length.

In the weeding process each worker could pick one or more rows to weed at one time. The hoes were long enough to reach right and left from center, from six to eight feet without too much stretching.

Jimmy, the man with one arm and one leg, was an oddity as a worker to say the least. The boys marveled at his dexterity as he moved along the rows as easily as any other worker. The boys made a point of working next to Jimmy whenever they could because of his constant joking, and kidding the boys along. His demeanor helped them forget the drudgery that this type of work represented.

By 10:00 AM, the boys had accumulated dust on their faces, they were hot, thirsty and tired. Davy relished the challenge and the friendly competition with the older men, yet he would only challenge as far as his ability would allow. His young and undeveloped body could withstand only so much torture. Soon he would slow down to a pace of his own and feel good about his accomplishments. Nick would look for any excuse to rest and stretch. Frequently he would stop to go for a drink of water and would offer to bring the canvas water bag to anyone in need of a drink.

By noon, Aunt Nena arrived with a deep metal pan filled with tacos, and a container of hot sauce. The flour tortillas were stuffed with chopped beef and diced potatoes, or with eggs mixed with *"chorizo"*, the Mexican sausage so popular in the west and southwest. She also had others stuffed with the ever present refried beans.

The men stopped work long enough to have a snack and then return to work by their own free will. The average lunch would take no more than a half hour of their time.

At mid afternoon, Nick and Davy would quit from sheer exhaustion and go to the house to await the return of Chamaco at near dusk.

Soon they would arrive home and have a good meal then sit in the yard to enjoy the cool evening air. Come the next morning, the routine would begin and end the same.

Thus was the work edict that every man in the crew observed while working for and with Chamaco.

NINE

The business at the Estrada farm near Wheatland, Wyoming had to be dealt with, so there would be one more trip. Chamaco and the boys made the trip one Saturday morning late in August. Francisca preferred to remain at home and prepare for the return trip to Denver.

On arrival at the Estrada farm, Chamaco found that all the marijuana plants had been cut down while the only thing remaining were short stubs showing sharp edges where the machetes had sliced through.

Puzzled, Nick stared at the crop stubs wondering where the plants were taken and by whom.

Chamaco spoke with a tearful Estela Estrada.

Her husband, Juan, had been arrested and taken to Cheyenne to await trial.

Chamaco and the boys did not linger.

By this time the cultivating of the sugar beet crop was nearing its end. The field had been weeded and the beet plants had been thinned. There would be a wait of a few weeks before the beets would be plowed out of the ground to be gathered and piled by hand then topped off with machetes, loaded on truck or horse wagon to be carried away to the refinery.

Francisca and the boys would not be around for the topping. By then the weather would begin to change and cold nights would start to set in. Francisca would have none of that.

Chamaco and the boys returned from their trip in late afternoon. Nick and Davy had the rest of the evening to run around Ragtown. Francisca gave them permission to stay out late as long as they remained close to the Martinez home and away from the entrance to the town tavern. They were eager to see Sally and Rosy again before having to go back to Denver.

The night was clear and cool as Nick and Davy walked slowly toward the main street of Ragtown. Still dressed in their better clothes, the boys felt as if they were going out on the town They joked as they walked.

"Let's go to La Cantina and have a couple of beers," Davy said as he stuck out his chest and swung his arms in a manly fashion.

"I want whiskey," Nick added, "with beer for a chaser."

They laughed out loud as they skipped downward on the embankment above the cattle track.

The girls were no where to be seen. There was a moment of disappointment in both boys as they walked to the front fence. Manuel was there. He was home waiting for the start of the topping season as was the whole crew.

"Hi Manuel, where's the girls?" Davy asked.

"They're out in back, I'll call 'em," Manuel volunteered.

Manuel disappeared through the front door and soon Sally and Rosy appeared wearing broad smiles.

They greeted one another and settled down to an evening of conversation and to criticize the local citizenry. It was after ten and La Cantina was in full swing.

The boys could see Jimmy sitting at the bar near the door. His wooden leg was resting against the bar next to him as he drank his beer with his one and only hand.

The music was loud and the patrons could be seen dancing to the western rhythms. The bar was full of cowboy types along with the same girls, that seemed to be part of the business. The drinking and laughing and continuous noise did not abate. Suddenly there was pushing and shoving and a beer bottle came flying out the door.

One of those in the argument was standing next to Jimmy's stool with his back to Jimmy. The other man was facing the first with a beer bottle menacingly in his hand. Out of nowhere the first man produced a switch blade that opened with a snap. In the meantime Don Jesus, the bartender, was on the floor trying to pacify the combatants.

As the man with the knife raised it with his right hand to strike, Jimmy picked up his wooden leg and brought it straight up with great force hitting the man's arm at the elbow causing the knife to fly up and over his head and landing somewhere behind the bar.

Don Jesus restrained the man with the bottle as the knife wielder walked out the door holding his right arm obviously in a great deal of pain. He went south to the corner then turned east, disappearing into the darkness still holding his damaged arm and in a highly inebriated condition.

The boys and the girls stood at the fence wide eyed as the action was occurring. The view from across the street was clear, as the four watched the action, and not missing a beat.

Soon La Cantina was back to normal. The drinking and dancing continued with no further interruptions.

Sally broke the silence as the four relaxed after the commotion.

"That guy that went home is Roy Valtierra, and the guy he was fighting with is his brother Joe," Sally explained.

"What!" exclaimed Davy, "They're brothers?" he could not believe what he heard.

"Yea, they're always fighting," she replied in a matter of fact way.

"Wow!" whispered Nick.

At that moment a figure came into view out of the dark, from the corner at the north end of the street. It walked ominously toward La Cantina as though floating just above the ground.

"Who's that?" Nick asked.

"That's '*La India*,'" explained Sally, "her real name is Susana but everybody calls her India."

The woman came into the light and could now be seen more clearly by the four at the fence.

Francisca and the Boys

She was wearing a long sleeved white cotton dress ending at the ankles, and tied at the waist with a long red sash that crossed her chest down from around her neck then around her waist and tied to one side. She wore tennis shoes without the benefit of socks. Her grey hair was tied in a tail and she wore a headband with beads, ending in a knot behind her right ear. Her face was wrinkled and scraggly.

Sally continued, "She speaks English and Spanish and when she gets drunk she talks in Cherokee."

"Is she really a Indian?" Davy asked.

"I think she is, but nobody knows what she says when she talks Indian," Sally answered.

As the woman stepped to the door of the tavern she spat into the street before entering.

Then Sally said, "She chews tobacco."

Rosy, who had been quiet most of the time, chimed in, "She's got at least three more skirts under her dress."

Everyone laughed loudly.

It was late and the boys must get home before midnight. The girls were ready to turn in themselves, so they said their goodbyes as the boys departed.

Walking home Nick turned to Davy and said, "Did you see Jimmy hit that guy with his leg?"

"Yea," replied Davy, "and he picked it up with only one hand. Did you ever try to lift his wooden leg? I did once and it was too heavy."

"He's a strong guy," Nick said.

Both boys felt proud of Jimmy because he was their friend and he done something good.

The next morning the church bell was ringing at about 9:30. That meant the priest was in and there would be mass at 10:AM.

Francisca decided to skip mass as she didn't intend to become a permanent member of East Eaton society. She would pray at her home altar for now, and attend church at a future date.

By the middle of the week, Francisca was ready to leave Eaton. She made arrangements for Nena and Jesse to move in with Chamaco until the end of the topping season, after that, everyone would go their separate ways.

Nena was left with plenty of food supplies to continue cooking for the crew, and Chamaco promised her extra money for her efforts.

By Wednesday afternoon the Ford pulled out one more time with Denver as its destination. As usual, Albert would be driving. The load back was much lighter since Francisca and the boys had only their personal belongings to contend with. With plenty of time to spare, Chamaco went along to make sure that the family was settled comfortably.

Chamaco was about to make his promise of a better home for his family become a fact. He had added money to Francisca's cache, and by not withdrawing from her savings, he gave her the signal to go ahead with her plans. He had kept his promise and Francisca was indeed grateful. After so many years of doing without, Francisca was determined to settle down to a more comfortable way of life.

Rental homes were not hard to find. Due to the economy of the time single family dwellings and apartments were unoccupied. With Goldie's help, Francisca found a five room house on Curtis near 26th, a few doors from Goldie's apartment.

The house was equipped with electric lights in every room, and there were gas pipe lines for stove and heater connections. It had a porcelain bathtub with washbowl to match in the water closet and a large sink with a drain board in the kitchen. The rent would be fifteen dollars per month, and the house was walking distance to 24th Street School. Francisca was pleased.

Within a few days time, Francisca had the house furnished with rug, couch, and armchair for the living room. An electric refrigerator and a gas cooking stove, along with table and chairs for the kitchen, and a dining set for the dining room were added.

Francisca and the Boys

She ordered a bedroom set for her upstairs bedroom, and single beds for the boys' bedroom next to hers.

Nick and Davy had been paid twenty dollars each for the work they had done in the beet field during the season, and were assured by their mother that they could spend their money as they wished. They each wanted a bicycle, so they sauntered over to the bike shop on 23rd and Larimer.

New bicycles were expensive, and the boys knew they didn't have enough money, but they also knew that the bike shop sold used bikes, and to them, a used bike was better than no bike at all.

Davy made a deal for a balloon tire bike with red painted fenders for all of his twenty bucks. It was an Ivor Johnson.

Nick acquired a newly painted blue bike with skinny tires, no fenders and no name plate for thirteen dollars. For an extra dollar, the owner of the shop exchanged the straight handle bars for curved racing handle bars on both bikes. They were promptly installed and turned upward, as was the style of the times. Nick paid the extra dollar without hesitation.

With receipts in their pockets, the boys rode away in their newly acquired bicycles. Nick and Davy enjoyed their bicycles for about two weeks before school started again in September. Their summer vacation was coming to an end and they would make the best of the last few days.

Ray Lucero now became somewhat of a leader to the boys, since he had owned a bike for some time and knew all of the interesting places to see and visit. The trio became closer now that they had something in common.

The brothers followed Ray's lead as they traveled by bike to areas not yet familiar to Nick and Davy. In the short period of time before school would start again, they had been to the Denver Mint, and visited the Capitol Building and the Public Library in downtown Denver. They had been to City Park and the Denver Zoo before, but not with the new found freedom afforded them by their bicycles. On one occasion they biked to the Platte River near Federal Boulevard to catch crabs.

The boys consumed hour after hour aboard their bicycles with great relish. Everything that appeared new to them was something that had never been on the family agenda. They were learning while exploring.

Now it was time to return to school.

School began the first Monday in September and Nick would now have to go to school without his brother. Davy had been promoted to seventh grade and would now be attending Cole Junior High School.

Nick was going back to 24th and enter Mrs. Davidson's 6th grade class for a full semester.

Mrs. Davidson was the most feared and the most hated teacher in the school. Nick's only encounter with Mrs. Davidson was a slap in the face he received one day for talking in class, adding him to the list of victims Mrs. Davidson had to her credit over the years. Nick was humiliated but he managed to live through it. The embarrassment would soon pass but her face slapping trademark had been established as a warning to the rest of the class. Nick now would carry the slapping incident as a badge of honor. Only those who dared would receive such attention from Mrs. Davidson.

After his first day, Davy came home filled with praise for his new school. He liked the idea of changing rooms for each subject and the contact he made with different students, especially the girls.

The school year was going by rapidly as the boys kept busy in and out of school.

Nick now had a paper route after school, and both, he and Davy joined the Boy Scouts. Meetings were held every Friday evening at the 24th Street School basement.

Davy had passed his test for Second Class Scout and had recently been awarded his badge. He was already into the studies required for the First Class test. Nick was still a Tenderfoot but he was also preparing for advancement to Second Class Scout.

The boys begged Francisca to purchase their Boy Scout uniforms, which she did without hesitation. Soon the boys wore

Francisca and the Boys

their uniforms proudly, with their badges pinned to their Scout hats.

At times they would attend Boy Scout conventions or jamborees wearing their Troop Number 65 patches on their sleeves.

Chamaco reestablished his position at Chon's during the next two week ends. The waitress never returned to work at Chon's after the fateful incident. Things had turned to a more or less normal pace as Chamaco was welcomed back.

Chamaco's winnings soared during his stay in Denver. Before his return to Eaton he had managed to add nearly two thousand more dollars to Francisca's savings. She had retrieved her wooden chest from her sister Lucy and it was again serving its required purpose.

Chamaco's coughing had subsided somewhat, and he refused to see Dr. Alanis any further.

Albert was alerted to be ready for the trip back to Eaton on Thursday of the second week. There was a contract to be fulfilled as the topping season was approaching.

It was the middle of November and the cold weather was beginning to sneak in. The field contract had been fulfilled and Chamaco and the crew were back in Denver.

Early one Sunday afternoon Nena appeared at Francisca's door, crying uncontrollably.

"*Que paso?*" she asked Nena.

"Jesse's in jail," Nena answered, "they picked him up last night, they caught him with a roll of *frajos*."

"Oh my God!" exclaimed Francisca.

Francisca did not know much about the law, but she understood that peddling, or even possessing marijuana was a major offense in the State.

"Come in the kitchen," Francisca said to Nena. She made coffee and the women sat down to talk it over.

"Let's wait for Chamaco to see what we can do," Francisca said, trying her best to console her sister-in-law. Nena stopped crying but remained nervous and irritable waiting for something positive to happen.

A few minuets later Albert and Goldie walked in the door.

Albert looked very pale and Goldie had a worried look on her face. Albert explained, "They raided Chon's place last night, and about half the people were arrested." He continued, "We spent the night in jail, Jimmy and me. They turned us loose just a while ago. They kept Chamaco. My brother Jesse was stopped and searched outside from Chon's and they arrested him, he was carrying a roll of stuff and they found it on him."

Francisca's heart dropped, "And what about Chamaco?" she asked.

"He was picked up for gambling but they took him to 'Federal Detention', was what one cop told me. I think it's Immigration," Albert told Francisca.

Francisca's world seemed to be coming to an end. Her mind began churning possibilities of every type imaginable. What would happen now? Would he be deported? Would he do time in prison? She wanted to cry with all her heart, but she contained herself so that she could think things out rationally. There was nothing she could do until she talked to Chamaco. She would try to see him Monday morning if it was possible.

Francisca offered Nena the opportunity to stay the night if she wished. Nena accepted graciously.

The boys were at the movies and Francisca was relieved that they were not present when the news about their father was brought in. In time she would have to explain to them what was happening and what course would be taken in the absence of Chamaco.

Before leaving, Albert gave Francisca a roll of bills held together by a rubber band. "Here Pancha." he said, "Chamaco told me to pick this up from his friend the Greek and give it to you."

As usual, the bills were in monetary disorder. Chamaco had somehow slipped the roll of money to his friend the Greek who was sitting at the bar. The bar patrons had not been arrested but were escorted out of the tavern during the raid.

Francisca took the money and almost broke down, but she held back the tears with as much restraint as she could muster. At bedtime that evening, she cried herself to sleep.

At the front desk of the detention center Francisca spoke with the attending officer. "Sir," she said, "can't I see my husband before they take him away?"

"I'm sorry ma'am," the officer replied, "that is not possible at this time. Processing will take a few days after the investigation. You will be notified as to the disposition of his case in good time."

It was explained to Francisca that her husband would go for a hearing before a Federal Magistrate and the disposition of the case would be decided at that time. If his police record was extensive, he would certainly be deported.

Francisca already knew that Chamaco would be deported because this was his second offense. He had been deported about five years previously and returned illegally for a second time. She was aware that there was no hope of his remaining in the States, and even if she hired a lawyer, it would only be a waste of money.

In desperation, Francisca tried a maneuver that often worked with city cops. She took a twenty dollar bill and held it folded in the palm of her left hand. Making sure that the denomination could be seen, she put her hand on the desk, and as she spoke she held the bill with her thumb and opened only her four fingers.

"Isn't there someway that I could talk to my husband?" she asked while flashing the bill.

The officer dropped his paper work and placed both palms on the desk as he looked down at her and replied in consternation, "Mrs. Delmonte, please, the Federal Government doesn't work that way. Put that away before you get in trouble."

Francisca became momentarily flustered at the refusal and at the same time relieved that the officer did not make a big thing of the offer. She thanked him and walked away. There were no longer any doubts in Francisca's mind as to what actions she must now take. The devastated woman of the day before no longer occupied her body. She thought of something that her mother had impressed upon her as she was growing into adulthood.

"There will be times in your life when there is no one to turn to but yourself, that is when you will have to make your own decisions." Something she, herself, impressed upon her two sons, by teaching them to cook and do house work and do their own washing and ironing, so they would learn independence and be self sufficient. In that vain she would tell her sons, "I'm not going to live forever, so learn to do things for yourselves," and as an afterthought she would say, "who knows what kind of women you will end up with."

Francisca hailed a taxi in front of the Federal Detention Center. On her way home she did a great deal of thinking.

If her mother had traveled halfway across Mexico with two children, and crossed the border to attempt to give them a chance at a better life, what was to prevent Francisca from accomplishing the same for her sons. The future had unlimited possibilities for them. They, her sons, were Americans.

Francisca's thoughts continued to emerge as she thought of her first child, born to her at the tender age of fifteen in El Paso. Her mother had been the midwife who brought her daughter into the world, without the aid of medical or sanitary facilities. She had been thankful that her mother was still around at the time. At fifteen she was still a child herself. Oh how thankful she felt even today, at a time that her mother was no longer present.

With the aid of the Catholic Sisters in El Paso, Francisca's daughter, Guadalupe, had been duly registered and baptized under the auspices of the Holy Catholic Church. The father, a young man of seventeen or eighteen years of age had quietly slipped back into Mexico never to be seen again.

Now her mother was raising two daughters for all practical purposes, and no one had to know any different. Silvina brought up Guadalupe as her own, but never denied to her own daughter that she was the child's true mother.

By age sixteen, Guadalupe had given birth to her own first child, making Francisca a grandmother in her very early thirties.

Chamaco had accepted Francisca's daughter, who was four at the time, as his own during his courtship of Francisca.

In her first year of school, Guadalupe was registered as Guadalupe Delmonte. A name she kept even after marriage and divorce.

The taxicab pulled up in front of her house and Francisca quickly returned to the present.

"Sixty five cents," the driver told Francisca as he stepped out to open her door. She rummaged through her snap purse and pulled out a dollar bill. She handed the bill to the driver and said, "Keep the change."

The driver was surprised at such a generous tip, but thankful. He said, "Thank you very much ma'am."

Francisca went into the house and made some coffee. Now she would sit and relax while waiting for her boys to get home from school. There were a number of decisions that had to be made Her first order of business would be to talk to Goldie and to Nena. She needed their opinions and their help in order to accomplish the actions that she was formulating.

TEN

Francisca, Nena and Goldie sat around the kitchen table sipping coffee and talking about the future. Francisca took the initiative with hopes that the other two women were in a mood of cooperation.

"Goldie," she said "I'm going to El Paso in a week or two, I'm not sure, but I want to know if you will take care of my house while I am gone."

"Of course I will, Pancha," Goldie answered.

Francisca continued, "There's two bedrooms on the second floor so if you want to move in while I'm gone, your welcome."

Goldie, not giving a yes or no answer, nodded as Francisca spoke.

She continued, "Nena is going to be alone for a long time, so if you can move in together it could help all of us."

Francisca was direct in her assertion regarding Jesse's fate, but as brutal as it might seem, she had to convince Nena that the situation was such, and must begin to make adjustments.

"I will give you enough money for six or eight months of rent and I promise to be back in at least that much time. I don't intend to live in Mexico, or even Texas. If I can't make some kind of arrangements to bring Chamaco back, I'm coming back with just the kids," she told Goldie.

Nena cut in for a moment, "I can move with Lucy or stay where I am until Jesse gets out of jail." She would not let go of expectations that Jesse would get out of jail soon and return to her.

This time Francisca was more direct and equally brutal to her sister-in-law.

Francisca and the Boys

"Nena," she told her, "Jesse was bound to the Grand Jury. That means prison time for sure in years, not months. I'd guess about five years or more. This state is tough on pushers of marijuana. If you are going to wait for Jesse, get ready for a long, long wait. What you should do is start thinking for yourself. If you need help or advice, I'll always be around where you can find me."

Nena put her head down looking at her hands. Tears rolled down her cheeks.

Francisca moved over and put an arm around her shoulders and said, "Nena, you're my sister-in-law, and I want you to know you can stay with me as long as you want. I know it's hard but we have to learn to stand on our own two feet."

"I understand, Pancha," Nena responded, "but it's just that I've been with Jesse so many years, I wouldn't know what to do."

"You will learn what to do," Francisca told her.

"Alright, I'll stay if Goldie don't mind." Nena said glancing at Goldie.

"Of course I don't mind, why should I?" Goldie retorted.

Goldie had seen the passivity in Nena's character and decided then and there that she could easily get along with her. They had known each other for a couple of years but had never really been involved in any intimate situations such as this.

Francisca told Goldie, "I'm leaving the car to you and Albert. Just make sure that he takes good care of it." As an after thought she added, "I know he will take care of it, but I want you to take the responsibility."

Goldie smiled and said, "Yea, I know, Francisca, I know what your talking about. I'll take care of your car and your brother too."

They all laughed, breaking the somber mood that had prevailed over the last few minutes.

There was a knock at the door and as Francisca was about to stand, the door was pushed open. Her brother Albert walked in accompanied by someone else.

"Oh, It's Albert," Francisca said.

The two men walked into the kitchen and joined the women.

"This is George Poloupolos, Chamaco's friend. He wanted to meet you and talk to you, Pancha," Albert said.

George offered his hand to Francisca who graciously accepted and shook it with a gentle grip.

"Me and your husband have been friends many years." He spoke with a heavy Greek accent. "I'm at your service if you need any kind of help. Money if you need it. I teach Chamaco how to play barbute. I teach him Greek too."

Francisca offered George some coffee but he thanked her and said, "American coffee is not strong. I drink Greek coffee. Thank you, thank you." George was not being rude but just practical.

George the Greek made a motion to leave as Francisca stood up from her chair. She walked with George toward the door. They stopped at the door and the Greek turned to her and said, "Alberto knows where I live, if you need help, send him to call me, I will come right away."

"Thank you very much, Mr. Poloupolos," Francisca told him.

"Call me George, no Mr., just George."

George took a glance at Goldie and quickly looked away.

Goldie remained seated with a slight, knowing smile on her lips, for George happened to be one of Goldie's best customers, and she couldn't and wouldn't have anyone here get the slightest notion that they knew each other outside of this immediate circle.

George walked out and Francisca noticed how short he was, no more than an inch or two taller than herself. Francisca was five feet tall at most.

Before leaving, George turned once more to Francisca and asked her, "Do you know what you are going to do now?"

"Yes," she said, "Chamaco will be taken by train to El Paso and then transferred to Mexican immigration in Juarez. I don't

Francisca and the Boys

know yet what day he is going, but if I go now, I will wait for him there. He has brothers in Juarez."

"Good, good, that is good," George told her.

"Thank you very much for coming over, George," Francisca said, "I'll tell Chamaco I talked to you."

"Very good," he said, "don't forget, I can help if you need." George was sincere about his offer to help.

Francisca smiled and said, "Thank you, thank you."

George left and Francisca returned to the kitchen to have more coffee and make plans. With Albert now present, the group went over the instructions one more time for his benefit. Albert was always ready to help in any way he could. He had no thoughts of abandoning his sister in her time of need.

Francisca's plan began to revolve slowly in her mind. She must first try one more time to secure the date of Chamaco's departure. If she could not accomplish that, she would go directly to the train station and make reservations for El Paso, Texas.

"I'm only taking two or three changes of clothes for me and the kids. Everything else will stay," Francisca told everyone. She had great confidence in all of those who were present. And now it was time to go to the Federal Detention Center.

Francisca arrived at the Federal Detention Center early the next day. She walked into the large office containing several desks occupied mostly by young women, but there were also, perhaps three or four young male typists and secretaries busily working at their appointed tasks. Guards in uniform came in and out of a doorway situated at the center of the rear wall of the office, carrying files back and forth.

On this occasion the person at the reception desk happened to be a matronly and bespectacled woman seeming to be in her early fifties.

"How can I help you?" she asked Francisca courteously.

"My husband is here and I wondered if I could to talk to him before he is deported," Francisca told the woman.

"What's his full name, please?" asked the receptionist.

"Estanislao Delmonte," replied Francisca.

Francisca's heart jumped an extra beat when there was no immediate refusal. She felt elated at the prospect of seeing Chamaco again.

The woman looked through the files as she murmured, "Hmm, let's see, here it is, Stanislaus!" pronouncing his name in English.

Francisca smiled and nodded without attempting to correct the pronunciation. She felt lucky to have gotten this far, so why spoil things.

"Wait here please," the woman told Francisca as she got up and walked to the rear and through the doorway.

Within three to four minutes she reappeared through the doorway and walked briskly toward Francisca. She smiled as she said, "You will be aloud to talk to your husband for ten minutes, then on your way out, be sure to stop here for information you are going to need. Walk through there," she pointed toward the door, "someone will be there to escort you in."

"Thank you very much," Francisca said trying to hold back the joy and glee she was feeling at this moment.

Francisca went through the doorway and was met by a guard who escorted her to a small room with three walls and a section of iron bars intertwined by thick screen wire. About four feet across from her side was another section of bars where she saw Chamaco holding the bars with both hands.

"*Viejo*," she said, "how do you feel?"

"Fine," he answered, "how are the kids?"

"*Muy bien*," she told him.

"We only have a few minutes to talk so it has to be fast. I'm leaving for El Paso as soon as I find out what day they are putting you on the train. I want to be there to meet you. I sent a telegram to your brother David so they can expect me and the kids. I talked to George, he said hello and good luck. He wished you the best." Francisca tried putting all of the important information into one exchange.

"This will be the only chance I get to talk to you until I see you in El Paso. I'm taking the kids out of school, and as soon as I know everything, we'll be on our way," she told him.

"I can't see you so good through the screen, I miss you," Chamaco said.

"You lost weight, you look skinny," Francisca said to him.

"Did George give you my message?" he asked

Instantly Francisca understood what he meant, the roll of bills that Albert had given her.

"Yes, I received it," she answered.

They continued to exchange information as fast as possible, but time elapsed quickly and soon Francisca was on her way back out the doorway.

"I love you!" she shouted as she was escorted from the visitor's cell.

Francisca stopped at the desk where the matronly receptionist still sat. She was handed an envelope containing all the information she needed. The disposition of the case, the date of departure and the arrest record containing a list of the offenses that Chamaco had committed over the years. At the bottom of the long sheet appeared in large print, Disposition: Subject to be Deported to Country of Origin as Undesirable Alien. Seal of the United States Department of Justice.

"Mrs. Delmonte," the receptionist told her, "if you plan to cross the border into Mexico, make sure you have a passport or you will have a hard time getting back across. You can apply for one in this building, right across the hall. If you are taking children with you, make certain that they also have passports. Good luck to you."

Francisca did not expect the kindness and consideration that this woman had extended her. She thought, perhaps it was luck or fate that she happened to be on duty this particular day. She preferred to believe that her prayers at her home altar had been answered. Yet, she thought, there are still some people in this world. that care.

Francisca left the office with mixed emotions. Her husband was still incarcerated, but at least he would eventually be released, and they would be together again, even if just for a short period of time. She had hopes but without hope.

Sitting in the taxi as it rolled toward home, Francisca went over the papers carefully. She found what she was looking for, it read; DEPORTATION GROUP U. A. - 12, Date of Departure: Wednesday, November 29, 1934, Time: 10:00 AM, Method: Passenger Train (Burlington)

* * *

All the guys were settled into their respective classes at school except for Ricky and Freddy. There stepfather, Alvino, had acquired permanent employment near Eaton and had taken Lucy and her four children to live there permanently.

Davy was attending Cole Junior High and had also graduated to a different level of friendships. He was beginning to spend less and less time with his brother Nick.

Nick, by now, had tasted Mrs. Davidson's wrath by absorbing the pain and humiliation of a slap to his left cheek. He had definitely learned to keep his mouth shut during class.

The changes to an upper class were interesting and challenging, yet, the comfort Nick had felt with Mrs. Crofton in the 4th and 5th grade classes was missing. The smiles and encouragement he once received in his former class had now been replaced by stern words and steely eyed glances.

He managed to adjust.

Nick and Emilio were still meeting after school to go roaming the streets looking for something interesting to do.

It seemed to Nick that everything of interest had to do with sex in one form or another. Like peeking through the keyhole at Goldie's apartment while she was entertaining a client, or watching from the roof of his former home down into the neighbor's bedroom while he and his wife were having sex. In which case it was more interesting after the sex because after each encounter there would be a knock down, drag out fight between the husband, a Japanese man, and the wife, a Black woman, and always ending outside in front of their house.

Then there was the Engineer at the Pump Station on 22nd, who lay naked on his back atop a long table while holding and fiddling his penis. A crack on the frosted glass window gave access to the neighborhood kids to the show of nudity, and the Engineer being fully aware of his audience.

Unknown to the children, they were receiving an education in areas such as sex and death, racial and ethnic and social stigma without the benefit of formality. Subjects forbidden by parents of this era, not easily avoided by children, with thriving curiosities, such as these.

Nick thought of Mary Moya. She had not reported to classes at Cole Junior High according to information passed on by his brother Davy. He had been to her home on several occasions looking for her without success. Nick asked questions of the kids on Mary's block and in the building on 22nd Street. Finally he put things together with help from the children in the area.

Several weeks earlier she had been taken by ambulance to the hospital, and had not been seen recently. Her mother had moved out of the building and had not returned. Upon further inquiry Nick learned that Mary had lost much blood from her female parts and had come very close to dying.

At hearing the news, Nick felt panic slowly building up inside of him.

What did it all mean?

How could he find out the whole story?

Who could he turn to?

Suddenly he had a flash of a thought Who better than Goldie. He ran most of the way home to 26th pausing now and then for short rests.

Arriving at the entrance of his house, Nick stopped and slowly pushed open the door. He was soaked in perspiration and breathing heavily. His mother and Nena and Albert were sitting at the kitchen table, but no Goldie. He went to the sink and served himself a glass of water. As he drank, he also tried to catch his breath. Suddenly he heard the toilet flush, the bathroom door opened to reveal Goldie. There she stood with her beautiful golden tresses and her beautiful blue eyes and her beautiful big busts and her beautiful everything else. Nick had to talk to her alone.

"Hi Nicky," Goldie half shouted as soon as she saw Nick, "you're all sweaty, what ya up to?"

"I was racing some guy," Nick lied.

Nick backed into the dining room while looking toward the kitchen table, making sure that no one was looking at him. He placed one hand next to his chest crooking his forefinger back and forth, motioning for Goldie to follow him.

Goldie nodded slightly and blinked her eyes in acknowledgment, then nonchalantly poured herself a cup of coffee averting the possibility of suspicion from the trio at the table.

Nick and Goldie walked through the dining room and into the living room, whispering.

"Do you know Mary Moya, Goldie?" he asked.

"Yea," she replied, "and I know her ma and everybody in her building."

"Well," Nick continued, "I found out that Mary got sick and she was taken to the hospital. She was bleeding from down there," pointing between his legs. "Do you think you can find out what happened?"

"Sure honey, don't worry," she told Nick, "I'll know everything by tonight."

There was an instance of relief as Nick sighed and said, "Thanks a lot Goldie."

Goldie, switching her coffee cup to her left hand, wrapped her right arm around Nick's head and pressed it against her bust while kissing him on the top of his head. "I'll see you tomorrow," she told him. With that she turned and went back to the kitchen.

In spite of his worries, Nick felt sexual arousal beginning to take hold as his cheek had touched Goldie's breast. He consciously suppressed the feeling.

Next day Nick arrived from school to find Davy waiting for him. As Nick walked in, Davy pounced on him and wrestled him to the couch with a headlock.

"We're going to Mexico!" Davy shouted.

Nick broke Davy's hold saying, "What's the matter with you, stupid, are ya nuts?"

"Ma just told me we're going to Mexico to live with Chamaco. She already got our transfers," Davy told Nick.

"Wow," Nick exclaimed, "for real?"

"Yea, for real," replied Davy.

Francisca came in and spoke to the boys in very serious tones. "Tomorrow you won't go to school," she told them, "we're going to '*el centro*' to take our pictures and get passports for Mexico."

Francisca had acquired school records to show proof of residence and citizenship for the boys. Davy had a birth certificate, Nick only a certificate of Baptism, but acceptable as a document for such a purpose. Francisca had an old tattered falsified birth certificate that had stood her well since she was a toddler. In all the years, never a question had been raised as to its authenticity. To this day she was an American in fact and in her heart.

Now Nick, more than ever, became concerned about Mary Moya's well being. Again he looked for Goldie.

Sure enough, Goldie walked in the front door. She had a somber look on her face. She went into the kitchen where Nick and Davy were busily having something to eat, and sat down next to Nick. It was difficult to see Goldie as a serious person, but the boys paid attention as she spoke.

"I've got all the lowdown on the whole mess about Mary," she paused for a second, first looking at one then the other. "She's at Good Shepherd, she was sent there by the Juvenile Court and if somebody from her family doesn't show up for her, she'll be stuck in there until she's eighteen years old."

It was common knowledge among the neighborhood kids what Good Shepherd Reform School for Girls and Golden Reform School for Boys meant, if anyone got caught up in the web of the Juvenile Courts. Just the mention of these institutions brought fear into every kid's heart. Davy, still ignorant of the tribulations Mary had been suffering, asked innocently, "How come, what did she do?"

"She didn't do nothin'," replied Goldie, "her ma did something."

Nick was about to ask the cause of Mary's bleeding as Goldie raised her hand in a motion for him to wait.

Goldie continued, "Her mother took her to see the woman over on Market Street, you know. *'la partera'*?"

Both boys nodded, for all the guys knew about *'la partera'*. She was a woman who in fact was a midwife, but performed abortions on young women who found themselves pregnant and in desperate straights.

"Well," Goldie said without too much detail, "after that she began to bleed and they couldn't stop the blood. Somebody called somebody and pretty soon the ambulance picked her up. He mother moved out the same day and nobody knows where she's at."

Davy looked puzzled at Goldie's explanation. He asked, "Did she have a baby?"

"No," replied Goldie, "there was no baby."

Goldie stood up cutting the conversation short. She was not inclined to go into detail about birth and sex, and she was in no mood to answer any more questions pertaining to the abortion. She walked out of the kitchen in great haste.

Nick and Davy needed no classes regarding sex. They both knew that it took a male and a female to conceive a child. Davy wondered who the male in Mary's case might be.

Nick remained quiet and pensive. He thought of three possibilities, of which one was himself.

Francisca and the Boys

The other two were Ray Lucero and Johnny Moreno, the guy that had raped Mary. He preferred to believe that the guilty party was Johnny Moreno. He kept everything to himself, not giving Davy the slightest hint that he might know something. Deep down Nick thought, was it possible that he, Nick, might be the....... He blanked out his mind purposely.

Nick was cognizant of the fact that Mary's internment at Good Shepherd was a direct result of her mother's lack of caring and perhaps other selfish reasons. Yet he felt a guilt that he couldn't remove from his conscience.

All necessary papers having been presented and registered at the Federal Building, Francisca and the boys were photographed and issued passports. Francisca read a line on her passport that said, Nationality: American. She smiled.

By Friday morning, November 3rd, Francisca and her two sons were on board a passenger train of the Burlington Railroad, heading for El Paso, Texas.

ELEVEN

The arrival and the border crossing by Francisca and the boys went without consequence. Francisca was granted a six months visitor's visa into Mexico with traveling privileges within the country. Finding living quarters was not a problem, for vacancies were in abundance near the west end of the city where two more Delmonte families lived.

Francisca and the boys spent two days sleeping on straw mats on a hard dirt floor while staying in the home of David and Maria Delmonte. Maria's family of four slept in the only existing bedroom and Francisca and her sons joined them, until she found a suitable place of her own.

The quality of homes in the area was not the best, but with extra effort, Francisca managed to find a vacancy just a block away from Maria's. She promptly rented the three room, single story adobe house.

A man recommended by Maria came in and built two bed frames of wood with crisscrossed rubber straps nailed to the edges in place of springs. With straw mats, plus heavy blankets over them to form a makeshift mattress, they were quite comfortable. Francisca's total bill was 20 pesos or 8 dollars American money. Her rent would come to another 20 pesos monthly.

Francisca thought she did very well in regard to all negotiations. Cooking facilities for the new home were located on the patio near the rear entrance to the kitchen. They consisted of a fire pit built of firebrick over a waist high stone structure. An iron grill, along with a large hot plate, completed the facility. A bamboo canopy hung overhead for protection from the sun.

Francisca and the Boys

A water well was a few feet away plus a hand pump, also for water distribution.

A large wooden table and two long stools were the total of kitchen furniture. Francisca furnished the house with only the bare necessities as she had no intentions of staying any longer than her self allotted six month period.

On Wednesday, December 1, 1934 at 2:00 PM, Chamaco was released from the immigration holding center in Juarez. He was thin and pale and still coughing slightly but was smiling and in good spirits as he hugged and kissed Francisca. His older brother David accompanied Francisca to the reunion. The brothers embraced and shook hands. The trio walked toward home, walking distance from the Rio Grand

Francisca's house was full of relatives when the three arrived. Maria and her two boys were there along with Chamaco's second brother Nicolas, who was between him and David in age, with his wife Alicia and their three children, two girls and a boy. The children ranged in ages from seven to ten years, all younger than Nick and Davy.

Relatives from the side of the wives were also there to greet Chamaco. Eventually it turned into a home coming celebration without intent. The women lighted the fire in Francisca's fire pit and soon food and drink began to appear in Francisca's house from all directions. The women got busy cooking while the men sat around the patio drinking tequila and cold beer. Francisca had no idea that anything like this was going to happen, but she was thankful that all of these people, relatives and non relatives, were so concerned about Chamaco.

Nick and Davy had greeted their father with their usual antics, treating their reunion like all the others that had occurred over the years. The boys had also finally met the two uncles for whom they were named.

The Delmonte families and the extended families ate and drank, celebrating toward dusk.

Before long Chamaco excused himself and snuck into the bedroom. Removing only his shoes, he fell on the bed and into a deep sleep. Francisca called her sister-in-law Maria to one side and asked her to take charge while she went to the drugstore for cough medicine. Maria agreed.

By the time Francisca returned about an hour later, the house was quiet and everything had been cleaned up and put in its proper place. Everyone was gone except her two sisters-in-law, Maria and Alicia, who were sitting in the patio waiting for Francisca to return. Francisca looked in on Chamaco then joined the other two women in the patio.

"Thank you for helping," Francisca said to the women, "I didn't know there would be such a celebration. I didn't expect it".

"All we need is an excuse to celebrate and we'll do it," Maria told Francisca.

"Yes, and we were all glad to see your family," Alicia cut in, "are you staying here for good.?"

"I don't know for sure," Francisca answered, "life here is just so hard, and not only that, but my boys have to go back to school in Denver."

"They can go to school here," Maria offered, "or across the border."

"It's just not the same," Francisca countered, "the schools are much better over there and my sons don't speak Spanish anyway. I think it would be too hard for them to learn here or in Texas."

The conversation switched to the husbands. Both women related to Francisca that their spouses were working for a commercial bakery near the plaza.

Alicia then told Francisca, "Nicolas has been building a baking oven behind the store at our house for about a year, but he never makes enough money to finish it."

Alicia's grocery store was a very small enterprise consisting of a short store counter and five or six shelves on a small wall containing canned goods. The biggest customers were children who came in to buy candy and cold soda. The building was located on a corner with the store facing east toward the plaza on one side, while on the other side was the entrance to the living quarters in the rear.

"Do you have any idea how much money it would take to finish the job?" Francisca asked.

"No I don't," Alicia answered.

Francisca let the conversation end without inquiring further. Here was the perfect solution to Chamaco's problems, thought Francisca. With a business to occupy his mind he might be able to make a decent living and leave the gambling behind. She was not forming illusions because she really believed that Chamaco would be willing to help his brothers as well as himself. She would speak to Chamaco first thing in the morning.

The women drank sodas left over in the ice tub as they conversed about their husbands and their children and their neighbors. The sisters-in-law asked questions about the United States, and in turn answered questions put to them by Francisca.

Dark was enveloping the streets and the women must be getting home, so they stood and excused themselves.

"We'll see you tomorrow, Francisca. We had a wonderful time," Maria told her.

"Yes, and thank you so much," added Alicia, "good bye."

"Thank you for coming and we'll get together again and talk some more," Francisca told them as they walked out, "good bye, until tomorrow."

The boys, being accustomed to their nine o'clock curfew, came in at about eight thirty. Francisca offered them something to eat before bedtime but they turned it down, since they had been stuffing their faces all day, and were quite full. They prepared for bed by removing their outer clothing and proceeding to wrestle in their underwear. They had been wearing underwear over the last few weeks, since their mother had reintroduced them to this horribly uncomfortable custom. The boys were warned by

Francisca that jumping on this bed could result in their return to the floor for sleeping because rubber straps were not as strong as metal springs. They stopped jumping and settled down for the night. The boys laid their heads in opposite directions on the bed, distributing their body weight more evenly, thus avoiding their sinking to the center.

Francisca doused all the lights and walked into the bedroom carrying a lamp. As she closed the drape on the entrance, Chamaco stirred and awakened. She gave him a dose of cough medicine which he welcomed. He had not slept with Francisca for two weeks or more, he welcomed her as well. She went to bed. Chamaco and Francisca made love with relish.

The next morning with everyone well rested, the entire family walked together to "El Mercado" where all the action usually occurred during the early morning hours.. They went sightseeing through the huge market place where everything conceivable could be found on sale.

Francisca purchased groceries for the day and a few pairs of socks for Chamaco. She had packed all of his clothes in a large suitcase on the move to Mexico, and just remembered he needed socks.

But the first and foremost purpose for coming to the market place so early in the morning was to stop for a breakfast of sweet bread and hot chocolate, a custom that was entertained by Mexicans of all ages, from coast to coast and from border to border.

During the breakfast in the outdoor food stand, Francisca took the opportunity to suggest to Chamaco that he and his brothers might form a partnership and open a bakery of their own, since all three were already experienced bakers. Chamaco was completely agreeable, for he too had similar ideas. He would speak with his brothers this very afternoon.

A baker's day started early and ended early, but a working day was usually a minimum of twelve hours. Therefore, by three o'clock in the afternoon of the same day, the Delmonte brothers, Chamaco, Nicolas and David were in Francisca's patio discussing the intricacies and the requirements necessary to open a bakery and run it as a profitable business.

An agreement was reached in less than an hour of conversation over tortilla chips, hot sauce and ice cold lemonade. The visiting brothers were here on a prearrangement that had been subtly initiated by Francisca the day before. She had suggested to the wives that it would be a good idea if the brothers got together. She also made a point of letting them know that financing could be available for completion of the oven. The message evidently got through.

As a gesture of courtesy, Francisca offered the brothers an invitation to stay for dinner, but the men, just as courteously declined the offer, knowing full well that their wives were at home already preparing their dinners. They left after agreeing to meet the next day at the home of Nicolas and Alicia. Tomorrow they would evaluate just what it would take in terms of money and labor to complete the construction of the half finished oven.

Nick and Davy came into the patio with two bundles of kindling wood each that had been purchased from a local peddler after successfully chasing him and his burro down a block away. They loaded the fire pit with wood and sprinkled kerosene over it, making it easier to ignite.

Francisca would light the fire when she was ready to start cooking.

"Go wash up," she told the boys. They complied without argument.

Not all homes in the area had access to water distribution of any type. Francisca felt lucky to have found a vacant house with both, a well and a hand pump. Some houses had water tanks built directly onto their roofs, receiving their water distributed by city water trucks. Some households with no immediate access to water relied on public wells found in various locations outside the populated areas.

While one boy held the wash pan near the pump spout, the other pumped. Placing the pan on a large flat stone they commenced to soap and rinse together, then splashing one another just to assure that their friendly rivalry was still intact.

Nick and Davy had been home since early afternoon. The streets had become deserted and all doors of homes along the street were closed to the outside world. It was siesta time. The brothers did not understand this particular custom but had no choice but to go along. They were beginning to accept this and other customs, and slowly conform to the ways of their extended family.

Francisca finished her cooking while Chamaco rested. She fed the boys and urged them to go out to visit their cousins who by this time should be home from school. After a reasonable length of time she ventured into the bedroom to wake Chamaco. He had not slept but rested well and was hungry enough to enjoy a good meal.

The couple sat down to dinner, each knowing that the conversation that was about to begin was unavoidable. Unknowingly, they both were thinking along the same lines regarding the immediate future of this family.

Nothing was said for the first few minutes as Francisca served and sat down to accompany her husband.

Chamaco dined quietly on "carne de puerco" in hot green pepper sauce, rice and beans on the side, and hot corn tortillas directly from the tortilla factory.

Francisca only had a little rice and beans as she had tid-bitted during the cooking process and was not particularly hungry.

The ever present *"molcajete"* containing extra hot sauce was on the table along with a clay pitcher filled with ice cold *"orchata"*, the rice drink that was so popular in all areas of Mexico.

Chamaco began the conversation by saying, "*Vieja*, tomorrow we start the final steps toward finishing the oven and we're going to need some money. How much can you spare?"

"How much do you think you'll need?" she asked.

Having already roughly calculated the cost of labor and materials, Chamaco told Francisca, "I think about two hundred American dollars should do it, and we might have some left over."

"Your going to need money for supplies and equipment for the bakery, so what if I give you five hundred," she said.

"That will be fine, but for now just give me two hundred. Any more than that and I'm liable to go out to the *jugada*," laughed Chamaco.

Francisca smiled and told him, "I don't think you'll be doing that for a long time."

She had faith in her husband when it came to handling money. She went to her cache in the bedroom and returned with the two hundred dollars.

The conversation shifted to the inevitable subject, their sons.

Chamaco had a serious look on his face as he spoke, "Have you thought about school for the boys?"

"Yes," she replied, "I've given it a lot of thought."

Chamaco paused for a moment not knowing exactly what to say or think. He found himself in a dilemma. He wanted his family at his side yet he understood that Mexico was not the place for the boys.

"Pancha, I know that you don't want to live here in Mexico, and I'm sure the kids don't want to attend a Mexican school, and I certainly don't want them going to school in El Paso," Chamaco told Francisca, "we have to take them back to Denver sooner or later. When that will be is your decision to make."

Francisca was elated at hearing Chamaco talking in that manner. She was so thrilled that she embraced him and held him very tight for a few moments.

"Thank you, *mi viejo*, she told him, "I'm so glad that you understand how I feel. For a while I thought we were going to have to fight about it."

"Fight?" Chamaco said, "there is no reason to fight. What must be done must be done"

Francisca kissed Chamaco as a tear rolled down her cheek wetting his face when he embraced and kissed her in return.

After a few minutes Francisca returned to normal and spoke, "The new semester for school begins in February. The boys will miss from now until then, but I know they can catch up on their studies. You know, they've done it before. We can leave after Christmas if it's alright with you."

"Of course," he answered.

Francisca got up and away from the table and began gathering the dishes to carry out to the patio for washing. Chamaco took her by the hand and said, "Leave the dishes, let's sit outside for a little while."

Francisca and Chamaco walked out to the patio and found a shady spot underneath the edge of the overhanging clay tiled roof. They sat on permanent stone benches built along the patio wall of the house. Holding hands and without speaking, they enjoyed the cool breeze blowing from above and finding its way along the wall to where they sat.

The afternoon shades seemed to slightly cool the atmosphere down from the ninety degrees plus heat that had prevailed since Francisca had arrived one month earlier. The sun was slowly moving down to the horizon on the western edge of the city.

Just over the top of the far patio wall, a mile or so in the distance, a long two storied building could be seen standing on the summit of a long hill near the river. The other side of the hill would drop steadily to the south bank of the Rio Grande. It was the barracks housing soldiers of *El Ejercito Nacional de Mexico,* the Mexican National Army.

Chamaco turned to Francisca and said to her as he pointed to the building, "There is one reason that Mexico is in such bad straights. You can't breath without a soldier sticking a bayonet in your ribs to see what you are up to. You can't go into a decent business without someone in government sticking out a hand for his share. Everything is government, government, and they have the army to back them up. Everything is going back to how it was before Villa and Zapata. Every thing changes but still stays the same."

Not having participated in any capacity on either side, Chamaco remained a revolutionary at heart. He still had a loathing for, what in his eyes was, a repressive government. He thought of Pancho Villa as the "Great Emancipator", for giving the peasants of the country, hope and reasons for living.

After a few minutes of silence Chamaco spoke again, "Francisca, I think that I will be able to join you in Denver in a year or maybe less. Then we can leave Denver and go east someplace where nobody knows me. I can get a job and get away from the gambling and all the rest of it."

Chamaco knew in his heart that it was a near impossibility to return and live any kind of life in the United States. The American immigration laws would eventually prevail and he would only be deported again or be sent to prison. Yet, he was trying to give his wife some kind of hope for the future.

Francisca went along for the moment, not wanting to spoil what she thought were mere illusions in Chamaco's mind. But she had that deep down feeling, that once she left Mexico, she would never see Chamaco again.

Tears swelled in Francisca's eyes as she put her right arm around Chamaco's waist and pulled herself closer to him. Chamaco stroked her hair and held her around the shoulders. They remained in that position until darkness fell.

In their skirmishes through the neighborhood, Nick and Davy had made new friends, and among them was a young man who was known as "Chino" because of his extensively curly hair. He was about the same age as the boys and about as tall as Davy but very thin. What made this boy unique was the fact that he had a singing voice that was exceptionally melodious.

Chino earned a very good income by singing in bars during afternoon and evening hours, charging half a peso per song. He had an extensive repertoire of songs that included the soft romantic "bolero" and the fast exciting "ranchera".

There would never be a pause in his melodic offerings, as long as there was an audience willing to pay. Most establishments would order him to leave after he captured the attention of the patrons, who would no longer feed the juke box as long as he continued to sing. On a few occasions Nick and Davy accompanied Chino on his trips into the world of the sex and alcohol culture, *La Zona Roja*, as the "Red Light District" of Juarez was called. It was located a few blocks east of the main bridge, as you crossed south over the Rio Grande into Juarez from El Paso.

One street at the center of "La Zona Roja" was the main hub of activity. For a distance of three to four blocks there were houses of prostitution on both sides of the street, where partially nude women stood or sat in their front doorways plying their trade. A bar named *La Consentida* occupied the south east corner on the block that was the commencing point into "La Zona Roja". Here Chino would spend an hour or two entertaining patrons of the bar, who also happened to be potential clients to the "working women" of the street.

All of this was new to Nick and Davy and they reveled in it. The boys knew about prostitutes and how they made their living, but they had never seen anything as organized as this.

To the boys, Goldie was their model. She worked singularly and without competition, and most of the time in secret. Oh, there were others who worked out of the dives in Denver that the boys knew about, but Goldie had her private clientele.

The women here at "La Zona Roja" were in abundance, and from the looks of things, with enough clientele to keep them continuously busy. It was evident that prostitution was legal in Juarez.

Chino offered Nick and Davy a chance to make some money for themselves, as long as they would be in his company. He placed his fully equipped she shine box on loan to the boys without charge. Now, while he belted out his tunes, the boys shined shoes and generated some income.

Francisca and the Boys

The newly found business endeavor did not last long. As all good things come to an end, the shoe shining establishment was abruptly shut down. The boys were alerted by their father that it was time to begin learning the bakery business. The oven had been completed and was ready to be fired up. The ten foot round oven was now enclosed by its dome-like roof with only the flue and the heavy oven door as openings. The fire pit rested just underneath the baking area, below the oven door, looking much like the boiler of a steam ship. There was enough room for eight, two by four foot, baking pans inside the oven when at full capacity.

Long paddle like poles were used for inserting and removing the full baking pans. Four of these were leaning against a wall near the oven door at the ready. All other necessary equipment had also been installed by Chamaco.

A long hard top table, with room for four bakers to mix, knead and cut, was placed in the center of the room. Wood barrels along a wall held flour and sugar, while yeast, lard and eggs were contained in a small ice cooler in a corner. Mixing bowls, all shapes of cutters, and baking pans were ready for the baking of the first batch of bread at the *Panaderia Hermanos Delmonte*.

Round wicker baskets three feet in diameter and six inches deep were waiting to be filled with a great variety of sweet breads. Once filled, they would be carried to the market place and emptied onto two long tables covered with clean white wrapping paper.

Before long Nick and Davy would become experts at balancing the bread filled baskets on their heads as they would carry them more than a mile to the market place.

The boys were given white cotton jackets and long white pants to be worn while serving behind the tables. They were also instructed by Chamaco, to keep their hands scrubbed and fingernails cleaned as long as they handled the product. Wooden tongs were used for serving. All rules regarding cleanliness were to be adhered to without question.

The Delmonte Brothers Bakery was finally in business.

Nick's and Davy's days were now starting at three AM, their waking hour. By four, the baskets were filled, by five the bread would be spread on the tables at the market. After a few days of this routine, the boys began to feel the pressure. It was more difficult to get out of bed each morning as time went by. The boys never uttered a complaint for, they thought, this beat going to school by a long shot.

Christmas came fast and the boys hardly noticed. Their birthdays also arrived and disappeared with out notice. There had never been a birthday celebration for either of them so the boys never missed them.

On Christmas Eve the boys attended *La Posada* in the city square of Ciudad Juarez. They were so tired that Nick nearly fell asleep while standing in the crowd watching the procession. They went home early and to bed and slept through Christmas morning.

Back to work after Christmas the boys performed their tasks with more precision and energy than usual.

Davy managed to get his hands into everything at the bakers table. Chamaco did not discourage him for he seemed to have the family knack to baking. In later years Davy would become a proficient baker himself.

On the other hand, Nick's interests were not in baking. He liked the sales part of the business and the handling of money. He was also fairly good at arithmetic, and while dealing with customers at the market, his Spanish began to improve.

Francisca had decided to remain in Mexico until the first of the new year, but kept everyone informed that her departure date was close at hand.

The boys did not leave Mexico without one final experience of note.

On a particularly hot morning on the way home from the market, Nick and Davy were walking down the street, empty bread baskets in hand. From the opposite direction three youths of about their own age walked toward them. As they passed, one of the three looked at Davy and remarked, *palos blancos,* words used to describe pimps who, in Mexico, usually dressed in white. Instantly Davy stopped and handed his basket to Nick.

"Hold this a minute," he said.

Nick took the basket and waited for the action to begin. He knew what was about to occur.

Davy walked up to the boy that had spoken and asked in English, "What cha say?"

The boy looked surprised then suddenly burst out laughing and saying, "Gringos!" as he pointed to Nick and Davy. Immediately Davy reared back and let go with a right fist that landed between the boy's upper lip and the tip of his nose. Blood splattered and teeth came loose as the boy covered his face with both hands and slumped away screaming in pain. Davy then stared at the other two as he motioned with both hands toward his chest and said, "Come on, you want some?"

The would be adversaries turned tail and ran.

On January 5, 1935, after tearful goodbyes and final embraces, Francisca left Chamaco standing on the Mexican side of the border as she and the boys crossed the bridge to El Paso. In a short time they would be on their way to Denver by rail.

TWELVE

The year 1935 arrived and departed without too much consequence. Times had improved since the election of President Franklin D. Roosevelt in 1932. New elections were imminent this year of 1936, and all signs pointed to the reelection of FDR.

Chon's bar had been temporarily closed after the gambling raid in which Chamaco was entangled. Not long after the closing, Chon's was remodeled, reopened and established as a legitimate business, sans the gambling.

Francisca's money became dangerously low. She found that working was her only alternative. She did not intend to return to the days of poverty that she had known in Texas With time, Francisca managed to rid herself of all fears and anxieties brought on by the incident outside of Chon's bar more than a year before. She had pride but she set it aside, for Chamaco was no longer around and she must earn a living for herself and her boys.

With the aid of George "The Greek", Francisca secured a job at the new establishment, ironically replacing the woman whom she had rendered helpless in their fateful altercation.

Francisca's brother, Albert, had now been working for WPA for a year. Workers Progress Administration was a program of jobs that Roosevelt had introduced the year before, and was helpful in bringing back self esteem to a great number of people in the country.

Francisca's older brother, Jesse, was into his second year of a five to ten year prison sentence at Canon City, Colorado State Prison. Jesse's wife, Nena, after a year or so, left the state in the company of a new man.

Francisca and the Boys

Goldie held strong to her selected vocation and was doing very well financially. She had tried quitting on several occasions but in the end would decide against it. She felt that the money was good for a minimum of effort. Her relationship with Albert had become a relationship of indifference and they were now living apart, seeing each other only on occasion.

The tree remained a meeting place for the guys but everyone had lost the verve for climbing.

Emilio had received a new bicycle for Christmas and now all the guys rode bikes during the summer.

Earl Ransom, the pharmacist's nephew, and the only Negro kid in the neighborhood, was now the soda jerk at his uncle's drug store and when not working in the store, he would be with the rest of the guys or at Francisca's house waiting for Davy. He spent so much time at her house that he eventually was considered a member of the family.

Nick and Davy were allowed to make up their lost lessons, with intensive home study for Davy, and after school study for Nick. Davy was promoted to eighth grade and Nick graduated to Cole Junior High School to begin seventh grade in the coming fall.

It was vacation time again and the boys were getting ideas about how to earn some money. They envied Earl because he had a job, and besides making money, he had all the ice cream and soda that he wanted whenever he wanted it.

Junking was no longer a priority, and stealing produce was unnecessary now that Francisca had a job and absolutely forbade the boys from bringing home pilfered goods.

One day, while the boys were having sodas at the Ransom drug store, Nick suggested, "Let's go look for a job!"

"Ah, nobody's gonna hire us, we're too young," Davy countered.

Earl walked over to the table and said, "I know some place you might get a job."

"Where?" the boys asked in unison.

"Well," continued Earl, "the chicken store on Champa kills chickens on Saturdays and they always need help."

"Kill chickens?" asked Nick, trying to picture in his mind what would a job entail that would also involve the killing of chickens.

"Yea," replied Earl, "they kill 'em and then they pull off the feathers so they can sell them in the store."

"Where do they kill 'em?" Davy asked.

"Out in back of the store," Earl answered feeling a little overwhelmed with the questioning.

"Why don't you guys just go over there and ask," he said.

"OK, let's do that Nicky," Davy said excitedly.

It was midweek sometime past noon as the boys finished their sodas and prepared to make the three block trip to the chicken store.

"We'll see ya after while, Earl," Nick said while exiting the drug store.

The boys mounted their bicycles and rode off toward Twentieth and Champa Streets. They arrived at the chicken store and dismounted. They walked up to the large store window and peered in, cupping their hands around their eyes as they did so.

"There's nobody in there," Davy said, "ya think their closed

"Let's find out," replied Nick as he stepped to the front door and pushed. There was a loud ringing of a bell attached to the top of the door that momentarily startled the pair.

A tall, thin and grey haired man came in from the rear of the store. "Hi kids," he said "what can I do for you?

The glass counter in the store was filled with a dozen or so of smooth, clean chicken carcasses resting on and partially covered with chipped ice. The clucking of live chickens could be heard coming from a room behind the store. The boys peeked over the counter in an attempt to establish the source of the incessant noise.

"Have you got something we can do around here?" Davy asked sheepishly but direct.

"You mean you want to work, a job maybe?" the man asked.

"Yea," Davy answered as both boys nodded their heads.

"Yes, I think I could use a couple of guys like you," the man said, adding, "if you're not too squeamish."

The boys looked at each other not quite sure of what to say or think but both were willing to take a chance.

"OK," Davy told the man.

"Alright," said the man, "come in back and I'll show you what to do, and if you think you can do it, you can come in Saturday morning."

The boys stepped around the counter and followed the owner to the rear of the store where, suddenly, the clucking became louder and to a point where you had to shout in order to be heard.

The stench of the chicken droppings was so strong that they coughed and automatically covered their mouths and noses with their hands. They continued through the rear room out to the back yard where they observed the paraphernalia used in the art of killing chickens spread under a wood canopy extending the width of the building.

Just outside the doorway, to the left, was a waist high metal table with inch high ridges on each side that was used for gutting the chickens. It was about three feet wide with an opening at one end for sliding chicken entrails into a large steel drum stationed just below the edge.

A chicken crate was on the cement walk, holding a half dozen live chickens. Next to the crate, a wooden table stretched a few feet to another steel drum, and finally a small sink with cold running water. A large, round and heavy iron pot filled with boiling water sat on a round gas burner to one side. Several sharp hook knives were on the table.

"Have you ever killed a chicken before?" the man asked the boys.

"Yea," answered Davy, "we chopped off the head with a axe."

"Well, I'll show you how to do it without chopping the head off," he told the boys.

The man proceeded by taking the chicken by the talons and holding it upside down. He picked up one of the knives and he swung the chicken under his left arm and held it tight to his body with the aid of his elbow. He then took his left hand and slightly twisted the chicken's head to one side exposing the neck to the plunging knife. He pushed the knife straight into it's neck just above the breastbone, gave the knife a slight twist then pulled enough to sever the jugular. He tossed the struggling chicken into the empty steel drum where it bounced around for about a minute then became still. He repeated the process and explained to the boys as he went along.

The boys looked on intently as the man killed four of the chickens, leaving two behind. He then dipped the dead chickens, one by one into the boiling water momentarily, then proceeded to pull out the feathers with ease.

"You want to try it now?" he asked the boys.

Nick and Davy looked at each other nervously but both agreed "To start, one of you can hold while the other cuts the throat."

"What cha wanna do?" Davy asked Nick.

"I'll, cut," he answered, wanting to get the more gruesome part out of the way first.

"OK, I'll hold the chicken."

With that said, Davy picked up the first chicken with both hands, fighting to keep the wings from flapping. He finally managed to hold it still but he couldn't hold it under his arm as the man had done. He placed the chicken on the table and held it down with his right forearm while holding the talons with his left hand.

"Can ya get it there, Nicky?" Davy asked.

"Yea," replied Nick, "just hold it tight so it don't get away."

Nick then took hold of the chicken's neck sliding his left hand to its head, pulling to reveal the spot where the knife was

Francisca and the Boys

to cut. He found the place above the breast bone and plunged the knife into the neck. He twisted the knife slightly, as the man had done, then pulled a little and the chicken abruptly stopped its squawking. Then the chicken began a convulsive struggle as Davy dropped it into the steel drum.

The boys reversed their positions as each took his turn at the others job. Each boy dipped a chicken in the boiling water and began the process of de-feathering and washing the chickens. The two felt proud of their accomplishments.

"Alright boys, you did good," the man told them, "come in Saturday morning around eight thirty. You'll get five cents for each chicken you kill and clean. I'll take care of the gutting."

The boys agreed to return on Saturday. They left the store and mounted their bikes for home.

On the way home, Nick began to figure how much money they could make if they killed so many chicken.

"Davy, we gotta kill at least twenty chickens Saturday so we can make a half a buck each," Nick said.

"We can do it," Davy answered with a tone of confidence, "watch and see."

The following Saturday the boys reported for work, and after the killing of eight or ten chickens, they would stop and de-feather them before going to the next batch. Eventually they each learned the complete process without the aid of the other and became expert chicken killers each in his own right. By developing their own system, the boys were able to meet whatever quotas were set by the owner in conjunction with sales in the store.

The boys were no longer on a weekly allowance. Now their spending money was earned, and it was gratifying to receive and spend money that one had worked for instead of depending on and waiting for the weekly dole that at times did not appear. The new job would last through the summer.

Francisca also developed her own style of "slinging hash" at Chon's Bar and Grill. In time she became a first rate waitress exuding confidence while on the job. Her income correlated with her personality, and it showed when counting the money received from tips. The tips, alone, were enough to maintain an exceptional income, notwithstanding the meager salary paid her by the establishment.

Another "on the side" income that Francisca enjoyed was a percentage payment from Goldie whenever a potential customer was referred to her by Francisca. The income, as a direct result of this arrangement, at times would surpass the earnings from the regular job.

Male customers began to notice Francisca, and on occasion she would be sexually propositioned, but always without success.

Again, the summer was nearing its end and before long school time would rear its ugly head. As much as the boys dreaded the thought, the attending of school was a foregone conclusion, an inevitability that could not and would not be ignored by Francisca.

Letters from Chamaco had dwindled from one per week to a short note every four to six weeks. His letters would always end professing his love for Francisca and great concern for his two sons.

One day in late August a letter written by Maria, her sister-in-law, arrived notifying Francisca that her husband was extremely ill with consumption and that he was being admitted to the State managed sanatorium just outside the city limits of Juarez.

Maria wrote; "You know what that means once you enter *El Sanatorio*."

Yes, Francisca knew very well what it meant, for it was common knowledge that a very small percentage of patients ever left the sanatorium alive.

Maria's letter continued; "The bakery is doing well but there is not enough income to continue treatment by private doctors for Chamaco."

Chamaco knew that he was dying, so as a last resort, he signed himself in at this public health institution on recommendations of his physician.

Francisca and the Boys

On reading Maria's letter, Francisca now realized why Chamaco's letters had become so infrequent. She had a decision to make. It would be one of the most important in her life.

Francisca closed the door of her bedroom and, while sitting on the edge of the bed, she buried her face in her hands and began to cry uncontrollably.

The next day Francisca wired three hundred dollars to Maria with this message: "Cannot go to Juarez. Use the money how you can. Write me."

From the telegraph office Francisca went directly to the Church of the Sacred Heart Of Jesus. She lit votive candles and knelt to pray. Two hours passed before she realized any time had expired.

On September 21st, 1936 at about 10:00 AM the inevitable telegram edged in black arrived by messenger at the Delmonte household in Denver. Tears rolled down her cheeks as Francisca signed for the message, trying her best not to break down while the messenger was still present. As she closed the door behind the messenger she began to sob while tearing open the envelope.

It was a short message: "Chamaco has expired.,"

Francisca then broke down completely. With no one present to turn to, she found herself alone.

Arriving home from school, the boys found Francisca at the kitchen table weeping softly. A towel was in her hands as she wiped away a river of tears that would not stop. Francisca stood up and took a boy under each of her arms as she announced, "Your father has died."

Nick was stunned as he heard the news and became immediately confused. He could not cry.

Davy burst into tears and went into the bedroom and lay on the bed face down on a pillow.

Nick put his arm around his mother's waist and held on for some time. He then walked out the door to take the bad news to Goldie. Goldie notified Albert and before long Francisca's house was filled with family and friends.

Francisca's daughter Lupe arrived with her three year old daughter, Sylvia, one of Francisca's greatest comforts whenever she was at a low point in her life, as at this very time.

Toward evening George the Greek and Jimmy "El Mocho" arrived to offer their condolences to Francisca. Other than his brothers-in-law, Jesse and Albert, of all the friends Chamaco had acquired over the years, George and Jimmy had become the closest and most trusted. Their appearance at Francisca's home on this particular day of mourning was not inconsequential, for both men had admired Chamaco a great deal.

After a few hours of conversation and general offerings of memories relating to associations with Chamaco, all visitors dispersed with the exception of Francisca's daughter Lupe and her granddaughter Sylvia. She had never felt so close to her daughter as she did on this day and the appearance of her granddaughter was a godsend.

"How are things going with you," Francisca asked Lupe

"Not good," replied Lupe, "I'm looking for somebody to watch Sylvia so I can go out and look for a job. I'm leaving my husband."

Francisca was not surprised since she had warned Lupe of the pitfalls of marriage at such a young age.

"You can come and stay here if you like," Francisca told her, "I think Mrs. Lucero will look after Sylvia if you want to try her out. She's a very nice lady, she likes kids."

"It sounds good except that I can't pay her right away, I don't have any money," Lupe said.

"Don't worry about that, I'll pay her until you get on your feet. Just go talk to her when you're ready and let me know," Francisca told her. She was already looking forward to having little Sylvia around the house.

"Thank you, Pancha," Lupe said to Francisca, having never learned to call her mother.

Before the end of the week Francisca had wired five hundred dollars more to Maria to cover funeral and burial expenses for Chamaco. She followed that up with a letter that read;

Francisca and the Boys

Dear Sister-in-law,

I want to thank you for everything that you have done to help me out at this time of crisis in my family. I don't know what I would have done without your help. I would not have been there on time to see Chamaco anyway so a trip would have been useless. I'm working now and if I would have gone, I might have lost my job. I loved my husband very much and I will hold his memory close to my heart until the day I die. The boys are back in school now. They took the bad news as well as could be expected for young boys like them. Thank you again for everything and I hope with all my heart that we might see each other again.

Your loving sister-in-law,

Francisca

Now Francisca went back to her thoughts for the future. What did it hold for her and her family? Her daughter was ready to return to the fold and she welcomed her with open arms. There would also be the addition of her granddaughter Sylvia whom she adored and wanted her near at all times. There was no crisis at this particular time so Francisca felt at ease.

Francisca had not been with a man since she left Chamaco in Juarez almost two years before. She often wondered if she could ever love another man after life with her husband. Her thoughts lingered on the possibilities. Should she actively seek companionship or should she let things happen at their own pace. Francisca smiled as she formulated Chamaco's voice in her mind.

'Go ahead, *vieja*, look around. Don't waist too much time on memories."

That was her husband's style. She continued to smile.

Francisca's daughter, Lupe, made the final break with her husband and came to live with Francisca and the boys.

Francisca's cache of savings had fluctuated during the last few months. There would be a high and a low, depending on necessities and other expenses. But in order to keep the savings intact, she must continue to work without letting up. Francisca needed a change in her life.

The country's economy began to show progress as a whole since the election of Franklin D. Roosevelt to the Presidency. He had initiated a great number of programs which were eventually identifiable by initials such as WPA, NRA, PWA, TVA, NYA, and CCC, just to name a few.

There was talk of war in Europe at Chon's Bar and Grill.

Steel mills in Chicago and Pittsburgh were hiring, and many of the local citizens were making the move to the Mid-West where jobs were plentiful.

Francisca made arrangements for her daughter, Lupe, to replace her at Chon's. She also made a promise to Lupe that she would send for her and her daughter Sylvia as soon as she became settled.

Francisca capitulated to the lure of the big city life and joined the exodus from Denver to Chicago.

THIRTEEN

The 1929 Ford coupe with rumble seat rolled along the highway just outside the city limits of Chicago. Nick and Davy were awakened by pelting raindrops that stung their faces as they slept in the open air. They quickly adjusted the canvas piece, making certain that it went over their heads and over the rumble seat backrest.

The boys could see lights in the distance and what seemed to be a ball of fire lighting up the sky in the horizon. They stared in awe.

Francisca leaned out the window on the passenger side pointing to the lights, and shouting to the boys in the rear in an effort to get their attention. Her voice trailed off into the wind making it difficult for the boys to hear what she was saying.

Pointing to his right ear and shaking his head, Davy shouted back, "I can't hear you!"

Francisca turned her head to the rear window, pointing to the lights in the horizon, then she mouthed the word, "Chicago."

The boys immediately tossed the canvas cover off and stood on the their feet to get a better look. Standing on the rumble seat they leaned forward against the roof of the car, laughing and shouting as they were hit by wind and rain.

As the car drew closer, the fire ball seemed to glow with more intensity.

The Ford continued in light traffic, winding its way to a part of the city called South Chicago. Stopping a few times to ask directions, the driver found his way to the 9000 block of South Buffalo Avenue.

It was 10:00 pm Sunday in mid April of 1937.

Antonio and his wife Helen were on their way to Indiana Harbor, Indiana, where Antonio had promise of a job at the Inland Steel Company.

As it were, the couple solicited passengers who were planning to travel east and willing to pay for gasoline in return for the ride. Francisca connected with the couple through mutual friends that resulted in the trip for her and the boys.

It was a long and arduous trip for everyone, but more so for the boys who rode the Ford's uncomfortable rumble seat. However, the lack of comfort did not faze the boys one bit, for they saw the trip more as a wonderful adventure than just a ride.

Since the decision to move to Chicago was made by Francisca, the boys were anxious to arrive in the big city to watch the gangsters shooting at each other in the streets. But alas, after all the propaganda they had absorbed from movies and newspapers, they found the streets of Chicago extremely quiet and calm, to their disappointment.

On South Buffalo Avenue Francisca walked up a flight of stairs to her friend Eulalia's second floor flat. The lights from inside could be seen through the slit between the floor and the door. A young woman, perhaps in her middle twenties, wearing a sleeping gown appeared at the door.

"Pancha, you finally made it!" shouted the young woman.

"Hello, Eulalia!" Francisca said as they embraced.

"How are you?" Eulalia asked, "Come in!"

"My friends are waiting in the car, they brought us here from Denver, they're on their way to Indiana."

"Oh my goodness!" Eulalia exclaimed, "Tell them to please come in, I'll make some coffee right away!"

Francisca returned to the car and invited the couple to come inside. She retrieved the boys who were running in and out of the alley alongside the building.

They all sat around the kitchen table having coffee while into a very short question and answer session.

During the conversation Antonio asked Eulalia, "Does your husband work in the steel mills?"

"Yes, he works at Inland Steel in Harbor," she answered.

"That's where we're going," Helen intervened, "Antonio has a job there as soon as we get settled, is it far from here?"

"It's only a few miles by car, less than an hour," Eulalia said, not knowing the distance in miles.

"Well, we have to be going," cut in Antonio, "we might as well get there as long as we are this close."

The couple stood up and thanked Eulalia for her hospitality. They shook hands all around as the couple stepped out the door.

All went out to help unload the car of Francisca's and the boys' belongings. Eulalia carried two candles and went down to the basement flat. On entering, she lit the candles illuminating the dreary three room flat. She opened a side door leading to the alley and walked to the street to show Francisca the way in.

"I talked to the landlord about this flat for you," Eulalia said to Francisca, "you and the kids can stay upstairs for the night. We have plenty of room, and anyway, Jesus will not be home, he works all night."

Francisca felt reluctant to accept her invitation, for she already felt like she was intruding.

"This is just fine, Eulalia," Francisca told her.

An old dilapidated couch leaned against the living room wall, and an old mattress lay rolled up on the bedroom floor.

"Look," she said, "we can use that mattress for at least one night, I have sheets and blankets."

Without further words, the women returned to the street for their final goodbyes to Antonio and Helen.

Francisca gave Antonio an extra five dollars in appreciation for allowing her to bring the boys' bicycles tied to the spare tire in the rear of the car.

"Which way do I go from here?" Antonio asked.

"Stay on this street going that way," Eulalia pointed in a southerly direction, "two blocks down is 92nd Street, you turn left on 92nd and go over the bridge. As soon as you cross the river, you will see signs. Take Highway 41 straight into Harbor."

"Thanks for everything!" Antonio told her.

Helen spoke to Francisca, "Pancha, I'll get in touch with you later. Once we settle down I'll look you up, goodbye!"

The car pulled away.

Francisca's knowledgeable attitude and her aggressive ways toward everything she attempted, seemed to draw other women's attention. Because of this, her friendship cup seemed to always remain full and overflowing.

The attributes that Francisca exuded had encroached her personality over time. She had inherited her stubborn ways and her willpower from her mother, Silvina, and from her husband she learned survival and how to recognize the motives of others in any and all relationships.

The boys finished the job of bringing in their belongings as the goodbyes were being said.

Francisca held a candle aloft as she surveyed the dingy, damp three room flat. With some cleaning and furnishings it could be made suitable for living.

"Pancha, you don't have to stay down here tonight," Eulalia said to Francisca. She was feeling some guilt about the poor accommodations facing Francisca and her boys, but knowing how stubborn Francisca could be, she did not insist.

"I'll help you clean up, but you know you're welcome to come up if you like," Eulalia said with finality.

"Oh, this is fine, one night won't hurt us," Francisca said.

With help from the boys, the mattress was dragged out to the back yard where the women pounded out the dust with a broom. They swept the living room floor and tossed down the mattress. Francisca covered the mattress with a sheet and two blankets.

Davy pounded the couch with his hands and raised a little dust. He felt around for protruding springs and found none. Deciding this would be his bed for the night, he removed his shoes, took a blanket and fell on the couch with his clothes on. Within minutes he was sound asleep.

Eulalia said goodnight and went upstairs.

Francisca and Nick shared the mattress on opposite ends.

"No kicking or I'll push you on the floor!" Francisca said to Nick with a smile.

Nick did not respond as he covered himself to the shoulders and immediately fell asleep.

Francisca whispered a short prayer then blew out the candle and soon, she too was sleeping soundly.

The sunlight broke through the kitchen windows the next morning warming the air in the flat, and ridding it of the dampness that prevailed from the night before.

Francisca and the boys awakened to face a new day, in a new home, in a new city.

By eight in the morning Eulalia was knocking on Francisca's door.

"Good morning!" Eulalia greeted when the door was opened.

"Good morning!" Francisca responded.

"I won't ask if you slept well, how could you, on the floor!" Eulalia remarked.

Eulalia was more inclined to speak English than Spanish, for she too was a product of a mixture of cultures, as were Francisca's two sons. Her background went back to Denver where she was born some twenty five year earlier. Although she preferred to speak English, she could still rattle off the Spanish when it became necessary.

"Oh, I've slept on harder floors than that," Francisca told Eulalia, "it wasn't so bad. We were all so tired we went right to sleep."

"Well, you got some rest anyway!" Eulalia commented.

"Except for one thing," Francisca complained, "there's bed bugs in that mattress, I woke up with tiny little bites all over me, I was really itching this morning."

Both women laughed, not considering bed bugs a great threat to Francisca's well being. Francisca would make a point of throwing out the mattress this very day.

"Come upstairs and have breakfast so we can talk and straighten things out for you." Eulalia was poised to help Francisca until she was completely settled.

"Wash up and come upstairs to eat," Francisca told the boys.

She and Eulalia went up the rear porch stairs.

Before long, they were all seated around Eulalia's kitchen table having fried eggs, fried potatoes, and refried beans. A typical Mexican breakfast with hot tortillas, and a very hot sauce of the green pepper variety.

Eulalia's husband, Jesus, came home from work, introduced himself then excused himself, for after working at the mill all night, he was ready for bed.

After breakfast the boys were given the task of taking out the mattress and sweeping and mopping the floors. The old couch was taken and dumped in the alley as well.

Meanwhile, Francisca and Eulalia took a walk down 91st Street to Commercial Avenue a few blocks west. They located a second hand furniture store that Eulalia frequented on occasion.

In a short time Francisca had purchased all of the immediate necessities to put the new home into operation. Included was a metal bed frame with spring and no mattress. The mattress, and couch with roll away bed would be bought new, thus eliminating further encounters with bed bugs.

With Eulalia's help Francisca was able to set up housekeeping once more. By now it had become second nature to Francisca in having to give up current living quarters in anticipation of something better. She was always willing to sacrifice in order to establish something new elsewhere, while still looking to the future and praying for the best.

However, establishing a permanent residence for herself and her children remained distant. The permanency that Francisca longed for was not in sight. Circumstances would continue to

Francisca and the Boys

interrupt whatever stability she was able to accomplish, but whatever the circumstances, Francisca's will of iron would not permit her to retreat.

The furniture was delivered the same afternoon and put in place by the boys, under the direction and watchful eye of their mother.

The utilities in the flat were now operational. Francisca made it feel and look as comfortable as she could, so that it could now be called home. To Francisca, this would do very nicely.

Two things remained predominant in Francisca's mind now, to find a job and to keep an eye out for a decent man.

The next day Francisca left home early, while the boys were still contemplating breakfast. After dressing, they settled for dry cereal and as long as their mother was not around, they made preparations for going out.

Nick and Davy, still curious about how and why the big fire erupted every night down the street, decided to investigate.

Riding north on Mackinaw Avenue aboard their bikes they felt the sting of tiny particles in the air hitting their faces. They soon learned that the particles were ash and soot escaping into the air from the blast furnace in full operation at the Carnegie Illinois Steel Mill.

As they neared the mill entrance they could see and hear activity in the distance. A high, thin, red and yellow flame would shoot up into the air momentarily, then seemed to extinguish itself, only to rise again a minute or so later. At each interval of rising there would be a huge roar emerging from the location of the flame.

Comparing the blast furnace to a Giant, roaring and spitting fire, the boys became fascinated with the noise and the fire from the mill.

Arriving at the mill entrance, the boys dismounted and moved in closer to get a better look. They leaned against the high wire fence holding on to the crisscrossing wire links and looking through diamond shaped spaces into the plant as far as they could see.

"Boy," Davy remarked, "it sure would be nice to work here."

"Yeah," agreed Nick, "I bet they pay big bucks, too."

Each boy with the same dream of leaving school forever, and going to work for a living. That was not to be.

The boys rode west on 89th Street and came upon the local school in the next block. Arriving at the corner they caught sight of Francisca leaving the entrance of the J. N. Thorpe Elementary School with papers in her hands.

Nick stopped suddenly and whispered excitedly to Davy, "There's ma!"

"Yeah, I see her you idiot, get back!" Davy responded, motioning for Nick to pull back his bike.

The boys waited for their mother to turn the far corner before emerging from around the corner of the building that blocked their view. They continued their ride past the school building, peeking into the large windows, where inside, students were busily engaged in their studies.

The streets in the neighborhood were empty and desolate. No sounds were evident in the immediate vicinity other than the muffled voices coming from inside the classrooms. The screeching sound of a trolley car could be heard at a distance, getting louder as the trolley traveled north on Buffalo Avenue.

The quiet atmosphere and empty streets gave the boys a sense of freedom that they could enjoy while it was still possible.

The boys continued south on Burley to 91st Street, crossing the empty lot on the corner. They went past "Garza's Groceries" and came to a halt in front of St. Jude Catholic Church. A reverent and uneasy feeling came over the boys as they each made the sign of the cross, a custom learned, and urged not to forget by threat of punishment from Francisca.

"We better go home or ma's gonna kick our ass!" Davy told Nick.

"Yea, I know, let's get goin'," replied Nick.

Francisca and the Boys

The boys knew the wrath Francisca could muster when antagonized, and they wanted no part of that. They turned toward home without further hesitation.

"I'll race you home!" Nick shouted to Davy while jumping to a head start.

Davy taking the bait, replied, "Shit, I'll beat your fuckin' ass!"

And took off after Nick who was already past the grocery store and about to cross the empty lot.

Nick, with an inferior vehicle, and smaller than his brother, knew he had no chance to win. He challenged Davy anyway, if only to irritate him. By the time that Nick had cut through the alley, with only a few feet from home, Davy went past him like a flash skidding to a stop at the side door of the house.

He taunted Nick, "I told you I'd beat your ass, stupid!"

Nick pulled up laughing loudly and responding to Davy he said,

"Shut up flat face, you were lucky!"

Davy's facial features were round with a slightly wide nose and a sallow skin tone, giving him the appearance of a seasoned pugilist. These features stood him well whenever he and Nick were involved in fist fights with other kids. Inevitably he would be accused of being a prizefighter and he would use this to a psychological advantage.

Nick would call Davy "flat face" whenever they argued, or just to irritate him.

Nick, by contrast, had a sharp nose and a fairer complexion and could easily be mistaken for a "gringo" providing he avoided the sun.

The boys parked their bikes against the building wall and went into the house. They looked through all the rooms in search of Francisca but she was nowhere to be found.

"Ma ain't home yet," Nick said.

"Yeah she is, ya dummy," Davy responded, "can't you see her stuff on the table?"

Francisca's purse and a small bag of groceries were on the kitchen table.

"She's gotta be upstairs by Eulalia, I'll go up and tell her we're home," Davy said.

Davy walked out the rear door and up the porch steps to Eulalia's flat. He could hear voices coming from the kitchen where Francisca and Eulalia sat at the table in deep and apparently serious conversation.

Eulalia was still in her sleeping gown sipping coffee, as Davy could see when he peeked through the screen door and knocked. Eulalia stood up to answer the door and, as she did, her pink satin gown opened at the lower half of her body, revealing her legs and much more.

Davy stared openmouthed as she came toward him. He took notice of her breasts as they bounced against the soft satin material of her gown. Davy stared unabashedly at her cleavage while Eulalia made no effort to cover herself.

Unlocking the screen door Eulalia said, "Come in Davy."

"No, that's ok," he said, "I just wanna tell my ma we're home."

Davy did not take his eyes off of Eulalia's chest. Her gown swung open once more, he took in her complete body staring straight at her. She was small and thin, an inch or so shorter than Davy, curvaceous and extremely attractive.

Eulalia turned toward Francisca and said, "It's your son David, the boys are home!"

"Ok," Francisca answered, "I'll be down in a little while."

"Ok, ma!" Davy called back.

Now Davy was staring point blank into Eulalia's eyes, then down to her breasts, and back to her eyes. Neither of them flinched. She gave him a half smile and a slant eyed look as she turned back toward the kitchen. In turning, her gown swung open one more time. Davy turned to leave but not before noting that Eulalia was wearing nothing underneath the gown.

Davy had felt an invitation in Eulalia's look. For the moment he stored the thought, but he became sexually aroused, to say the least. His hands automatically went to his pockets.

Davy was about halfway through his fifteenth year of life and, by now, his interest in the opposite sex had grown immensely as he approached maturity.

Nick was not in the house when Davy returned. He looked out the window and spotted Nick crossing the empty lot. Davy knew what Nick was up to, he decided to join him.

By the time Davy arrived Nick had already lit up his cigarette and was practicing to blow smoke circles. He picked the darkest corner under the sidewalk so the smoke could not be detected from a distance.

The boys no longer picked butts from the street like they did in Denver, now they would buy cigarettes by the pack, or Prince Albert tobacco by the can and cigarette paper to roll their own.

"Wanna a butt?" Nick asked Davy.

"Yeah," Davy answered.

The boys sat on the ground with their backs against the stone wall. They smoked quietly until their butts burned to their fingers. The air was damp and musty, but cool and comfortable as far as the boys were concerned.

"This is a good spot for a clubhouse," Nick suggested.

"Yeah," Davy said, "It's a good place to hide."

Davy sat quietly thinking for a few moments. He pushed down on his penis with his hands in his pockets and said, "I got a fuckin' hard-on!"

Nick laughed loudly at hearing Davy's comment.

"Not so loud, stupid, they can hear us!" Davy reprimanded.

"I went upstairs to look for ma and.....," Davy started to say but was interrupted by Nick.

"Was she there?" Nick asked.

"Will you shut up and let me talk!" Davy told Nick in frustration.

"Ok, go ahead and talk," Nick said, giggling at seeing his brother become irritated.

"Well, when Eulalia opened the door," continued Davy, "she was wearing a silk gown and I could see right through it, she didn't have nothing under!"

"Wow!" exclaimed Nick, taking hold of his penis from the outside of his pants.

Davy continued, "I saw the nipples on her tits, and when she was walking, her gown opened up and I saw the hairs on her pussy. I had to get outta there fast, my dick got hard and it started to show through my pants."

Nick covered his mouth with both hands trying to hold back a laugh. He did not succeed, he laughed until tears came to his eyes.

"Then what happened?" Nick asked, still trying to control his laughter.

"Nothin'," Davy said, "but the way she looked at me, I think she likes me!"

Now both boys were trying to control their erections, but the more they tried, the more exited they became. Nick went to a distant corner, and while he pictured Mary naked in the clubhouse in Denver, he masturbated with his eyes closed.

Davy was doing his own thing against the wall a few steps away.

After a time the boys returned to their original location under the sidewalk, sitting with their backs against the wall and legs popped up. They lit up one more time and continued their conversation.

Nick asked Davy, "Are you gonna screw Eulalia?"

"Fuckin' ay," replied Davy, "first chance I get!"

Suddenly Francisca's voice could be heard in the distance, "David, Nicolas!"

The boys could see her head sticking out the door as she yelled. As soon as she pulled her head back inside, they scampered from their newly found hideaway out into the sunlight. Knowing

Francisca's temper, the boys ran home so as not to keep her waiting.

"We're coming, ma!" Davy shouted.

"Don't breath in ma's face, Nicky!" Davy said.

"Yeah, I know!" responded Nick.

The boys walked in the side door directly into the kitchen to find cold meat and cheese sandwiches, along with four hard boiled eggs in a bowl in the center of the table.

"Wash up before you get near the table," admonished Francisca.

For Nick and Davy it was perfect timing, now they needed no excuse to enter the bathroom. While washing up, they also gargled to get rid of the tobacco odor. This done, the boys sat down to eat while Francisca sat in the living room counting money.

Francisca had replaced her wooden chest with a small metal cash box to hold the savings she had accumulated up to the final days with her husband Chamaco. These savings had diminished considerably within the last year, now she was feeling the pressure and anxiety that came with being a mother without a husband.

She closed the cash box and went into the kitchen.

"Tomorrow we're going shopping for your school clothes. You start school Monday morning at nine o'clock," Francisca announced.

At the mention of school the boys groaned simultaneously.

"You know where the school is don't you, right where you saw me this morning when you were on the bikes," Francisca told them with a controlled half smile.

Nick and Davy, looking at each other, grunted and giggled. Their mother was still that one step ahead of them.

"Ma, can we go out now, we only got today and tomorrow?" Davy asked his mother, as if they had just been sentenced to time in jail.

"You can go out, but be back in time to eat by six," she told the boys.

Now she must really get down to business and find a job, Francisca thought. She was not quite sure what her next step would be.

She had learned the art of waiting on tables with good precision, and not having any other skills, she would pursue this particular type of work as far as it would take her.

For now, Francisca would have a little talk with Eulalia who was familiar with South Chicago and this neighborhood in particular. Perhaps she might be able to supply some ideas as to where to look for a job.

"Pancha," Eulalia said, using that nickname again, "let's make the rounds tonight after Jesus leaves for work. We can have a few drinks and talk to the owners of some of these "joints", you can make good money working in a tavern!"

Francisca knew that much already, but now she must use diplomacy in explaining to Eulalia the apprehension she was feeling. After all, Eulalia was a married woman and Francisca did not want to be the cause of any marital problems that were sure to develop.

"Ok," Francisca said, "but what about your husband?"

"Don't worry about him, he doesn't have to know," Eulalia responded.

"Oh, Eulalia, aren't you afraid to get caught?" Francisca asked, a little surprised.

"Hell no!" she replied, "What the hell can he do, beat me up, I'll throw his ass in jail!"

Francisca smiled at Eulalia's rash, and somewhat tough behavior. She now saw a side of her friend that she had never seen before.

Francisca did not want to be judgmental and would not question other peoples values. In fact, she admired Eulalia's attitude and her boldness in making this decision. Besides, she thought, it would be a break and a change from all that had happened since Chamaco had passed away. The decision was made, they would go out tonight.

Francisca and the Boys

Friday was a busy night for most drinking establishments, and workers from the steel mills would be out in force. It was a time when most working stiffs looked for entertainment and relaxation after a full week of hard work. Whether a bar or a lounge or a tavern, call it what you may, It was a place to consume alcoholic beverage in an attempt at escaping the realities of life.

Green Bay Avenue at 91st Street would be the first stop for Francisca and Eulalia. At about mid block on the east side of the street stood the "Green Bay Lounge." The women walked in to the sound of polka music blaring from the jukebox, and a bar full of men, sitting and drinking various mixtures, and well past their cups.

A woman in a white apron cleaned and wiped tables in a poorly lit section of the lounge. Francisca's hopes of securing a job here as a waitress were dashed, as anyone could see, this place was not in need of one.

The two women sat at a table and ordered drinks, a rum-and-coke for Eulalia and a straight coke for Francisca. They would sit and discuss the situation.

"This is the first time that I've been here," Eulalia said, "it sure is dead. I don't think you would want to work here, Pancha, you wouldn't make any money!"

Francisca's thoughts were running along the same lines.

She remarked, "Boy, you're not kidding!"

The waitress appeared with two more drinks as the women were preparing to leave. A customer at the bar had sent drinks to the ladies, so they courteously accepted and remained seated.

Eulalia, who was not accustomed to complete independence and was testing the night life for the first time ever, asked Francisca, "Now what do we do, Pancha?"

"Just sit and relax and drink slow," Francisca responded.

Eulalia sat nervously tapping her glass with her fingers, for in spite of the facade she presented, she still worried that somehow her husband would know that she had betrayed his trust.

Francisca's experience from the days at Chon's in Denver was about to be tested.

A burly steel worker sitting at the bar looked in their direction and raised his glass in a toast. Francisca raised her glass in return and Eulalia followed suit Both women touched their drinks to their lips and smiled.

"He'll be coming to our table pretty soon, just watch," Francisca said.

Sure enough, the man left his stool at the bar to join the ladies, and in so doing, he almost fell over. He wobbled toward them with an empty shot glass in one hand and a full bottle of beer in the other. The man was quite drunk.

"Francisca, here he comes!" In her excitement Eulalia uttered Francisca's true name instead of her customary "Pancha."

"Try to be calm and act natural," Francisca said.

As the man arrived at the table he spoke to the women in a foreign language.

Eulalia again looked at Francisca for some kind of help.

"No speak Polish," Francisca told the man.

The man pulled out a chair and sat down directly in front of both women.. He raised his arm in a motion to the waitress and circled his forefinger around the top of the table. As he leaned forward toward the women he asked, "You got husband?"

Immediately Eulalia responded with an up and down motion of her head. Francisca only smiled.

The waitress returned with another round of drinks and placed them on the table. The table was now cluttered with full glasses. The man pulled a billfold from his left inner coat pocket and paid with a ten dollar bill. His change was placed next to him on the table.

Francisca took two of her full glasses and moved them across the table, placing them next to the man on his left. She turned to Eulalia and said in Spanish, "Don't move from here, I'll be right back."

Francisca and the Boys

Taking a dime from the man's change Francisca went to the jukebox and played three polkas in succession.

On her return, Francisca sat to the man's left side with the bar now situated behind herself and the man. Eulalia faced Francisca and the steel worker with an eye on the bar and in a very nervous condition. She was not sure of what to expect next.

After another shot of whiskey and his beer chaser, the man could hardly keep his eyes opened.

Eulalia, still unaware of what Francisca was up to, asked why she had changed her seat.

Again Francisca spoke in Spanish, "Keep looking toward the bar and act like you're talking to our friend here, and sort of lean over like he knows what's going on, and hold on to your purse so we can leave when I tell you."

Eulalia, without a clue to the reason for all the preparation, did what she was told.

Now Francisca leaned toward the man and spoke to him as if he were able to understand what she was saying.. With her right hand on his shoulder she leaned in a little closer, and with her left hand deftly removed the wallet from his inside coat pocket, removing its contents in one motion and replacing it immediately.

Francisca threw back her head and laughed while giving the man a friendly shove. The man opened his eyes momentarily, rolling them and smiling broadly, he then closed his eyes one more time.

Eulalia was dumbfounded at what she had just witnessed. She sat speechless, waiting for further instructions from Francisca.

Still speaking Spanish Francisca said to Eulalia, "Get up slow and walk out in front of me, be sure to smile."

The women stood up and walked toward the door with Eulalia in the lead. Francisca waved goodbye to the bartender while remarks and whistles followed them out the door.

The pair crossed the street and made their way to the next block where the neon signs of *El Jalisco* came in to view on the corner.

Eulalia was now in a state of jittery nerves as she remarked, "Pancha, you scared the hell out of me!"

Francisca looked at her smiling and said, "That guy probably has a wife waiting for him at home and he's at a bar spending his pay. He deserves what he got. To me he's just another sucker.

Eulalia, looking down and shaking her head from side to side could only say, "Pancha, Pancha!"

Walking slowly down the street Francisca counted out sixty five dollars resulting from the short encounter. She offered thirty dollars to Eulalia.

"Oh no, Pancha, I don't want any money, what would I tell Jesus if he found it on me?" said Eulalia.

Beside the fear of being discovered Eulalia still had that feeling of having done something wrong, and by refusing to share, she would be free of any guilt associated with this encounter.

Francisca, still smiling, understood her situation perfectly and did not press any further.

As the women walked along, Francisca thought of Chamaco. She thought of the things that she had learned from him, and him alone, over the years.

"Never feel sorry for a fool!" he would say, and Francisca recalled his words as if he were saying them at that very moment.

She was taught to realize that everything involving money was a business in one form or another. That there was more to the liquor business in particular, than just selling and consuming.

To the consumer of alcohol a bar was a place for relaxation and enjoyment, while subconsciously looking for something new and different in his life.

To the proprietor, the consumer was nothing more than an emotional weakling, ready for exploitation. 'Get him drunk, take his money, and send him on his way', was the unspoken motto. The *sayo*, the sucker, the mark, whatever name it happens to be known by, is eventually recognized in the person who becomes a habitual consumer of alcohol.

Francisca and the Boys

Francisca learned these little inconsistencies of life as taught her by her husband, Chamaco. Yet, she found the ills of alcoholism and drug addiction in Chamaco himself.

Was there no end to the contradictions? No, of course not, this was life!

Chamaco's weaknesses had contributed to his demise, along with anxieties and pressures brought on by his endeavors to overcome poverty. He had become the *sayo*, or the sucker to the retailers of alcohol as well as the drug dealers of his time, reversing the phenomena of the 'easy marks' that he, himself, had looked for in the culture of the habitual gambler. It was a vicious circle that was difficult to recognize.

Francisca Delmonte thought she might have an idea to what it was all about. She had now entered that vicious circle on her own.

The women arrived at the entrance to *El* Jalisco. It was late in the evening and live music could be heard through the open door. This was one of the few bars in the neighborhood that offered music for dancing played by live musicians.

The dance floor was filled with couples dancing to the rhythm of soft bolero music being supplied by a quartet consisting of a violinist, a guitarist, a base fiddler and a vocalist swinging a pair of maracas back and forth as he sang.

All the tables were occupied and the bar was filled to capacity.

Two bartenders on duty worked feverishly to keep up with the demands of the patrons. The one working the bar at the open end worked double duty since he was also serving tables.

Francisca squeezed into a slightly opened space at the bar in an attempt to order drinks. A bar patron made room and offered his stool to Francisca. She declined the offer since she needed a place for two.

The bartender, noticing the ladies' dilemma, signaled for them to meet him at the other end of the bar.

"Wait here and I'll fix you up in no time," he told them.

He disappeared into the rear of the establishment momentarily and soon returned with a small table that he placed near the bandstand along with two chairs. The ladies could not have asked for better seats.

No sooner were the women seated when Eulalia was asked for a dance and drinks were offered by someone seated at the bar.

A rum and coke and a straight cola were served and Eulalia was dancing even before tasting her drink.

The bartender who seated them told Francisca, "These drinks are on the gentleman at the bar," he nodded in that direction. A man raised his glass in a toast as did she.

"Would you care for something a little stronger?" the bartender asked Francisca, with a knowing smile on his face.

"Well, ok," she replied, "but bring me a shot of Southern Comfort straight, I'll chase it with coke."

As the bartender returned to the bar Francisca poured half of her coke into an empty glass. The bartender returned with her drink, spilling some of the liquid on the tray.

"If you use a double shot glass you won't spill any," she remarked to the bartender playfully.

"Oh, you know the business!" he exclaimed.

"A little bit," she replied.

"Have you ever waited on tables?"

"Yeah, that was my job where I come from," retorted Francisca

"We could use a waitress, if you're interested," the bartender told her.

"I'm interested, I'm looking for a job," replied Francisca.

"Well, if you can come in tomorrow and talk to the boss, he's here by twelve noon. I'll let him know you're coming in. My name is Frank, what's yours?" he asked as he gave her his hand to shake.

"Francisca," she answered.

"Oh, we're *tocayos*," he said, using the Spanish word for namesake, "I'm glad to meet you!"

"See you!" Francisca remarked as Frank walked away.

The music stopped playing and Eulalia returned to the table. She was waving a hand in front of her face in an effort to cool off.

"Pancha," Eulalia said, "I'm all tired out from that last rumba, I need a drink!"

"You have two of them right here, but you better take it easy, I don't want to drag you home drunk, you'll get in trouble then," Francisca warned jokingly.

"I don't want to drink anymore anyway. If Jesus smells liquor on me I'll have a lot of explaining to do, so I'll just have one," she said.

Eulalia took a glass of rum and coke and drained it in a series of gulps. She then took a deep breath and released a sigh of relief. She noticed the shot of whiskey on the table and said, "Look at you, Pancha, are you drinking straight whisky now?"

"No," Francisca replied, "watch what I do."

Francisca picked up the drink and looked toward the bar at the customer who paid for it. She raised the glass in a toast as the man nodded approvingly. She put the whisky in her mouth then raised the chaser to her lips, letting the whisky run from her mouth into the half filled glass of coke, while keeping the glass covered with her hand.

"Ai, Pancha, you're something else!" exclaimed Eulalia. They giggled and laughed.

After a few more drinks the two decided it was time to go. Their table was littered with full and near full glasses. Very little of the liquor having been consumed.

"Let's get out of here," Francisca told Eulalia, "I start work tomorrow, I think I've been hired."

On their way home, Eulalia, being curious about how Francisca handled her drinking asked, "Why did you take those shots if you didn't want to drink?"

"Well, Eulalia," Francisca told her, "in this business you never want to refuse a drink because you don't want to offend the customer, so you just let the customer believe you are drinking, but you have to be very careful that you don't get caught.

"And that way you don't get drunk either, huh, Pancha?"

"Yes, that's the way it is when you work in a bar, you wouldn't last two hours if you drank everything they offered you."

It was well after 1:00 AM when the women arrived at their flats. By Eulalia's calculation she would have enough time to sleep a few hours and still wake up and tend to her husbands needs. He would be home no sooner than 10:00AM. His arrival was like clockwork.

Before going to bed, Eulalia washed her face with soap and water, then applied cold-cream to her neck and shoulders, wiping and removing all traces of makeup and perfume odors that might be lingering She brushed her teeth, and rinsed and gargled with Listerine Antiseptic Mouthwash, then hung her dress in the farthest corner of her closet and went to bed.

Francisca checked on the boys. Satisfied that they were safe and comfortable, she tiptoed into her bedroom..

The candles on her altar were burning low and flickering. She took two votive candles from her supply, lit them and placed them on the plate at the altar. She knelt and prayed for a few moments, made the sign of the cross and went to bed.

FOURTEEN

Indoctrinated into their latest institution of learning, the boys settled down to the routine of daily class attendance at the J. N. Thorpe Elementary School.

While Davy had not had too much time to catch up with the required curriculum, he still managed to complete all studies in preparation for his approaching graduation in June. If all went well, Nick would also be a member of a graduating class but not until the following year of 1938.

The classes at Thorpe were of an ethnic mixture corresponding to the people living in the surrounding area, and as much as the teachers tried to promote ethnic tolerance among the students, the school environment was the only place it was ever practiced, simply because it was quietly enforced. Once school was dismissed, ethnicity would take hold and each kid would return to his or her own ethnic enclave.

In time, Nick and Davy made friends in and out of school.

Francisca's new job at El Jalisco kept her busy Fridays through Sundays into the early hours of the morning. On occasion she was asked to work extra hours during the week, which she would accept enthusiastically, as the extra income came in very handy. However, because of her late working hours, Francisca was losing time normally set aside for her sons. She felt the boys were old enough to take care of themselves, but she was losing the "hands on" control that she usually exercised.

Two distinct and separate avenues of learning were becoming evident in the course the boys were about to follow. There was school with its academic environment that the boys constantly complained about, and there was the streets of Chicago, where a different type of education was offered at any time of the day or night, and which the boys would heartily embrace.

The southeast corner at 91st and Brandon, opposite the church, was in perpetual occupation by the juvenile delinquents of the neighborhood. The wood railing surrounding the wood frame building offered a perfect seating arrangement with a view in every direction, and a good position for ogling the female church goers on Sunday mornings.

Here is where Nick spent much of his time in company of his fellow delinquents.

The front door to the building was permanently nailed shut, making it much more convenient for the guys to occupy the area and practically take up residence without protest from the local populace.

At this corner of notoriety Nick became acquainted with guys having such ominous names as, "The Shadow", "The Claw", "E.P.", "Freckles", "Pecker Head" and "Lonny", each name having its own personal background. There were others with ordinary names such as Oscar, Mike, Johnny, Joe and another Nick.

Set apart from this group was a young man known as "Caldo". Now, Caldo was called Caldo because of his love of home made soup. As you might have guessed, Caldo is Spanish for soup.

Caldo was dark of complexion and extremely muscular, with jet black hair that hung loosely over his ears, ending at the back of his head like a thick rug seemingly pasted to the skull. His eyes were squinty with bushy eyebrows, his nose was hooked and his thick lips were in a constant smile. The smile hung to one side of his face, as if he knew something no other kid knew. He was a "loner" who knew everyone and was known by all, yet he kept to himself unless he thought someone was worthy of his friendship. He avoided any type of altercation, for his activities required neither fighting nor arguing.

Francisca and the Boys

Nick looked at Caldo as an imaginary Indian Chief who hardly spoke unless spoken to. Caldo looked at Nick as a student who needed to learn the street life of South Chicago, and he, Caldo, was willing to take up the task of teaching him the finer points of his "trade".

As fate would have it, the two boys took to each other and became fast friends.

There was a third party completing a triumvirate of delinquents that would become a trio to be reckoned with. His given name was Dominic but few of his friends knew it. On the corner he was referred to as Nick, a name resulting from his pet family name of "Nico".

The coincidence of two friends having the same name was not unusual, but at times confusion would result when referring to either or both Nicks.

The two Nicks were equal in size, skinny and agile, and devotees to the art of self-defense and always willing to mix it up in a street fight. There was an abundance of aggression stored in the minds and bodies of both of these boys, and they would constantly release their tension by "slap boxing" with each other in the street. After each session of "slap boxing" there would be an agreeable ending without a winner or loser.

Caldo would watch these antics with amusement, smiling his crooked smile, shaking his head, and wondering what was wrong with these guys.

The two Nicks, always ready to prove how "tough" they were, would usually be the ones to pick the street fights with opposing neighborhood toughs, such as the "Pollacks" from "the bush" across the tracks.

"Mexicans" were not necessarily admired by other ethnic groups in the South Chicago area, thus there were conflicts with opposing groups at any time of the day or night.

Nick was beginning to learn more and more about ethnicity, since that was the forefront of all that mattered in the neighborhood. If you were not a "Mexican", you didn't belong.

The word Mexican itself gave Nick a slight problem whenever he used it, for he was still self conscious about its use, after being subjected to continual reminders that the words Spanish-American were more suitable to describe his Mexican background in the Public Schools of Denver.

The word Mexican, when used by those who were not of that particular persuasion, was almost always used in harsh and disdainful tone, as if it were a word to describe something particularly bad.

There was an outlet in avoiding the use of the word Mexican, and that was to describe ones self as a "Chicano" instead, but that was done only while out of school.

The word Chicano was introduced by the Spanish-speaking minority of the western United States, offering a subtle reminder to the English-speaking majority, or "Anglos", that Chicanos were still Mexicanos in a more accepted form.

Most of the boys on the corner were guys that had been born and raised in Chicago or somewhere nearby, their fathers having been employed by the Railroad Companies or outlying farmlands since the late "20's and early '30's. Other than the little Spanish they spoke at home, English was their first language. Few of these boys had ever heard the word Chicano before, and considered themselves Mexicans whenever backgrounds were discussed.

One particular afternoon when several of the local guys gathered at the corner across from the church, Nick arrived and soon became involved in a conversation regarding ethnic backgrounds.

"I'm a Chicano from Colorado," Nick proudly told his listeners.

"Chicano, what the hell is a Chicano?" someone asked.

'Well, you know," Nick replied, "a Spanish-American, just like you guys!"

Suddenly there was a burst of laughter and jeering from the entire group on the corner. Nick, momentarily bewildered, wondered what he had said to cause the uproar.

Nick's newest and closest buddy, the other Nick, confronted him with ridicule.

"Spanish-American your ass," he said, "around here you're either a fuckin' Mexican or something else, like a 'Nigger' or a 'Polack', or a 'Wop'.

Nick winced a little at hearing the tirade, but managed to conceal his reaction. He laughed it off and felt relieved, for now he realized there was no further need to avoid any discussion concerning his true heritage. Suddenly he could say the word Mexican without a second thought.

Nick would now be able to present himself as a Mexican anywhere at any time, regardless of repercussions, hidden or otherwise. Nick suddenly felt a freedom that was hard to describe, yet he knew it was there, somewhere within him.

Meanwhile, Davy was in the process of solidifying his friendship with the "older crowd". This group's hangout was the clubhouse, or Grande's Pool Room near the Illinois Central Railroad tracks, a half block down the street from the church.

At the pool room, if you were big enough, you were old enough to shoot pool. It took only the first time to convince the attendant that you were old enough, then you would become a regular without further question. Here, Davy polished his game of 'eight ball' and 'straight pool' and soon became very efficient and competitive.

Davy's friends were guys with names like "Spinks" and "Lefty" and "Gonzo". Nicknames that were acquired for obvious reasons or were "earned "in one way or another. This day Davy would earn his nickname and it would end in a crowning glory.

Davy walked into the pool room and found but one lone shooter.

"Where's all the guys?" Davy asked Hyman.

"I don't know," Hyman answered., "maybe at the clubhouse. Wanna shoot some eight ball?"

"Yeah, rack 'em up," Davy answered.

After the second game Hyman suggested they might take a walk to the clubhouse to see if the guys were around. The clubhouse was located two blocks away on Burley Avenue, across the street from the school.

Arriving at the clubhouse, Hyman stepped to the door and jiggled the knob.

"I don't hear nothin'," Hyman said, "maybe they're out in back."

Davy stepped to the gangway to check, he heard nothing and saw no one.

Hyman opened the door and walked in and signaled to the guys inside. Spinks, a hulk of a young man who was into bodybuilding, stood blocking the doorway with a sly smile on his face.

As Davy went through the doorway he slipped past Spinks and raised his arms with clenched fists and announced "The King is here!"

Suddenly Spinks and Hyman took Davy by one arm each, lifted him bodily and carried him into the clubhouse. Out of nowhere Lefty and Gonzo appeared along with five or six more guys.

Davy was forced to the floor on his back and held tightly by the arms and legs. He felt someone unbuckling his belt then felt his pants sliding off.

"What the hell are you fuckers doing?" shouted Davy who was now in great distress.

"Initiation time!" somebody shouted back.

By now the clubhouse was in an uproar of laughter and shouting..

Davy's pants were pulled down to his knees exposing his genitals. As his legs were held open, the guys took turns spitting on his penis. Someone took a mouthful of water and sprayed it between Davy's legs.

Finally Davy was turned loose as the laughing continued. He pulled up his pants while swearing at all the guys.

Francisca and the Boys

"You fuckin' ass holes!" Davy shouted, then turned to Hyman and said, "You fuckin' Hyman!" and shook his head from side to side in exasperation.

Hyman only laughed louder, holding his stomach with both hands.

Spinks stepped up and placed a hand on Davy's shoulder and announced, "Hey you guys, I now present his majesty the King!" He bowed low swinging one arm out while holding the other to his chest.

Davy had now been initiated into the club and inadvertently given himself a nickname. From that day forward his name had changed to King and he would be known as such thereafter. Davy had earned his nickname.

One Saturday morning Nick was in the kitchen having his usual cold, dry cereal and milk for breakfast when there was a shrill whistle penetrating the early morning quietude. The whistle came from just outside the kitchen window. Looking out, Nick saw Caldo and the other Nick standing in the alley near the window. He tapped on the pane and put his forefinger to his lips, motioning to the guys to be quiet. He swallowed what was left of the cereal and tiptoed out the door so as not to disturb Francisca from her deep sleep.

"We're goin' swimmin'. Ya wanna come with us?" Caldo asked.

"Yeah, let's get outta here before my old lady wakes up!"

The trio headed toward the bridge connecting South Chicago with the East Side.

"Where we goin'," Nick inquired, "to Calumet Beach?"

"Naw," the other Nick answered, "that's too fuckin' far to walk, we're goin' to the river."

"The river!" Nick said in a surprised tone.

"Yeah, just stick with us, we'll show you the ropes," Caldo said, with that crooked smile on his face.

It was about ten o'clock in the morning and the sun was shining hot. The trio crossed 92nd Street just before the bridge.

They entered a high weeded prairie that separated the street from the loading tracks that ran along the bank of the South Branch of the Chicago River. A grain elevator stood a short distance away, and several rail cars filled with coal nuggets rested on the tracks a few yards from the river's edge.

Crossing the prairie, the guys reached the rail cars. They climbed up between the cars examining the hitches as they went over.

"We got enough coal here for all winter," Caldo said to Nick.

Nick looked at Caldo curiously, wondering what he was talking about.

"We steal the coal for the house, when it gets cold," Caldo explained, "it belongs to the steel mills, but they have a lot, they can spare some. There's always full cars here, summer and winter."

On reaching the river's edge, Caldo and the other Nick began to undress immediately.

"I ain't got no trunks!" complained Nick.

"We don't neither," Caldo said, "can you swim?"

"Fuckin' aye I can swim!" Nick replied.

"Ok, so take off your clothes, come on!"

By the time Nick had removed his shirt, the other Nick was already diving into the river, completely in the nude.

"You mean we're goin' in bare ass?" Nick asked, surprised.

"Yeah, bare ass, whatsa matter, ya chicken?" Caldo retorted as he dove into the water.

Nick followed close behind, diving in and hitting the water with a splash. At first touch the water felt very cold, but in a very short time his body became accustomed to the water temperature.

Looking up from the water Nick could see cars crossing the bridge and wondered if he could be seen from that distance. Well, he thought, if the others don't care, why should he?

Thick logs lined vertically and tightly set together formed a narrow dock about four feet above the water level, now serving as a diving platform for the guys. An empty barge, tied to a

Francisca and the Boys

dock serving a material service company, floated on the surface directly across the river. A thin layer of oil floated on the surface of the water, which no one seemed to notice, and if they did, no one really cared. The water was cool and refreshing, it was deep and the current was very slow making it ideal for swimming.

After an hour or so of diving and swimming, the trio dried off under the hot sun. They dressed and prepared for their return to the neighborhood. Caldo supplied the comb that was used by each boy, testing the strength of the comb to its limit when running it through their still wet, thick and unruly hair.

Retracing their steps the boys crossed the prairie once more to the street just at about the time a streetcar was slowly screeching its way from the turnaround then heading north on Buffalo Avenue.

"Come on," shouted the other Nick, "let's hitch a ride!"

Only once had Nick been aboard a streetcar in his life, and that was in Denver on his way to a Boy Scout Jamboree. Now he was on the verge of riding one on the outside. How, he wasn't sure, but he would soon find out as he followed Caldo and the other Nick in pursuit of the trolley car that was slowly gaining speed.

By hanging by their hands from the open window frames and placing their feet on the butting skirt of the streetcar, the guys jumped on the rear end and held on. As the streetcar gained speed, so did Nick's heart. Now it was going too fast to let go.

The guys hung on for two blocks, and the trolley was not making any stops. Nick pressed his forehead to the back of his hands, closing his eyes very tight, he hung on. At mid block near the school, Caldo reached up and pulled the trolley rope, disconnecting the contact rollers from the cables above and breaking the electric current. The streetcar slowed, and before it came to a complete stop, the boys jumped off and ran through the school yard.

The operator stepped out of the streetcar shouting and swearing at the boys. He reattached the trolley to the electric cables above and returned to his motorman's position once more to continue his journey.

Walking down the street Nick cut through the alley for home.

"See you guys on the corner later," he told his buddies, "I gotta check in". They separated.

On entering the flat, Nick found Davy sitting at the kitchen table He was unusually quiet and looking very perplexed. Francisca was in her bedroom readying herself to go to her job. The sound of running water could be heard in the bathroom. Nick soon realized that there was someone else in the flat beside the three of them.

Davy, looking at Nick, held his forefinger to his lips and signaled Nick to follow him out the door. The two walked out very softly.

"There's some guy in there, I think he's ma's boyfriend," Davy said.

"So what?" responded Nick.

"So I don't want a fuckin' stepfather!" Davy answered.

"That's ma's business, what do you care?" Nick said.

"Well, I don't like it!" Davy said with an air of authority.

Francisca and her friend were sitting at the table having coffee when the boys returned.

"I want you to meet Miguel," she said to the boys.

The boys responded with a simultaneous, "Hi". Neither boy offered to shake hands.

Miguel half smiled, nodded slightly and said, "You can call me Mike."

The boys did not respond further as neither boy cared to continue a conversation with this interloper.

Nick took notice that Miguel was wearing a suit and tie and that his shoes were mirror clean. To Nick, this was reason enough to dislike the man, but he managed to conceal the feeling.

Davy concealed nothing, he turned abruptly away and went into the living room.

Francisca and the Boys

"What have you got in your hair?" Francisca asked Nick, breaking the lull.

"Nuthin', why?" replied Nick.

Francisca reached over and took a handful of Nick's thick, black hair and pulled her fingers through it.

"What's this stuff?" she asked rubbing her fingers together.

"I don't know, what is it?" Nick replied.

Francisca smiled and said, "You have a lot of garbage or something in your hair. How did you get it, where were you?"

"I went swimming with the guys," replied Nick.

"Where?" she asked. Francisca was now astonished and amused at the same time.

"In the river," Nick answered rather subdued.

"Are you crazy?" Francisca laughed out loud, "You know you're not supposed to swim in that river, *mijo*!" Francisca used the Spanish word for son to emphasize the seriousness of the situation.

"Look," Francisca said, gently reprimanding Nick, "in the first place, it's too dangerous to go swimming in the river with nobody watching over you. Second, the river is nasty and dirty. It's full of a lot of stuff coming from the steel mill, and even shit from the houses!"

Francisca's explanation was a little crude but effective. She wanted to get through to Nick, and that was the best she knew how.

Finally she said to Nick, "Take a hot bath and wash your hair good with lots of soap, before your head starts to stink!"

"Ok, ma," Nick said with a smile. He was pleasantly surprised and relieved that Francisca had not lost her temper. He immediately began to prepare his bath.

As Francisca and Miguel turned to leave, Davy called to his mother, "Ma, there's a dance at Eagles Hall tonight, can I go?"

Nick's voice boomed from the bathroom, "Me too, ma!"

"Yes, both of you can go, just make sure you're home by twelve. Take a dollar each from the box, but no more," she said,

"I know how much is in there, and make sure you lock the doors when you go!"

"Ok, ma," Davy told her.

Nick emerged from the bathroom with a towel tied around the waist. Picking his underwear from the bureau drawers, he put on a pair of jockey shorts and a pair of argyle socks. The socks were of large red and white diamond design, that would go well with his loafers. His blue denim pants would be rolled up above the ankles, one slightly higher than the other. He put on a polo shirt with red and white inch wide stripes that ran horizontally around the front and back of the shirt.

Davy ironed his white dress shirt over a carefully folded bed sheet on top of the kitchen table. Next, he took his blue, pinstriped "pegs" and pressed a sharp crease on the front of the pant legs using a damp cloth under a hot iron. He decided not to use the coat, since the weather was turning very hot. He would also forego the necktie.

Davy also put on white socks and a pair of long, pointed, brown oxfords. If the weather should turn cool, he would return for his "drape" suit coat before going to the hall. However, as it looked for the present, the weather was not about to change.

The boys entered Francisca's bedroom. Davy pulled open a drawer that was positioned to open toward the wall. The small table containing the drawer also served as the altar that held Francisca's religious figures and the candle plate, which at this moment contained three burning votive candles.

From the drawer, Davy retrieved a small metal box with a bobby pin across the link on the latch serving as a lock. As he pulled the bobby pin, the box cover popped open and the bills inside expanded causing the cover to rise. He pulled the box cover back on its hinges.

"Wow, look at that!" Nick exclaimed.

"Yeah, I know," Davy said rather unconcerned.

Davy removed two single dollar bills and set them aside. He then lifted all the bills in the box and shuffled them. There were a number of fives, tens, and twenties stacked in numerical order.

"Ma knows how much she's got," Nick said in a matter of warning.

"I know she knows!" retorted Davy with sarcasm in his voice.

The temptation to take more money was present in both boys, but by weighing it against Francisca's probable punishment, they restrained the urge. They knew full well there would be hell to pay if their mother found any money missing.

Closing the cash box and replacing the bobby pin, Davy returned the box to the drawer. They left the room and prepared to leave for separate destinations.

The doors at Eagles Hall would not open until eight o'clock. The boys had time to spare.

"I'm going to the clubhouse, I'll see you at the dance tonight," Davy said to Nick, and he walked out the door.

"Ok," Nick replied, "see ya later!"

Nick returned to the bathroom to check his hair more closely.

He looked in the mirror, running his fingers through his hair. It was clean and smooth, but too bushy and too dry. With the first two fingers of his right hand he pulled a wad of petroleum jelly from a jar. He slapped the jelly to the other hand and rubbed them together then applied the jelly to his hair. After a thorough application, he combed his hair to his ultimate satisfaction. One more glance in the mirror, then he left the bathroom.

Nick, remembering Francisca's final instructions, pulled the two slide bolts on the kitchen door closed, placing them in a locked position. He checked all the windows making sure that all locks were closed.

Nick checked his pockets in search of his key to the self locking latch on the rear door. He found it among a variety of junk in his pockets, which included a wrist chain, a St. Joseph religious metal, a small safety pin and two pennies. Then he realized that he was still holding his dollar bill in his hand. He folded it and stuffed it into his watch pocket. Now he was ready to walk out the door.

On his way out, Nick slammed the door shut and pushed in to make certain it locked securely. He walked to the alley and turned in the direction of the church. It was time to meet the guys.

* * *

Francisca stepped out of the car and walked around to the drivers side to talk to Miguel.

"Are you stopping by tonight?" she asked him.

"I will if I can, there's some things I have to do, I can't promise," Miguel told her.

Francisca knew instinctively that Miguel would not return. His lack of an explanation made it obvious to Francisca that he had other plans. She did not press the conversation further, she must report to work.

The bar at El Jalisco was filled with clientele and the juke box blared. It was past six toward evening and the afternoon crowd was still there. By eight or nine this crowd would be replaced by the dancing crowd and the festivities would continue until closing at three o'clock the next morning.

Francisca would start early to make a few extra dollars. The tipping was extremely good on Saturday nights and she was almost certain to encounter a fool that was willing to part with his money.

* * *

The Royal Castilians were playing at Eagles Hall this Saturday night. The tuning of their instruments could be heard as the Nicks arrived together. The rest of the guys from 91st and Brandon began to show up in twos and threes and some alone. When the

Francisca and the Boys

band was ready to begin playing, the guys gathered in front of the high stage for a better view of the band and for making better connection with the girls.

Nick stood around the bandstand with an overwhelming urge to get on the dance floor, but he could not work up enough nerve to ask a girl for a dance. He milled around the hall as did the rest of the guys.

About halfway through night the band leader announced a "Jitterbug" contest.

Shadow and Claw were nearby. Shadow motioned to Nick to come closer.

"We got some wine, you wanna slug, Nick," Shadow said exposing a pint bottle he carried in his belt under his shirt.

"What kind of wine?" Nick asked, as if he knew the difference.

"It's Muscatel, you want some?"

"Fuckin' aye!" Nick responded.

The three walked into the washroom at the rear of the hall. Shadow pulled the bottle from his waistline and handed it to Nick. It was more than half full.

"Here, you go first," Shadow said to Nick.

Nick gave Shadow a dubious look, wondering why he should go first.

"Take a slug," Claw told Nick, "it ain't piss!"

Shadow put the bottle to his lips and took a swig to convince Nick that it was not a trick.

"Ok!" Nick agreed as he took the bottle.

First he smelled it and looked away, grimacing at the odor of the contents. He took a quick taste and found the wine to be sweet but strong.. He held his breath and took a long drink, leaving a half empty bottle. Nick's eyes became teary as the hot wine took its course from his lips to his stomach. His stomach turned hot for a few moments, then he experienced a titillating feeling going through his body. Nick wanted more.

"Let's get some more," Nick suggested.

"Ok, let's chip in," Shadow countered.

Everyone chipped in and with the toss of a coin, Claw became the courier. There was always someone of age willing to buy beer or wine for the guys at Loncar's Liquors.

Claw returned with the new bottle of Muscatel. Nick number two had now joined the guys in tasting the liquid heaven. Shadow had acquired a paper cup somewhere and used to measure each guys' drink in the interest of equality.

Nick forced one more drink and decided it would be his last for the night. He left the washroom feeling drunk and a little bit out of control.

The jitterbug contest was in full swing. Nick slowly made his way through the crowd looking for the exit. Watching the dancers on the floor, he spotted Davy with his partner as he went by.

Nick's head was starting to feel fuzzy from the effect of the alcohol and things were beginning to rotate in front of his eyes. He had to get home while he could still stand.

Nick wobbled down the street for six blocks, from the dance hall to the alley near the house. He stopped every now and then to check his location, all the land marks seemed to be in place, he was sure that he was on the right track for home.

On reaching his home alley he stopped and leaned against a light pole. Looking up at the street light he saw it fade away and return instantly. He felt a sudden urge to vomit. He placed a hand on the light pole and leaned forward spraying the area with contents from within. Groaning, he continued in quest of his goal, the door to the flat, and finally his bed.

Nick had difficulty finding the keyhole to the latch on the rear door. Finally succeeding, he pushed open the door, and while doing so he accidentally rubbed the door jamb and caught a splinter on the side of his right hand. In his inebriated condition he felt no pain. The splinter imbedded in his hand went unnoticed.

Slamming the door behind him Nick ran to the bathroom and found the toilet bowl in the dark. He fell on his knees and embraced the bowl with his arms and discharged another spray of vomit. Before long there was nothing left to release from his stomach. After a few dry heaves, he stood up and found the light string.

Looking into the mirror Nick could see his image as a whole, but he could not focus his eyes enough to see who was staring back at him. His eyes remained teary as he wiped his mouth with the back of his hand. His hair fell to the sides of his face, effecting a ghostly appearance of his entire countenance. Nick managed to throw cold water on his face.

The dizzy feeling subsided some, and with a little effort, Nick was able to walk without wobbling.

What time was it?

Nick suddenly pictured Francisca walking in the door and catching him in this drunken stupor. He went to the kitchen looking for the clock. It was eleven forty five. He was relieved that he made it home before the hour that his mother had set as limit.

Realizing that Francisca would not be home for a few more hours, Nick relaxed and continued the business of getting sober.

It was almost twelve o'clock and Davy wasn't home yet.

Where was Davy when he needed him most, Nick thought.

Nick removed his shirt and returned to the bath room. He stooped over with his face toward the toilet bowl one more time. He heaved, but nothing came up. The smell from the bowl was unbearable. He heaved a few more times but there was nothing left.

Nick finally had the sense to flush the toilet.

Now Nick was beginning to concentrate a little better.

When was he going to sober up?

How would he get rid of that smell?

Would he be able to hide it from his mother?

Questions that he could not answer immediately.

Nick stuck his head under the bathtub faucet and let cold water run over the back of his neck until it felt numb. He dried off feeling much better. He cleaned the wash bowl and toilet bowl with a mixture of Lysol and water. He brushed his teeth twice then with a mixture of water and tooth paste, he gargled.

Finally Nick pulled out the bed from the couch, straightened the mattress and blankets and fell into bed.

Nick, in a deep sleep, felt a nudge. He opened his eyes to find Davy lying next to him.

"What time is it?" Nick asked Davy.

"I don't know, about three maybe," Davy answered.

"Three o'clock?"

"Yeah, why?"

"Where were you, you were supposed to be home by twelve!"

"I was," Davy replied, "I was upstairs."

"No shit, with Eulalia?" Nick excitedly asked.

"Fuckin' aye!" Davy answered, smiling..

"Wow, you fucker you!" Nick half shouted. He felt good for his brother and smiled as he turned over to go to sleep.

"Who won the contest?" Nick asked before closing his eyes.

"Peckerhead and Peewee, me and Jenny came in third."

The boys fell asleep.

Nick felt a sharp pain in his lower legs while in a sound sleep. He awakened to see his mother with the ironing cord in her hand. He sat up just as Francisca was swinging the cord at Davy.

"Whatsa matter?" Nick asked, scared and confused.

"Alright," Francisca told the boys, "I want you to get out of bed and go to the kitchen!"

The boys did what they were told and sat at the kitchen table wondering what was going on.

"Now, before I beat the shit out of you two *hijos de la chingada,* I want to know where the money is!" Francisca said to the boys, swearing in Spanish for more emphasis, and knowing full well that she was only swearing at herself when she called them sons-of-a-bitch.

Francisca had found the box empty when she went to make her weekend deposit.

Francisca and the Boys

"Ma," Davy said, "it was in the box!"

"Well, why isn't it there now?" Francisca asked in a rage.

"I don't know, ma, I went out before Nicky, ask him!" Davy said flinching in fear.

Now the burden of truth would switch to Nick.

Francisca raised the cord one more time, this time intended for Nick.

"Well, what have you got to say?" she asked Nick, with fury in her eyes.

"Ma, wait!" Nick pleaded while holding both hands up in self defense, "Before I went out I made sure that all the doors and windows were locked like you said ma, and I didn't take no money honest-to-god!" he raised his right hand to emphasize his plea.

Francisca by instinct felt the boys were telling the truth. She sat down exasperated, wondering how the money had disappeared. Could it be Eulalia who has a key, or maybe the landlord who most certainly would have a key. She dismissed both as farfetched.

Nick rubbed his left hand over his right and felt a stinging pain.

The sliver was still lodged in the meaty part of his hand.

"Ma, I got it!" shouted Nick.

Nick, remembering something unusual about the rear door from the night before, jumped up and ran to the rear entrance and opened the door.

"Look ma!" Nick half shouted pointing to the edge of the door frame.

The door jamb looked as though it had been chewed next to the latch. Clearly, a knife or other sharp tool had been used to force the latch open to gain entry into the flat.

Francisca saw the logic in Nick's discovery and became very calm, now realizing that the boys could not be guilty. Returning to the kitchen she sorted things out in her mind and understood instantly what had really happened.

Miguel was now the only possible suspect, for he was the only other person who knew that there was money in the house.

"Alright, now go back to bed," Francisca told the boys, "I'll look into it."

The boys, feeling relieved and reprieved, returned to bed in hopes of accumulating a few more hours of sleep.

Francisca, in need of sleep herself, went into the bedroom and leaned back on propped up pillows, removing only her shoes. She thought of the dilemma she now found herself in. She had accepted a relationship with Miguel hoping to perhaps build from there. After this day there was no possibility of that happening. In her mind he was the guilty party.

As she compared Miguel to Chamaco, her eyes swelled in tears She wiped her eyes convincing herself that this was no time for crying. She reached over and placed the intended deposit in the now empty box. All was not lost, this was only a set back, she would start anew. She placed the box back in the drawer and closed it, closed her eyes and dozed off.

FIFTEEN

June of 1937 was into its third week and Davy's graduation day was less than a week away. He had passed his final examinations earlier in the month, making him confident that he would receive his diploma and go on to high school in September.

However, at this time of the year there were recruiters in the neighborhood looking for field workers to help in the harvest of crops on nearby farmlands. Most of Davy's friends signed up for tomato picking at a farm in the state of Ohio.

After begging and finally convincing his mother to let him go, Davy signed up along with the rest of the guys. He would miss his graduation but his interest in school was not overpowering anyway. He departed for the tomato fields of Ohio in the company of his friends.

Nick found himself alone for the first time ever. It seemed so strange to have the bed all to himself and not to have Davy to fight with and to be pushed around as always. Now he did not only have the bed to himself, but he had the whole house.

Between working and sleeping and other duties such as church and shopping, Francisca's time was spread pretty thin. Now she was seeing less and less of either boy. For Nick things worked out well, for now he had all the time he needed to concentrate on his own activities.

In the evening while his mother slept or worked Nick explored the neighborhoods of the South Chicago area in company of his good friend and buddy, Caldo. In time Nick would learn the intricacies of sneaking through dark allies, climbing rear porches, and going through ice-boxes while relieving them of their contents.

Nick had an excellent teacher in his friend Caldo, and Caldo had an excellent student in his friend Nick.

Nick was not short of experience when it came to the appropriation of other peoples property. If it was out in the open and looked like it might have some value, then it was free for the taking.

Things such as tools or bicycles or anything else not locked down would usually end up at the "buyer", or more commonly known as the "fence", located in the "Bush" north of the tracks on Burley Avenue.

Nick had learned a great deal in the streets of Denver, although self-taught, and unknowingly attempting to survive a depression that he was not aware of. The small things that he had accomplished in his bold but innocent way were done in the light of day. However, with his friend Caldo, everything had to be done with care and precision, and without question, after dark.

On his first excursion with Caldo, Nick was a little bit nervous but absolutely unafraid. The agenda had been planned by Caldo in advance and he would explain to Nick as they went along.

"We're going to the rich part o' town," Caldo told Nick, "where all the good stuff is at!"

"Where's that?" Nick asked.

"Over on Exchange Avenue."

Caldo was pulling a four wheeled red metal wagon that brought memories of Denver to Nick. He thought of the rickety old wooden wagon, with crooked wire wheels that he and his pals carried their loot in back in Denver. Caldo's wagon had rubber wheels and could be pulled with a minimum of effort. What a difference! It was like comparing a Model T to a brand new 1937 Ford.

The pair walked along 91st Street, then west toward the park on Exchange Avenue. Crossing Commercial Avenue, the boys turned into the first alley. After a few steps, everything to see could be seen by moonlight only.

Caldo was wearing tight fitting, black leather gloves, and carrying a flashlight in his belt next to his stomach. Nick understood the reason for the flashlight, but why was he wearing gloves in this hot weather? He would soon discover why!

As the boys walked along, a black cat suddenly appeared crossing the alley just ahead of them. Caldo stopped and motioned to Nick to be quiet. The cat climbed a fence and stopped momentarily atop the fence boards.

"Wait here for me," Caldo whispered to Nick, "I'll be right back, don't move."

Superstitions, black cats, and bad luck being synonymous kept Caldo on the alert for situations such as this.

Nick stopped and became very quiet and wondered what Caldo was up to.

Caldo very quietly opened the fence gate and stepped to the other side, disappearing into the darkness. Nick remained motionless.

Suddenly there was a great commotion coming from the other side of the fence. The rustling of bushes and the meowing and hissing of the cat could be heard. The noise stopped suddenly. The gate opened slowly and Caldo walked out cradling the cat in his arms. He petted the cat while he whispered softly, "Kitty, kitty," in an effort to keep it calm.

He seemed to be succeeding.

Nick saw for the first time, and realized, why Caldo wore gloves.

"What you want the cat for?" inquired Nick

"Just watch," replied Caldo.

Caldo gripped the cat's tail with both hands as it hissed and tried to wiggle free. Caldo turned his body round and round imitating a shot putter, swinging the cat around he released it upward. On the way down the cat hit some electrical wiring but still landed on all fours on the alley pavement. The cat disappeared into the darkness.

"See," Caldo said, "you can never kill a cat, they got nine lives, and they always land on their feet."

As far as he was concerned, Caldo proved the axiom of cats having more than one life. While Caldo laughed uproariously, Nick just shook his head in disbelief.

Continuing down the alley, Caldo picked out a three story building with apartments on two sides. Center railings divided the common porches on each floor. Lights shown through windows on one side at the top floor. The boys would start from the second floor and work their way down.

The wagon was parked in the shadows. Caldo pulled a paper shopping bag from a back pocket and opened it ready for filling. Handing the bag to Nick, Caldo said, "Here, you carry this, we'll fill it with the small stuff." Then he pulled a smaller bag and said, "This is for eggs."

The two climbed the porch stairs to the second floor quietly. They ravaged the ice-boxes on both sides of the center railings as they descended.

Reaching the alley, the boys placed the full shopping bag in the wagon along with the smaller bag containing at least two dozen eggs. They pulled the wagon to the end of the alley and stopped to arrange the goods separately on the wagon bed. The shopping bag was now ready for filling once more. Again the pair surveyed the area and prepared for the invasion of the next apartment building.

By midnight the boys had filled the wagon with everything for the table. They zigzagged their way home, in and out of alleys to avert suspicion and to avoid any roaming police squad cars.

Both boys were full from stuffing themselves with a variety of foods from the ice-boxes, such as pie, Jell-o and puddings, and fried chicken, all washed down with cold milk.

Along with the eggs, the boys carried home foods such as butter, milk, lard, cold cuts, cooked and uncooked steaks and chops, and a completely stuffed raw chicken that was ready for the oven.

Francisca and the Boys

Nick had now been initiated. In time, with Caldo's tutelage, he would refine his style.

There would be more trips in the offing.

On another occasion, Nick, with a continuing curiosity in Caldo's abilities as a thief, would accompany him on a short expedition closer to the home neighborhood.

This trip would take them north of the steel mill's loading track at about 86th Street and Burley Avenue, into what was unofficially known as "The Bush", or the Polish neighborhood.

A grocery store owned by an elderly couple, and the only store in the vicinity that did very good business during the day, was picked by Caldo on a previous visit.

Caldo had been at the park a block east from there and on his way home decided to stop for cigarettes 'for his father he said'. He was there long enough to "case" the store and the surrounding area.

As he paid for his purchases over the counter, a huge, black, ill tempered mongrel dog stood up on its hind legs and placed its huge front paws on the counter top, growling ferociously and exposing its fangs. Caldo jumped back in surprise!

The dog's jaws were so large that it gave the impression of having the ability to bite off a human head in one bite.

Caldo left the store thinking of ways of to cope with a situation such as this. The "smiling" dog presented a small problem. Caldo was not necessarily concerned about the dog's ferocity, but more about the noise it would make with its barking once it became disturbed.

On the after dark visit of this particular night, Caldo came prepared.

Parking the wagon just outside the backyard gate, the pair tiptoed along the backyard walk, very quietly approaching the basement rear door. Caldo carried a package under one arm that Nick had failed to notice until now.

"What's in the package?" Nick asked, frowning curiously.

"You'll see in a couple o' minutes," Caldo responded reassuringly, "relax!"

Nick handed Caldo a crowbar that he had been delegated to carry. There was no sound from within. As Caldo pushed the flat edge of the crowbar between the door and the jamb, there was a low single bark that emerged from within the basement. Caldo held his breath and put his forefinger to his lips, motioning for quiet. Nothing more could be heard from within.

"Unwrap the package!" Caldo instructed Nick in a very low whisper.

Quickly, Nick unwrapped the contents of the package that revealed several good sized chunks of fresh meat and a large beef bone.

"When I bust the door open, have a piece of meat ready, here goes!" Caldo whispered.

Caldo, deftly and swiftly, pulled on the crowbar to snap open the door in one try. He gave the bar to Nick and took a piece of meat and threw it at the barking dog. The meat landed at the dog's front paws. To their advantage, the boys found the dog tied to the railing of the stairs leading to the basement from the first floor.

The dog wasted no time to begin enjoying the unexpected treat that fell from nowhere. While the dog chewed on its morsel, the boys stepped gingerly into the basement. As Caldo shined the flashlight beam on the dog, the dog stopped chewing momentarily, and growling, poised itself as if to attack. At that moment a larger piece of meat landed at the dog's paws. Between the growling and the chewing, the chewing won out. The dog's tail now had a noticeable wag and continued to chomp on the meat between those huge jaws.

Nick stood back and watched in disbelief, something that to him was absolutely impossible.

Caldo held a piece of the meat over the dog's snout and dangled it, then reached over with his free hand and actually

Francisca and the Boys

petted the dog behind the ears. By the next piece of meat Caldo had the dog literally eating out of his hand.

Again, Nick further recognized the logic in Caldo's penchant for wearing leather gloves.

Caldo left the huge beef bone for the dog to entertain itself with, while he and Nick would go about their business.

Nick and Caldo carried out canned goods, boxed goods, bottled goods and about a little of everything they could see. They filled the red wagon to capacity and slipped away without a sound.

* * *

Graduation time came to J.N. Thorpe School and there was no one there to represent Davy. However, to every one's surprise, a few weeks after the ceremony Davy's diploma arrived in the mail. Francisca was a very happy mother that day.

To Francisca, this was the culmination of a goal she had worked and prayed for. Even though it was only Grammar School, it was the first step in the right direction and something to be proud of. Her son Davy had earned his diploma.

At this juncture, Francisca was satisfied that Davy had finished eight years of school. Eight years with many interruptions in the process, and at age fifteen, a little older than the average graduate. Nevertheless, it was a goal in completion and an enormous step on the way to a better life.

Francisca was fully aware of her own shortcomings due to the lack of an education. Her own formal education was completed after being expelled from the fourth grade in the Public Schools of El Paso, Texas. She planned to see that her sons did not remain in this difficult way of life.

Francisca would encourage both of her boys to attend High School, and finish if it was at all possible. She did not dwell on it, but the better the education, the better the chances were of surviving an uncertain future.

The weather had turned hot and September was just around the corner. Davy would be returning from Ohio before the end of August. Nick had a birthday early in the month that went by without notice, no one ever kept track of such things.

Weeks after the break in at Francisca's home, Miguel appeared at El Jalisco, evidently depending on expired time to heal whatever animosity might exist between him and Francisca. He exhibited no guilt while speaking to Francisca and she, in turn, succeeded in hiding her displeasure by being civil.

Miguel's good looks and easy going demeanor still appealed to Francisca. She had no qualms about continuing their relationship, for in spite of everything, there still remained that physical attraction between the two. However, the relationship would not be a forgone conclusion should she become convinced that he was guilty of the break-in.

Almost sure of Miguel's guilt, with little room for doubt, Francisca set a plan in motion to entrap him and perhaps catch him in the act. Francisca began to build her systematic plan of revenge. She would enjoy this meddling Lothario until the time was right.

Miguel had inched his way back into Francisca's good graces, or so he thought. He stayed with Francisca on several occasions believing that everything was back to normal. The last weekend that Miguel spent the night at Francisca's was a turning point in this hectic love affair.

Francisca had changed location for saving her money but she purposely left a small amount of bills in the table drawer.

After a hard Saturday of serving tables at El Jalisco, Francisca was at home enjoying a well deserved rest. Miguel was alongside her as she slept. She felt movement as Miguel sat up in bed. Initially, Francisca thought nothing of it.

There was more movement when Miguel decided to leave the bedside. He moved very slowly and deliberately. Francisca remained quiet while feigning sleep.

Francisca and the Boys

Francisca heard the sliding of the drawer in the altar table as it was opened, then closed. Miguel returned to the bed as if nothing had happened.

All hell was about to break loose!

Francisca confronted Miguel and accused him outright of breaking in and taking the money on that particular weekend. Miguel became very angry and began to argue with Francisca. Feeling insulted, he shouted, "What do you think I am, you're accusing me of being a thief!"

Francisca shouted back, "You are a thief, and not a very good one either!"

The words of anger bounced back and forth, first one then the other.

The argument had become very heated when Nick sat up in bed. He left the bed and walked to the bedroom door. He peeked in to see what was going on.

"Go to bed, Nicolas!" his mother said sternly.

Nick stepped away from the door, but instead of returning to his bed he went to the kitchen and picked up the tortilla rolling pin. It was not much of a weapon but Nick thought it might serve the purpose.

Suddenly Nick heard a loud slap and a scream from Francisca.

As he was about to run in to defend his mother, she came through the door. Pointing her finger at Nick's bed she said, "Stay right there!"

Francisca went into the kitchen, and in a matter of seconds she was back, carrying a long sharp kitchen knife in her right hand.

Miguel had his pants up to his knees, and he was hurriedly in the act of tying his shoes while sitting on the edge of the bed.

Francisca walked in, her temper flaring.

"Get the hell out of my house, you son-of-a-bitch!" Francisca shouted, brandishing the knife.

"Ok, I'm going, I'm going!" Miguel replied with fear in his voice.

"Who the fuck do you think you're hitting?" Francisca continued to shout.

"Take it easy, Francisca!" Miguel pleaded.

Miguel had all of his clothes on but had yet to buckle up his pants. As Francisca waved the knife in his face, he dropped his pants to the floor and picked up a pillow for protection. She slashed at Miguel and sliced a long cut on the pillow. Feathers were literally flying.

"Francisca, please!" Miguel shouted.

"I'll please you, you bastard!" she yelled back.

Francisca pushed the knife toward Miguel's genitals, he backed away, turning his body to one side. Francisca lowered her sights and plunged the knife into his right leg, just above the knee. He screamed as Francisca pulled out the knife instantly.

Miguel, pulling up his pants, ran limping through the living room, through the kitchen and out the alley door leaving a trail of blood along the way.

Francisca slammed the door shut and leaned her back against it. The knife was still in her hand. Walking slowly to the living room, she sat on the edge of Nick's bed and dropped the knife to the floor. She put her hands to her forehead and took a deep breath. The rage within her slowly diminished and she became very thoughtful and calm.

All during the commotion Nick had stood near the bedroom door watching the action unfold. He was still holding the tortilla rolling pin that he had been ready to use should it have become necessary.

Nick sat next to Francisca, with his arm around her shoulders he said, "Don't cry, ma!"

"I'm ok, *mijo*," she said, "I'm not going to cry."

Francisca turned to Nick and said, "Get dressed so we can go to Mass."

Nick groaned at the mention of Mass but he was not about to dispute Francisca's word, especially in her present condition.

As Francisca dressed and went through her makeup ritual, she spoke to Nick, "After eleven o'clock Mass we'll go to a nice restaurant, then we can go to the show."

Nick smiled at the restaurant idea, but he wasn't too keen on the accompanying of his mother to the movies. However, at this point Nick no longer had a voice in the matter.

Mother and son walked out to a warm and sunny Sunday morning on their way to their first stop, the bar where Francisca worked.

Arriving at the front door of El Jalisco, Francisca cupped her hands around her eyes to look through the plate glass on the door. She knocked. The door was opened by Frank, the bartender.

"Hello Francisca, what are you doing here so early?" he asked.

"I'm on my way to church, I just stopped to let you know that I can't come in until Friday, I found a new place and I'll be moving all week," Francisca told him.

"Ok, I'll let the boss know," he said.

Before leaving, Francisca quickly related to Frank all that had happened with Miguel.

"Aye, Franny, you don't fool around do you?" Frank said after hearing all the sordid details.

Francisca smiled and said, "Look out for that bastard, let me know if he comes around while I'm gone, see you Friday."

"See you!" he responded.

Francisca took Nick by the arm and pointed him in the direction of the Shrine of Saint Jude Thaddeus, Holy Catholic Church on 91st and Brandon Avenue.

As they walked along Nick thought of the old days, when he and Davy and his mother and father would all get together and do what he and Francisca would do today.

Things sure had changed since the passing of Chamaco, his father's memory was still fresh in Nick's mind and he would not easily be forgotten.

After Mass Nick walked across the street to hang with his friends while his mother was in deep conversation with a thin, matronly woman. Their conversation seemed to be of a serious nature, for it was highly animated as far as Nick could tell from a distance.

Francisca waved to Nick that she was ready to leave. Nick walked across the street as jeers from his friends followed him.

"See ya later mama's boy!" the other Nick shouted.

Nick turned and gave the other Nick the finger and silently mouthed the words, "Fuck you, ass hole!"

As Nick walked along he asked his mother, "Whose that lady, ma?"

"She's the teacher of catechism at the church," Francisca replied.

"Oh, I see," Nick said nodding his head.

The fact was that Nick did not see at all, not in this case for he was about to get walloped with some totally unexpected news.

Francisca continued, "She is also the lady that's going to teach you the prayers that you need to make your First Communion.

Nick suddenly stopped in his tracks, dropped both arms to his sides and exclaimed, "What!" Nick could not believe his ears.

"Come on, come on, "Francisca scolded, "the world is not going to end, you're going to make your First Communion whether you like it or not."

"But ma," Nick complained, "that's for little kids!"

"First Communion is for everybody!" she said.

"Aw, ma!" Nick responded.

"Shut up and let's go eat!" Francisca had the final word.

* * *

By Wednesday of that same week Davy had come home from the tomato fields of Ohio. He had seventy eight dollars that he had earned over the last two months of picking tomatoes.

Francisca and the Boys

When Davy walked in the door, the greeting he received from Nick was, "Man, are you black!"

"I was working in the fuckin' sun, you idiot!" Davy shot back.

Suddenly Davy realized that he had sworn and put his hands over his mouth. He asked Nick in a whisper, "Where's ma?"

"She ain't here," Nick told him with a cynical laugh, "I think she's upstairs by Eulalia."

Davy looked around to find that most of the kitchen was empty.

"Where's all the stuff?" he asked.

"We're moving," Nick said, "all the stuff is at the new house already, except for the heavy stuff, we saved that for you!" Nick laughed tauntingly.

"Aw shit, I shouldn't of come home so soon," Davy said in mock anger.

Francisca walked in the rear door and immediately embraced Davy, "*Mijo*," she half shouted, you're back!"

Touching Davy's cheeks with her fingertips, Francisca said, "You sure are sunburned!"

"Ma, you and Nicky keep tell me about my color, just for that I ain't gonna work no more," Davy said with a smirk on his face. Davy handed Francisca all of his earnings except three dollars that he would keep for spending money.

Davy arrived home on time to help in the moving by coincidence, but he was prepared to do his share. "Are just you and me gonna move everything by ourselves. Where's the truck?" he asked.

"There ain't no truck, besides, the new house is only a block away," Nick explained, "It's next block on this same street, across the street from Thorpe."

"So you and me still gotta move all this shit, don't we?" Davy asked again.

"Naw," answered Nick, "the guys will be here in a little while to give us a hand."

"That's more like it!" Davy exclaimed.

The boys would now get down to the task that confronted them at the moment, that of getting the couch through the rear door. Turning the couch on its side seemed to be the best fit. The boys slowly pushed the couch to the door and managed to get the first armrest through, the bedspring fell open sticking the couch in the doorway.

Eulalia's husband, Jesus, was kind enough to offer his services when Francisca mentioned the problem that the boys were having with the couch. He came down stairs without hesitation and gave the boys a much needed hand.

As they moved about, Davy avoided looking at Jesus in the eyes for he was not sure of what to expect, therefore he was not taking any chances. Eulalia had been on his mind for a while and the presence of her husband did not help matters much.

The couch was eventually extricated from the doorway.

The boys thanked Jesus and let him know that they could handle the rest of the moving.. The couch was left in the backyard temporarily.

Before long Nick's buddies arrived to lend a hand. These guys had been recruited by Nick since early in the week and so far had helped without complaining. There was so much horsing around that it turned out to be more fun than work.

The guys had decided that they could move everything by hand and just walk it over to the new house. Davy, Nick, Caldo and the other Nick each took hold of a corner of the couch and carried it down the street.

Caldo volunteered his red wagon and it was used to wheel the kitchen stove since it was the heaviest of the furniture.

When the moving was all done, Francisca had sandwiches and soda for everyone plus two dollars each for Caldo and the other Nick.

By nightfall everything was in place and all that remained was the making of beds and the hanging of clothes..

Francisca and the Boys

Francisca purchased a new electric refrigerator leaving the old ice box behind. Now she would not have to contend with buying ice and having to dump the water from underneath the ice box.

By the next week Lupe and Sylvia would join Francisca and the boys, bringing the family back together once again. She furnished a bedroom for Lupe and Sylvia, leaving the boys to still occupy the living room as their sleeping quarters.

Francisca returned to work and finished out the weekend without repercussions from the incident with Miguel. She felt confident that Miguel was gone for good and would not be seen around El Jalisco again.

Francisca rode the Illinois Central Train to Downtown Chicago to meet Lupe and Sylvia at the Greyhound Bus Depot. The three returned to South Chicago within three hours, and on their return the festivities would begin. There was a lot of hoopla as they walked up the front steps to meet Nick and Davy, who were waiting impatiently at the door.

Nick swept four year old Sylvia up, tossing her into the air. Everyone hugged and otherwise greeted each other. No sooner had they arrived and Francisca began preparation for cooking a festive meal.

Lupe, after not seeing Davy for so long, could not resist picking on him. "How come you're so dark, stupid?" she asked.

"Shut up dummy," he retorted, "I worked like a dog to get this beautiful tan."

Nick stuck his two cents in, "He went to work so he wouldn't have to go to school!"

"Shut up, you idiot, nobody asked you!" Davy said.

Stupid, dummy and idiot were descriptive words used by these three whenever they got together. It was all camouflage to hide the true feelings that existed among the three. An understanding between siblings that traversed from childhood to adulthood.

Meanwhile, Francisca was in the kitchen enjoying her granddaughter.

"Can I help you, Gramma?" little Sylvia asked her grandmother.

"Yes, baby, you can help Gramma."

Francisca took a cupful of flour and mixed it with water to form a ball of soft doe, then divided the ball into several smaller one's. She showed Sylvia how to roll then left her to exercise her own abilities. Sylvia became occupied while Francisca went on with the business of cooking the meal.

There was animated conversation between Lupe, Davy, and Nick as the boys helped Lupe unpack.

Lupe related some of her experiences as a waitress at Chon's Bar and Grill in Denver. She summed it all up by saying, "All those guys were like dogs, they just wanted one thing –!" Lupe did not finish her sentence, she just sort of let hang in the air.

The boys understood what she meant without her having to elaborate. They nodded at her elucidative assessment of men.

Davy's tales about picking tomatoes in Ohio were few since that was all there was to do. He complained about having a sore back from bending over so many hours at a time, but he enjoyed the hard work in the open fields. He even spoke of going back to Eaton, Colorado to work beets again. Maybe next summer.

Nick detailed what happened the previous Sunday between Francisca and Miguel at the other house.

"He slapped ma, and boy he should uh never done that," Nick related, "ma went to the kitchen and grabbed that long meat knife," he spread his hands visualizing the length of the knife, "then she stuck the knife in his leg around here," pointing at his own leg, "and it went all the way through to the other side, then he ran out yelling like a stuck pig!"

All three laughed but all were conscious of the fact that it had been a serious act and all were in agreement that their mother had acted in self defense.

The family sat down to a meal of chicken in *mole* sauce, with rice and refried beans. A treat that only came once in a great while.

Francisca looked at her children together for the first time in such a very long time. For the moment she felt very blessed.

Now that Lupe and Sylvia were at home certain changes would begin to take place. These changes would effect the freedom of movement that the boys had enjoyed for so long.

Davy was still visiting Eulalia late at night, but Lupe was asking too many questions and he was tiring of making excuses to her.

Nick's excursions were cut short, for now he had to be home on time or Francisca would hear about it from Lupe.

Now the boys were making deals with Lupe, for instance, baby sitting Sylvia in return for her silence.

September came around once more, bringing the inevitable opening day of school. Davy began classes at Bowen High School and Nick returned to Thorpe for his final year.

Lupe combed the area in search of a job.

Little Sylvia became the core of the family's activity, in her own innocent way she controlled all of the family's movements. Someone always had to be at home watching over her until she would become of school age, which would not be for at least another year and a half.

Taking care of Sylvia became routine with each family member taking a turn, with or without protesting. Deals would be made between Lupe, Davy and Nick, involving baby sitting time Sometimes with money involved, sometimes by exchange of hours. At times Francisca would relieve everyone by taking care of her granddaughter for a full day or more.

Francisca spoiled her granddaughter to extremes, and in sensing all the attention, little Sylvia took advantage. Whenever she did not get her way, Sylvia would go to grandma for help and protection. Yet no one seriously complained for she was the darling of the family. Nick and Davy would refer to her as the "brat"

Cold weather was setting in. Francisca purchased a potbellied stove for the living room at the second hand store. Coal and wood were bought by the bushel from street vendors. On extra cold days the stove had to be fed continuously. At times the fuel would run out and everyone would be wearing coats or would wrap themselves in blankets until the crises would pass.

The street vendors could not always be depended on, so Nick decided he would correct the situation. He would go looking for coal. Caldo would have to be called on.

Nick took his first trip to the coal cars with his pal Caldo, who came prepared with empty gunny sacks, a long rope and several strands of twine inside the red wagon. He also had a flashlight stuck in his back pocket and wore his ever present leather gloves. They waited for dark then began their trek to the coal cars near the river's edge.

Nick and Caldo crossed the prairie pulling the wagon to the tracks where the coal filled cars stood in the dark. Caldo tossed three of the empty gunny sacks up into the coal car. He put the rolled rope over his shoulder and told Nick, "Let's go!"

The boys climbed the iron ladder near the car hitch up onto the coal pile, sinking ankle deep into the soft coal nuggets.

"Look," Caldo told Nick, "you fill the sack like this." He pushed the sack opening into the coal and proceeded to fill the sack by pulling in the coal with his hands and arms in a sweeping motion while he straddled the sack.

Nick commenced by imitating Caldo and before long found the knack to filling the sack.

The three gunny sacks were filled and tied with twine at the openings. The rope was looped around the center of the sack and the full sack was lowered.

"You go down and untie the rope and stay down there, I'll send the other two down," Caldo said.

"Ok!" Nick responded.

The boys loaded the wagon by placing one sack inside the long way and the other two on top crosswise for balance.

"We can only take three at a time 'cause their too heavy, I'll pull, you push."

"Ok," agreed Nick, "let's go!"

As Nick pushed, the wagon temporarily stalled. He put his shoulder to it and the wagon began to move. Now he understood what Caldo meant by "too heavy".

The boys struggled through the high weeds in the prairie, but once across, they reached the pavement where the wagon then rolled easily along. Walking in the direction of Nick's house Caldo had a thought. "You know what," he said, "this coal is better than that shit those guys sell from the trucks!"

Nick was not sure but he agreed with Caldo anyway, "Yeah!"

As they approached the house Caldo told Nick, "You take two sacks and I'll take one, I still have coal at home, next time I'll take two!'

The boys arrived at Nick's and unloaded two of the sacks onto his back porch.. Caldo continued on his way home.

"See ya later," Caldo said to Nick.

"See ya," responded Nick.

As the weather would turn colder, there would be many more of these trips to the coal cars.

Francisca now had her cache of savings on the top shelf of her bedroom closet Her savings continued to fluctuate and seeming as though she would never attain the goal she had set for herself, that of going into business for herself.

Francisca daydreamed of working in her own establishment and having people working for her, so she could give orders and instructions on how to keep the clientele happy. In all of her experiences as a supplier of liquor and food services, she learned that a satisfied customer would always return.

Her thoughts were primarily affixed on starting a tavern business or a restaurant, or maybe a combination of the two, like Chon's Bar and Grill in Denver.

Francisca had much experience in the dispensing of food, but the cooking part of the business was a very hard job. She leaned toward a bar. A bar was certainly a business with many more headaches, but the restaurant was much harder physically.

She would finally set her sights on the tavern business in spite of any obstacles she might be confronted with.

Francisca left for work at her usual time one Saturday evening.

As usual, El Jalisco became filled to capacity during the late hours of the evening. The musicians were playing to a crowded dance floor at around the midnight hour.

As Francisca made the rounds serving tables and picking up empties she saw Miguel come in the front door. Her heart sank, immediately she went looking for Frank. He was not in the immediate vicinity.

Miguel ordered a drink at the far end of the bar near the door.

When Frank returned to his post Miguel had already been served, so he could not very well refuse him at that point. He assured Francisca that he would watch Miguel closely.

Miguel continued to order drinks in rapid succession, eventually consuming enough alcohol to put him in a highly inebriated condition.

"He seems to be ok, Franny," Frank said to Francisca.

"Maybe so," she answered, "but he's a no good sneak and I don't trust him!"

"Well, we'll keep an eye on him," Frank reassured Francisca once again.

Francisca stayed close to Frank when she could, but in the confusion of serving, giving change, picking up empties, plus the music and the dancers, Francisca tended to relax her observance of Miguel as did everyone else. Francisca concentrated on her job and no longer preoccupied with Miguel's presence.

Miguel left his barstool unnoticed and walked to the men's room and remained there for some time.

Frank, who had been busy washing glasses behind the bar, noticed that Miguel was no longer at his stool and assumed that he had left the premises. Francisca, unaware of what had transpired, continued waiting on tables.

Miguel cracked the washroom door slightly, enough to see all of the crowded dance floor. Francisca came into view not more than a step or two from the door.

Miguel kicked the door open and rushed out taking Francisca by the neck from behind. She screamed and swore at Miguel as she struggled, "Let me go you son-of-a-bitch!"

Miguel held her tight.

The musicians stopped playing and the dancing crowd moved away from the altercation.

Miguel had an open switchblade knife in his right hand while holding Francisca with his left arm.

She dropped a tray full of empty glasses and continued to scream as she attempted to break the hold on her neck. She pushed on his arm with both hands when she caught sight of the blade flashing a few inches from her face. She ducked her head digging her chin into Miguel's left arm. As he struck the blow, the blade caught Francisca just below the left ear, slicing down the left cheek to the tip of her chin..

There was pandemonium as people ran in all directions. In the confusion, Miguel pushed his way through the crowd and out the door to freedom.

Instantly, Francisca's head was wrapped in towels while the wound on her cheek continued to bleed profusely. Someone in the crowd with knowledge of first aid managed to subdue the bleeding.

Frank immediately jumped into action.

"Take over," he told the other bartender. "I'm driving her to the hospital, and no cops!" he warned.

By now, half the clientele had departed. The musicians continued to play.

"How you doin', Franny?" Frank asked Francisca as he drove.

"I'm ok," she replied, "I told you he was a sneaky son-of-a-bitch! But it was my fault for not being more careful."

"Franny, you think we can keep this from the cops?" Frank asked, "I don't want to see the tavern get involved, but it's up to you!"

Pressing the towel against her cheek made it difficult to speak but Francisca managed.

"I don't want to involve the tavern either," she told him, "but the hospital will make a police report and they are going to ask me questions, so we have to keep our stories straight."

Francisca's knowledge of the business came in to play in spite of the pain and the confusion. In Frank she found a person she felt she could trust and that their friendship would be valuable in the future.

"Just say I went home to check on my kids and that I ran back in a few minutes later asking for help. I can take care of the rest," Francisca said, then she added, "You might have to pay off the cops, you know how they are!"

Frank smiled at her forthrightness way of looking at things and said, "Franny, I won't forget this, thanks a lot."

Francisca was admitted by way of the emergency room at South Chicago Hospital. She was placed on a surgical table and preparation for the repair of her cheek began instantly. Very concerned nurses moved rapidly to get her ready for the doctor on duty. After swallowing a sedative in capsule form Francisca became light headed and began to drowse.

"Wash the wound and prepare for closing," the doctor told the nurses. Francisca felt sleepy but could still hear and feel the activity around her. She felt her head being covered with towels and the cutting and shaving of hair around the left ear. Cold liquid placed on the wound caused her to jerk slightly as a stinging sensation followed.

She heard the doctor's voice, "We are going to apply a local anesthetic now, you will feel a pinprick at first then there will be no pain at all.

Francisca acknowledged the doctor's words with a short moan then dozed off.

The next day Francisca awakened feeling drowsy and in a great deal of pain. Slowly she began to recollect the events of the previous night.

Francisca and the Boys

The nurse was busy attending patients in the four bed ward.

With great effort Francisca looked over at the nurse and said, "Nurse could you get me a mirror please?"

The nurse smiled and said, "Sure, but all you're going to see is bandages!"

Francisca tried smiling at the nurse's humorous comment but felt excruciating pain on the left side of her face. Instead she exhaled and released a low moan.

A mirror soon appeared in the hands of the accommodating nurse. Francisca managed to grunt a "thank you". Looking into the mirror she saw exactly what the nurse said she would see, bandages.

Francisca's cheek was swollen to a point that caused her eye to turn purple, and the swelling of her lips made it very difficult for her to speak. There were strips of white tape across her forehead, her nose, and her chin, all part of the arrangement of the entire bandage covering the wound on her cheek. Her hair was cut and shaved above and behind the ear where more tape was attached.

Convinced that she would be disfigured for life, Francisca put the mirror aside and closed her eyes.

She heard the nurse's voice, "Would you like to be propped up?" Francisca gave her a slight nod and blinked her eyes in affirmation. The nurse cranked up the head of Francisca's bed and rearranged her pillows allowing for more comfort. Before leaving the ward the nurse told Francisca, "If you need anything just push the button."

Francisca again closed her eyes. With her mind in a turmoil she made an effort to relax so as to release the tension that was beginning to build.

She felt a presence near her bed and opened her eyes to find her daughter Lupe looking down at her.

"Pancha, how do you feel?"

Francisca did not answer the question as put to her, but commented, "Look what I got myself into! How's my granddaughter? How are the boys?"

"Everybody is fine, they're all in the lobby waiting for me. They weren't allowed to come up," Lupe told her

Lupe felt like crying but managed to hold back the tears. She was reluctant to ask her mother for details on how she had been cut on the cheek but Francisca volunteered a partial explanation.

"Some guy I was seeing some time ago came back and did this to me." she said, "he grabbed me from behind and tried to cut my throat, but he couldn't raise my head to do it. Everything happened so fast....her voice trailed off.

"I know about that guy, the kids told me what happened," Lupe said to her mother.

"*Mija,* if you need money it's in the closet on the top shelf. It's in a long box with a lock on it, and the whole thing is wrapped up in a towel right behind the sewing basket. The key is in my purse, you'll have to go to the tavern to pick it up. Tell them it's behind the bar, Frank will get it for you."

Now, instead of crying, Lupe wanted to laugh at Francisca's continuous dialogue and the methods of hiding her money.

"I already got your purse, Frank brought it to the house, he told us what happened," Lupe said.

Francisca's cash holdings had graduated from a small box to a larger cash box with a lock. The savings would have to pay for her hospital stay and whatever other charges might be included.

"I'm not staying here very long," Francisca said, "I got to get out of here!"

Thinking of the hospital bill and the loss of time from work, Francisca felt desperation engulfing her. She felt that time was of more importance than the physical healing of her wound. This was a setback that would take time to overcome and she could little afford too long of a recovery.

"Don't rush things Pancha, you gotta take it easy for a while, we'll manage somehow!" Lupe reassured her.

Lupe realized she was not helping Francisca's condition with her presence. After a few minutes of conversation Francisca's eyelids began to droop. She was feeling tired.

While Francisca slipped into a gentle sleep, Lupe tiptoed out of the ward.

On the third day the attending physician entered the ward to check on Francisca's progress.

"How are you Mrs. Delmonte?" he said. "How do you feel?"

"Not very good," she responded.

"Oh, it will be a few more days before things get back to normal," the doctor commented.

Standing at Francisca's bedside the doctor reached over to her bandage and said, "Let's take a quick look here." He pulled gently on the tape below Francisca's lower lip until it came loose, he raised the bandage slowly and carefully until the entire bandage was removed.

"It looks fine," the doctor said.

Francisca groaned and gave the doctor a dubious look, suspecting that he was only trying to make her feel good.

"Mrs. Delmonte," he continued, "you have a very bad cut The blade of the knife went deep, damaging the muscle just below the ear," he pointed to the corresponding area on his own face, "in time it will heal to almost normal.".

Francisca, taking the hand mirror from her side table asked the doctor, "Can I look?"

"Of course you can, Mrs. Delmonte," the youthful doctor responded very politely.

Seeing her scar for the first time, Francisca gave a sigh of relief. It did not look as bad as it felt, but it was reddish throughout a rather wide area around the scar.

Francisca was about to touch her face with her fingertips but was advised by the doctor not to.

"The scar is still fresh and is susceptible to infection," the doctor warned.

"Why is it so red all around?" she asked.

The doctor smiled and told her, "That's the color of the iodine antiseptic that we used when your wound was repaired."

Francisca studied her face closely in the mirror. There was a slight swelling around the scar tissue that was held together by twelve individual stitches. The stitches, made of a silk suturing material, were about a quarter inch apart and tied with tiny knots on the surface. The scar ran parallel to the jaw line, starting under the ear and ending at the chin.

She examined her face thoughtfully, with plans cascading through her mind on how to conceal her newly acquired disfigurement.

After some cleaning and wiping with alcohol, the cheek was covered with a fresh bandage that would be much less cumbersome than the first.

By the end of the week Francisca was notified to ready herself for departure, she would be discharged sometime Thursday afternoon. There would be someone to pick her up.

While Francisca readied her belongings, Lupe came in to the ward.

"Hi Pancha, are you ready to go home?" Lupe asked.

"Yeah *mija*," she answered, adding a question of her own, "Did you ask about the bill?"

"That's already taken care of," answered Lupe.

"What, who......" Francisca was about to ask when Lupe cut her off.

"El Jalisco took care of everything, Frank's in the lobby waiting for us.

Francisca felt a sudden lifting of weight from her shoulders on hearing Lupe's comment. Raising her eyes upward, Francisca softly whispered, "Thank you dear God!"

She closed her eyes momentarily then resumed her preparation to leave the hospital.

SIXTEEN

For a minimum of one hour every Sunday afternoon Nick would pray with Dona Purisima, his catechism instructor. She was now visiting regularly to prepare Nick for his First Communion.

Dona Purisima arranged for Nick to be excused from regular catechism classes and separate him from the eight and ten year olds who would take their first offerings of the host at the altar railing. He would miss all the fanfare that went along with the traditional celebration of First Communion. Nick was relieved and thankful that he would not be embarrassed by having to appear in public with so many little ones.

Dona Purisima, who's name translated to "very pure", drilled Nick until he learned every prayer without faltering. The fact that the woman could speak only Spanish made it more difficult for him to learn However, not being completely fluent in Spanish, Nick managed to satisfy Dona Purisima by memorizing every word phonetically.

The day for confession finally arrived and for Nick this would be the very first time he would be so close to a priest, much less speak to one.

According to Dona Purisima, Nick would have to confess to the priest every bad thing he had done in his lifetime. Nick sorted out the sins he had committed over time. There were many, but he had no intentions of confessing everything. Nick went down his mental list of sins:

He talked back to his mother—well, not really but he would confess it anyway.

Stealing coal and other stuff— he would confess.

Drinking wine — he would confess.

Having bad thoughts about girls, like having sex—he would confess.

Smoking and swearing—he would confess.

Having sex with Mary in Denver—he would NOT confess.

Masturbating—he would NOT confess.

Nick prepared himself for whatever punishment God would administer, but he was not ready to tell his deepest secrets to another human being, and anyway, God already knew about his sins! If he was watching from up above then there was no way Nick could hide his indiscretions.

Nick entered the confessional and knelt facing a small screened window. He looked around and found himself in a dark telephone booth without a phone. He coughed a couple of times to let his presence be known. He heard a deep voice from the other side of the screen say in Spanish, *"Favor de proseguir!"*

Nick wasn't sure what he had heard, but the voice sounded like God himself. Was God a Mexican?

He heard the voice again, "Go ahead please!"

Nick, now aware that the priest could understand both languages went ahead with his prayers in Spanish as he was taught by Dona Purisima.

He began nervously, "Uh, uh, bless me father for I have sinned........" or whatever its equivalent happened to be in Spanish.

Nick's confession went well. He was told by the priest to repent and endeavor to become a better person. All of his sins were forgiven and he was to do a good Act of Contrition, plus three Hail Mary's and three Our Fathers.

In less than ten minutes he said his prayers and walked out of the church none the worse for wear. Sunday morning he would take communion with the regular parishioners and, other than his mother and Dona Purisima, no one would know it was his first.

That Sunday after Mass, Nick walked across the street to where most of the guys were already milling around and acting

Francisca and the Boys

useless as usual. He sat on the wooden railing without saying a word to his friends, just feeling rather pious.

Nick tried to recall the words the priest uttered when he placed the host on his tongue. He remembered something about "The Holy Eucharist" and "The Body of Christ." Anyway it was all over now, and Nick felt like he was the same as everyone else and that his soul had been cleansed. Now he felt free to start all over again.

Nick heard someone call his name.

"Nicky, hey Nicky!"

He felt a slight shove. It was the other Nick saying, "What the fuck's wrong with you?"

"Hey, fuck you!" responded Nick with a loud laugh.

"You got any money for the show?" asked the other Nick, "Let's go down to Commercial and see what's on!"

"Fuckin' aye I got money, let's go!" Nick replied.

Leaving the group on the corner they walked west toward the business district. They were going to see what was showing at the Commercial Theater. The boys crossed the IC tracks and went past the YMCA building on the next corner.

"Have you ever been in there?" Nick asked his namesake.

"Where?"

"In there, the Y," Nick said pointing to the building.

"Just once but they kicked me out!" replied the other Nick.

"Why?" asked Nick.

"The guy that runs it said I was too dirty to take a shower in there, but that was just a lot of bullshit. They just don't like Mexicans, so none o' the guys ever go there."

"What a bunch of fuckin' ass holes," Nick said with anger in his voice. "we should go looking for Polacks and kick some ass!"

"Ok," the other Nick concurred, "but not until after the show!"

The boys arrived at Commercial Avenue A line of kids had already formed at the box office waiting for the theater to open.

"I ain't waitin' in no fuckin' line!" Nick said.

"Naw, me neither," the other Nick agreed, "what we gonna do?"

"Yah hungry?" asked Nick.

"Yeah!"

"Let's go to White Castle until the line is gone," Nick suggested.

A block south, at White Castle Hamburgers, they each had two of the minuscule square hamburgers and a bottle of coke at a cost of seventeen cents to each boy.

Walking back to the theater the other Nick made a suggestion.

"Let's sneak in the show, you wanna?" he said.

Nick thought for a moment and asked, "Why, are you broke already?"

"Naw, I ain't broke," he answered, "but why pay when we don't hafta?"

A large poster with the picture of a horse was hung outside the theater. Across the front in large lettering appeared the announcement of the movie showing inside. Roy Rogers and his horse Trigger in 'Rustlers at Mesquite Creek'.

"Roy Rogers is cool, man," Nick said, "until he starts singing that love shit, after that...forget it!" Nick swung his arm to emphasize his remark.

"Yeah!" the other Nick concurred.

With just a few kids now waiting in line, the other Nick came up with an idea.

"I got it, let's go downtown!" he half shouted.

"Hey man, that's kinda far ain't it?" Nick asked.

"So what, I know how to get there!"

"Ok, how do we get there?"

We take the fuckin' streetcar," the other Nick said, "come on follow me!"

It was one o'clock on Sunday afternoon and there would not be many passengers aboard the trolley car. The boys waited on the corner.

Francisca and the Boys

Screeching and clanging announced the arrival of the big red streetcar. A sign across the top on the windshield in large white letters read, DOWNTOWN. A large number 5 appeared next to the sign. Black lettering on the red background of the streetcar advertised the name of the company, Chicago Surface Lines.

Boarding the trolley, each boy paid his three cents fare and walked to the rear of the car. They made themselves comfortable on hard wicker seats.

"This will take us all the way downtown and we won't even have to transfer," the other Nick said.

"Where do we get off?" asked Nick.

"We get off right in the middle of downtown," the other Nick answered, "right on State and Madison!"

This would be Nick's first excursion outside the limits of the South Chicago neighborhood since arriving from Denver. He felt some excitement as he made the trip downtown to the Loop.

The screeching of the streetcar on the rails, and the clanging of the bell each time the motorman kicked down on the floor pedal, added to the excitement. Now Nick would get a good look at the city that he had heard and read so much about.

The trolley traveled north on South Chicago Avenue to Stoney Island, to Cottage Grove, zigzagging its way finally to State Street heading into downtown.

"Madison, Madison street!" the conductor shouted loud and clear an hour into the trip.

"Come on, this is our stop!" the other Nick said as he pulled his namesake by the sleeve. They disembarked and stepped down to the sidewalk. Nick was captured by the thrill of the moment as he stared in awe at his surroundings.

There were huge store and theater signs along both sides of State Street. Nick took note of the clock on the Marshal Field Building and the big sign further south reading, Goldblatt's. The most noticeable of the theater signs were the Chicago, north on State and the State Lake directly across the street from the Chicago.

Behind the theater signs he saw for the first time the elevated tracks that formed the loop around the downtown area of Chicago. Looking south, Nick took in another elevated track crossing at Van Buren Street.

"What show we goin' to?" inquired Nick.

"None of these," the other Nick answered, "they cost too much, come on, I'll show you where the cheap shows are."

The boys walked west on Madison, crossed under the elevated tracks at Wells street and continued to the Madison Street bridge. They walked to the Chicago river and stopped on the bridge. They looked over the railing and watched their spittle fall several feet down to the water.

"Is this the same river that goes through South Chicago?" Nick asked Nick number two.

"Yeah, the same one we went swimming in, remember?"

"Yeah, but it looks a lot cleaner over here," Nick answered. "My ma said there was shit in the water where we swam, from the sewers and the houses!"

"No shit!" the other Nick remarked

"Yeah, shit!" Nick said with a laugh.

Both boys suddenly burst into laughter at the humorous connection of their expressions.

"How many more blocks?" asked Nick.

Pointing west, the other Nick said, "Just a couple more blocks, you can see the shows from here."

A few blocks west three large signs could be seen above the marquee of each theater, with cascading lights and looking as if they were suspended in mid air.

The Haymarket, the Star and Garter and the Empire were located within a half block of each other just west of the river.

Once the boys crossed Canal Street from the bridge, the environment in the new surroundings became quite a change as compared to the downtown area.

"This is skid row, starting here," commented the second Nick, "all the way to the other side of the shows."

"What do you mean by 'skid row'?" asked Nick.

"All the bums hang out here," the other Nick answered without emotion and explaining the situation to Nick as a matter of fact.

Like a tour guide, the other Nick took the initiative to explain to Nick every aspect of skid row that he knew.

As they walked, the other Nick pointed across the street and said, "See where all those guys are going in and out, they go in there to eat and at night they go in there to sleep. Sometimes they run out of beds and the 'winos' have to sleep on the sidewalk."

The store front where the activity that the other Nick had just described, had a large red and white sign painted across the top, just above the plate glass windows that read, The Salvation Army.

Continuing their walk, Nick stared in bewilderment at a row of small buildings with signs that read, Rooms $2.00 Weekly, and Beds 25 Cents all Night A few had signs designating a hotel, but most were one and two story buildings that had been converted into the well known 'flop houses.'

Bearded and disheveled men lined the street, some with wine bottles in their hands, others just looking downward with their hands in their pockets.

The Star and Garter Theater still had dancing girls and comedians on the stage, and musicians in the orchestra pit. Two performances nightly on weekends, after the feature motion pictures were over.

These were theaters that had been slowly converting from vaudeville to motion pictures in the last few years.

"Let's go to the Star and Garter, they got girls on the stage after the movie, the first stage show starts around six," the other Nick said.

The boys went straight to the box office window and each paid his admission fee of twenty cents, not checking to see what movies were showing, for they were more concerned in seeing the dancing girls.

They stocked up on the usual popcorn and candy and found seats in the very front row.

The Nicks watched the news, a cartoon, a comedy, and a gangster movie starring George Raft. The movie ended and the screen went dark. A collective sigh of anticipation could be felt throughout the auditorium. Coughing and whispering accompanied the paper rattling and squeaking of seats as the audience grew restless.

The musicians tuned their instruments in the dim lights of the orchestra pit. There was activity behind the huge stage curtain evident by the noise and by the movement of the curtain when touched by someone on the other side. At last, a master of ceremonies stepped out to announce the program of the evening.

"Ladies and gentlemen, tonight we have with us......," he went on, speaking into the microphone as he adjusted it for height.

The boys, not paying attention at the moment, continued talking in low tones.

"Hey Nicky," the other Nick said, "I ain't got no more money, how about you?"

Nick feeling through his pockets said, "I got a nickel left, I saved it for carfare."

"Aw shit, now what?" blurted the other Nick.

At that very moment the orchestra blasted out with fanfare music then the master of ceremonies introduced the next personality. A comedian stepped out from behind the curtain and began his routine. The boys paid no attention as they continued searching their pockets for the penny they would need to complete the necessary carfare.

"Let's wait 'til after the show," Nick suggested.

"Ok," answered the other Nick.

Neither boy seemed too concerned at the moment.

The dancing girls came out with more fanfare from the band. A line of ten girls danced their way across the stage holding each other by the waist and kicking high. The boys looked up into the bevy of legs in high heeled shoes, knees rotating, feet sliding, and heels kicking up.

The Nicks compared the dancing girls in size, in leg length, hair color and all around beauty.

"I like the little one on that end, the one with the black hair," Nick said, pointing in the general direction where the girl danced in line.

"I like the blond, the third one from that end." the other Nick said, also pointing, "Look at the tits on 'er!"

The show came to an end and the lights went on in the theater.

"Come on, let's go," Nick said as he stood up to leave.

The other Nick pulled him down by the arm and whispered, "Wait a couple of minutes until my hard-on goes down." They laughed and waited for the crowd to thin out.

Outside the theater the boys contemplated on how to get the penny they needed to complete carfare for the two of them.

"Let's look around for a penny, maybe we can find one around here somewhere," the other Nick suggested.

"Ok, but we gotta keep goin', let's walk to the Loop," Nick said. The two Nicks walked in the direction of the downtown area reaching the bridge once again.. They looked over the railing one more time. They had no luck in finding the elusive penny thus far.

"Hey man, why don't we ask somebody for a penny," suggested the other Nick.

"I ain't askin' nobody for nuthin'," Nick retorted, "I got my carfare, you ask!"

The other Nick looked down rather discouraged and said, "Yeah, I know, but I'll walk it, I ain't askin' nobody either."

The boys arrived at the corner of State and Madison Streets once more. It was nearing eight o'clock and the evening theater crowd was active, as people walked hurriedly to their destinations. The street lights were turned on in the Loop. Standing on the corner of the world's busiest intersection, the boys felt lost.

"Do you know how to get back?" Nick asked his counterpart, softening the tone of his voice just a little.

Mistakenly believing that Nick was about to abandon him, the other Nick asked very solemnly, "Aw, man, ya gonna leave me by myself?"

"No, you fuckin' dummy," Nick answered, "but I should! Come on, let's start walking, we gotta follow the streetcar tracks."

The other Nick's feelings were not hurt in the least in the dressing down he received from his buddy. He was aware that it was his own fault that they were now in this situation.

The trek to the south side would now begin.

Nick attempted to calculate the time it might take to get home on foot. If it took one hour by street car to get from South Chicago to the Loop, how long would it take to get back to South Chicago on foot. Figuring ninety blocks from Madison Street to 90th Street, and about thirty more blocks east, that would be a total of one hundred and twenty blocks. He asked himself, how many miles would that be? He gave up.

Looking at the other Nick, Nick threw up his hands and said, "We ain't gettin' home until tomorrow, man!"

Walking south on State street the boys stopped to look at posters of scantily clad women at the small theaters south of the elevated track at Van Buren Street. The barkers on the outside exuded the wares that were offered on the inside. Sailors and old men gathered at the box offices.

"Girls, girls, girls," a barker shouted, "come in and see the girls!.

The two Nicks stopped in front of one of the strip tease joints as the barker continued his spiel.

"Run along boys," the barker said to them, "you're too young for this sort of stuff, come back when you're twenty one!"

The boys laughed as they continued their walk. Looking south on State Street they saw no end in sight.

At 22nd Street they turned east to Cottage Grove Avenue, where they would follow the street car tracks south.

Francisca and the Boys

"This is the Colored district," the other Nick said, "I hope we don't get 'jumped'."

Now they had to worry about getting jumped Nick thought, what next.

Nick asked, "Why, do you have trouble with the Coloreds?"

"Naw, but you know!" the other Nick faltered not knowing how to explain it. In reality it was nothing more than deep rooted prejudice that built up over his young life.

"Don't start that shit," Nick reprimanded, "if you don't bother nobody, nobody will bother you!"

The statement was of a philosophy that Nick tried living by but, unfortunately, it never rang true. There would always be someone to bother you, at any given time, regardless of race or ethnicity.

Despite his philosophical remarks, Nick felt apprehension walking through a Colored neighborhood after dark. Yet he felt the same when walking through a Polish neighborhood. What the hell was the difference, he thought! The fear inside both boys did not subside and they increased their pace.

A few more blocks down the street the boys went by the Savoy Ballroom where the marquee read, ROY ELDRIDGE AND HIS TRUMPET, Fri., Sat., and Sun. Roy Eldrige, one of the hottest Negro trumpet players on the music scene, had top billing over the rest of the all white band.

It was near nine o'clock and the box office of the ballroom was very busy, as Colored guys and girls paid their way in. The girls in high heels and frizzy dresses or tight skirts and bobby socks. The guys in *Drape Suits* and long pointed oxfords, and wide brimmed hats of various colors.

At 63rd Street the boys went by the Trianon Ballroom. The marquee was lit up announcing the Tommy Dorsey Band, and about this time of the night the band could be heard on radio on the 'Aragon-Trianon Way' program.

"Hey man, how much farther is it?" Nick asked with a complaining attitude, "I'm gettin' fuckin' tired!"

"Well, I'm not sure," responded the other Nick, "let's see, if this is 63rd Street, and we have to go to 92nd Street, how many blocks is that?"

"That's thirty blocks, man!" Nick answered.

Nick was tired and irritable, but there was not much of a choice but to continue.

It was eleven o'clock when the Nicks approached 92nd and Cottage Grove Avenue. Unknown to them, at some point, they had missed a turn and followed the wrong street car tracks.

"This is 92nd, we gotta turn here don't we?" Nick asked.

"Yeah, I guess so," the other Nick replied with uncertainty.

They turned east on 92nd and walked a half dozen blocks to a dead end.

"Hey man, there ain't no more fuckin' street, what do we do now?" Nick asked.

The other Nick already lost for some time answered, "I don't know, I've never been around here before."

They jumped over a short wire fence and into a swamp that they had failed to see in the pitch darkness. There feet sunk to above their ankles into soft, slimy mud hidden by tall weeds. A slope banked upward just beyond the fence. Climbing the embankment they discovered a rail bed running north and south. In the dark they made out another track a few feet from the first. Straining their eyes they could make out the outlines of buildings and large machinery across the tracks.

"I ain't crossing these tracks." Nick said.

"Look, there's a bridge, there's cars goin' under it!" shouted the other Nick.

The boys walked in the direction of the viaduct where car lights could be seen as they seemed to float across the underside of the track.

Arriving at the stone and cement bridge they scrambled down a path along the embankment leading to the street below. A street car passed as they reached the sidewalk.

Francisca and the Boys

"Look, we're on 95th, this goes all the way through!" commented the other Nick.

"Let's rest a while, I'm fuckin' tired," Nick told his buddy.

The two sat on the sidewalk, knees popped up, backs resting against the stone wall that held up the bridge. It was well past midnight but the boys were not yet sure of the time. More lights could be seen down the street toward their final destination.

"That's gotta be Stoney Island over there, where all the lights are at," the other Nick said, "we're not too far now!"

He tried soothing Nick's discomfort, still feeling guilty for having caused their predicament in the first place.

The boys removed their shoes and pounded them on the sidewalk to remove the mud that was slowly drying and caking on the outside. They removed their socks and shook them as well.

"Look, I got mud on my feet all the way inside, and it stinks, how about you?" Nick commented.

"Yeah, me too," the other Nick answered.

The two Nicks looked at each other and suddenly the whole situation became very funny.

"Nobody will ever believe this shit," Nick said, "we walk a thousand fuckin' miles just because we're short one fuckin' lousy penny!"

Nick laughed as he complained.

The other Nick felt relieved to hear his buddy laugh, things were not so serious after all. He also laughed but without comment.

"Come on, let's get the fuck outta here!" Nick said as they stood up.

"Ok, I'm ready," the other Nick remarked.

The pair continued their march in the direction of the lights to the east.

Finally arriving at Commercial Avenue and 95th Street, the boys turned north and crossed under the viaduct that supported the Northern and Western Railroad tracks, incidentally, the same tracks that they had encountered during their mud stepping experience at the 92nd Street dead end.

Most businesses on Commercial were closed except for a tavern or two, and White Castle Hamburgers. The pair looked through the plate glass door at White Castle. There was one customer at the counter.

"Man, I could sure use one of those little shitty hamburgers right now!" exclaimed the other Nick.

"Me too," countered Nick, "you got a dime?"

They laughed and continued their stroll toward home. They stopped at the corner near the school.

"Ya goin' to school tomorrow?" asked Nick.

"I don't know," the other Nick answered, "if somebody wakes me up, maybe, how about you?"

"I gotta go," Nick answered resolutely, "I don't have a choice!"

"See ya later," Nick said

"See ya," responded the other Nick, as they parted.

The electric signs were still burning brightly at El Jalisco, it was not yet 2:00am, the closing hour. It didn't much matter, for Francisca was at home convalescing from her injuries resulting from the ordeal of the week before.

Nick would have to face Francisca sooner or later. He thought of what he might tell her when the time came. After a pensive moment he came to a conclusion, he would tell the truth even if it would be the hardest thing to believe.

As it turned out, Nick had to explain nothing, since no one was awake at the time of his arrival. Francisca was sound asleep in her bedroom with little Sylvia cuddled next to her with the door closed. Lupe was not home yet, and Davy only stirred as Nick tiptoed into the house.

Nick had removed his shoes before entering, and sat on a chair to remove his muddy socks. He took off his socks and tossed them behind the couch. He hoped to hide them temporarily in hopes that no one would find them before the day was over.

He slid slowly into bed next to Davy, who never became aware of Nick's presence during the night.

Minutes later Nick heard the front door open. It was Lupe coming in from a night out. Now Nick realized that he had made it home just in time to avoid questioning about his whereabouts of the night before. He would relate his experiences to Davy later. Nick fell asleep.

Nick's eyelids were heavy the next morning as he attempted to open his eyes. He raised his head in an effort to get out of bed but dropped back on the pillow closing them once again. With a greater effort he finally sat up. He looked around for the clock, finding it across the room on a table. It was seven thirty. He could sleep one more hour and still get to school on time, but he thought better of it. It would be best to just get up and act normal and go about the business of getting ready for school.

Davy had been up for sometime and was on his way out. Bowen High School was about eight to ten block distance and Davy must walk. He would make his first class with time to spare.

Francisca prepared hot oatmeal for Sylvia while she waited for her coffee pot to boil.

Lupe's bedroom door was closed indicating that she was in a sound sleep and evidently did not wish to be disturbed.

Nick took up a corner of the kitchen table to set up ironing pads for pressing his shirt and pants. The ironing routine had not changed from how he was taught at a very early age, except that now the iron was electric and did not have to be heated up on top of the stove.

Nick washed his face in cold water in an effort to eliminate the drowsiness that persisted. Before leaving the house he took a bowl of oatmeal and diluted it with milk, so that he was able to drink it down without stopping.. He went off to school hoping to be able to stay awake in class. Nick was successful.

Francisca was back to work and Nick and Davy would return to their way of life on the streets of South Chicago.

On one particular Friday evening the guys stood around on the corner, laughing and joking and jostling one another as usual, when one of the guys came up with the bright idea of going looking for a fight.

With mention of a fight, Nick suggested, "Let's go over to Commercial and look for Polacks!" suddenly remembering his conversation with the other Nick concerning his ouster from the YMCA building.

"Yeah, let's go!" the other Nick concurred.

"I'll go!" Lonny volunteered.

Joe, the oldest of the group, and also the respected leader, more or less, offered a warning.

"All you guys are gonna do is get your ass in a sling. If you don't get your ass kicked you'll get thrown in the can!" Joe told the guys.

"So what, nobody's gonna catch us!" Lonny retorted as he alternately rubbed each knuckle with an open hand.

"We need another guy," the other Nick said, "come on with us Oscar."

Oscar, who was considered the toughest guy in the group, and who also had a little more sense, would not commit himself but he was certainly aching for a fight.

"Come on, Osc," Nick said. "Just in case we run into some big guys."

Oscar needed no more coaxing, he capitulated showing feigned reluctance.

"Ok," Oscar finally agreed, "let's go!"

The four went west to Commercial Avenue, the neighborhood shopping area. They didn't have to go very far before spotting a tall gangly looking youth walking toward them from the far corner.

"There's a guy, he's coming this way!" Lonny said.

"Don't scare him away," Oscar told the guys, "let's cross the street until he gets to the alley, then we'll jump him. Nicky, you go meet him by the alley and start the fight."

"Ok," Nick agreed, "but don't leave me alone too long, that guy's kinda big, he'll kick my ass!"

The youth and Nick walked toward each other, closing in on the alley between Commercial and Houston Avenues. The rest of the guys walked on the other side of the street waiting for the action to unfold.

Nick reached the mouth of the alley first and stopped. The youth, unaware of what was about to transpire, walked nonchalantly down the street holding a gym bag in one hand. On reaching the alley he was confronted by Nick, now intentionally blocking the way.

"Whatcha got in the bag, Polack?" Nick asked him.

"Gym clothes, and I ain't a Polack!" responded the kid. "What do you want?"

Nick pushed the kid hard against a garage door and reached for the bag.

The boy recovered and grabbed Nick by the shoulder, and in turn, shoved Nick against the garage door. Nick dropped the gym bag as he slid down the garage door to the pavement from the force of the push.

"I don't want to fight," the youth pleaded, "I ain't got nothing against you!"

By this time the rest of the guys appeared on the scene. Each guy took a turn in pushing and shoving the youth.

"Wait a minute," the boy continued to plead, "I'll fight anyone of you guys, I can't fight all of you at the same time!"

The guys stopped the shoving and looked at each other, all eyes rested on Oscar. Oscar took up the Challenge, after all, he was the toughest of the bunch, He was not about to blemish his reputation.

Oscar had received instruction in the art of self defense and had even boxed amateur in the ring for the CYO. This would be the time for him to prove his worth.

Oscar was short, husky and muscular, and packed a pretty good punch, but in this case, the difference in the height of the opponents would tell the tail.

The young man was at least six feet tall and seemed at least two heads taller than Oscar. Oscar was lucky to measure five and a half feet in height.

The pair stepped into the alley so as not to attract attention. They eyed each other as they began to spar by bobbing and weaving. The difference in height of the combatants presented a humorous combination.

Suddenly Oscar attacked, ducking under the long arms of the other boy and landed several punches to the mid-section and to the ribs. The boy withstood the punches and covered up the pain by keeping a straight face.

Oscar stepped back and prepared for another attack. As Oscar lunged forward, the kid stuck out his left hand, landing a jab directly on Oscar's nose. He stepped back one step, then came forward again, landing two more jabs in succession on Oscar's nose. The nose cracked under the punishment from the tall boy, and an unstoppable flow of blood was released by way of Oscar's nostrils. Again and again the boy hit Oscar on the nose with his left jab. In the last series of punches, the boy stepped in with a one-two punch, landing a left and a right on the battered nose once more.

In the few minutes that the boys had been fighting, the tall boy had clearly and decisively beaten up on Oscar, leaving his face a bloody pulp.

The youth finally asked Oscar if he had enough.

Reluctantly, Oscar said yes, but in turn he asked, "How about you?"

The boy nodded his head and dropped his arms to his sides and stepped back. Oscar did the same. The fight was over and quickly the guys went to offer aid to Oscar, who at this point was in dire need of assistance.

"Hold your head back and the blood will stop," Nick suggested.

The tall kid pulled a towel from his bag and offered it to Oscar, who accepted gladly and immediately pressed it against his bleeding nose.

Francisca and the Boys

"If your not a Polack, what are you?" Nick asked the boy.

"I'm Irish," the boy responded with a smile and walked away.

Oscar's eyes began to swell. He felt his proboscis gently with his finger tips, trying to determine the amount of damage inflicted upon his nose. The bones or cartilage were grinding as he moved the nose from side to side. His nose had been broken and re-broken several times before.

Everyone praised Oscar for a good fight that, according to the guys, nobody won. He would never admit to losing anyway, but he did not claim victory.

For all practical purposes it was called a draw by all the guys.

Oscar's ego was still intact, and he was still the toughest guy on the corner, with no one daring to dispute it.

The guys walked slowly to the corner across the street from the church.

Oscar headed for home with his outer wounds needing attention and his inner soul needing consoling.

SEVENTEEN

The year 1938 arrived, and to no ones surprise, Nick followed his brother's footsteps when graduation time came around. He joined the tomato pickers and also missed his graduation from J. N. Thorpe School in June of that year. His diploma was also delivered by the U.S. Postal Service and he would become eligible for entry to Bowen High School the following September.

With Francisca's permission Davy took a bus to Eaton, Colorado to spend the summer working in the beet fields, where now he could earn a full man's pay and contribute to the support of the family as a whole.

Lupe, after scouring newspaper want ads, finally landed a job with the Florsheim Shoe Company near the downtown area of Chicago. It would pay thirty five cents per hour, totaling, to perhaps fifteen dollars weekly. The difficulty would arise in traveling to and from the job by streetcar, which would take one hour each way of traveling time.

Lupe took up the challenge with enthusiasm, for getting a job of any kind in these hard times was extremely difficult.

For Lupe, having a job and being somewhat independent after four or so years of marriage, it was a new and exciting experience. She now had the freedom that had escaped her during the years that she should have been growing into adulthood, instead of being saddled with a marriage that she had been too young to cope with in the first place.

But such were the times, as each individual member of the Delmonte family struggled toward an imaginary goal that was vague and uncertain.

Lupe became acquainted with neighborhood girls of her age, or near her age group. She was usually a year or more older than the average eighteen or nineteen year old. Lupe, being of small stature, did not appear to be any older than most of the girls, and she would never confess to being the oldest nor the more mature of the group.

On Sunday afternoons the girls would play softball in the school yard, eventually forming a team which they named the "Amapolas", in deference to the poppy flower, and to the song "Amapola", so popular at the time.

Games would be scheduled with surrounding area teams, such as the west side of Chicago and Indiana Harbor, Indiana, at times referred to as East Chicago.

On occasion, little Sylvia would want to go watch her mother play ball. That was fine with Lupe, as long as Sylvia would adhere to a promise.

"Remember," Lupe would say to Sylvia, "when I play ball, I'm your big sister, and here at home I'm your mama. Can you remember that?"

Sylvia would laugh and say, "Ok, mama!"

Lupe looked for an even chance in the competition for dates with the local guys, and a young woman with a child would have a first strike against her. The competition was very strong.

Lupe would date for the next couple of years with no intentions of getting seriously involved with anyone. She was enjoying her freedom and planned to stretch it as far as possible.

Inevitably, Lupe's life would change considerably. She knew very well that she would not remain single too much longer. There were men out there, but she had to be very careful when deciding to pick a partner.

Lupe's life continued in a pattern that was routinely the same from day to day and week to week. She would go to work, go out on weekends, play ball on Sundays, date now and then, and hang around with the girlfriends when it suited her.

Lupe laughed and fought with the same vigor that Francisca displayed when happy or angry. She had inherited that mean demeanor that was so apparent in Francisca, and was not afraid to express herself in the same manner as her mother.

The job at Chon's Bar and Grill in Denver, that Lupe had inherited from her mother, gave her experiences normally attributed to much older women. Lupe, therefore, had become established in the alcohol culture of her contemporary generation. The nightclub or the neighborhood Bar would be the culmination of an evening of fun and frolic.

Her new job now afforded Lupe a night out on any given weekend and she took advantage of the opportunities whenever possible. At times she would return home in her cups, but never to an extent that she did not have her wits about her. On occasion there would be a girl friend of Lupe's that would come home with her and stay overnight after a night out.

On one particular Sunday morning after a Saturday night of celebrating Lupe was accompanied by a girlfriend coming home, both girls slightly inebriated and having an excitedly happy time. The loud laughing and giggling caused Nick to budge a little as he lay in his couch-bed, but not enough to awaken him completely.

"Who's that?" Lupe's friend asked as she pointed at Nick.

"That's my little brother!" replied Lupe as she turned on a table lamp.

Nick raised his head enough to look at the girls with his squinty eyes and immediately rolled over and closed them again.

Hortense, Lupe's friend, took a closer look at Nick and remarked, "Oh, he's cute!"

The girls retired to Lupe's bedroom, still laughing and joking as they went to bed. Before long the fun of the evening came to an end for Lupe, who went into a deep and sound sleep. Hortense purposely remained awake, for she had designs on Lupe's little brother.

While Lupe slept, Hortense left the bed in search of the bathroom. On her way back she stopped at Nick's bedside.

Looking down at him she decided at that very moment that she would like to join him.

Wearing nothing more than her slip, Hortense gently slid in under the sheet and into Nick's bed. Nick, half asleep, complained at the intrusion as the young woman's arms slowly encircled his waistline.

"Davy, what the....!" Nick suddenly cut his words short in realizing that Davy was not at home. He turned to face the intruder.

Hortense gently covered his mouth with one hand and held a finger to her lips in a sign for Nick to be quiet. By the moonlight penetrating the window panes, Nick could vaguely see Hortense's extraordinarily pretty features. The odor of makeup and perfume, and a slight mixture of the smell of alcohol on her breath, plus the warmth of her body next to his, gave Nick the ultimate sensation of sexual arousal.

Hortense took Nick's chin in one hand and held his face steady. She placed her lips on his, kissing him roughly while running her tongue in and out of his throat.

Nick was no longer in a mood to complain. He decided to let nature take its course.

Before Nick could utter a word, Hortense pulled down his shorts and took his genitalia in her hand. Nick's penis was completely erect. Hortense moved her face to his chest, kissing and sucking on his skin as she moved downward. Nick held his breath and said nothing.

Nick had now experienced oral sex for the very first time. The young woman quietly left his bed as Nick looked upward and very softly whispered, "Wow!"

This would go on his list of non-confessing sins. No mortal man would ever hear of this except, of course, his brother Davy.

Eventually, Nick attended Bowen High School and dropped out after completing a little more than a year of the required curriculum.

He convinced his mother that a job was of more importance than attending school. Francisca, seeing the logic in her son's argument, complied with his request for freedom to look for a job. But jobs for sixteen year olds were not in abundance, so Nick was destined to wander the streets for a few more months.

Nick was outgrowing his penchant for roaming the streets of South Chicago. The necessity for supplementary aid to the family had slowly diminished with contributions that Lupe and Davy were now making. Now he was spending more time alone. Nick dug deep into his subconscious mind. What was life really all about?

Still hanging around on the corner with the guys, Nick began to take note of how each of his pals handled their personal lives.

Some depended entirely on family, doing nothing to help their own cause, not even attending public school. Others, like his friend Caldo, continued their particular methods of survival by stealing.

For Nick it had been exciting when he was robbing porches and breaking into stores, but now he felt that those actions were actions of a boy who now seemed distant. He condoned what he did in the past with the excuse that it was done by necessity. It no longer felt good to do, and the necessity was no longer a factor. He sensed that somehow he had outgrown the past and that there had to be a future. He thought about going back to school, but to spend three more years in High School was not very appealing. In spite of himself, Nick was growing into adulthood.

One day, in a conversation with Joe, the recognized leader of the guys on the corner, Nick thought he might have found a solution to his dilemma.

"How did you get your job?" Nick asked Joe.

Joe worked nights as a busboy and dishwasher in a downtown restaurant and was learning to be a full fledged waiter.

"A guy I know that works there helped me get the job," Joe answered.

"I quit school and now I gotta find a job," Nick said.

"Man, Nicky, you should of never done that!" Joe told him. "There ain't no jobs out there, especially for young guys like you, how old are you?"

"I'll be seventeen in a few weeks," Nick answered.

"You gotta be at least eighteen to land any kind of a job," Joe told him.

Nick pondered Joe's words, wondering at that specific moment whether to return to school or not. He still had the opportunity to return if he so decided. He also had the desire to learn, but not to attend daily classes in a boring routine that continued day in and day out.

"Why don't you join the C's?" Joe asked.

"What's the C's?" Nick asked in turn.

"It's government camps for guys seventeen to twenty one," Joe answered.

"What do you do there, how much do they pay?" Nick continued his questioning of Joe.

"You work out in the open and get paid the same as the army,"

"I don't wanna join no fuckin' army!" Nick said with a laugh.

"Naw, it ain't the army," Joe said, "It's run by the army, you join for six months then you're out, unless you sign over. They pay twenty one bucks a month besides your clothes and food."

"That don't sound so bad," Nick said, "maybe I'll check it out."

The Civilian Conservation Corps was one of many programs that President Roosevelt had initiated at the start of his administration in the early 1930's. This particular program had been designed to give young adult males the opportunity to become socially productive, and simultaneously give the country the resources needed to rebuild after a long and devastating depression.

The Corp became commonly known by its abbreviation as the CCC, or by what it was called by the recruits as simply the C's.

Much like the WPA, or Workers Projects Administration, which had been designed by the Government to give jobs to heads of families, the CCC trained young men in such things as building dams and roads, cutting trees, and fighting forest fires. Above all, the Corps was very effective in teaching discipline Army style.

At home Nick presented the situation to his mother.

"I think it's a real good idea," Francisca said rather enthusiastically, "why don't you join and see how you like it?"

"I'll be gone for six months, ma!" Nick told her in a not so enthusiastic tone. He felt his mother was too quick to agree.

"It will do you some good," she told him, "at least it will get you off the streets and I won't have to be worrying about you all the time!"

Nick now knew that Francisca would back him in his decision to join the Corps. So his next step would be to travel downtown to the recruiting office to sign up and to bring back the necessary papers for his mother to sign.

By early August of 1939 Nick was aboard a passenger train on his way to La Crosse, Wisconsin, where he and his fellow recruits would transfer onto US Army trucks that would carry them to Camp McCoy, Wisconsin.

Davy would be returning from his second year of working in the Colorado beet fields, but that would not be until December. Nick, therefore, would not see his brother for another few months.

There was so much to discuss between the boys, information that could not be shared with anyone else. Each boy looked forward to seeing the other but that would not take place in the immediate future.

Davy was in the process of honoring his commitment to the crew that was now headed by Alvino, his aunt Lucy's husband. They were working from dawn to dusk every day, with Sundays off. By the end of the season, ending in mid November, Davy would return to Chicago with a few well earned dollars in his pocket.

Francisca and the Boys

Davy enjoyed working in the fields and it seemed that the harder the job the more vigorously he would apply himself. But his vision for the future did not include field work. Eventually he would land a job in Chicago and make a life for himself. He would turn nineteen before his return home and he vowed not to come back to Colorado as a field worker ever again

With the threat of war, jobs in the mid-west were beginning to open up in the steel mills and foundries. Finding a job in Chicago would not be a problem for Davy.

Back in Eaton, however, Davy had blended into a group of families that had been brought together by common ideals. He was given room and board by his aunt Lucy for a minimal consideration, thus avoiding the bunkhouse where other workers were housed.

Manuel, the youngest of the Martinez Brothers, and Davy had become fast friends over the last couple of years, and for good reason.

Davy's cousin, Mary, the eldest of Lucy's children had been romantically involved with Manuel for a year or more and were already making plans for the coming marriage. Davy paired off with Manuel's younger sister, Rosy, and the four would sometimes go dancing where ever there happened to be something to celebrate. Romance for Davy was not yet a possibility, so at this point in his life he still avoided being tied down. However, his sexual drive was alive and well.

When there was no particular reason for going out, Davy and Manuel would sit in La Cantina and drink a few beers on their tabs, usually on Sunday afternoons when their was not much going on. On one of these Sundays the bar of La Cantina was filled with patrons with the usual noise and the juke box playing very loud.

At the opposite end of the bar was a group of men, drinking and arguing and discussing whatever drunks discuss. The jukebox had suddenly stopped playing. One of the men stepped to the jukebox and dropped in a few nickels for the music to continue.

On his way back to his seat, the man stopped at the end of the bar where Davy and Manuel sat.

"Hi, you guys, how are you?" he asked, but not in a very friendly way.

"Ok Tony!" Manuel answered.

The man was wearing a tight fitting polo shirt, neatly pressed black dress pants, and brown shiny loafers. He was looking like a male model out of a magazine. His arms were muscular, and he had a flat, wide nose, showing all the signs of a professional boxer.

"I know you," he said to Manuel, "but I've never seen this guy before!" He pointed a finger at Davy.

"This is my cousin Davy, we work together. He's here from Chicago for the summer season," Manuel explained, making Davy his cousin in the process.

Davy had felt the animosity this guy was releasing. He prepared himself for an altercation but he would try to avoid it if he could, he turned away facing the bar and took a sip of his beer.

"Oh, Chicago gangster, huh?" Tony commented sarcastically.

With that comment Davy turned and pointed a finger at the intruder and said, "Get the fuck outa my face before I lose my temper!"

Tony smiled and said, "Would you like to step outside?"

Davy's temper was already at a boiling point. He answered, Fuckin aye, let's go!"

Manuel attempted to hold Davy back by the arm, saying, "Don't go out with him Davy, he's the--"

Davy pulled his arm away, not hearing or even paying attention to what Manuel had to say.

The pair stepped out into the street with Tony in the lead. Manuel followed closely behind, hoping to stop a fight he was sure Davy would lose. Finally seeing Davy's determination to continue, Manuel threw up his hands and gave up trying to stop the potential action.

Tony took his stance with arms and fists up looking every bit the fighter that he was.

Davy, with both hands low in front of him just stood and moved them from side to side. Davy then stepped back and dropped his hands down to his sides, in a sign that he was not going to fight at all. At that, Tony also dropped his hands figuring there would be no fight.

Suddenly Davy turned and faced his opponent along with a swinging overhand right that landed square on Tony's jaw. Tony went down and out.

"Come on, let's get outa here!" Manuel told Davy.

As Manuel and Davy walked toward home Manuel said, "Do you know who that guy was?"

"Hell no," Davy said, "just another fuckin' asshole as far as I'm concerned!"

"Davy," Manuel said with excitement in his voice, "you just knocked out Tony Penco, the Rocky Mountain Welterweight Champion!"

Davy laughed and said, "No shit, really?"

Manuel assured him that what he was saying was the truth.

Davy clenched his right fist and looking at it he said, "That was a pretty good right, wasn't it?"

The two laughed hysterically.

Davy's notoriety spread through towns and farms where field workers congregated.

At Saturday night dances Davy became very popular with the girls once they knew that he was the guy that knocked out the champ. Davy reveled in all the attention and took advantage by making dates, and in many cases, satisfying his aforementioned sex drive in the process.

Topping season arrived in late November, and in three weeks time the contract was satisfied and closed. Davy was paid for the full season. He paid his tab at La Cantina and a week before Christmas he was on a Greyhound Bus to Chicago.

* * *

At Camp McCoy, the recruits were issued summer and winter clothing. For dress they were issued khaki, and denim fatigues for work. They were assigned to companies and to barracks by number and to bunks in alphabetical order. The training at Camp McCoy consisted of all necessary methods in sustaining one's own person, such as the washing of individual clothing, sweeping and scrubbing down barracks, making of bunks, and keeping up personal health habits. Marching and exercise drills were part of the early morning routine before the call to breakfast.

All training at CCC camps were, in effect, the same as the regular army except that no fire arms were ever present. After two weeks of preliminary training, all trainees were shipped to parts of the country where they were most needed.

Nick's first assignment was to Elko, Nevada, where he would join CCC veterans in the building of roads and dams. Nick's pay was equal to that of a regular army private, at twenty one dollars per month. His cash dole on paydays amounted to five dollars, while the balance of sixteen dollars was sent home to Francisca as per prior arrangement.

Five dollars per month were enough to cover such necessities as tooth paste, soap, razor blades and shaving soap. Incidental items such as candy and Bull Durham smoking tobacco were included. It was cheaper to pay five cents for a bag of Bull Durham than ten cents for a pack of cigarettes, and it lasted longer. After all necessities were accounted for, Nick always had the two dollars he would need to visit the brothels in town.

The first three months of Nick's six month "hitch" were spent at the Elko camp, where he soon became very proficient in shoveling dirt and pushing a loaded wheelbarrow, and at breaking hard rock with pick and sledge hammer.

The work was hard and tiring, but with the aches and pains that were consistently apparent after a day's work, it was still satisfying to an extent.

Nick's life was slowly changing as he matured from a skinny little runt to a strong and healthy young man. He would sometimes stand in front of a mirror to look at his upper body. It was still skinny, but a little more sinewy if not completely muscular.

Every so often there would be a surprise "short-arm" inspection The short arm inspection consisted of dropping the pants for inspection of the genitalia by the doctor or other medical personnel on duty.

A group of a half a dozen or so recruits would enter the dispensary at one time. "Alright, line up and drop your pants, skin it back and milk it twice," the medical assistant would shout.

The medical assistant, a tall thin youth with a long sharp nose and very squinty eyes, wore a perpetual smile during short-arm inspection. He had a gold tooth that glistened as long as the smile was in place. He seemed to take great pleasure in doing the inspection, making Nick fidgety and uncomfortable when his turn came around.

There was always joking going on during inspection among the group, to which the doctor would react by saying, "Save the jokes for the barracks!" There were rumors that the doctor and the assistant were an item. The snickering would continue.

Anyone having been in town during a specific recreational period was required to appear for inspection to insure that no venereal disease was contracted during visits with the prostitutes in town.

Although condoms were issued to recruits, and the ladies in town were regularly inspected, the inspection of recruits was done for purposes of assurance.

Time went by normally for Nick. As friendships would build, so would animosities. He soon became comfortable that he was not the only Mexican in camp. In any case, he felt that he was no different than the average guy, but there were others who thought differently.

One morning at reveille, all recruits jumped out of their bunks to prepare for call to breakfast. Everyone rushed to latrines to claim a washbowl for shaving and brushing,

Nick arrived at an empty sink moments before another fellow who, unfortunately, had his eye on the same sink. As Nick was about to put his toothbrush into his mouth, he was given a shove that sent him sprawling to the cement floor.

"I was here first!" announced the pusher.

Nick recognized the intruder as a fellow recruit who bunked in the same barracks just a few beds down the line from his own. His name was Donato

After hitting the floor, Nick rolled over and stood up at once.

"Oh no, not another Dago," he said to himself, *"what is it with these Italians?"*

He remembered the fights with the Spino kids in Denver.

Donato had the kind of upper body that Nick often thought of having himself someday. Broad shoulders, thick forearms, and biceps that bulged without flexing. Nick and his new adversary were the same height

Suddenly Nick was engulfed with fear at the sight of this guy, but there was also anger that he could not control. He thought again, *"Now what the fuck do I do?"*

Anger, overpowering fear, took precedence in Nick's mental state. He went back to the washbowl and shoved Donato, pushing him away from the sink, but with nowhere near the force that his opponent had used on him.

"This is my fuckin' sink.!" Nick shouted.

The fight began in earnest with a sudden uproar in the bathroom. Donato attacked Nick with flying fists without pattern but landing hard all around Nick's head. Nick tried ducking, but to no avail, the punches continued to land on his head. Finally, stepping back from close quarters, Nick bobbed and weaved and landed a few punches of his own including an overhand right that landed squarely on the other guy's left eye.

The two rolled to the floor, wrestling and punching with Nick losing ground and about to lose the fight. Suddenly a pair of army boots appeared near their heads.

"Alright, cut the shit!" shouted the '36'.

Francisca and the Boys

Thirty six was the rank equivalent to a an army corporal and designating the monthly pay of thirty six dollars per month.

The '36,' standing at about six feet two or three, toward over the combatants. He was dark of complexion and had short, black, wavy hair.

Taking each boy by an arm he stood them up and spoke in a calm firm voice, "If you guys don't stop this bullshit, you'll both end up in the stockade. Now shake hands and go about your business. I don't want to write you guys up, but I will if I have to."

The uproar and confusion that was caused by the encounter soon died down. The latrine was calm and quiet.

Nick, with verification from others who had seen the fight from the beginning, was awarded the washbowl by the thirty six.

Donato walked away in search of an empty washbowl.

Once again Nick started to prepare his toiletry for the morning routine. After brushing his teeth and combing his hair he would shave his face whether he needed it or not. All recruits had to shave daily by orders of the Camp Commander.

As Nick looked into the mirror he saw the reflection of the '36'go by. He glanced at Nick with a quick smile, that to Nick was a sign of approval. Nick believed he had made a friend.

As it turned out, the '36' was a Puerto Rican from New York City who spoke only English by choice, as did Nick. There would be no close friendship, but there was an understanding of sorts between the two thereafter.

Donato also became a friend after a second encounter behind the mess hall. While Nick was completing his assignment of KP duty one day, he was dumping garbage into the large containers outside in back of the kitchen. Suddenly he was startled by a loud voice, "Hey, Delmonte!" It was Donato.

Holding the empty garbage bucket in his hand and ready to use it in self defense if necessary, Nick was ready for a second fight.

Donato raised both hands with palms out and said, "Hold it, Delmonte, I came to apologize, I just want to be friends!"

"Ok, if you're sure!" Nick said rather dubiously.

"I'm sure, man," replied Donato "You're a Dago aren't you?"

"Naw, why?" Nick answered.

"No reason," Donato answered, "you must be Spanish then."

Nick was beginning to get peeved by all the questioning and was on the verge of losing his patience.

"I'm Mexican," Nick said, "but what the hell's the difference what I am?"

Donato noticed anger building in Nick's facial expression.

"Look, we're almost the same anyway so let's forget about all this other shit!"

Nick's anger almost reached a limit when he said, " No, we're not almost the same, we're not even close to the same. You're you and I'm me and there's a lot of difference!" Nick was prepared to go at it one more time if need be.

"Ok, ok," Donato exclaimed " I'm sorry about everything, let's start over!"

He stuck out his hand to shake, and finally Nick accepted the truce and shook Donato's hand.

Once more they continued a conversation and exchanged information from back home. It turned out that both were from Chicago, Nick from the far south side and Donato from the near west side at Taylor and Halsted Streets, reputed to be the toughest section of all Chicago.

Now Nick understood the reason for the rough and tumble attitude that Donato carried. On Taylor and Halsted, if you could not take care of yourself physically, or be speedy of foot, then you were in for an "ass kicking".

In the long run, Nick decided it was best to become friends, this way he would not have to always keep looking behind his back.

By early December all friendships were dissolved. The inclement weather would no longer permit working on roads or dams, and the forest fire season had ended. The Elko camp was dissolved and all recruits were transferred to camps in other parts of the country.

Nick would find himself traveling northeast by train once more, to a town called Kemmerer, Wyoming.

The Kemmerer camp would turn out to be a hell that Nick, never in his darkest dreams, ever thought might exist.

It was a cold morning when the half dozen recruits disembarked from the ever present US Army vehicles. They were escorted to their new quarters and advised to hurry and settle down, for that very morning they would be indoctrinated into their new duties.

"Be sure to wear 'long johns' and two pair of pants" was the advice given by the '36' in charge, "you have exactly one hour to be ready!" There was finality in his voice.

The boys unpacked after selecting their bunks and proceeded to follow instructions.

Nick decided to wear one pair of pants only, since the long underwear was thick enough to ward off the cold. He would soon find that wearing two pair of pants was an integral part of the job.

The army truck pulled up in front of the Administration Building on the main street of the camp. The '36' in charge issued the order for the men to fall in next to the truck. This done, he then handed each man a pair of heavy canvas gloves with high wrist guards.

"You're going to need these once you get started, and I would advise you to wear the heavy boots when working on this project," the '36' told them. He continued, "You will have just one day to learn the job so you will have to pay close attention. After today you will be on your own. You are relieving the men that will instruct you for today.

The men boarded the truck and were on their way. After fifteen minutes of highway travel the truck turned off a side road and came to a stop. The truck was covered by a canvas tarpaulin, therefore the passengers were unable to see exactly where their journey had ended. The smell of tar and oil was very strong even before the truck came to a stop. The rear gate to the truck was dropped and the men filed out.

Nick noticed that the ground in the immediate area was black and thick with oil. As they stepped out, they looked around and spotted what they presumed would be their station.

A huge steel tank held up by a steel and iron frame stood in open farmland. A crane as high as a two story house was alongside with a long telephone pole in a grip that pulled the pole out of the creosote filled tank. The boiling hot liquid dripped from the pole and splashed in all directions.

The tank was at least fifty feet in length and about twelve feet across. A steel mesh walkway, about two and a half feet wide completely surrounded the tank. A waist high railing was built along the inner side of the walkway. It resembled a swimming pool, except that the liquid in the six feet deep tank was melted tar and oil.

Some days there would be telephone poles to dip, other days there would be railroad ties, depending on orders.

The new guys climbed the ladder to the walkway where they were met by the retiring crew, and before long Nick and the rest of the guys were dipping poles and logs in creosote.

By the end of the day Nick's pants were soaked in the greasy stuff and he could feel the burning sensation on his skin from the waist down. The creosote had penetrated to the lower half of his body.

By the end of two weeks Nick thought of going AWOL even if it meant hitch hiking his way home. That would not be necessary because, unknown to him and the rest of the crew, there was a two week limit of working on the creosote tank for everyone, as set by the Commanding Officer.

A new crew would arrive before long and Nick would be assigned to another project.

However, the hot tar had done its damage. Nick and the rest of the crew had to be treated for burns and blisters of the lower body, the face, neck and scalp.

The clothing that had been worn by the crew on this job would be burned and replaced by new issue.

If there was a Hell on Earth, Nick had finally found it at the creosote tank.

Christmas was around the corner and Nick was feeling homesick. There had been no communication with anyone at home for some time. Nick was feeling sorry for himself, but he was not alone. There were several guys in the same situation. Some of the old crew members got together to plan a little Christmas party in the barracks.

They solicited the services of Kruczewski, one of the permanent truck drivers in the camp. Kruczewski had just reached the age of discharge with the option of leaving the C's for home or joining the regular army. He was twenty-one.

Kruczewski was a short, muscular young man with straight, bright blond hair and blue eyes. He pronounced his name 'Kra-shef-ski' and he would correct anyone that called him "Kra-zoo-ski'. He was a veteran of the C's and had been in the Corps since its inception and had reached the pay scale of $36.00 per month. He was called Kru by all who knew him.

With Christmas still a few days away, Kru, making several trips into town brought in a fifth of rum, two bottles of wine, and a case of beer for the coming party.

Kru was paid for his services by each guy chipping in a share.

More than half the camp went on leave for the holidays.

The '36' in charge warned everyone to keep their noses clean. There would be someone from the Administration Building in charge while he was gone. With tongue in cheek he said, "When you go to the canteen for your Coke, you tell the guy to give you all the ice you need"

The attendant already had the word.

On Christmas Eve, everyone sat around the potbellied stove singing Christmas carols and getting drunk with their choice of liquid.

Nick did not care for the taste of beer, and after having his bad experience with wine, he opted for rum and coke. Three six ounce glasses of the mixture later, Nick was ready to pass out. A little after midnight he 'hit the sack.'

On waking Christmas morning Nick found that he had just a touch of a hangover. He decided from here on, rum and coke would be his drink. New Years Day came and left with the usual festivities By the last week of February, 1940, Nick was on a train back to Chicago. His 'hitch' in the C's had been completed and, after expenses, he still had thirteen dollars in his pocket.

EIGHTEEN

Francisca had now reached her fortieth year of life, and to date had not been able to accomplish her goal of establishing her own business. At times she would go into a state of depression wondering if the dream would ever become a reality. She had managed to add to her savings and felt that she might now be in a position to take the plunge. But how and where would she initiate the process?

Francisca was into her third year as a waitress at El Jalisco and was now a trusted employee. She had been given the freedom and the opportunity to run the entire business from all its aspects, giving Frank the bartender time off that he so desperately needed.

Frank was Francisca's greatest source of information regarding the liquor business as a whole, for he had become one of her closest male friends without a romantic attachment. He introduced her to local business men and politicians who, in turn, directed her to the right people to talk to in regard to her aspirations. Francisca, no stranger to political type maneuvering, quickly caught on to the do's and don't's of the liquor business.

By mid 1940, Francisca moved the entire family to the near West Side of Chicago, not far from the center of the liquor and restaurant industry in the city.

From Halsted Street west, for more than a mile, and from Madison Street south for another mile, there were restaurants, bars and nightclubs, all night joints, and hidden enclaves of prostitution and backroom gambling. Other than the theater area of Downtown Chicago, the corner at Madison and Halsted

Streets was the hub of nightlife activity for those of lesser means and anyone with money willing to enter the territory.

Highly recommended by Frank, Francisca was hired as a waitress by one of the better known establishments along Halsted Street called El Castillo, owned and operated by old country Spaniards. This was the only bar on the street with a Spanish name, but remotely connected to anything Mexican other than its costumers.

The Mexican population of the time was settled in an area surrounding the St. Francis of Assisi Roman Catholic Church located just around the corner from El Castillo.

On Sundays, when bars were not allowed to open before noon under State law, by nine a.m. El Castillo would be filled to near capacity by Mexican husbands waiting for the families to be let out of church. Of course, the doors were locked and windows covered, but entry was offered by way of an adjoining hallway door.

Francisca's tenure at El Castillo lasted one year or more, and the knowledge and experience that she would accumulate during this period was immeasurable. She felt she was ready to take up the challenge of going on her own. She decided to take the plunge.

Davy and Nick were hired by the Inland Steel Mill in Indiana Harbor, Indiana. The pay was good, but the ride to the job from the west side of Chicago was long, approximately two hours in one direction. Transportation was a slight problem but the boys arranged to be transported by car in a share-the-ride proposition which would cost a nominal weekly fee for the sharing.

Davy's first job at the Inland Steel Mill was in new construction, where the Mill was building new blast furnaces in preparation for the expected conflict in Europe. As a laborer, his job consisted of pushing a wheelbarrow filled with fire brick to the brick layers who were building the outer walls of the new furnaces

Loading his wheelbarrow, pushing it up wooden scaffolds that were built in spiral arrangement, and unloading at the work

Francisca and the Boys

site of the bricklayers was no easy task for Davy, but he seemed to revel in it. For Davy, the harder the job, the harder he would attack it.

Nick worked alongside Davy for a month or so then he was transferred to another department by request. Nick saw no point in working so hard, particularly if there was a remedy to the situation.

However, the remedy turned to poison when he reported to his new job in the sheet mill. Here, Nick's job was to catch red hot steel sheets that were eight feet by twelve feet and two inches thick with a heavy iron fork as they rolled down on upright floor rollers. With the aid of another laborer the hot sheets were then pushed to where they would be lifted by cranes and carried to another department.

Nick wore a steel helmet with a window that covered his face and asbestos gloves as thick as baseball mittens.

Nick thought of the creosote dipping job in the CCC camp. As in the old saying, Nick went " from the frying pan into the fire". The creosote job was only the pan, the fire was in the pushing of the wheelbarrow and now the fire was only getting hotter in the sheet mill.

The Selective Service Act of 1940 had placed Nick and Davy in a position to be drafted into the Armed Forces of the United States due to the threat of war with Germany. The boys had duly registered for the draft but did not expect to be called up in the immediate future.

On December 7, 1941 a surprise attack was launched by Japan on Pearl Harbor that astounded the world. The war was closer to home now and both boys became immediate candidates to be drafted.

Lupe met and fell in love with Ben, the man of her dreams. Their marriage was imminent.

Davy was the first to receive his congratulatory notice to appear before the Draft Board. Immediately Francisca went into action by pleading before the Draft Board that her son be excused from military service. presenting to the Board how Davy was the sole support of the family. She was asked by the Board if she had any other sons of draft age. Reluctantly she admitted that she did. She was advised to have Nick report to the Draft Board, then her son David would become exempt.

On learning the news, Nick decided to take the next logical step on his own. He had already mulled over the possibilities of volunteering, for now his number would be coming up and he reserved the right to pick his choice of Service. Nick had tired of working in hell holes and nothing could be any worse than what he already knew.

One day in October of 1942, Nick, on a ruse that he was reporting to the Draft Board, decided instead to go directly to the recruiting office where he enlisted in the Navy. He always wanted to see the world and here was the opportunity. After taking the oath to serve and protect his Country, Nick was given three days to settle his affairs at home and prepare for his trip to "boot camp".

Davy was exempted from Military Service without further question.

Francisca looked ahead pondering the future. She decided she would forge her own.

NINETEEN

Davy's exploits back in Eaton were just memories now, and he no longer had a desire to return to Colorado. His job at the Inland Steel Mill was secure, which meant he would have a paycheck in his hands every other week.

The work at the mill was hard, but to Davy, it was very satisfying. He felt he was doing his share for the war effort now, and the negative feelings of guilt slowly disappeared. At times he still noticed looks of disdain from those who did not know his personal circumstances, because most young men of his age had already volunteered or had been drafted. He learned to cope by ignoring the ignorant.

The paycheck did not last too long in Davy's possession on paydays for he had a ritual that he adhered to religiously. He would collect his check, examine it, then tear off the stub. He would then endorse it and hand it over to Francisca without any qualms. Francisca, in turn, would give him a reasonable amount that both would agree upon, and the remainder would go toward household bills and savings.

Davy still spent time with the guys at Grande's Pool Room when he could. His job took up much of his time and the majority of the guys had either been drafted or had volunteered for service; thus, his partners at the pool tables now were either too old to serve or were 4F, meaning that they were not physically or mentally up to the military's standards, or, in cases where the individual was sole support of the family.

Davy was not drafted after the Draft Board was notified that his brother Nicolas had volunteered to join the Navy.

Davy turned his interests elsewhere, attending Saturday night dances and dating many of the girls that were left behind by husbands and boyfriends. Being one of the better dancers in the neighborhood, Davy was hardly ever without female companionship. At one of those Saturday night dances Davy met Isabel, one of seven beautiful sisters, and soon the courtship began.

Needless to say, the courtship continued at fever pitch, and the couple became inseparable. By early 1943, Davy and Isabel were married while Isabel was well into her pregnancy. Even so, the couple was not inclined to hurry into marriage, however, at the insistence of the ever watchful Francisca, they exchanged vows and received the Holy Sacraments of Matrimony given by the pastor at the Holy Roman Catholic Church of St. Francis of Assisi.

Soon after the wedding, the arrival of their firstborn became a fact. It was a boy, and he was duly baptized and named after his grandfather, Estanislao. His name would soon be Americanized to Stanley.

As in most marriages, the bumps of life began to appear to the couple, and as fate would have it, the first incident occurred soon after the birth of their first child. On this particular occasion on a Sunday morning while on their way to Mass, Isabel and Davy were walking down the street. As they walked, a young man coming from the opposite direction on the other side of the street crossed over to their side.

As the individual approached, Isabel turned to Davy and said, "Here comes this guy that kept pestering me to go out with him. I don't want to talk to him. Let's cross the street."

"We don't cross the street for no asshole!" Davy exclaimed with anger in his voice.

Isabel took hold of Davy's arm and held on tight as the individual came closer.

With a smile on his face, the man stepped in front of Isabel and stopped abruptly. "Hi, Iz," he said, "how you doin'?"

Francisca and the Boys

"Hello," Isabel replied trying her best not to be rude.

Davy pulled Isabel by the arm and placed her directly behind him. "Get lost before you get hurt."

"Who the fuck are you?" the intruder asked.

Davy could smell alcohol on the man's breath as he came closer, apparently, the man had been drinking for some time. The intruder stepped forward in an attempt to get past Davy. Davy gave him a slight push with the palm of his left hand on the man's chest. The man resisted and pushed Davy with both hands. At about this time, Davy's patience had vanished, and the inevitable was about to take place.

Isabel knowing Davy as well as she did, while wringing her hands said to him, "Davy, don't, don't!"

Ignoring Isabel's plea, Davy reared back and landed an exploding right cross to the intruder's jaw. The man went down hard from the punch, one side of his face hitting the sidewalk and blood splattered on the cement walk. Davy took Isabel by the hand, calmly saying, "Come on honey, let's go to Mass!"

At this moment Isabel was feeling very proud of Davy, yet she was trembling in fear after what had just occurred.

After a few months of his daily routine of traveling to and from his job in Indiana, Davy became weary and tired from lack of sleep. He explored alternatives to his present job and decided to look for work closer to home. Defense jobs of every type were opening up everywhere, so finding a new job was not too much of a problem. Eventually Davy was hired by a steel-forging company that was making artillery shells for the federal government. Getting there took a streetcar ride of about fifteen minutes from home, thus making a great deal of difference in his traveling time to and from work. After some on-the-job training, Davy became proficient at forging artillery shells, and with "overtime" and other incentives, Davy had nearly doubled his previous salary at the mill.

Davy and Isabel became accustomed to married life and with a little help from Francisca, life became routine once more and with much better results. However, fate still lurked in the shadows!

One early Friday evening on a festive time at home in celebration of his son's first birthday, as the supply of beer was dwindling, Davy went out to buy more. He walked the same route he usually took on his way to church on Sundays, South on Morgan Street to Roosevelt Road. The sun had just gone down and it was rapidly getting dark as Davy walked to the liquor store. Walking past the alley entrance near Taylor Street, he was confronted by a figure who had jumped out of the darkness. Davy stopped at the sudden intrusion. "What the hell!"

A man wearing a short coat with a turned-up collar and a hat pulled over his eyes shouted, "Now I got ya, you motherfucker!"

At that instant, Davy felt a sharp pain in the left side of his abdomen, where a pointed blade entered when the man shoved his right hand in Davy's direction. Davy immediately recognized the figure as the intruder that had confronted him and Isabel one Sunday on their way to church. Instinctively, Davy hit the man with a left and a right that knocked him down. While the man lay stunned on the pavement, Davy gave him a tremendous kick to the head. The man remained unconscious for a few moments.

Davy looked everywhere for some sort of weapon as he bled profusely from the abdominal wound he had just received. He found a heavy stone that he could lift with one hand just inside the alley entrance. He returned to where the man, beginning to stir, lay and straddled his victim. With the stone in his right hand, he pounded the man several times on both sides of the head until the man was bloodied and again unconscious.

Davy was now beginning to feel weak due to the loss of blood. He stood up and turned toward home on very wobbly legs. Blood poured from the wound, drenching his clothes. He held both hands to the left side of his abdomen in an attempt to hold back the flow of blood to no avail. When Davy reached home, he pushed open the door and fell into the living room floor. Screams resounded and tears flowed as reality sank in to

Francisca and the Boys

the family and guests. Someone ran out and called police, and a fire department ambulance soon arrived. Before long Davy was in the emergency room at Mother Cabrini Hospital.

Hours later Davy opened his eyes in the intensive care unit with Isabel and Francisca standing next to his bed looking down at him. As he attempted to move as if to sit up, he groaned and fell back in pain. He looked at his arms, secured by straps to the bed with needles and rubber tubes protruding from his forearms. A steel tank nearby fed oxygen to his lungs through a mask tied over his nose and mouth.

Davy closed his eyes temporarily and reopened them in an attempt to figure out why he was lying here in this condition. His eyes darted from side to side as he looked in turn to his wife, then his mother. He tried to speak but what he thought were words sounded like grunts to Isabel and Francisca. Isabel cried continuously while standing at Davy's bedside, and as Francisca wiped his brow with a towel, she admonished him to close his eyes and rest. At this early stage after surgery, Davy was still under the influence of the anesthesia, but it was slowly wearing off, and pain was spreading from his injury.

A nurse walked in holding a syringe, and as she spoke to no one in particular she said, "I'm going to give him a shot for pain so that he can get some rest."

The intramuscular injection of a sedative was administered by the nurse into Davy's left arm just above the elbow. Within minutes, Davy was in a deep sleep.

"The doctor would like to speak to you," the ward nurse announced, "follow me please."

Isabel and Francisca followed the nurse to a small office down the hall from the intensive care ward. They sat on chairs provided as they waited for the doctor to speak.

"The news is not very good," the doctor told the women as they sat listening with great concern. "At this point, his chances of survival are still fifty-fifty, very much depending on his will to live."

Isabel let out a loud scream and began to cry loudly while holding a handkerchief to her nose and mouth. Francisca twitched slightly but managed to control her emotions and hold her composure. Suddenly she became very stoic and firm.

"Thank you, Doctor," Francisca said. "I think I'll take my daughter-in-law home and come back a little later. Would that be all right?"

"Yes, of course," the doctor replied. He wrote down some numbers on a pad and handed the sheet to Francisca. "You can call the hospital anytime to check on your son's condition, and this is my number in case you have questions."

Francisca thanked the doctor one more time, then walked over to Isabel and put an arm around her shoulders. "Let's go home. We can come back tomorrow when we are calmed down."

The women left the hospital.

In the following days, Francisca spent many hours at the Church of St Francis of Assisi praying to all the saints for guidance and help in this hour of need. She had much faith in St. Francis himself since he was her namesake after all.

Two and a half weeks had passed since Davy's arrival at the emergency room at Mother Cabrini Hospital. Now he was being administered nutrients intravenously and discharging waste by way of a catheter and a rubber tube through a nostril to his stomach.

From his normal 170 pounds, Davy was down to between 90 and 100 pounds. His bones showed through his sallow and seemingly thinned skin. His eyes were sunken and he spoke weakly with great effort.

"Ma," Davy told his mother, "I don't want to die here. You gotta get me out of here. Take me home."

"Yes, I'll talk to the doctor," Francisca said.

"No, Ma. Just take me out!" Davy pleaded.

"All right, all right" Francisca responded. "I'll take you home."

Francisca and the Boys

There was a great deal of activity as nurses came into the ward to attend to Davy's needs and a few young doctors also visited to observe and study his case.

Francisca and Isabel left the ward while this activity continued.

A few steps out the door Francisca heard a soft voice behind her say, "Mrs. Delmonte, would you give me a call when you are able." The youthful-looking doctor handed Francisca his business card. A surprised Francisca instinctively accepted the card and knowingly cupped it into her hand and swiftly placing it inside her purse while simultaneously pulling out a handkerchief. By the look on the young doctor's face Francisca had immediately understood that this short communication was to remain confidential.

At home Francisca studied the business card that the young doctor had handed her. Dr. Henry L. Bertucci read the top line. Further down it continued, Surgeon—Internal Medicine, with an address and telephone number on the bottom line. That same evening, Francisca placed a call to Dr. Bertucci's office somewhere downtown in the Loop. The doctor would not be in his office until the following morning at nine.

The next morning, Francisca told Isabel to go to the hospital by herself and to let Davy know that she was making arrangements for his release from the hospital. She was to stay by his side until Francisca arrived arrive later that morning. Finally Francisca made contact with Dr. Bertucci.

"Mrs. Delmonte," the doctor told her over the phone, "what I say to you must be kept strictly confidential. You know, if our conversation were to leak out to anyone involved in medicine, I could theoretically lose my license."

"I understand, doctor," Francisca replied.

"You must get your son out of the hospital immediately and take him home or he may die of malnutrition!" the doctor told her.

"Yes, I'm going to bring him home sometime today whether the hospital lets him out or not," Francisca said to the doctor.

"All right then," Doctor Bertucci said, "listen carefully. Your son is suffering from a blockage of the large intestine, and he cannot pass waste from his body. What you must do when you get him home is to give him a soft soap enema to induce peristalsis. Do you think you can do that?"

Francisca didn't have the slightest idea what the doctor meant when he said "induce peristalsis," but she certainly knew how to give enemas, since that had, for years, been her favorite cure for anything that ailed her children.

"Yes, Doctor, I know how to give enemas," replied Francisca.

"Good," the doctor continued, "start out with a very small amount of soap and warm water at first, and if there is no reaction, you wait a few minutes, then add a little more. If it still doesn't work, you turn him on his back and let the fluid drain out naturally. Once the water is out, try again with a little more soap and water, and continue doing this until you get results. If none of this helps, give me a call and I'll come down to see your son at no charge."

"Oh, thank you very much, Doctor," the overwhelmed Francisca responded, "I appreciate it very much!"

They hung up precisely at the same time.

When Francisca arrived at Mother Cabrini Hospital, she found Davy dressed and ready to leave regardless of the circumstances and sitting on a chair looking very tired. The nurses were in conversation with Davy attempting to convince him that he had to get back in bed. Davy absolutely refused and notified the nurses that he was going home this day, and if he wasn't discharged, he would walk out of the hospital on his own. Eventually Francisca signed papers at the front desk taking full responsibility for Davy's well being. Davy was discharged. Isabel had called a cab from the lobby, and it was now waiting for them in the driveway. The three boarded the cab for home.

Immediately on arriving at home, Francisca began to prepare the enema that she would give to Davy. Isabel helped Davy undress and get into bed. Soon Francisca was there with the hot water bottle with its long hose and hard rubber tip.

In all the years that Davy had taken enemas from his mother, this was the first time ever he welcomed the coming event. Just as Dr. Bertucci had predicted, on the second try the enema did the job. There was feces from sometime back in Davy's discharge along with bits of intestinal tissue. Davy gave a great sigh of relief and smiled broadly at Isabel when he suddenly felt his stomach shrink and gasses gush out of his body.

Within a short time Davy was taking nourishment by mouth, and within a week or so he began to eat soft foods. He was on his way to complete recovery.

TWENTY

Nick's letters to Francisca were about a week apart whether he received an answer or not and her responses were always in his sister Lupe's handwriting. Although Francisca could read well enough, her spelling and her handwriting in general were not the best.

Nick and Francisca corresponded all through his time in training and his time in the Hospital Corps School in San Diego, California, and through his hospital ward duty at the U.S. Naval Hospital in Bremerton, Washington.

At Bremerton, during training, Nick learned the nuances of surgery by attending surgical procedures and a few autopsies. After an autopsy, he and other corpsmen were given the privilege of closing the cadaver by stitching up the open cuts. On these particular occasions, Nick's thoughts would become a scramble of life, death, religion, science, and the possibilities of truth in Darwin's theory of evolution. Eventually he would remove these thoughts and move on to learn more.

The only thing of any consequence that had occurred during Nick's training time at Bremerton was an incident that came about during his duties in one of the wards. One particular patient was isolated in a corner of the ward, separated and enclosed by a partition, and was on twenty-four-hour watch. The patient was a Marine of huge proportions whose body covered his bed almost to its entirety. He was well over six and a half feet in height and weighed close to four hundred pounds with no evidence of fat on any part of his body and had a fairly dark complexion. He suffered from pernicious anemia, and his heart was in a very weak state. He received vitamin injections every four hours.

The Marine and Nick became friendly during the few weeks of Nick's ward duties, because both happened to be from Chicago. They often talked about the neighborhoods in Chicago and the different ethnic and racial groups that existed in the city. During these conversations, Nick learned that the Marine, of Lithuanian descent, had been a Chicago police officer and was still carried on the police roster in his precinct.

One day while Nick was on duty, the hour for the patient's vitamin shot had arrived, but the Marine happened to be sleeping. Nick had already prepared the syringe and entered the medication and the hour it was to be administered into the ward's medical logbook. Nick was due to be relieved within the next ten or so minutes, so he decided to place the medication on the side table and let the relieving corpsman administer the shot.

When the corpsman in relief arrived for duty, Nick attempted to explain the situation to him, for any sudden disturbance of the patient might cause a dangerous fibrillation of the heart. The new corpsman refused to cooperate and immediately reported the incident to the ward nurse who was in charge and happened to be a commissioned officer.

Nick woke the patient and administered the shot while the other corpsman was away. The damage had already been done as far as rules and regulations were concerned, but Nick saw no problem as long as his duties had been performed. The nurse and the other corpsman saw it differently and subsequently accused Nick of breaking the rules. In attempting to explain further, Nick entered into a heated discussion with the nurse that ended with tempers rising and words being exchanged. The nurse lost her temper and called Nick "blackie" referring to his deep and dark suntan. In defense, Nick responded angrily by calling her a stupid "broad," thus escalating the argument.

"Spick!" the nurse retorted

"You fuckin' bitch!"

At that point, all ward patients were sitting up to listen, some in awe and others just smiling and laughing at the commotion taking place at the nurse's station.

Nick turned to leave. On his way toward the exit, he stopped momentarily near the other corpsman on his way out and said to him, "Watch yourself, you fuckin' asshole. I'm gonna kick your fuckin' ass!"

The other corpsman did not respond, looking downward he quickly walked away.

Nick was put on report and brought up to a captain's mast, a military court in the Navy that handles administrative discipline without a full courts-marshal. At his trial Nick pleaded guilty to insubordination without the argument in the ward being mentioned, and was sentenced to five days in the brig "on bread and water."

Nick served his sentence, losing fifteen to twenty pounds in the interim. On his release, Nick was informed by one of the other corpsman that the patient in question had died one day before Nick's release from the brig. Hearing the news, Nick, looking downward, just shook his head, attempting to understand the irony of it all.

One more interesting occurrence during his time at Bremerton was a telephone call that he received by way of the officer of the day's line. Nick was notified that he had a phone call from Washington, D.C. Thinking that someone was trying to play a joke on him, Nick attempted to dismiss the whole thing as such. That was not to be, for within minutes, the chief in charge came, walking in his direction.

"Delmonte" the chief half-bellowed, "go answer your call. That's an order!"

Nick followed the order without question. He picked up the phone and to his surprise, Nick heard a man say, "Are you Nicolas Delmonte?"

"Yes, I am," Nick replied.

"This is the Internal Revenue Service calling in regard to an outstanding income tax payment of two hundred thirty dollars," the man on the other end of the line said.

Nick's heart and jaw seemed to drop simultaneously. He couldn't believe what he was hearing. Nick stammered and coughed looking for an answer that he could not come up with when the man spoke again.

"Mr. Delmonte, we understand that you are now in the Navy. Is that correct?"

"Yes," Nick answered, bewildered that the IRS would go to such lengths as to track him down all the way to his barracks.

"Well, we have been informed that you will be going overseas in a short time, and since you will be fighting for your country, the IRS will forgive your outstanding balance."

"Thank you, sir!" Nick responded with great enthusiasm.

"Good luck, Mr. Delmonte," the man said, and then line clicked.

Nick walked back to the barracks smiling to himself while still in disbelief at what had just occurred.

Eventually the dreaded list of names was posted on the hospital bulletin board of those corpsmen who were being transferred to duty somewhere overseas in the Pacific theater. Nick found his name on the list. His point of departure would be Port Hueneme, California, where he would board a transport ship to San Francisco It was now early April of 1943.

While he waited for orders at Port Hueneme, Nick's duties would be the same as all other sailors in transit. His dreams of special treatment for being a hospital corpsman were shattered when he realized that all personnel in transit were treated as nothing more than cargo.

In his letters to Francisca, Nick detailed his duties, which consisted mostly of kitchen duty and guard duty in the wooden tower at Point Mugu near the beach in an isolated corner of the California coastline. Guard duty in the tower at night, by moonlight only, was divided into four-hour watches, which made it a little easier to endure.

As for kitchen duty, or KP, aside from cooking, peeling potatoes and washing dishes, these were the two most important jobs and the most dreaded. However, these jobs had their good side, for whatever time spent in the kitchen was well rewarded. One could eat whatever one wanted whenever the occasion occurred. One day, after a week or so at Port Hueneme Nick was called to the office of the CO on duty.

"Delmonte," the CO announced sternly, "you have been granted three days' liberty. Make sure you're back on time or suffer the consequences!" As an afterthought he added, "Someone will be waiting for you at the gate, so shake it up and get going!"

Somewhat confused as to why or who would be waiting at the gate for him, Nick quickly ran back to the barracks, changed into his dress blues, and walked toward the gate with Liberty Pass in hand and a few dollars in his money belt. As Nick approached the gate he could see a taxicab parked a few feet away and someone waving a hand from inside the rear passenger seat. The back door opened and a woman stepped out still waving. Nick recognized his mother Francisca as she ran toward him.

"Ma!" Nick exclaimed.

"*Mijo!*" Francisca half-shouted as she embraced her son.

"What are you doing here, Ma?"

"I came to see you once more before you go across the ocean."

Nick fumbled for a response and found none.

Mother and son seemed to be thinking along the same lines. Implanted somewhere in the back of Nick's mind were the possibilities that he would never come home alive. All the evidence leading to his approaching departure only made it more of a sure thing. The war in the Pacific was raging and heating up more and more each day. Nick thought about the liberty pass given to him out of a clear blue sky. "Ma, how did you do it?"

Francisca and the Boys

"Do what?" she asked.

"How did you get me a pass to go on liberty?"

"Don't worry about it!"

In fact, Francisca had used her mysterious persuasive powers to convince the guard at the gate that it was important that she speak with the commanding officer. After a few minutes of cajoling by Francisca, the guard capitulated and made a call to the CO's office. She was granted a visitor's pass, and in the CO's office, she was assured that Nick would be at the gate ready for liberty. In Francisca's mind, she well understood that Nick might be killed in the war, but she had great faith in God and thus prayed daily for his safe return.

Nick and Francisca entered the cab and were driven to Oxnard, a short distance north of the Navy compound. In Oxnard, Francisca introduced her son to a couple whose son was a Marine and overseas somewhere in the Pacific and whose seventeen-year-old daughter was at home and about to graduate high school.

Francisca's magic had been at work once more! On her arrival in Oxnard that morning, she had stopped to read a bulletin board at the entrance of the local drugstore that announced ROOM FOR RENT with a telephone number to call in hand printed black lettering on a half page of notebook paper. Francisca was on a public phone almost immediately. She explained her situation to the woman on the other end of the line and arrangements were made for Francisca to see the room. Eventually Francisca rented two rooms for an extra two dollars for a two-night stay. Nick would occupy the son's room, and Francisca the daughter's room, while the daughter would move to the couch in the living room. Everything worked out well for all concerned.

In the two days that Nick and Francisca stayed with the family in Oxnard, they were treated as family themselves, following a tradition of treating travelers with respect that went back to the Spanish influence of a couple of hundred years. The young daughter, Estelita, and Nick became friendly immediately and soon became involved in long conversations. These conversations always covered what each had experienced in their relatively short lives. She would talk about school, and he about his experiences on the streets of Chicago. Nick was attracted to Estelita mostly for her intellect, as opposed to her physical beauty. Estelita had a beautiful thin face attached to a very thin, underdeveloped body.

During the last of the conversations between Nick and Estelita, she handed Nick a photograph of herself, saying, "Here's a picture of me. I hope you don't mind."

"Oh, no! Thank you," Nick replied. "In fact I was thinking of asking you for one, but I thought you might not like the idea!"

They laughed together as they felt a mutual understanding.

The two days and nights went by slowly and Nick was somewhat relieved when time came to return to the Navy compound in Hueneme. On the final day of Nick's liberty, goodbyes were said to the accommodating family and mother and son made their way to the bus depot in Oxnard.

It was early evening when the Greyhound bus arrived at the depot, the letters above the windshield read Los Angeles, where Francisca would transfer to a bus heading for Chicago.

In tears, Francisca pulled a cloth scapular from her purse that showed the image of St. Christopher, patron saint of travelers, and handed it to Nick. "Here," Francisca told Nick. "Put this in your wallet and always carry it and it will bring you home safe."

Nick took the scapular without protest, for he wasn't about to oppose Francisca's religious beliefs in any way, and if he came back alive, he would certainly give credit to his mother for her faith in God and all the saints.

Mother and son hugged one more time before Francisca boarded her bus. Nick struggled to hold back the tears until the bus pulled away. The tears then flowed as Nick watched the taillights of the Greyhound Bus disappear into the darkness.

It was about eight-thirty, giving Nick three and one half hours left on his liberty pass. By midnight, he had to be past the guards

Francisca and the Boys

at the Navy compound gates or, as the CO had warned him, suffer the consequences. Nick walked toward the business section of Oxnard where lights shown on both sides of the main street. He strolled while watching people going about their business. As Nick walked he heard laughing and loud conversation behind him. He turned to see three sailors, two in dress whites and one in dress blues, walking animatedly in his direction.

"Hey, mate," one of the sailors shouted, "where you heading?"

"Nowhere, just killing time," answered Nick.

"We're going to the local bar for a few drinks. You wanna come along?" one of the trio offered.

"I'm not twenty-one yet," Nick answered rather timidly.

The sailor talking to Nick was a boatswain's mate, a hash mark on his sleeve indicating six or more years of Navy duty. He noticed that Nick had a red cross on his left sleeve and referred to him as "Doc" thereafter.

"Don't worry about that, Doc," the boatswain's mate answered. "If you're old enough to fight, you're old enough to drink! I'm stationed here at Port Hueneme and I'm fairly well known in most of these bars, I'll take care of that age business."

Nick didn't think twice. "Sure, why not. I could use something to drink right now."

After introductions all around, four sailors walked into the nearest bar. Inside the bar, they each took a stool, ready to order. The boatswain's mate walked around to the end of the bar and motioned to the bartender. He cupped his hands and whispered something in the bartender's ear while glancing in Nick's direction. The bartender nodded a couple of times and walked away. Beers were served all around, and as much as Nick disliked the taste of beer, he soon acquired a taste for it as he guzzled and watched the time on a wall clock.

At eleven fifteen, Nick's mates helped him board a taxi and gave the driver directions to get him to the base on time. The taxi driver was paid in advance, tip included, "just in case." By the time

Nick reached the base, he was extremely drunk but still able to control himself. The taxi pulled up to the gate with fifteen minutes to spare just as Nick was beginning to feel like vomiting.

Nick gave the driver an extra two dollars for being so careful and for taking such good care of him. As he slammed the taxi door after stepping out, the taxi pulled away and Nick let out a spray of vomit. Nick checked in with time to spare and slowly made his way toward his barracks as the world turned before his eyes.

As he walked into the barracks, he stumbled and made noise that woke a few of the sleeping occupants. Voices came from the dark: "Hey, knock it off!" Then he heard, "Delmonte, over here. Your bunk is over here." He found his bunk and fell into it clothes and all only to hear, what seemed almost immediately, the sound of a bugler blowing reveille.

Nick's guard duty time had been fulfilled, and his turn would not come up again for a few days. However, he would have to show up for muster by six in the morning. Nick quickly changed into his denims and went out to line up for muster, skipping breakfast. He sneaked back into the barracks and fell into his bunk one more time.

Later in the day he felt someone shaking him by the shoulder, one of his barracks mates.

"Delmonte, wake up" the person said. "Orders are in. We'll be aboard ship by Saturday morning."

If the scuttlebutt were true, and Nick had no reason to believe that it wasn't, it being a Thursday, the men scheduled for overseas had but one day to prepare for boarding, ample time to pack and write letters to loved ones.

Thursday afternoon, all occupants of Nick's barracks were ordered by the chief petty officer on duty to stand at attention near their bunks and listen to the latest orders from the office of the commanding officer. A short speech by the chief reminded them of what they had learned in boot camp regarding firearms and that they would now be issued rifles individually. After falling into formation outside the barracks, the entire group was marched to the armory to receive their Springfield 1903 single-action rifles and steel helmets.

Nick became momentarily confused, for he had learned that medical personnel were not supposed to carry or use firearms during any conflict, according to the Geneva Convention. He never raised the question to anyone and accepted his rifle without objection.

By early dawn on Saturday, several small boats filled with sailors were launched from shore in the direction of the huge transport ship that had anchored a short distance from shore the night before. Ocean water splashed onto Nick's face as he gazed at the giant ship he was about to board. White hats bobbed up and down in unison with the motion of the small boats that carried the sailors. As the bows of the boats broke the short but strong waves, they approached the ship.

Rifle and helmet hanging by straps to his back and his sea-bag over his left shoulder, Nick climbed the side ladder, suddenly realizing that he was going to war. He quickly stepped ahead of the group that he was with and found his way down a ladder at the forward section of the transport to the second deck. The group scrambled in search of empty bunks. Nick felt lucky when he spotted an empty bunk on the second tier and quickly dumped his gear on it.

Looking around his new quarters, Nick noted that a majority of the ship's passengers were army personnel, and he was not certain as to why this small group of sailors was mixed in with soldiers of the army. Eventually, this uncertainty would be cleared up on arrival at their destination.

By late afternoon of that day, the huge transport ship weighed anchor and began to move slowly in a northerly direction. Nick enjoyed the lights along the California coastline from the bow of the ship as it cut the waves, pushing smoothly toward its destination. The scuttlebutt lines were again busy with information that the ship was heading to San Francisco to pick up troops and equipment, and as usual, the scuttlebutt was about 99 percent correct. The only thing missing was that the ship would also be joining a convoy of several ships destined for the Pacific theater.

By 0600, chow time was whistled over the ship's loudspeakers.

"Now hear this," the boatswain said over the loudspeakers. "All transient personnel will line up on the port side toward the bow with mess kits for the serving of breakfast!"

The line on the main deck formed swiftly, but Nick had alertly moved just as swiftly to be one of the first ten or so men in line. As he waited, Nick could see the Golden Gate Bridge behind the ship as it headed toward a rendezvous point for loading. Another bridge could be seen ahead, it was the bridge connecting Oakland to San Francisco from across the bay.

By ten o'clock that morning, the ship was teeming with army personnel, all having boarded the same as Nick did the day before. All sleeping bunks aboard ship were now occupied; thus, most of the soldiers were obliged to make themselves comfortable on the main deck by propping up their equipment as support for blankets to be used as miniature tents. The afternoon heat brought out shirtless men, some in shorts, forming into small groups, some just talking, others playing cards, and still others shooting craps for money stakes, on the top deck of the ship. Nick roamed the main deck for a while, making friends with a few of the army guys while engaging in conversations and more or less acquiring a feeling of what it was really like to be aboard a truly sea going vessel.

Nick went below decks at just about sunset. He climbed up to his bunk, removed his shoes and shirt, went through his old mail, and reread some of the letters that had accumulated over the past few weeks. Drowsiness took hold as he read, and with the aid of the humming of machinery throughout the ship, and the warm air cascading through the compartment, Nick fell asleep.

TWENTY-ONE

Back in Chicago, Francisca's determination began to produce reality in her efforts to initiate the necessary ingredients for the opening of her long-awaited business venture. She negotiated for an empty store located south of Madison on Halsted street, and just around the corner from the hub of the old vaudeville strip, for the purpose of selling alcoholic beverages to the public. With her instincts in full throttle and fully realizing what exactly was needed to begin operation of the business, Francisca went ahead and signed a five-year lease for the store with a real-estate company. The necessary applications for licenses to run the business were filled and filed with the city and state once the empty store was converted into a viable establishment to sell beer and liquor.

The empty store soon became a hub of activity and a family project in its conversion. Lupe, Isabel, and Davy became intensely busy with putting together a serving bar and a back bar with mirrors. Sinks and beer-draft equipment, which Francisca had negotiated with local wholesale dealers, were installed by Davy with the very appreciated help from his sister Lupe. Davy, in a mode of "learn as you work," did carpentry and plumbing, and most of the heavier work, while Lupe and Isabel painted walls and ceilings. All of this activity took place in late afternoons and continued through evenings since Davy was not yet ready to quit his job at the steel-forging company.

Meanwhile, Francisca made the rounds visiting or calling politicians and officials whose political pull was so necessary for her to acquire the licenses to open her new business establishment. In a corner at the rear of the establishment hidden by protruding walls was a shelf serving as an altar for Francisca's religious figures. There she lit several votive candles and prayed quietly as she knelt on a makeshift cushion.

By mid-January 1943, the doors to the original Club Delmonte were opened to the public. Sporadic customers occupied the barstools daily for the first two to three weeks until word got around that Francisca had opened a Bar. Soon business began to boom.

Being the only man in the group, and because, by city ordinance, women were not allowed to work behind the bar, Davy became the evening bartender of choice. A family friend was hired for day duty, giving Davy the opportunity to hold on to his day job. The long sign tacked above the mirrors on the back bar advertised, in black letters on a white background, draft beer for five cents a glass, mugs for ten cents, and bottles for twenty cents.

By the end of the first half-year license, Francisca's Club Delmonte was in full swing, and it was time to consider a "grand opening" for the establishment. Francisca and her "crew" began preparation for a big party. After several meetings held in the place of business, decisions were made on what and how things were going to be done.

Family relations suddenly came into play. Davy's new brother-in-law, by marriage to a younger sister of Isabel, was a musician of note. Arrangements were made for his five-piece band to appear for two nights, Friday and Saturday, to celebrate the grand opening of Club Delmonte. In one of the store's double windows hung a white sign saying "Grand Opening" with the dates corresponding to the days of the week. In the other window hung a similar sign that read Manolo and His Cuban Rhythm Boys, Manolo being Manuel Vasquez, Davy's brother-in-law.

Manny, as he was known to family and friends, had a following of fans who were interested in the musical sounds of Latin America. He also had a reputation of presenting a good show when appearing on stage at local nightclubs. At this particular time, he was free to do small jobs while waiting for his coming 'gig' at the new Club Copacabana that had opened recently on State Street in Chicago.

The grand opening was such a success that Manny and his band were hired for weekend entertainment permanently at Club Delmonte, that is, permanently until the band was ready to move on to bigger and better things. By the time that Manolo and his Cuban Rhythm Boys were ready to move on, another band had already been hired to replace them.

Francisca's club flourished. Eventually Davy quit his job at the steel-forging company and directed all of his energy into helping run Club Delmonte.

Little Stanley was a toddler now, running around when turned loose by his mother within the confines of home. Isabel thus became a full-time wife and a stay-at-home mother.

With the club now running at a fast pace, Davy began to utilize his position as head bartender to make himself available to some of the females that came into the place unescorted. As things stood in this time of war, there were a great number of unescorted females. Davy took advantage of the situation with fervor. It wasn't very long after the business became stabilized that Davy's time at home with Isabel became less and less frequent.

Davy soon became cantankerous and ill tempered to such a degree that for any little thing that Isabel said or did out of the norm, he would attack her verbally and physically to "keep her in line." His demeanor had changed dramatically from a loving and caring husband to that of a cruel and demanding spouse. Isabel would frequently appear battered and bruised, with blackened eyes and puffy lips from beatings by Davy after his temper flared and falsely accused her of one thing or the other.

Isabel now was with child for the second time and into her second month of pregnancy. When Francisca became aware of her daughter-in-law's pregnancy, she took steps to stop the beatings. She warned her son that the next time it happened, he would do jail time. There was a next time a few weeks later and, true to her word, Francisca arranged with the captain at the local precinct to hold Davy in the lock-up for two days and nights.

On his release, Davy promised Francisca that he would stop drinking and to control his temper. Francisca acquiesced and reserved the right to repeat the process if Davy were to break his promise.

Davy continued to drink but managed to remain relatively sober and henceforth refrained from beating on Isabel again.

The business continued to flourish.

TWENTY-TWO

Nick was awakened by the sound of the warning sirens and loud activity on the top deck of the ship. He dressed quickly and made for the hatch leading to the top deck. Abruptly, the hatch cover slammed shut before he reached the top of the ladder. He felt the ship slowing and making a sharp turn to the right. The sirens continued to blare and shouting by ship personnel could be heard from above, though indistinguishable as to what was being shouted. This activity on the main deck lasted about a half hour, then eventually slowed back to normal after the all clear was sounded. Nick saw daylight break through as the compartment hatch was opened.

Nick climbed the ladder and went through the hatch. The sun cast bright rays making him blink several times. He heard the humming sound of animated conversation among the crew and passengers. The scuttlebutt was alive and well. Nick learned immediately what had caused all the commotion. It seemed that the lookouts on the bridge had spotted the wake of a fast-traveling torpedo coming in the direction of the convoy. Alerts had been sounded, and all ships acted accordingly by zigzagging to avoid the danger. Nick got his first taste of the war and now was convinced that where he was going would not be a picnic.

Lazy warm days went by as the ships sailed in dangerous waters, and the convoy grew larger as it went along. Fighting ships of every sort surrounded the convoy, sailing toward the battle zone of the South Pacific. Days later Nick, standing on deck, spotted land in the distance, and soon all the bow and side railings were filled with personnel, some looking through binoculars while others just stared, all looking for signs of activity on land. American fighter planes were now buzzing the convoy as it sailed closer and closer to the bay at Pearl Harbor. Hours passed as the land beyond seemed to grow very slowly. It would be at least one more day before the ships reached the bay.

Nick wisely went below to write home and prepare for landing. He wrote a few pages to his mother with messages included for his brother and sister. Nick placed the folded letter in the envelope, and as per previous instructions, he left the envelope unsealed for the censor. He found the mail slot on the upper deck and sent his letter on its way. How long would the letter take to arrive in Chicago? Nick wondered about that for a while but quickly put it out of his mind for he knew that it would get there eventually. He went back to his bunk and into a sound sleep.

Once more, the sound of the boatswain's whistle was heard over the intercom. "Now hear this," the man said, "all transient personnel with designated orders for Acorn report topside at port bow by thirteen hundred!" The message was repeated one more time.

By one o'clock in the afternoon (thirteen hundred in navy vernacular) the port-side area toward the bow of the ship was filled with about thirty or more sailors dressed in denim uniforms and wearing white hats. As the sailors roamed on deck, Nick talked to a few of the guys, asking questions to see who happened to be assigned to his new outfit. Almost immediately he found two other hospital corpsmen assigned to his destined group which became known as Acorn 11. A chief petty officer soon appeared and began to call out names and assigning each name to a corresponding group. There were a dozen or so that were assigned to Acorn 11.

By making inquiries here and there, Nick soon learned what the designation of Acorn 11 meant. It was the code name of a naval construction battalion that would be landing on an island somewhere in the South Pacific for the purpose of building a landing strip for navy fighter planes, which also meant that Nick and the medical group would not be far behind, for the medical group was a detachment of this particular group commonly known as the Seabees.

Soon the transport was a beehive of activity. Nick surveyed his new surroundings while preparing to disembark. There were sunken ships of many types throughout the harbor, some sticking out of the ocean's surface and still smoldering after nearly two years after the attack on Pearl Harbor.

By nightfall small boats with lights swaying in the dark began to show up near the transport. Shortly thereafter, Nick was aboard one of the small boats with the swaying lights along with the other two men he had befriended earlier that evening. Of the three, Nick was the youngest at age twenty, then there was a twenty-five-year-old named Geib (pronounced *gibe*), and the third, very close to age fifty, was known by the name Swanson. First names were seldom used between service personnel, but in cases of close friendships, that custom faded and either first names or nicknames were used. In the near future, a strong relationship would be formed between these three, basically founded on the fact that all three were Roman Catholic. Soon the three friends soon referred to each other as "Monty," short for Delmonte; Geib; and, out of respect for Swanson's age and previous experience in the navy, and whose first name happened to be Christopher, Chris.

The small boat pulled up alongside a long wooden dock that stretched from dry land across the sandy beach for about thirty or so yards, ending in perhaps ten feet of water depth. A total of fifteen hospital corpsmen assigned to Acorn 11 lined up just off the beach on orders from the chief boatswain's mate in charge. From the beach, at the point where the small boats were unloading, the vast extent of the naval base could be seen straight ahead. On the boatswain's mate's orders, the corpsmen lined up in twos with the extra man bringing up the rear.

"Attention!" the boatswain's mate bellowed.

As the group lined up and stood at attention, he again called in a strong voice, "In lock step, forward march!" "In lock step" meant that the group would march in a normal walking step. Within a few minutes and about a half-mile of walking, the group arrived at the barracks compound where all new arrivals were quartered until further notice. There was no particular order for the men to pick their bunks; therefore, the three new buddies, Swanson, Geib, and Delmonte picked bunks next to one another.

After chow that evening, the group was notified that early next morning all would be assigned to work details. Sure enough, soon after breakfast the hospital corpsmen were lined up in front of the barracks. With the usual orders from a boatswain's mate first class, the group of corpsmen was marched to a work site. Once at the site, the corpsmen began to complain that hospital personnel were exempt from working outside of a medical environment

The boatswain's mate smiled. "You are transients like anyone else until you arrive at your destination, so let's get to work!"

Nick surveyed the work site and what he saw was devastating to say the least. There were hundreds of oil drums, full and empty, strewn throughout a huge field just off the ocean's edge being loaded on to trucks by Japanese prisoners of war. These prisoners were being closely watched by U.S. Navy guards carrying loaded rifles at the ready. Observing the scene before him, Nick just could not believe what he saw. *How could his country allow American service personnel to labor in the same atmosphere as the enemy?* he thought. Nonetheless, the contingent of third-class pharmacist mates was put to work just yards away from where the Japanese prisoners of war were loading trucks.

After a day of loading drums onto trucks, the corpsmen were returned to their barracks in a mood of despair and incredulity. However, good news awaited them; their orders had arrived! Chris, who had been exempted from the work crew because of his pharmacist mate second class rating and his advanced age, presented Geib and Delmonte with the news.

Nick had mixed feelings now that he knew he would be going into the zone where the action against Japan was taking place. He had already experienced a little danger with the scare of the earlier torpedo incident aboard the transport, but he knew that henceforth he would be doing the job he was trained to do, that of caring for the sick and wounded somewhere on the field of battle.

All hospital corpsmen destined for Acorn 11 were assembled in front of the barracks for muster one more time. Soon after muster, a short, thin-looking individual with squinty blue eyes and reddish hair, wearing the hat of a naval officer as indicated by the gold braid above the beak of the hat, stepped out of an army jeep that had just pulled up.

"Gentlemen," he announced, "I'm Warrant Officer Jonas Walker, and I will be in charge of this contingent until further notice."

The men had been at ease and therefore relaxed while the warrant officer spoke in a gentler voice than the commands they had been accustomed to in the last few days.

"You will be packed and ready to board ship by oh six hundred," the officer continued. "And if you have letters to write, now is the time to do it. You will be notified of your destination aboard ship."

The scuttlebutt had already been through the barracks that a battalion of Seabees was scheduled for the Solomon Islands, but no one was sure which battalion it was. For some unknown reason, Nick had a strong feeling that it would be Acorn 11, the battalion that his group would eventually be attached to. He refrained from writing home at this particular time because he didn't want to worry the family back home more than they already were, and, anyway, his previous letter written aboard ship had already been mailed.

As Warrant Officer Walker had announced the night before, by 0600, the contingent of hospital corpsmen was lined up in front of the barracks wearing their steel helmets with their sea bags on one shoulder and their Springfield '03 rifles hanging by a strap to the other. The group marched to the beach and boarded a small boat that headed toward one of the smaller ships. A landing ship tank—known as an LST for short—served as their transportation to their yet-unknown destination.

Sirens blared during the morning hours, and American fighter planes could be heard and seen taking off the runways, evidently going out to reconnoiter, to seek out and meet the enemy if need be. There were a number of fighting ships in the harbor and their silhouettes could be seen through the early-morning fog. The sunken ships of December 7, 1941, stuck out of the water surface in a dreary and somewhat spooky way. Nick suddenly felt a deep sadness come over him at the sight. He felt as though he wanted to cry, but with a forceful effort, he managed to hold back the tears.

The LST was a long, flat ship with the bridge overlooking the expansive deck that ended in a point at the center on the bow. There, a 40mm antiaircraft gun stood poised for action at all times. There was a small cannon aft of the bridge and six more antiaircraft guns, three on each side of the bridge. These were of smaller caliber, at 20mm each.

The hospital corpsmen were immediately notified to make themselves comfortable on deck, for they would be sleeping there until their arrival at their destination. The corpsmen located spots to camp out toward the bow of the ship until their arrival to wherever they might be going.

The LST was loaded down with army jeeps and trucks loaded with heavy building equipment, all chained to the steel deck and covered with huge sheets of canvas. Below deck, in the hollow of the huge landing ship, were more trucks loaded with equipment along with two army tanks located next to the exit ramp. By noontime the deck of the LST was teeming with soldiers of the infantry and army engineers. At roughly 1800 hours, six in the evening, the ships began to form into a convoy out at sea. The LST began to move ever so slowly while turning starboard and getting into position toward the center of the convoy.

Francisca and the Boys

Warrant Officer Walker appeared from nowhere. "Gentlemen," he said, "for your information, we are headed for Guadalcanal in the Solomon Islands. The island has been secure for some time, so they tell me, but we have to keep our eyes and ears open for there is still some heat in the area."

Everyone understood what Mr. Walker meant by "some heat".

"Guadalcanal?" Nick thought. "Wow, now we are really getting closer to the heat!" Nick had heard about the battle for Guadalcanal that had occurred not too long ago, with great losses to the Marines. He wasn't sure of what he would see once he got there, but he mentally prepared himself for any situation.

After hot days and warm nights and, and at times some pretty rough seas, the convoy slowed to about half its normal speed. Then the convoy seemed to stop completely. Signals were flashed back and forth by the escort ships, four destroyers and one destroyer escort; then the convoy began to pick up speed again. The scuttlebutt was soon doing its designated job. Word came down to the hospital corpsmen that the American fleet was chasing Japanese fighting ships in the area, the reason for the slowing and stopping of the convoy.

As on the arrival at Pearl Harbor, land was again spotted one early afternoon by the men on the deck of the LST. Three of the landing craft broke away from the convoy and headed toward the island of Guadalcanal. As American fighter planes circled the skies above, the LST carrying the Hospital Corpsmen hit the beach. While time moved ahead, early afternoon was soon late afternoon before the huge front doors of the landing ship opened and the ramp slowly dropped, causing a splash of seawater in all directions. The two tanks rolled out of the LST depths and quickly disappeared along a road leading into the jungle of Guadalcanal. The corpsmen leaned over the railing at the bow of the ship to watch the unloading while waiting for orders to disembark. Trucks, jeeps and army personnel moved out slowly but without hesitation.

Afternoon turned to dusk and as darkness fell, the Corpsmen received their orders to disembark. With sea bags on one shoulder, Springfield '03 rifles hanging by a strap on the other, and steel helmets on their heads, the corpsmen filed down the upper-deck ramp to the entrails of the landing craft and out the main ramp below into about two to three feet of seawater. They walked through water soaking their legs well above the knees, Warrant Officer Walker leading the pack.

It was quickly turning dark as the army engineers set up gasoline-powered transformers and electric lines along the beach with lights at about twenty to thirty feet intervals. The contingent of corpsmen continued inland for perhaps fifty or so yards to a clearing past bushes and trees just off the beach. To their surprise, tents had already been set up for them. The army had already done its designated job by the time the hospital corpsmen arrived. Several army cots lay folded a few feet away from the tents.

"Pick your spots, men," Mr. Walker announced. "There is no particular agenda here."

The three buddies each picked up a cot and went on to find a tent. The rest of the corpsmen followed suit, and after they had spread out, all eventually settled down to three men per tent. Warrant Office Walker had a tent all to himself

The sky was clear, and the moon shone brightly down on the camp. Chris, Geib, and Monty were settled. Their gear piled in the center of the small tent, all three lay back on their bunks after removing their wet boots and clothing.

Then all hell seemed to break loose. Shouting came from the beach where the army personnel were still moving equipment about. Then the drone of a plane could be heard from above. It was an enemy dive-bomber getting in position to strike. A whirring could be heard as the bomber began its dive. More shouting and swearing came from the beach.

"The lights" someone shouted, "cut the fuckin' lights."

As the lights went out the loud swishing of the dive-bomber could be heard. When the first bomb struck, all three friends dived to the ground. The plane's engine could now be heard very loud and clear as it went over and past the corpsmen's new camp. A few yards past the camp, a second bomb exploded, missing the camp by at least fifty yards.

The first to speak after the scare was Geib. "Chris, you okay?"

"Yeah, I'm okay!"

"Monty, how are you doing?" Geib asked.

"I'm in good shape," Nick answered. "but it scared the shit out of me, I'm still shaking!"

Everyone laughed.

On further investigation by Walker, he found that there had been no casualties on the beach or in the corpsmen's camp. As luck would have it, each bomb exploded harmlessly in two areas that were not occupied by personnel, which happened to be between the beach and the corpsmen's camp, and beyond the camp at the clearing. A long tear was spotted on the upper part of the trio's tent by Chris. No one was sure if it had been from shrapnel or from the air pressure force from the exploding bomb. In any case, all three had now received their first real taste of the war.

The activity on the beach continued through the night while the Hospital Corpsmen's camp went into a mode of silence as every corpsman gave in to fatigue and finally fell asleep. Nick awoke to the distant sound of a bugle's reveille, the unmistakable signal that it was time to get up. The bugle could have been coming from any camp in the interior of the island, for contingents of Marines, army, and navy construction battalions had occupied it following the initial landings of August 1942 by the Marine Corps. After many losses since the first landing by the Marines, the island of Guadalcanal had been finally secured and the construction of Henderson Field (formerly the Lunga Point Airfield) by the army engineers had been completed.

As the trio of friends sat up on their cots, Warrant Officer Walker could be heard outside the tent. "Up and at 'em, men. Get up and step outside with mess kits!"

The men stepped out of their respective tents, and gathered around Walker, mess kits in hand.

Walker introduced a young boatswain's mate from one of the navy construction battalions on the island. "The boatswain's mate here will take you to mess, and we will meet back here right after chow."

Nick noticed that most of the strict military order was slowly beginning to fade. Walker spoke to the men in a mostly friendly and nonmilitary manner, something that the men greatly appreciated after experiences through boot camp training and Hospital Corps School and all the rest of it. After all, Walker had also been an enlisted man at one time and had literally come up through the ranks.

As the corpsmen followed the boatswain's mate, they saw through the trees, for the first time and up close, the devastation caused by the pounding the island had received by navy firepower from the sea and by navy dive-bombers and fighters from the air before the initial invasion of August 1942. The invasion of Guadalcanal had been the first major offensive action of the war in the Pacific by the United States and its allies. At times, there were sea battles going on between the Japanese naval forces and the U.S. fleet, with much help from the Australian navy, and the Japanese were clearly the dominating factor, because they were the superior naval power at the time. At this late date, after the initial invasion of Guadalcanal, fighting was going on by land, sea, and air throughout the Solomon Islands, with the United States and its allies trying to close the gap against the Japanese. That gap was closing slowly, but it was closing. Guadalcanal had been officially secured in February 1943, but here it was May 1943, and bombs were still being dropped by Japanese dive bombers.

The Seabees were building a compound with Quonset huts for offices and eventually a field hospital, but it was not nearly finished, so in the meantime, long field tents had been erected as temporary hospital wards and operating rooms. Here the hospital corpsmen would do their designated job.

By the third day after the landing of the latest contingent of army and navy personnel, the hospital corpsmen had set up operating room facilities and one long tent with cots for hospital ward accommodations. That very day, the hospital corps received their first casualties from the fighting that was going on in the surrounding area. Nick had yet to know who the doctors were that were a part of the group that he was attached to. There were a number of doctors in the officers' quarters, perhaps eight or ten, and they all seemed to get involved when casualties started to appear. Walker was the head pharmacist, and he was the one to hand out the particular duties to his corpsmen.

The ward was slowly filling with casualties, mostly Marines and Army suffering from gunshot and shrapnel wounds. There was only one navy man among the casualties. He had been caught in an explosion from below decks that had caught him on his way out of a hatch on the top deck of his ship.

Mr. Walker was talking to the sailor as Nick was coming into the ward.

"Delmonte," Walker called to Nick, "come over here, and see what you can do for this man. Stick with him, and if you need advice, talk to Doctor Comer; he's around here somewhere."

Nick felt good and somewhat proud that Mr. Walker had such confidence in him to leave him by himself to attend to a burn patient. Nick was a little bit nervous, but he said to himself, "Well, that's what the hell I'm here for."

The young sailor was sitting up on his cot with legs stretched to the ground and his arms out as he held onto the edge of the cot. He could not lie back because his entire body was blistered from the neck down. At the time of the explosion, the sailor had been wearing only a pair of shorts that had protected him from burns to his genitals and buttocks. His legs were burned from just above the knees down to his ankles. His upper body was burned from the neckline to the waist. His left arm was burned, but his right arm was unscathed; evidently, it was the arm he used to open the hatch.

Nick introduced himself. "Hi, buddy. My name's Delmonte. I'll be the corpsman taking care of you for a while."

"Hi, Doc. I'm in a little bit of trouble here. Can you do something for me? My name's McClellan, Boatswains Mate Second."

"Oh, I'm also second class. Let's see what we can do for you." From then on Nick referred to his patient as "Boats." "What are you feeling right now Boats, I know it's a stupid question but your answer can help in the healing process."

"Well," Boats answered, "it's not as painful as it was earlier, but I feel numb all over; it just hurts when you touch the skin."

"Okay, just sit tight while I go pick up some necessary equipment. I'll be right back."

"Okay, Doc," Boats said.

Nick went out to the medical supply tent and returned with all the tools he needed to help heal his patient. He brought back a container of petroleum jelly, a few large rolls of gauze and tools such as scissors and tweezers, rubber gloves, alcohol, and the latest medical discovery used to fight infection called penicillin in the form of a powder. Everything that Nick brought back had been sterilized, including the rubber gloves. He could not scrub his hands because there was no water available nearby so he washed them with alcohol.

"We're going to pull off all these blisters the best we can. If it hurts to where you can't stand it, just let me know and we'll stop," Nick told his patient.

Nick had brought in all his equipment on a small portable table with wheels. He also had managed to conjure up some army blankets, which he used to build up the cot along with a rubber sheet and a white sheet to absorb any drainage.

Doctor Comer walked in at a short break from surgery. "How are things going, Delmonte?"

"So far, so good. We're about ready to start pealing the burned skin."

Doctor Comer walked closer to Boats and introduced himself while looking closely at his burned body. The doctor was wearing a surgical gown and hat and was still wearing rubber gloves. He didn't touch Boats anywhere; he just inspected his upper body to see how deep his injury had been.

"Most of it is superficial," the doctor commented. "I believe you will heal very well. You're in good hands." He turned and left abruptly.

Dr. Comer, a man about six and a half feet tall with slightly stooped shoulders and in his early thirties, was one of the younger surgeons in a group of perhaps a half-dozen doctors who were also slated for Acorn detachments. Militarily, he was ranked as a lieutenant in the navy. Nick was quite sure that Dr. Comer would eventually be a member of Acorn 11, because he noticed that the doctor and Warrant Officer Walker seemed pretty much to pal around together.

Nick went back to his job. After the cot was prepared, Boats again sat in his original position on the edge of the cot. Nick began the work of painstakingly removing dead tissue from Boats' body. With his gloved fingers and occasionally with tweezers, Nick managed to remove all of the loose tissue within an hour. In that time, other than a twitch now and then, there was not one whimper from Boats.

Nick washed residue from his gloved hands with alcohol as he prepared to bandage Boats' body. He removed all equipment from the table and spread a sterilized towel on the surface. He then cut an arm's length of gauze three inches wide and placed it on the towel. He took a wad of petroleum jelly and smeared it the length of the gauze. He then took some powdered penicillin and sprinkled it on the gel; then he placed the first piece of bandage across Boats' back. When the medicated gauze touched his body, Boats flinched slightly and then let out an enormous sigh of relief.

"Ah, Doc, that feels great," he muttered.

Nick repeated the procedure until every burned section of Boats' body was covered with the medicated gauze.

TWENTY-THREE

After a month or so, Boats was ready to return to duty. His body had healed completely, but a reddish tinge remained on his skin, which, with time, would disappear.

Nick had other duties to perform, particularly in surgery when he had the watch. Now there was a little more order and calm since his arrival at Guadalcanal. By the middle of June 1943, the Quonset huts for the new field hospital had been put together and set up, so all of the casualties were now taken there for emergency treatment. The cots in the tent that had been used as a ward for the injured had now been removed, and the tent was converted into a reading room. On Sundays, it was sometimes used for lectures by officers representing different religions.

Deeper into the island there was a valley that was being used as a dump by all of the surrounding outfits. Nick sometimes went there for target practice, mostly to kill time and to get some use out of his rifle.

There was a theater built on a slope about a half-mile inland. The movie screen was set up at the bottom, and long benches had been built on the slope for the audience. Saturday nights were movie nights. On Sundays it was used for church services. One Sunday, Nick decided it was time to go to Mass and perhaps to confession. His two buddies, Geib and Chris, were regular churchgoers, and they had more or less convinced him to go to confession.

The priest listened to confessions after Mass at the bottom of the slope near the movie screen. There was no confessional, so the priest sat with his back toward those confessing so as not to see each other face-to-face, because confessions are private and confidential matters.

After Mass, Nick walked down the slope to where the priest was hearing confessions. When his turn came, he knelt with his face slightly turned away from the priest. "Bless me, Father, for I have sinned."

"Yes, my son."

Nick continued with his confession. Since coming overseas, Nick had not had too much to cause him to sin except that he thought a great deal about women and sometimes masturbated. So he made up something about bad thoughts and confessed the masturbating. At that instant, the priest turned to Nick and, with anger in his voice, half-shouted, "What did you say?"

Nick didn't have time to answer as the priest very sternly gave him a high penance of ten Our Fathers and ten Hail Mary's. Nick turned and left the area without fulfilling his penance, convinced that he would never go to confession again, much less to Mass.

On the other hand, among the officers was a young navy lieutenant who was also a Roman Catholic priest. He appeared at the reading tent one day to give a talk on religion versus atheism, not to say Mass. Catholics and Protestants alike attended the lecture, for the scuttlebutt had it that the lecturer was pretty good. Nick and his two buddies were also there.

The young lieutenant began his lecture by going back to the days of the crucifixion of Christ and to all the different gods of the ancient Romans, Egyptians, the Aztecs and Mayans and how the Jewish faith began. Then he turned to Darwin's theory of evolution and spoke at length about prehistoric man. The young priest's audience was held spellbound for close to two hours.

When everyone left the tent, there were discussions going on within groups of three or four, including Nick, Geib, and Chris. Chris did not say much about the lecture because he avoided discussions about religion or politics. At around fifty years of age, he knew better. Geib, a staunch Catholic, argued that in spite of Darwin's theory of evolution, it did not mean that there was no God.

Nick argued back that Darwin's Theory was more logical, but he would not argue that God did not exist. What he would say while looking downward and shaking his head from side to side was "I don't know!" However, Nick mentioned to Geib what had happened to him at confession that Sunday morning.

"What?" Geib remarked when Nick told him he did not do his penance. "God's gonna punish you!" Geib said with a grin.

"Well, so be it, but that priest was not supposed to look at me when I was confessing," Nick said. "Then you wonder why people want to change religions." As an afterthought, Nick said, "That priest is an asshole!"

Everyone laughed.

Late in September 1943, the trio learned that they were moving out one morning. The navy construction battalion, or Seabees, had already arrived at their destination further north into the Solomon Islands. No one in the medical group knew exactly what the destination was, including Walker, and if Walker did know, he wasn't saying.

The day before their departure from Guadalcanal, all the corpsmen were prepared for the worst, for they were going into territory that had not yet been completely secured. Warrant Officer Walker called the group together.

"Gentlemen," he said, "we are going into a hotspot where the Japanese are still shelling from the sea and bombing from the air. It is worth repeating that we must all remain focused. Get as much rest as you can. We will be boarding a small ship around midnight tonight. Pack your sea bags and be sure to load your rifles. Put your helmets on before boarding. Do I make myself clear?"

"Yes, sir!" the group shouted in unison.

In spite of the suggestion by Walker to get some rest, with all the nervousness in each corpsman, they all remained awake in anticipation of the coming action. By this time, all the corpsmen had gone up one rating having taken their examinations during their stay at Guadalcanal. Now Chris was a first-class pharmacist mate, and all the rest went up to second class.

A little bit after midnight, Walker assembled the men and lead them down to the beach to where small boats were waiting at a loading dock recently built by army engineers. The contingent of corpsmen was divided into two groups, and each group boarded a small boat. A few yards out from the beach, a ship that looked like a tugboat waited for its passengers. On closer look the silhouettes of three antiaircraft guns could be seen mounted on the ship, one at the bow, another aft, and the third on the bridge. Within a few minutes, all the corpsmen were aboard, and soon were on their way.

Turning in a northerly direction the tug soon rendezvoused with a destroyer escort and followed it out to sea. Before daybreak, perhaps five or six hours later, the islands could be seen in the distance. Flashes of cannon fire could be seen from a distance to the north, and explosions could be heard just ahead in the direction that the corpsmen were headed.

The ship carrying the medical group came to a stop a short distance from the beach. The destroyer escort remained farther out to sea and patrolled north to south while the tug waited. Within minutes, a small landing craft appeared and pulled up the side of the small ship and tied up. Rope ladders were dropped over the side and the Hospital Corpsmen began their descent into the landing craft utility, called an LCU for short. Right behind them were Walker, Dr. Comer, and the Chief Surgeon, Dr. Cushman.

The LCU was equipped with a 20mm antiaircraft gun mounted in the center, directly in front and slightly below the helmsman. The gunner sat comfortably in the steel saddle. The LCU was untied, pulled away, and turned south. Morning was beginning to break, and now the jungle along the beach could be seen clearly. About a half-mile south, the LCU made a sharp left turn into a long, wide strip of water leading into a large bay surrounded by land and jungle all around.

Lights could be seen to the right as the landing craft traveled along near the beach. For a distance of about two or three miles, where the island made a slight turn, no lights could be seen; then more lights appeared almost directly on the beach. The helmsman turned his craft directly toward the lights and the beach. When the craft hit the beach, the ramp dropped. The men followed Walker off the LCU past a road that was being built by the naval construction battalions and into the edge of the jungle. The LCU backed away from the beach, turned, and disappeared in the direction from which it came.

There was a large area past the road where trees and brush had been cleared. This area was littered with equipment and materials used in the construction of Quonset huts. Tractors and road plows were already pushing earth, building of the road south toward the mouth of the bay from where the LCU had entered was in progress. There was movement in the area around the unfinished road. The Seabees were up and about.

A chief petty officer who seemed to be in charge of the Seabees crew walked over to Walker and introduced himself. "We set up two large field tents as temporary quarters for now. You may be there for a week or so until we finish your compound," the chief told Walker. "Follow me and I'll show you where the tents are located, and you can take it from there."

"Okay," Walker responded as he followed the chief and signaled his men with an arm to follow.

As the two walked together, the Chief gave Walker some vital information, something that every corpsman in the group was concerned about. "Up to now, we haven't been hit in this particular area because the Japs don't know we are here yet, but the airstrip we are building has been bombed and strafed a few times, and shelling from Kolombangara has hit the strip but without any serious damage."

Walker knew that they were now somewhere in the New Georgia Islands north of Guadalcanal, but he didn't know exactly which island they were on. He also knew that Kolombangara was in New Georgia. He asked the chief about that, and the chief explained it to him in a rather seemingly complicated way.

"Well," the chief began, "this island is called Ondonga, and it's not actually a part of the New Georgia group. It is some type of monarchy with a head honcho, perhaps a king. The island is separated from New Georgia by a body of water a few miles north of here that is slowly drying up; it's closer to a swamp now. South of here about four or five miles is the landing strip that is only half finished. This road we are working on will connect the airstrip to your compound in just a few more days."

Sirens sounded from the direction of the airstrip. Planes could be heard overhead. New Zealander fighter planes flying from Guadalcanal circled above unchallenged. When the sirens sounded, the group was already in the tents, which were hidden from above by surrounding palm trees. The chief showed Walker where cases of canned foods of different types, including canned peaches were: temporary food supplies until the mess hall was built. There were four large jugs of drinking water, and several army cots still folded and piled just outside the tent.

"If you need anything, like more information," the chief said, "I'll be close by. Just let me know." The chief turned to leave then stopped abruptly and said, "Oh, by the way, the word *ondongo*, with an *oh*, means 'the place of death' in the native language." The chief smiled and walked away.

Within days, an operating table had been built by the Seabees and placed in one of the tents. Operating tools and equipment and medicines followed, and the OR was open for business. All the Quonset huts were not quite finished, but there was one that could be used temporarily as a ward for the injured. There was fighting going on all through the islands and casualties started coming into the Naval Medical Dispensary, as it was formally known. During the shelling and bombing of the airstrip, not one shell or bomb fell in the area of the dispensary.

Gunshot and shrapnel wounds were the most common. There were a few with internal problems, such as bleeding ulcers or other types of injuries such as dislocated or broken bones. All patients were placed in the ward and kept until healing was accomplished.

Within a week's time, the compound was complete. The first two Quonset huts were built to form a *T*. The top of the *T* was divided in half, one side containing the operating room and the other side becoming the officers' quarters. The connecting Quonset hut became a ward that could accommodate sixteen cots for the sick and wounded. The third Quonset hut, located about twenty to thirty yards inland from the operating room and the ward, was used as a barracks for the enlisted men. It was built not more than ten feet from the edge of the jungle.

More material was brought in for Quonset huts, and a long structure began to take form about one hundred yards north of the dispensary. Through the scuttlebutt line of information, the corpsmen learned it would be a mess hall that could accommodate a large number of personnel. That signaled that more troops were expected in the very near future.

After perhaps a month or so, the naval dispensary was complete and well organized. Four-hour watches were set, according to navy regulations, with every corpsman in the group trained to take responsibility for any medical or surgical emergency on his watch. The island became more populated as army and navy personnel and Marines moved in to establish camps and compounds. The Seabees had by now added a second landing strip to the airfield, which became the base for a New Zealander fighter wing flying P-40s.

Since entering the warzone, the corpsmen had most often seen Lockheed P-38 double fuselage fighter in the sky. One other fighter plane, the P-39, which had been built with the engine behind the cockpit, had been seen for a short time in the area, but it was recalled because of errors in design.

On one occasion, a tragic accident occurred to a P-39 coming in for an emergency landing at the airstrip. The pilot misjudged the distance to the end of the strip and overran it crashing his plane. A call was immediately relayed to the dispensary for a team to investigate for injuries.

Warrant Officer Walker poked his head into the barracks doorway and half-shouted, "Delmonte, take a jeep and go up to the airstrip to check for injuries. A plane just crashed. Pick up a kit and take somebody with you."

Nick jumped up from his cot. "Let's go, Geib!"

Geib was on his feet even before Nick shouted. Geib ran into the OR and picked up an emergency kit, and Nick jumped into a jeep and started it. The jeep raised some dust as it traveled toward the strip.

At a distance, they could see the tail of the plane sticking up in the air. It took less than ten minutes to arrive at the air airstrip. The strip came to an abrupt ending at an embankment that sloped down to the road. At the end of the strip were rocks and rubble left there purposely during construction. Beyond the rubble were palm trees and bushes on the slope. Nick stopped the jeep and both men jumped out and ran up the embankment to where the airstrip came to an end.

The fighter plane was smoking from behind the cockpit, and the pilot was hunched over in his seat. Nick outdistanced Geib by a few feet as they ran up the embankment. He climbed up on the wing of the plane and looked in the cockpit. Nick was aghast at what he saw. The pilot's head had been cut away from the back of his neck, through the skull between the ears, only the face remained intact. Blood spurted from arteries leading into the body. The fuselage had been cut open by the force of the engine ripping away from the plane and consequently hitting the pilot behind the head.

"Geib," shouted Nick, "this guy is gone. His head was torn off!"

Geib climbed up to take a look. "Holy Mother of God!" Geib remarked, his Irish half was showing.

Before coming down from the plane, Nick looked out past the embankment and spotted a trail of torn and burned brush leading to the plane's engine a few yards away. The two Corpsmen got off the wing and went over to look at the engine that was smoking hot. They returned to the compound to make their report. In the months to come, Nick learned that the P-39 had been taken out of service after a few similar accidents had occurred.

Wounded men of every service in the area soon filled the hospital ward. The operating room was in constant use by Dr. Cushman and Dr. Comer. Besides patients that had been wounded in armed conflict, others had been seriously hurt or killed by foolish mistakes. For example, a soldier was wounded in the legs while fishing with hand grenades. One of the grenades exploded prematurely in his boat before he could toss it into the water; consequently, both his legs were shattered from the ankles to the knees. He died on the operating table from loss of blood. Another time, a young sailor on liberty from the cruiser *Montpelier*, which happened to be in the bay, climbed one of the palm trees near the dispensary to pick coconuts and fell thirty feet, landing on his head. The result of the fall was a fractured skull, which caused bleeding in his brain. He died a few hours later.

At times the operating room was so busy that it was divided by a hanging sheet and both surgeons worked simultaneously. On one occasion while Nick had the duty, a soldier was brought in with a bullet wound to the chest. He was bleeding profusely, but he was still alive.

Chief Surgeon Cushman, a man in his middle to late fifties who wore glasses on the tip of his nose, received the patient in the OR. The doctor only had time to put on his mask and rubber gloves. The patient was in critical condition and was swiftly turning pale. There was no time for anesthesia for the soldier was fading fast.

The patient was placed face up on the operating table and his blood-soaked shirt was cut away from his body. A handful of blood-soaked bandages were pulled away from the wound, and blood squirted out, hitting Dr. Cushman in the face covering his glasses with blood. The doctor opened the man's chest and cut away tissue to get to the patient's heart. There was no time to cut into the rib cage. The doctor could see where the carotid artery had been nicked just above the aorta by the bullet.

Nick handed him a threaded curved needle on a clamp. Dr. Cushman dug his fingers in between two ribs in an effort to pull out the artery. He failed. As he decided to cut away on the ribs, the soldier's heart stopped beating. The blood flow slowed to just drainage. The doctor pounded the patient's chest in a futile attempt to restart the heart. The soldier died on the operating table. All the hospital corpsmen attended the autopsy, scheduled for that afternoon. After the autopsy Nick and two other Corpsmen remained behind to sew up the body and wrap it in canvas. The body was later picked up by the army.

One more incident occurred that rattled Nick's thoughts on the sanctity of life. While strolling through the jungle with free time on his hands, Nick stumbled onto a figure lying on his back in the deep brush. It was a navy lieutenant junior grade in full dress uniform. There was a bullet hole in his right temple, and on the left side of his head was a large blob of brain matter that had exploded out when the pistol shot went through his head. The end of a life perhaps caused by a "dear John" letter, or just because the young man could not withstand the consequences of war.

TWENTY-FOUR

By mid-December 1943, the island of Ondonga was completely occupied as U.S. and allied forces continued their advances northward in the South Pacific. Fierce sea battles between American and Japanese ships were going on throughout the Pacific. Gaines and losses were chalked up by both sides. But the U.S. Navy held strong and slowly gained superiority over the Japanese.

The ward at the dispensary was now about half filled with patients. The OR was down to about one operation per week, but the dispensary was still tending to the sick and injured on the Island.

Christmas and New Years came and left with celebrations at the dispensary with cold beer and pure alcohol supplied by the pharmacy. The corpsmen were obliged to do something with their spare time, of which there was plenty. A space just outside the OR was cleaned and raked, and a net was erected to form a volleyball court. A softball team was organized, and games were booked with teams from other services. Nick played shortstop and was a "good field, no hit" in the twelve-inch fast-pitch games.

Geib and Nick entered all races in the half-mile run at track meets. Geib usually set the pace, with Nick following right behind; then Geib would drop out from exhaustion and cheer Nick on to the finish. Nick never won a half-miler, but he usually placed second or third.

The Seabees built a boxing ring about a half-mile inland and were about to begin to have smokers. They were short of boxers, so one of the organizers went out looking for men who might be interested. Nick immediately offered his services when a chief from one of the construction battalions asked for volunteers to try out. As luck would have it, Pizzuto, a thorn in the side to Nick since they trained back at Hueneme, also volunteered.

Nick and Pizzuto were friendly enough but Pizzuto had a character about him that was sort of braggadocio. Whenever he saw the opportunity to ridicule Nick, he would do so. Pizzuto was from the Bronx in New York, and Nick was from the West Side of Chicago, two neighborhoods with a history of poverty and tough kids. It was inevitable that these two would someday butt heads in one form or another.

Nick, at five feet eight inches in height and 126 pounds asked to be matched with Pizzuto, who was taller and at about 135 pounds. Besides, of the guys that volunteered, these two were the closest to a match in weight. Now Nick could exhibit the skills he had learned from his ex-brother-in-law Louie, the ex-professional fighter who had taught Nick how to defend himself under any circumstances.

Pizzuto grinned at Nick while both were being fitted with boxing gloves. Nick looked downward as the trainer tied his gloves, not giving Pizzuto the slightest inkling as to what was about to occur.

"All right, men," the trainer said as he held each one by a wrist. "When I say, 'Break,' you step back until I tell you to continue boxing. You will box for two minutes, and the tryout will be over. No hitting after I say, 'Break,' no hitting below the belt or in the back of the head, and no head butting. Step back and when I say, 'Box,' start boxing." The trainer looked at both men, who were standing a few feet apart. He raised his right hand, then brought it down swiftly and with a soft tone said, "Box!"

At the word, Pizzuto rushed toward Nick with his hands in position of a boxer. He came in fast, and Nick sidestepped, and as Pizzuto went by, Nick gave him a slight shove on the elbow. Pizzuto went flying forward, almost falling over from the momentum. Pizzuto turned around and had a ferocious look in his eyes, ready to beat up on his opponent. This time, Nick gave Pizzuto a slight grin and began walking backward in a circle with hands in position.

Again, Pizzuto rushed at Nick. This time, Nick knocked his lead hand out of position with his left hand, then landed a right hook between Pizzuto's eyes. Pizzuto's eyes watered, and he recovered and positioned himself to continue. Now Nick was about to put on a show.

Pizzuto wasn't rushing anymore, so he struck his stance as a boxer and waited for Nick to throw a punch as he circled to his left. Nick did not throw a punch; he threw several punches. Nick stepped in close and feigned a right to the head, and Pizzuto stepped back dropping both arms to his sides. As Pizzuto dropped his arms, Nick stepped in and landed several blows to the head with both hands, one after the other. Then he stepped back and threw an overhand right to the head that landed squarely on Pizzuto's nose. Pizzuto was covered with blood and had to quit before the two minutes expired.

The gloves were removed from both fighters. Pizzuto was given a wet towel to place on his forehead, and his nostrils were stuffed with cotton.

"It's nothing serious," the trainer told Pizzuto. "The bleeding will stop pretty soon, and you'll be fine." The trainer pulled Nick to one side. "Nice exhibition, where did you learn those moves?"

"My brother-in-law taught me; he was a fighter a while back," Nick replied.

"Are you interested in fighting in the ring?"

"Yeah."

"Okay," the trainer said. "Come over to the ring first chance you get, and we'll get you started training and maybe get you a fight for our next smoker, okay?"

"Yeah, okay." Nick walked over to Pizzuto. "How you doing, Piz?"

"I'm all right; the bleeding stopped," Pizzuto replied. "Monty, you never told me you knew how to box, you fucker!"

Nick laughed. "You never asked, stupid!"

After that little encounter, Pizzuto sort of blended somewhat and thereafter, he and Nick became closer friends. Pizzuto was still more or less the clown, but he refrained from being repulsive and obnoxious toward Nick.

Next day Nick went over to where the boxing ring had been erected and found the trainer inside the boxing gym, a double tent equipped with punching bag, a heavy bag, and other boxing paraphernalia. The trainer was of Polish descent and was named Borackowski. He had been middleweight champion of the State of New York years back and had suffered a broken left arm in a car accident. The break was a compound fracture that healed with the forearm to hang only halfway down the side. He had managed to convince the navy that he could handle any job regardless of the condition of his arm. Being a former navy man was the biggest reason the navy wanted to enlist him. Because his arm was no longer in a normal position, Borackowski had quit boxing. He continued training and developing young fighters and, as a consequence, had carried his career into the service. Everyone in the area knew Borackowski as Borac.

"Where do I start?" Nick asked.

"Let's see you hit the punching bag," Borac said.

"Okay," Nick answered.

The punching bag was a little bit too high for Nick, so Borac adjusted it to accommodate Nick and gave him a pair of leather mittens. Nick was rusty at punching the bag for it had been about four or five years since he had been to the YMCA. However, once he got started and into a rhythm, he showed Borac that he could handle the bag.

After a few minutes of punching the bag, Borac stopped Nick. "Have you ever fought inside of a boxing ring?"

Nick replied that he had not. Borac picked up a pair of the gloves and told Nick to follow him into the ring. In the center of the ring, Borac put the gloves on Nick's hands.

"I noticed that you fight out of a crouch. Have you ever tried fighting standing straight up?"

"Yeah," replied Nick, "but most of the guys I had fights with were always bigger than me, and it always made it harder for them to hit me when I crouched. My brother-in-law taught me that."

"All right then," Borac said with a smile. "We'll do a little sparring and I'll show you some things that might help you when you get into the ring. Take your normal stance. You see that your left hand is out in front and the right hand is back inside toward your body."

Nick nodded in agreement after taking his stance. Borac, not wearing gloves took the same stance opposite Nick.

"Now notice that we both are standing the same facing each other. My left hand is out, and my right hand is inside, which means that it's cocked and ready to strike at any opportunity."

Nick nodded that he understood what Borac was saying.

"Now," Borac continued, "if I throw my right hand at you, and you are circling backward to your left, I will be able to catch you with an overhand right or a right hook in an instant by feigning with my left, which would cause you to drop your guard. I noticed that you did exactly that when you gave your friend that bloody nose at the tryouts."

Nick raised his eyebrows because he didn't know exactly how he did it.

"But here is the kicker," Borac continued. "The same effect will not come about if you happen to be fighting a southpaw. So what do you do? You do exactly the opposite. You circle your left-handed opponent to your left, or his right, making his left hand less effective."

Borac and Nick sparred a few minutes, with Borac changing positions from a right hand to a left hand giving Nick the opportunity to test both positions.

"Here's another little move that is very important," Borac said. "When you are in a clinch with your opponent and you break the clinch, gently push his lead arm by the elbow away from you and that will put him off balance to prevent him from striking you after the break, and remember one more important thing: always keep your eyes on his hands, not his feet, not his eyes, but his hands!"

Borac demonstrated the clinch move from left and right several times until Nick became accustomed to both.

"Okay," Borac announced, "remember what you learned today, and next time we will go over some more stuff." Borac lead Nick back to the gym tent and put him on a scale. "One hundred twenty-five-and-a-half pounds. We may have a tough time finding someone your weight to fight. We'll see."

Nick left the compound elated that he was going to fight in the ring and a little befuddled that there was so much detail to boxing.

One Sunday afternoon, most of the Corpsmen were playing volleyball when Nick showed up after his watch was over. He entered the volleyball game as soon as there was an opening. After the game Nick met up with Geib and Pizzuto just to talk and to go into the jungle to explore. Pizzuto had decided he would not enter into boxing after his experience at the tryouts, but he was curious about Nick's involvement and wanted to know what was going on at the boxing tents.

"What's the latest with the boxing thing," he asked Nick.

"Borac is trying to get me a match for the next smoker," Nick answered.

Geib cut in. "When will that be?"

"The next smoker is a week from Saturday, so that gives me about two weeks to get ready," Nick answered.

Pizzuto, ever the clown, said, "Are you scared? You're not chicken, are you?"

Nick turned to Pizzuto with feigned anger. "Fuck you, Piz. If I was scared, I wouldn't have kicked your ass to get in!"

"Okay, okay, I was just fuckin' with you!" Pizzuto remarked.

All three corpsmen laughed it off.

When the trio returned to the barracks Pizzuto spread the news. "Monty's gonna kick some ass," he shouted into the barracks as the three walked in. "He's fighting next week!"

Nick became the talk of the barracks. Then the officers got the word, and it spread to the air strip. Former patients who had gotten to know him in the ward heard about the coming event. Nick had met some of the fighters at the gym but could not make any friends. Most of the guys acted like prima donnas and would literally look down on Nick, because of his size.

But Borac's interest in Nick's boxing ability did not waiver. As the smoker date came closer, Nick prepared himself according to the regimen set by Borac. A week before the Smoker Borac called Nick to one side.

"I want you to go a minute or so with that fellow over there, but I want you to hold back your punches, just box him without actually connecting."

Nick did not understand why Broc wanted him to hold back his punches, but he would do it. The other fighter was a head taller than Nick and was at least fifteen pounds heavier. He looked at Nick with hatred in his eyes, but Nick did not flinch.

"All right, guys," Borac told them. "When I say, 'Go,' start boxing."

Then Borac said, "Go!"

Immediately Nick's opponent attacked him, forcing Nick to go into his crouch. Only a few punches were thrown, but several landed heavily on Nick's head. Nick counterpunched, trying to hold back his punches like Borac had told to do. When he could not hold back, Nick let go with a few fast punches, infuriating the other fighter. At that moment, Borac stepped in and stopped the sparring.

"Okay, fellas, that's all for now. Don't leave yet, Monty," Borac said. He dismissed the other fighter who left with a smirk on his face. "How would you like to fight this guy in the ring?"

"No, the guy's too big. All he would need is to connect a good punch, and he would knock me out. He's just too heavy!"

Francisca and the Boys

Borac smiled with a knowing look on his face. He had just given Nick his personal test for courage and intelligence. "We have a fight for you for Saturday, and I'll be in your corner. You'll be in the preliminary, which starts at eight o'clock sharp. Don't be late!"

Fighters in different weight classes from all around the islands appeared at these smokers. Now and then, there would be a fighter from a nearby ship. Each trainer had one or sometimes two fighters to ensure a full complement of participants at smokers. Nick arranged for his buddy Geib to be a second at his corner on fight night. He would assist Borac in the corner.

Saturday morning Nick went for breakfast at the mess hall and turned down everything on the menu except oatmeal with powdered milk. At lunchtime, he stopped in to see his bakery buddies who already knew about his approaching bout. They gave him a loaf of French-style bread, hot off the pan, with butter and a can of cold grapefruit juice. He ate half of the loaf and sipped the juice just enough to wash down the bread. That held him until fight time.

Geib and Nick arrived at the ring site at a little after seven that evening. A crowd had already gathered, and a steady flow of new arrivals was filling the expansive area way back into the trees. Spectators brought stools and cushions or anything else they could sit on. The late comers climbed surrounding trees for a better view

"Holy shit," Nick exclaimed, "look at all the people, Geib!"

"Yeah, you're a celebrity."

"Hell no. These guys don't even know who the hell I am. They're just here for the fights."

"Well, you better win so they know who you are," Geib replied.

Borac was already there when Geib and Nick walked into the training tent. The weather on the island was always the same, usually at a temperature of 100 degrees or more. At night it might drop a little but not very much. This particular night was no different; after so many months in the South Pacific, Nick was accustomed to it. Nick wore cutaway shorts and his denim shirt and white gym shoes. In the training tent Borac told Nick to lie back on a cot and to just relax. Well, he did lie on the cot, but relaxing was another thing. He just couldn't do it.

Finally it was time.

Borac, Nick, and Geib walked out of the tent with Borac in the lead and Nick behind him with a towel over his back and shoulders. Geib followed carrying a bucket with water and a sponge and extra towels. From above, huge spotlights shone brightly into the ring, making the heat even seem hotter.

Borac climbed up to the ring first and held the ropes apart for Nick to go through. Nick went through and sat on a stool provided. Nick's nerves were on edge, but he managed to hide his anxiety as Borac smeared petroleum jelly above his eyebrows and on his cheekbones. Borac talked to Nick continuously as he prepared him for his first fight.

The bell rang about eight or ten times in a row to quiet down the crowd. The announcer introduced each fighter by name as he pointed to each corner. Nick was introduced as "Monty" Delmonte as he looked across to the other corner. His opponent was sitting, so Nick couldn't tell too much about his size, but he did look kind of skinny.

The referee called the combatants to the center of the ring. His opponent stood up and walked to the center, as did Nick, and that was when Nick finally noticed how tall he really was. He had to be at least six feet tall and perhaps six to eight pounds heavier than Nick. Nick immediately dismissed that fact from his mind and prepared to do battle.

Instructions were given like those at the tryouts. Nick didn't pay much attention to them. Finally the referee said, "Shake hands; go back to your corners; and when the bell rings, come out fighting."

The bell rang. Both fighters took their stances and circled each other for a few seconds. Nick's opponent jabbed at him with his left, barely tapping Nick on the forehead. Nick bobbed and weaved, then stepped in under the long arms of his opponent and landed a left and a right to each side of his opponent's head. The fighters stalked each other, both landing punches when and where they could. Nick went into his crouch and stepped in and out of his opponent's reach. After a few feints from each fighter, Nick's opponent jabbed a left to Nick's head several times connecting two times, on the third jab, Nick went under his reaching left arm and scored a half dozen punches to the jaw that made the other fighter step back. A roar went up from the audience. The bell rang ending round one.

"You're ahead," Borac told Nick as he sprayed water from a wet towel into his face, then wiped him down in his corner. "Keep your eyes on his hands."

Nick nodded in the affirmative as the bell rang for the second round. Nick stepped in to meet the opposing fighter and took his stance as usual. Suddenly, his opponent led with an overhand right that landed squarely on Nick's left temple. Nick stood legs apart as he began to lose his balance. The lights seemed to circle around his head as he waited to fall to the canvas. He shook his head violently trying to clear it. Just as it did, the other fighter came in for the kill. Nick ducked under and clinched his opponent, giving him enough time to make sense of where he was.

The referee broke the fighters from the clinch. The fighters went back into their fighting stance. They circled each other. Nick suddenly remembered an old trick that he had learned in the streets of Chicago. His opponent's left hand was out in front as usual, and Nick made a move to go in but stopped suddenly and hit his opponent's lead hand sharply with his left. At that moment, the other fighter dropped his right hand, and with both of his opponent's hands at his sides, Nick took advantage. He stepped in, landed several shots to his opponent's head, and backed the other fighter against the ropes. Nick pummeled his opponent who in turn caused a clinch by holding Nick's gloved hands between his own arms and rib cage. The crowd was going wild, and through the din, he could hear his buddies screaming, "Monty! Monty! Monty!" The round ended.

The third and last round was much of the same. Nick's style of boxing became too difficult for his opponent to solve. The judges' cards were collected by the announcer, and as he read them, he walked to the center of the ring holding a microphone. The referee held both fighters by a wrist waiting for the announcement.

"The winner by a unanimous decision—'Monty' Delmonte." The referee raised Nick's hand to be recognized as the winner.

The other fighter walked away toward his corner.

Borac whispered in Nick's ear. "Go shake his hand and congratulate him on a good fight."

Nick did what Borac told him, and the other fighter graciously responded, saying, "You're pretty good pal. Nice going."

They shook hands.

All fights during wartime were limited to two-minute rounds and only three rounds per bout. To Nick, he felt as though he had fought for hours and that it would never end. He was exhausted but felt very good about himself. Nick's popularity had now risen by a couple hundred percent. Nick won another four fights in a row. There were no fighters in his weight class to be found in the surrounding islands, so he had continued to fight heavier fighters.

One day Nick received word through the scuttlebutt system that the dispensary was going to cut personnel and many corpsmen would be reassigned. Most of the corpsmen wanted to move on anyway, including Nick. Life at the dispensary was beginning to feel boring. Nick kept training at the ring site to see if there might be another fight for him in the near future. And so there was.

"This guy is a southpaw; that's all I can tell you," Borac told Nick.

It was a Sunday, and the fight was for the coming Saturday, so Nick had time to prepare. He sparred with Borac as he would against a left-handed fighter. Borac told Nick, "I want you to try and knock this guy out."

"I'll try my best, but there's no guarantee that I can do it."

Borac smiled and said nothing. There's that smile again, Nick thought. Whenever Borac smiled, Nick always felt that the man had something up his sleeve.

The Saturday-night fights came again, and this was Nick's first main-event fight. The crowd was unusually large, much larger than for any of his previous fights. Nick was on top of the world, knowing that he and his opponent would be the main event.

It was well after ten when the last bout on the fight card was over. It was time for the main event. Nick felt a little more nervous than at any of his other boxing matches. The fighters' names were announced as usual. At the announcement of "Monty" Delmonte, the crowd went wild, for he was the local favorite, hometown favorite, one might say, from Ondonga. The other fighter had been brought in from aboard one of the fighting ships that were in constant surveillance throughout the South Pacific islands. The scuttlebutt carrying information about the undefeated kid from Ondonga had traveled far and wide. To Nick, the most notable thing about his new opponent was the fact that he was closer to his own size than any of his former opponents had been. He was perhaps an inch or two taller than Nick, but physically the two were very closely matched.

Nick sat in his corner waiting for the bell while Borac and Geib went through their usual motions in preparing their fighter.

"Remember the things that we went through in training," Borac told Nick. "Try to knock him out as soon as you get the chance."

Nick wondered why Borac was so adamant about knocking out his opponent. Nick stood up from his stool and Geib pulled it out of the way. Nick, with his elbows on the ropes in his corner, tried to size up his opponent from a distance.

The bell sounded.

Both fighters rushed to the center of the ring. Nick felt awkward facing the left-handed fighter who began circling to his left, and Nick backpedaled in the same direction. Nick threw a right that was partially blocked and landed on the left shoulder. Nick left himself unprotected when he dropped his left arm just a fraction, giving the other fighter an opening for several right jabs and hard hook to the jaw. The crowd roared, and from Nick's fans came a low moan. The jabs landing on Nick's head were very light and did no damage physically, but points were gained by the other fighter.

Thus, went the whole first round. Nick could not immediately calculate his opponents attack, for not once did he use his left hand. His right hand was his only weapon. Nick now understood why Borac wanted him to try for a knockout.

"You're a little bit behind. Try to rush him a little bit," Borac said as he gave Nick water and wiped his face at his corner.

Nick just nodded, but now he had his own idea of what he was going to do. He thought of saving some of his energy as he formed his plan in his mind.

Round two.

The other fighter came out and continued peppering Nick with his right jabs and occasional hooks. Nick calculated that the round was about half over, so he went into action. His thoughts went back to the street fights he had as a kid on the south side of Chicago. When his opponent came in for more jabs, Nick suddenly knocked down his lead right hand, and as his opponent dropped his left hand, the fighter was left wide open. Nick tore into him. Nick hit his opponent with lefts and rights to the head, and as the other fighter tried to clinch, Nick stepped back and attacked again, swinging both hands at the face and head of his opponent. The other fighter complained to the referee about Nick's tactics, but the referee dismissed his complaints. There was nothing illegal about Nick's methods. The cheers from the crowd were deafening. Round two ended.

Nick did not sit on the stool after the round. He stood waiting for the bell to ring for the start of the final round.

Francisca and the Boys

At the bell, Nick ran to the center of the ring to meet his opponent. They stood toe-to-toe, exchanging lefts and rights, and clinched. The referee separated the fighters, and before the referee could turn around after the break, Nick was already pounding lefts and rights to the southpaw's head. The lefty attempted to complain once more, but the ref just shook his head, no With his opponent against the ropes, Nick attacked one more time with devastating rights and lefts and with a knockout on his mind. The bell rang. The crowd was going berserk.

Borac threw water on Nick's face in the corner as they waited for the scorecards, then the decision. The announcement was made.

"The decision is a draw!"

Immediately boos could be heard. The crowd did not like the decision. Loud boos continued to resonate, and then, "Monty! Monty! Monty!"

Nick, at Borac's urging, went to his opponent's corner and congratulated him on a good fight. The crowd cheered the gesture and began to dissipate as Nick left for the training tent.

In the training tent, Nick notified Borac that the dispensary was cutting down on personnel and that he would be getting his orders soon.

"Monty, if you ever come to New York and you decide to continue boxing, look me up. We can make some money," Borac said as he handed Nick a piece of paper with his name, address, and phone number.

"Okay, Borac," Nick said. "Thanks a lot for everything."

Nick did not think about becoming a professional boxer ever. He had seen too many boxers and ex-boxers walking around shaking their heads and otherwise acting punch-drunk. He thought more about other things, like getting home and maybe getting married and settling down. When he was alone, he would pull out Estelita's photo and look at it. She had never become his girlfriend, but she was gracious enough to give him her picture.

The scuttlebutt continued to churn. It was early August 1944. American forces were steadily working their way in the direction of Japan. The next logical invasion would have to be the Philippine Islands or the Japanese mainland. All the corpsmen were anxiously waiting for their orders.

August 6 was Nick's birthday. The day had come and gone without Nick paying attention. He remembered weeks later and kept it to himself.

TWENTY-FIVE

From the scuttlebutt, the corpsmen deduced that the next invasion was certainly the Philippine Islands, for they also knew that General Douglas MacArthur was somewhere in the area, and as the Supreme Commander of the Southwest Pacific, he would not waste time.

Once more the hospital corpsmen boarded a small ship to travel to an unknown destination. However, it turned out that they were going back to Guadalcanal for reassignment. When they arrived at Guadalcanal, the corpsmen were marched to a barracks along with other groups of hospital corpsmen to report for muster, the Navy equivalent to a calling of the roll. After chow, the entire contingent was again called to muster.

Chris, the senior member of the group of friends at Ondonga, had stayed behind with an entirely different group. Pizzuto, Geib, and Nick were still together at muster. Names were called, and each corpsman received his reassignment orders. The three buddies were separated, each receiving orders to different destinations.

Nick was ordered to pick up his gear and to stand to one side. Now Nick found himself with an entirely new group of Corpsmen that were headed to the same destination. He waved good-bye to his buddies. Before long, Nick found himself aboard a new LST commissioned just recently, along with five other corpsmen with whom he had yet to become acquainted.

Six hospital corpsmen and one doctor comprised Surgical Team 13 aboard LST 746. The six Corpsmen were lead to an open booby hatch on the port side of the ship.

"Pick your bunks and make yourselves comfortable," the boatswain's mate announced. "Someone will be here to escort you to the mess hall at chow time."

Nick, who had wisely followed directly behind the boatswain's mate down the hatch, threw his sea bag on the first lower bunk he saw. It was one of two bunks located in the forward compartment near the bow of the ship and was nearest the ladder leading to the top deck. The next six bunks were located in the next compartment, three high, anchored to the port bulkhead.

Nick decided to check out the rest of the port-side interior leading aft toward the ship's engine room. In the next compartment past the corpsmen's quarters, a long operating table, with its legs welded to the steel deck and a thin navy mattress strapped to the flat surface, occupied about one-third of the space with little room to maneuver around it. The next three compartments held six bunks each and served as hospital wards for casualties. All compartment hatches were kept open except the last one, which lead to the engine room. Only engine room personnel were allowed through that hatch.

Dr. Simon Adler came below and introduced himself to the corpsmen. Dr. Adler was a surgeon and held the rank of lieutenant commander in the navy. "Who among you is the registered pharmacist?" he asked.

A tall, thin corpsman raised his hand and responded in a soft voice, "I am, sir." Edward Wilson, a little more than six feet tall, with graying blond hair. His face was wrinkled, giving him the appearance of being fifty or more years of age. He wore eyeglasses that rested near the tip of his nose. At first-class pharmacist mate, Wilson was the top-rated corpsman in the group, all the rest were second-class pharmacist mates.

The doctor and Wilson conferred for a few minutes, then walked together to the last ward compartment and returned a few minutes later. The doctor continued up the ladder and out the top hatch.

Francisca and the Boys

Wilson looked toward Nick. "You want to give me a hand, Delmonte?"

"Sure," Nick replied.

The two walked back through the ward compartments and returned with a large wooden box. The box contained all the tools necessary for surgery, as in any operating room in a civilian hospital. As senior corpsman, and because of his extensive knowledge of drugs, Wilson was put in charge of all aspects concerning the OR, including all drugs, and he become the official anesthetist. All the other corpsmen, having been duly trained to assist in surgical procedures, were given their respective watches, or schedules, following navy regulations.

Wilson got in touch with a crew member who was a welder and gave him a sketch of an instrument table needed for the OR. A few hours later, Wilson had his instrument table that could be adjusted up and down and was movable in a full circle with floor rollers that could be locked. The OR was now ready.

On the fourth day after the corpsmen had boarded the LST, the anchor of the LST 746 was hauled up and the ship began to move. It slowly turned starboard and headed out to sea to join three other LSTs plus three escort ships consisting of a destroyer and two destroyer escorts.

The small convoy headed north in the Coral Sea, where the now-famous battle of American and allied navies against the Japanese Navy, involving aircraft carriers, fighter planes, and dive-bombers, had taken place in the spring of 1942.

In that battle, the American carrier USS *Lexington* was sunk by the Japanese, but the Japanese were eventually routed, and the battle went down in Australian History as "the battle that saved Australia."

Nick could never keep track of time pertaining to days and nights while in the open sea. He still needed quite a number of points in order to qualify for his return home; therefore, he made it a point not to think of time, just to continue forward and hope for the best.

By mid-September 1944, LST 746 and its sister ships anchored off the shores of New Guinea. They eventually hit the beaches along the shoreline to load up with army personnel and equipment. By late September, the ship was loaded with personnel and equipment of the U.S. Sixth Army. By now the scuttlebutt had confirmed that the 746 would be landing somewhere in the Philippines with its contingent of the Sixth Army.

In mid-October, the invading American forces were fully formed into a convoy of fighting ships and landing craft of every size and shape. In the early morning of October 20, the convoy approached the Philippine Islands from the east. In the meantime, shelling of the island of Leyte by American battleships had continued nonstop, effectively forcing Japanese troops inland and making way for the landing of American troops.

LST 746 hit the beach at dawn with no enemy troops within sight. The huge doors began their slow opening, followed by the ramp coming down just as slowly; then with three to four feet to go, the ramp dropped into the water causing an enormous splash. By full daylight, the two tanks in the hollow of the ship had made their way out of the ship and inland toward the palm trees. Heavy-duty trucks filled with equipment and ammunition followed. Trucks and jeeps on the top deck were lowered by elevator to the lower level and driven through the opened doors. Soldiers carrying packs and rifles left the LST in orderly fashion by way of the ramp.

The beach was littered with Japanese bodies rotting in the heat of the sun while others floated in the shallow water.

Nick and two other corpsmen were looking over the railing on the bow at the starboard side of the ship.

One of the Corpsmen pointed. "Look down there. That guy is alive. He's moving."

"Let's go down and see. He might be one of our soldiers," Nick suggested.

The three picked up a stretcher and a first-aid kit and went below and down the ramp. A few yards to one side of the ship was

Francisca and the Boys

a Japanese soldier, wounded in both legs and attempting to stand, but all he could do was to push himself up by his hands and arms and fall back down. The corpsmen checked him for weapons, then wrapped the wounds on his legs with gauze and placed him on the stretcher. He kept saying something in Japanese, shaking his head up and down, and moaning. The corpsmen had been taught that according to the Geneva Convention, all prisoners of war were to be treated with respect when taken prisoner. So, with that in mind, they picked up the stretcher and started up the ramp with their prisoner.

Suddenly someone from above at the bow shouted, "Put that slant eyed son-of-a-bitch down. I don't want him aboard this ship!" It was Dr. Adler.

The corpsmen turned and carried the soldier back to where they had found him. They looked at each other, wondering if they had done something wrong. The Japanese soldier pleaded with his arms out, as if to say, "Please don't leave me here!"

After the incident, Dr. Adler never mentioned his outburst, nor did the corpsmen.

LST 746 slowly pulled away from the beach with its huge doors closing as it went astern. A few yards from the beach, it dropped the anchor. American and allied planes continued to bomb enemy positions in Leyte as darkness fell. Flashes from explosions on the island could be seen in the dark.

It became quiet and calm for a few hours. The corpsmen went up to the main deck to escape the heat below. From their position at the railing, they could see flashes of explosions occurring on the island. Suddenly they heard and saw a tremendous explosion from deep into the island, followed by a series of smaller explosions, giving the impression of a Fourth of July fireworks display in the States. The small explosions continued for several hours. The scuttlebutt, as usual, brought the news that a munitions dump or a warehouse had been hit by an American bomber, causing all the ammunition to explode and go up in smoke.

The empty LSTs remained in Leyte Gulf awaiting orders. Word came in that General MacArthur had gone ashore at Palo, Leyte, south of Tacloban City, where the main landing had taken place. All landing craft were ordered to remain in the gulf until further notice. All escort ships left the gulf, except for a couple of destroyers and destroyer escorts that maneuvered in a continuous arch to protect the LSTs. Scuttlebutt came through again; the Japanese fleet was on its way to Leyte Gulf.

"General Quarters will remain in effect continuously until further notice" was the message over the loud speaker of LST 746. On October 23, 1944, the word was that the American and Japanese fleets had encountered one another and that the battle for possession of the Philippines had begun.

On October 24, three Japanese kamikaze aircraft appeared in the late-morning hours. Two were immediately shot down by antiaircraft from the LSTs. The third managed to sneak through the antiaircraft firepower and aimed itself directly at the 746. The gunner at the antiaircraft gun at the center of the LST related later that the plane came so close that he could see the pilot's face as it flew past him.

Corpsmen were not allowed on deck during any action, but Nick and the others could hear the bullets from the kamikaze bouncing off the steel deck of LST 746. The kamikaze missed the 746 by inches but managed to crash into the LST fifty or more yards away on the starboard side of LST 746. The plane hit the bridge of the ship and remained stuck, nose down, tail up. Several crewmen of the wounded LST jumped into the water on impact while those on the bridge perished. The number of killed and wounded was not verified immediately. Lifeboats from the 746 and other LSTs picked up those who had jumped into the water. All returned to their ship once the danger of attack decreased.

The ship that was hit was in the 900 series, making it a later addition to the fleet of LSTs. It was similarly equipped with its own surgical team as the 746; therefore, it was capable of attending to its own dead and wounded. In retrospect, it was noted that the kamikaze had expended its bombs elsewhere, hence why there was no explosion on the targeted LST.

The Battle of Leyte Gulf actually took place outside the gulf itself, but it was attributed to the American landings that the Japanese fleet was determined to stop and destroy. The corpsmen were not exactly oblivious to the naval action going on out at sea, for the action could be heard faintly and, at times, flashes and smoke from cannon fire could be seen in the distance.

The battle began on October 23 and came to an end on October 27. In essence, the depleted Japanese navy had been no match for the American naval forces, for the carrier task force and the rest of the surface fighting ships of the United States had destroyed it.

The 746 remained in Leyte Gulf for approximately one month. Toward the end of November, the island of Leyte was close to being secure, because the army of the Philippines and guerilla fighters were prepared to take over the ground defenses of Leyte.

The LST's once more hit the beach and opened their doors and dropped their ramps. Army engineers began the loading of the ships one more time. There definitely was one more landing somewhere in the Philippines.

Tacloban City, located just beyond the beaches of Leyte, was coming alive. The corpsmen were given permission to go ashore on a four-hour Liberty with strict orders not to go beyond the town. Wilson opted to remain aboard ship and stay on watch. It was early in the afternoon when the Corpsmen walked in to Tacloban. Makeshift tables filled with native wares and trinkets for sale were already set up on the edge of town. The Corpsmen walked through the town that seemed to have survived the action of the recent invasion, for there was very little evidence of damages to the town. The corpsmen were invited to enter a newly opened brothel on the main street, but all declined. The Liberty served more as a leg stretcher than anything else, for it had been some time since the corpsmen had walked on solid ground. All eventually returned to ship.

By late November, the convoy was again ready to move on to its next landing. Contingents of the Sixth Army were again aboard. Early in December, the convoy pulled out of Leyte Gulf, its destination unknown. Only the officers knew where the next landing would take place.

The convoy moved southward into the open sea. After a few days out to sea, the convoy was attacked by kamikazes that were quickly eliminated by P-51 Mustang fighters of the U.S. Army Air Force. The American convoy cut through the Surigao Strait as if heading to the island of Mindanao where the Japanese expected the next landing, but instead went through to the far western side of the Philippine Islands and turned north in the direction of the Island of Luzon and the Capitol, Manila.

The convoy eventually landed on the island of Mindoro, just south of Luzon on December 15, 1944, with little or no resistance. Supplies were left aboard meant another landing farther north was in the offing. Once again, the convoy continued north, and on January 9, 1945, the 746 found itself in Lingayen Gulf at the Island of Luzon, landing and dropping off men and equipment. Later in the month, the 746 pulled into Manila Bay, where the U.S. Army was cleaning up and securing the city of Manila.

On February 3, 1945, paratroopers were dropped on the outskirts of Manila on the south. From the north, two U.S. cavalry divisions moved in on Manila. The Japanese troops had left the area, leaving Manila free of Japanese forces. The scuttlebutt was at work again bringing news that our next stop was to be Japan proper. The 746 remained in Manila Bay until early April 1945. During that time, Nick and the rest of the corpsmen used the time for the well deserved R&R, or rest and relaxation. On several occasions, Nick and the other corpsmen were granted liberty to go into the Manila.

Nick had already made friends with some of the business people in the city. Tagalog was the primary language of the

Francisca and the Boys

area, but many spoke Spanish, a hangover from when the Philippines were under Spanish rule. When Nick encountered people speaking Spanish, he would stop and ask questions in the language, to the surprise of his fellow corpsmen. He managed to get information regarding location of drinking establishments and local brothels.

Toward the end of their stay in Manila Bay, Nick and two other corpsmen were on liberty when they decided to visit one of the local bars. Under American government regulations, hard liquor sold in bars must be 5 percent or less per volume of alcohol. The trio ordered one bottle of cognac each at one dollar per bottle. After the second round, the three were feeling pretty good. They decided to visit the nearest brothel and found one with a line of sailors trailing out the door from the pay counter. All three were slightly drunk and were about ready to leave when Nick spoke up.

"Wait a minute, guys. Stick around. I'll be right back."

Nick walked up to the pay counter and spoke to the man collecting the fee. He said something to the man and pointed to his left sleeve, where the two stripes and a red cross were stitched in. Nick had a five-dollar bill and two singles folded in the palm of his right hand. As he talked to the man behind the counter, he slipped the money into his hand as he put up three fingers for himself and the other two corpsmen and pointed at the collector, signaling that the extra dollar was his. No one in line complained simply because all sailors had respect for the little red cross and for the men they called Doc.

The brothel's interior was but a short hallway with three rooms on each side without doors. The room that Nick entered had an army blanket on the floor and a basin of water to one side. The room was no more than a large closet but long enough to accommodate an average man. A type of sheet covered the doorway.

"Hello, Joe. Come in, Joe," the young girl, who didn't look more than fifteen or sixteen years of age, said. In the Philippines, all American servicemen were called Joe.

Nick did what he came to do, walked out of the brothel, and looked around for his buddies. The other two walked out a little behind Nick; they all had smiles on their faces. "You guys owe me two bucks apiece," Nick said. They cheerfully handed over the payment.

"What did you tell that guy at the counter?" one of the corpsmen asked.

"I told him we were health inspectors, but I winked when I gave him the money."

They all laughed. The corpsmen went back to the bar and repeated the whole process two more times.

The 746 hauled anchor and began to pull out of Manila Bay along with three other LST's.. It was the last week of March in 1945. The 746 had no cargo.

Along with the usual escort ships, the convoy headed south past Mindoro Island, then west to the Sulu Sea. The next port for the 746 was Puerto Princesa City in Palawan Island, where contingents of the U.S. Eighth Army came aboard with the usual fighting gear and heavy equipment. The last of the equipment to come aboard was three army tanks, completing the cargo in the hollow of the ship.

Another invasion was in the making. Newer LSTs had joined the convoy for this coming invasion. Most were now in the 1000 series. The old reliable scuttlebutt came through one more time. Next stop, Mindanao island on the southernmost tip of the Philippine group and one of the larger islands.

On April 17, 1945, the LST 746 landed on the beach at Mindanao with its load of fighting men and equipment. The first to go through the open doors and over the ramp were the three army tanks just inside the huge doors. American fighter planes roamed the sky but found no opposition. The Eighth Army began its advance against stubborn resistance. Casualties on the American side began to arrive at the beach and were promptly placed aboard the LSTs. The 746 received nine soldiers with wounds ranging from serious to life threatening. The most serious was a soldier who had been hit in the legs by machine-gun fire and was bleeding profusely from below the knees. He had a tourniquet on each leg just above the knee. His legs were shattered, and one leg was hanging by the skin.

The soldier was transferred directly to the operating table in the medical compartment aboard the 746. Dr. Adler and Wilson immediately went to work. Nick, who happened to have the watch, scrubbed up and was prepared to assist in minutes. The soldier was awake and in much pain, moaning loudly and struggling to get loose from the operating table he was strapped down to. Wilson prepared a syringe with morphine and administered the shot to one of the soldier's arms. Wilson then began to drip ether into the mask on his face. The soldier's struggling stopped, and he went into a deep sleep. A bottle of plasma was hung on a pole, and the needle on the end of the rubber tube was inserted into one of his arms.

Dr. Adler began to cut away what was left of the right leg, and with Nick's help, he tied off protruding arteries below the knee and then switched over to the other leg tying those arteries as well. Another corpsmen took the soldier's blood pressure with a sphygmomanometer.

"His pressure is way down," the corpsman announced.

"Stop the ether," Dr. Adler said calmly. He sponged the open wounds, but the blood continued to flow.

"I can't find a heartbeat," the corpsman reported.

Dr. Adler checked the soldier's heartbeat with a stethoscope and could not hear a beat. The soldier's heart had stopped beating! The doctor made a fist and pounded the soldier on the chest once, twice, as he listened with the stethoscope. He tried to find a heart beat several times more without success. The soldier died on the operating table.

Dr. Adler pulled off his rubber gloves in desperation. "Take the data from his dog tags and prepare him for burial."

After removing the soldier's dog tags, the corpsmen proceeded to wrap the body in canvas. The canvas was sewed up with heavy cord, and the body then placed in a wire stretcher. With very little room to spare in the compartments below, they decided to carry the body up and out to the main deck. As they were placing the wire stretcher on the deck, the loudspeaker from the bridge came on and the booming voice of the captain was heard.

"Take that body back down below, *now!*"

The Corpsmen, startled by the captain's voice, immediately complied. The body was placed at the bottom of the hatch ladder not more than a foot or so from Nick's bunk.

The 746 pulled back from the beach and dropped its anchor to await orders. For two days, Nick slept next to his dead companion. On the first day, his fellow corpsmen kidded him and attempted to frighten him. Nick only felt sorrow over the dead soldier and wondered about the meaning of life and death.

Looking at the body across from him, Nick wondered if he would survive the rest of the war. Japan was be the next invasion for certain. Would he make it home? he wondered.

The anchor of LST 746 began to rise, it would be moving out soon. The convoy was divided in about half, as ships began to move in opposite directions. The ship moved east and north toward Leyte. While out at sea, the body of the dead soldier was brought up on deck and placed on a flat board. The body, wrapped with heavy chains and weights, was covered with the American flag. The captain of the ship said a few prayers; then two crew members stepped up, one on each side of the body, and a third held the flag. With the captain's final words, "We commit this body to the deep," the crewmen raised the board and the body slid from under the flag and into the ocean.

The ship pulled in to Leyte a few days later and discharged the wounded soldiers who were aboard. They were eventually moved to army headquarters somewhere on Leyte. The LST was now doing what was called occupation duty until further orders arrived. The corpsmen and the rest of the crew were under the impression that the next action was the invasion of Japan. The

746 and other LSTs in the gulf took practice runs and landings so that the crews stay tuned to whatever action might be in the future.

Late in June, Dr. Adler came down to the corpsmen's quarters and pulled Wilson and Nick to one side. With a smile on his face, he said, "You're going home, guys. It's been a pleasure serving with you. Congratulations!" He shook Wilson's hand first, then Nick's.

Nick didn't know whether to cry or laugh he was so stunned.

After saying their good-byes to everyone in Surgical Team 13, Wilson and Nick went aboard a small ship that looked like it might be a sub chaser. Within hours, the small ship pulled into Samar Island, just north of Leyte, and dropped the corpsmen off at a dock where a first-class pharmacist mate waited in a jeep. They were taken to Fleet Hospital 114 on Samar to wait for their departure. The date wasn't until early August, when they were alerted to prepare for evacuation within hours.

The second week of August Nick and Wilson were driven by jeep to the airstrip, where an army transport plane was unloading material and being refueled by tanker truck. A small group of servicemen from the army and the navy waiting to board the plane.

The plane had been converted from passenger plane to transport plane; therefore, the windows were still intact. The seats had been removed and replaced with benches that were attached to the sides of the plane and folded up. All together, there were about twelve to fifteen servicemen aboard the plane headed for the island of Guam. The men boarded the plane and looked around for seating accommodations. The floor was the best place to sit, and Nick found a spot next to a window.

The plane finally took off. It was Nick's first plane ride ever. He felt his stomach drop on takeoff. Flying low, the plane remained at a few hundred feet above the ocean all the way to Guam. From Guam, where more men on their way home waited, the next stop was Pearl Harbor by way of a Merchant Marine troop transport. More men were picked up at Pearl Harbor, and then the ship backed out and turned in the direction of the United States mainland.

On arrival at San Francisco Bay, the hoopla had already started. There was a crowd on the dock with horns blowing and flags waving as well as a marching band playing loud music. The ship moved very slowly toward the dock, was pulled in by ropes, and tied down. Wooden ramps were pushed up to the ship and made ready for disembarking.

After all the waiting and transferring from one port to the other, Nick finally boarded a train from San Francisco to Great Lakes Naval Training Station, north of Chicago, where he was processed and given a thirty-day leave with orders to return to base no later than his last day of leave. A local train took him from Great Lakes to Canal Street Station in Chicago.

Nick had not written to anyone that he was coming home because he wanted to make his arrival a surprise. When he stepped off the train, who was there? No other than his mother Francisca herself. They embraced, and tears flowed over Francisca's cheeks as she held on to Nick. After she finally let him go, he asked her, "Ma, how did you know I was coming home?"

"I just knew," she replied, giving no other explanation. Francisca hailed a cab on Madison Street, and in fewer than five minutes, the cab dropped them off on Madison and Halsted Streets, only four blocks west of the train station.

The entire family was at Club Delmonte. Davy, Isabel, Lupe, and a bar full of costumers greeted Nick when he walked in the door. Davy and the girls were surprised to see Nick, because Fransica had not told anyone that she had been going to the train station every day for the last two weeks. It was Friday, so Manolo and his Cuban Rhythm Boys would be playing at the homecoming celebration.

At the end of his thirty-day leave, Nick returned to Great Lakes and was directed to report to the navy hospital on the compound. Nick thought it would be a routine examination at the hospital, but he was surprised at what he learned next.

"We have a report here from Dr. Simon Adler," the doctor in charge said, "that you have a hernia that you sustained while lifting heavy equipment aboard ship."

Nick nodded.

"If you want it repaired, all you need to do is give your consent and it can be done before your discharge from the navy."

Nick agreed and signed a consent form.

"Fine," said the Doctor, "we'll set you up in the surgical ward and have you ready for surgery in a couple of days."

Nick thought back to the day that he had come back to the ship after the drinking spree in Manila. He had visited the brothel so many times that he had sustained the hernia without knowing until days later when he felt a slight stinging pain in his groin. At the time, he had confided in Dr. Adler, who in turn had covered for him on the health report.

It was December, and the surgery had gone well, but he had to spend Christmas in the hospital. Nick did not mind that at all for he thought he needed the rest. During his stay at the Great Lakes Naval Hospital, Nick had time to think about his three-plus years in the navy and about what the future might hold for him.

The war had essentially ended when the atomic bomb was dropped on Hiroshima. That action saved Nick from one more invasion and, perhaps, had saved his life. Ironically, the bomb had been dropped on August 6, which happened to be Nick's birthday.

By January 1, Nick was on his way to Charleston, South Carolina, for discharge. On January 14, 1946, he was discharged from the navy with payment of $100.00 mustering-out pay and $32.00 for train fare back to Chicago.

EPILOGUE

Nick's thoughts returned to reality when there was a tap on the front-door glass. It was the mailman. Nick opened the locked door and greeted the man, who handed him a handful of letters. Nick ignored all the mail except the big square envelope with the return address City of Chicago.

His tavern license had arrived, and he immediately took it from the envelope and taped it to the glass on the cabinet behind the bar. He then jumped over the bar and opened the front door, propping it open with a doorstop. He taped a large hand printed sign to the large glass window that read Open for Business.